night of the animals

An Imprint of HarperCollins*Publishers*

night of the animals

bill broun

Epigraph from *The Golden Legend or Lives of the Saints*. Compiled by Jacobus de Voragine, archbishop of Genoa, 1275. First edition published 1470. Englished by William Caxton, first edition 1483, edited by F. S. Ellis, Temple Classics, 1900. Excerpt slightly edited for clarity.

HarperCollins books may be purchased for educational, business, or sales promotional use. For information, please e-mail the Special Markets Department at SPsales@harpercollins.com.

FIRST EDITION

Designed by Suet Yee Chong

Library of Congress Cataloging-in-Publication Data has been applied for.

ISBN 978-0-06-240079-6

16 17 18 19 20   OV/RRD   10 9 8 7 6 5 4 3 2 1

For Annmarie

And every night when his brethren were abed, Cuthbert would go and stand in the cold water all naked up to the chin till it were midnight, and then he would come out, and when he came to land he might not stand for feebleness and faintness, but oft fell down to the ground. And after a time as he lay thus, there came two otters which licked every place of his body, and then went again to the water that they came from. And then Cuthbert arose all whole.

—from The Life of Saint Cuthbert,
The Golden Legend, ca. A.D. 1260

author's note

The novel employs language from both fading and emerging dialects and slang of Birmingham, the Black Country, old Worcestershire, and the Clee Hills region of England, from Guyana, as well as future-set, speculative words and phrases along with common phrases from British English. With more arcane or esoteric regionalisms, or opaque terms, footnotes are added where I felt they would help readers better appreciate the story.

one

listening to the zoo

ON THE LAST DAY OF APRIL OF 2052, AS A NEWLY discovered comet, Urga-Rampos, neared Earth, a very ill, very old, and very corpulent man started to shoulder his way into the thick hedges around the last public zoo on earth. Cuthbert Handley, a freshly minted nonagenarian—and a newly homeless one—clambered into the shrubbery as fast as his large, frail bones allowed (which wasn't very). As the tough branches of yew and hazel abraded his arms and neck and face, he hardly felt them: what stung him was consciousness, every last red, lashing ray of it.

"Crack on," the old man grumbled to himself, struggling to guard his eyes with his immense hands. "Go, you two-boned bletherhead—you get a wriggle on!"

It hurt Cuthbert to think, and it hurt to feel. Most of all, it hurt to remember. For a moment, he saw the boy's face—that sinking face, with black, deep-river eyes. He saw the long lips, as purple and frail as iris petals, and the pale forehead wreathed in rushes. He glimpsed again the tiny clawing hands, grabbing at fronds of ferns from the brook-side, and all of it, the whole creature, tangled in green threads of time, plummeting, twisting, swimming, down to the depths, right down through the misery of the last century.

There, or somewhere, was his lost sweet brother, the otter-boy. Here, now, eighty years later, he would be found.

Cuthbert had never stopped looking.

"Drystan," the old man whispered aloud. He paused for a moment, gulping for breath, pulling a twig off his ear. "I'll find my way to you. And to tha' others."

And what of this comet?

All the world jabbering about it, and it was the worst of omens, Cuthbert felt; Urga-Rampos seemed to presage a frenzied phase of the mass-suicide pandemic that had already wiped out tens of thousands of Britons, and abroad, millions of other people—and animals.

For the most powerful and largest of the suicide cults—a group named Heaven's Gate, originally from California—had also let it be known that animals occupied a "Level Below Human," as the cultists put it, and must be exterminated to enable suicided cult members to travel more readily to the "Level Above Human." Earth was a "dead vessel," they claimed, a mere technical impediment to spiritual ascension. They also claimed God had "revised" Jehovah's covenant with Noah. Instead of revering the "bow in the cloud" of Genesis, that ancient sign of His promise never again to destroy Earth's living creatures, the cultists said to look to the white comet, to a new covenant in which animals didn't fit, and on one continent after another, they found ways to tip already endangered whole ecosystems toward their bowls of ashes.

The international response had been, so far, slow and uneven. America, where most of the cults had begun and where the self-murders and animal killings seemed to be accelerating, had organized a "cognitive policing" effort, but it wasn't authorized outside New York, despite being under the control of the new "national police," an extension of the U.S. Army. Only a few other larger countries—Korea Hana, India, the Nigerian Federation, and Britain—seemed up for a fight.

As the last great repository of living "whole" animals on earth—genomic clones were available but also dwindling in numbers—the London Zoo now ranked as the cult's biggest target, at least as Cuthbert saw it. The animals had awakened—for him, he believed—because Britain, and indeed the world, stood in desperate danger. Waves of species were being wiped from the wild at a level not seen since the end of the Mesozoic era. So few nonhuman animal species existed in the deforested, bulldozed, and poisoned planet, the London Zoo had truly become a kind of "ark" for all interconnected life—an ark, and a death row prison.

The animals, wisely, wanted Cuthbert to help them escape before it was too late.

CUTHBERT WAS BIG, big, big—twice the size of most Britons and half as dainty. Despite his semihomeless state, he always, somehow, managed to find food, especially his favorite—cold kidney pies and kippers. His love of England was outsize, too, nearly as great as his respect for its ruthless king, Henry IX. His fingers were as thick and dirty as parsnips, and his feet as long and narrow and slippery as eels. An old set of EverConnector™ muscle-sleeves bound his old body together, but he heaved around a fat tummy on the lankiest of frames, and his enlarged heart, thick-walled with cardiomyopathy after decades of high blood pressure, struggled to siphon his gallons of blood around a porpoise-shaped body. And yet this most unlikely of recipients, Cuthbert Handley, a lowly Indigent born long ago in the Black Country, the son of a machinist, was the most recent, and perhaps final, recipient of a gift given only to a few people through human history—the Wonderments.

Earlier that day, he had bided time until the right moment came
with the long sleeving shadows of evening and the zoo visitors beginning to disperse for the day. When the nearby Broad Walk and
the adjacent playground emptied of people, he had made his appalling gambit, unbandaging caution from his long limbs in one rip of
movement. He could not scramble fast enough now. A branch jabbed
his neck. Another struck his thigh. He scrunched his eyes shut. He
kicked his filthy way forward, a man powering an immense spinning
fan of rags and anguish. The hedge's branches felt far stiffer than
he remembered, and much sharper. He flung his ancient forearm at
them. He ducked. He sidestepped. He puffed his chest out. He threw
another chunky forearm out. It was as if he were trying to taunt a
mob of thin men all threatening to stab him with a yew stick.

And there *was* a kind of horde about him, after all. Cuthbert,
who had lived much of his life on the dole* and, later, "the Sick"
(disability benefit), and who could not stop drinking Flōt, was
not simply disturbed. He heard things—*loads* of things. For half
of the past year, his mind had inhabited, like a terrified moth in
a candle lantern, a phantasmagoria of mental tiger-shadows and
ghost-smokes. It was far worse than even the renowned horrors of a
typical first Flōt withdrawal. Every time he saw an animal, whether
a stray moggy or the rats running along the New Tube rails before
trains burst into the station, he felt sure the creatures were preparing to do or say things to him, or both—until they finally did just
that. He *could* hear the language of animals—or so he believed—
and he was doing this.

And here he was, attempting to break into the old London Zoo.

"Almost there," he said, panting. "Break a leg, mon!"

Cuthbert had no money, no friends, and no possessions, but
he had learned through the Wonderments to listen to England's

---

* Welfare benefit

animals. It was something even the powerful king he so revered couldn't comprehend, and through this skill, he was going to save Britain and its creatures.

Unfortunately, Flōt addict and madman that he was, not a living human soul on earth believed him.

And on Flōt, as everyone knew, one could *believe* that microscopic violet-quiffed visitors from Planet Flōtica kept castles on the tips of every blade of grass. One could *believe* that the last Tasmanian tiger didn't actually freeze to death in 1936 because of an incompetent zookeeper. When Flōt was good, it was hands down the best legal hallucinogenic and sedative on earth. It offered more than intoxication, more than a release: it took you rippling across whole new planets of purple-white euphoria. Like the old rave drug ketamine, or "Special K," from the 1990s, it offered a sense of being utterly, and sometimes pleasantly, alone; but uniquely, it also gave the proprioceptive illusion of having extremely long, lissome, and powerful legs. To "get up" or "spire" on Flōt, as it was often called, was all about total self-possessed elevation. On Flōt, the world stood miles below you alone, a distant purple and white field of violets you could only feel tickling your ankles, and you needed nothing or no one else—not God, not a lover, not your pet cat.

CUTHBERT HAD DONE the proper prep for his assault on the zoo, or at least he thought so. A few meters through the dense shrubbery lay a secret grotto that he had fashioned earlier that month inside yew and hazel hedgings and a few coppiced beeches, scooping dirt with his dry hands and charily snapping twigs. He kept an emergency bottle of Flōt stashed there, and a powerful pair of bolt cutters. His plan was to wait until darkness, cut his way in, then break open as many enclosures as possible—especially the otters'. It was the most organized thing he had done in decades. One couldn't spot the grotto from either the park or the zoo's interior. It sat a meter from the zoo's sturdy iron perimeter fence, close to the jackals— and to a rare gap in the iron fence. But the grotto might as well have been in France, such were the difficulties of getting to it now.

Cuthbert shoved forward a few more paces until the crisscrossing hazel branches budged no more and encapsulated him in a green foliate cage. For a moment, he thought he saw a boy, a thin boy with dark hair, shoving along with him a few meters away in the shrubbery. "Dryst," Cuthbert said. "Look at me. Over here!" Then the boy vanished. Every so often, a stressed branch would crack and loosen the cage's "bars," allowing Cuthbert to move again. At one point, tiny twigs jammed up both nostrils and his mouth, making it appear as if he were disgorging leaves from his face like some kind of garden goblin.

"Oh, shittin 'ell," he gasped, spitting out flecks of shredded leaves. The beast of first Flōt withdrawal was upon him, too, pulling him downward, tearing at his nerves, seizing his muscles—including his fragile heart. A singularly vicious facet of Flōt addiction was its two-bell-curved dual-withdrawal syndrome. It crushed the newly and the long-term sober alike with two acute phases sometimes a decade or more apart. Yet the dual-withdrawal also allowed ex-addicts past the initial psychosis-laden hell of withdrawal No. 1, an island of peace and sanity, before dragging them into the furies of withdrawal No. 2.

For so many years, from the last days of the era of the powerful prime ministers and the European Union, up through the Great Reclamation and the Property Revolts and the slow rise of the various suicide cults of the 2020s, and on through the Second Restoration to the new king in 2028, the ramshackle Cuthbert had somehow survived. All those decades, he'd searched doggedly for his long-lost elder brother, Drystan, who, in his mind, had vanished when they were children, way back in the late 1960s. Since then, after leaving the Black Country, he had learned to suck in and oxygenate himself on London's quotidian pathologies as naturally as breath. The filthy old town seemed to nourish him, to fuel the hunt for his brother. He took in every coarse *'oi* of speech, ate every chip-butty* bag of cheap potato joy, learned every mucky machination to blag† Flōt—all of it, fluently and helplessly, and it had all led to this brambled corner beside the beasts. If the entire history of London, from the Iron Age to the age of digital skin, had a meaning, this spot, as far as Cuthbert knew, was precisely where it stood. This, he was certain, was where his dear long-lost brother Drystan would come back and stay.

GOD KNOWS, the paroxysms of the 2020s and Henry IX had sucked nearly every other last drop of energy from Britain's tired veins. While thousands of artists, philosophers, and authors had joined the suicide cults or the ranks of brazen self-promoters on WikiNous—the implanted, all-purpose comm-network that grew within human tissue—the most original minds faced almost total indifference.

WikiNous had long ceased being freely moderated by "Wiki-Nousians." Its inner workings were no longer open-sourced; they were "open-branded" and edited vertically by subeditors obedient to Henry IX and the aristocracy and rules, rules, rules. The sending of messages in Britain had become expensive, tightly centralized, and censored; in America, India, Scandinavia, and parts of the Far East, WikiNous's relative freedom had brought its own set of problems (particularly, the cults), but even there, open network protocols were dead and the Internet golden age was long gone. Cryptographically protected WikiNous "stalks" had replaced the

---

* A buttered bread roll stuffed with French fried potatoes, i.e., chips, often served with brown sauce or ketchup

† To obtain for free, often by trickery

URLs. Among Britons, WikiNous mainly spread Harry9's official views and a boorish brand of light "newsertainement."

"Oh, Dryst," Cuthbert said aloud, reaching with his hand toward the fence. He clutched a shock of tender, faintly serrated hazel leaves, pulling himself forward. "Dryst!"

Finding the boy wasn't just the search of a lifetime for Cuthbert—it was a command, a direction, a holy destination.

That his lost brother would have been aged ninety-two, were he alive, was entirely meaningless to old Cuddy. Drystan was, in his mind, always a child.

CUTHBERT TURNED AROUND and leaned against the crosshatching branches he'd just plunged through. He found that they supported his full weight—all twenty-two stones of a man wattled together with crylon mesh and half-poisonous nickel rods. He took a deep breath and closed his eyes. It had rained the night before, and a few drips of water coursed slowly across his cheeks and down his neck.

"Gagoga," he gasped, breathlessly, repeating the most mysterious of the various phrases he had been sent a few months before by the zoo animals. "Ga! Go! Ga!" he cried, sounding as raw animal as he knew. How he knew this watery, gurgling phrase, what it meant, where it came from, why he ought to repeat it—none of those things were quite clear. But he knew he must say it.

Gagoga.

The zoo wasn't the only source of animal voices, though it was the strongest. He heard them all over the place these days. England roared and screeched with them, especially those of cats. He could hardly make it down the street lately without a moggy telling him that moths in the moonlight were enchanting, or saying that those blue mallow flowers along garden walls in Holloway smelled of petrol, or asking him to touch me here, no touch me there, no here yes there here between the ears there here there—workaday cat-thoughts, really.

Britain's dogs had much to say, too: a Seeing Eye Labrador on a bosonicabus* had told Cuthbert that invisible grid lines criss-crossed every pavement, street, house, New Tube, or bosonicabus entrance in the city. From its point of view, London was impeccably Pythagorean and soothing. A wirehaired fox terrier, on the other hand, who yelped behind a wooden gate that Cuthbert often passed in Islington, would shrill with impish pep, *Happyfury! Happyfury! Happyfury!* Cuthbert did not know what it meant—but he believed it.

And on and on they went, voices from across Albion. The black-eyed ponies of the New Forest wanted larger pastures. The fat gray seals off the Isles of Scilly wanted cleaner breeding waters. That autumn, down from the craggy Black Carls of Beinn Eighe came the angry voices of red deer stags in rut, barking for sex. Then there were Britain's forty million head of sheep, and each head, Cuthbert suspected, had a gentle idea of its own.

All these animals didn't *talk* to him exactly, not like Virginia Woolf's Greek-uttering birds or Kipling's noble, contraction-averse wolves. Words did not pass through snout, proboscis, or mandible. But nonetheless, the animals asserted themselves toward him. They sent messages, some limpid, some inscrutable, but all appreciable. Some were preverbal, others expressive and exact. Most were enigmatic—but they all nipped at him, if only just a little.

They spoke so tersely, too. Often the zoo animals imparted just one or two expressive words. "*Saliq,*" the sand cats would whisper. "Murkurk," rumbled the hippos. "Progress and dominion," the imperial—and often verbose—lions would intone, and so on. On more and more days, these occult reductions popped into

---

* A form of public mass transport with bosonic particle-based engines

perfect sense within Cuthbert. For example, *murkurk,* as Cuthbert grasped it, clearly meant "let the hippopotamus make its way to the Thames." He'd think: how much clearer could it be?

HE LIFTED UP a tangle of the thin, elastic branches in the hedge with his arm, spun around, and tried backing in. He needed to make sure no one was watching. He felt he could not be more prepared for today, considering his circumstances. He'd put on his black weather-buffer and green trousers for cover. He wore the hood on the buffer, and cinched it tight around his swarthy face. He looked like a big, dark Teletubby from the old TV program—a new one, Boozey, with a smashed television screen on its tummy and two purple Flōt bottle-tops for eyes.

Getting to this secret spot, a maneuver he had practiced twice that week, seemed far more difficult this evening; he felt as if he were crawling under a duvet stuffed with plaited, stinging sticks. He had ducked and shoved in, stolid and elephantine, but come to a real sticking spot. He must move fast. If a passer-by spotted him—a fat man splayed in the hedges—undoubtedly a commotion would ensue. If that happened, everything ended. His grand plan to free all the animals would die.

It was with this realization that something truly unaccountable appeared before Cuthbert, within the hedges. All at once, a broad and robust figure, in the shadows of the leaves and branches, crept upon him. A nimbus of golden-green air surrounded him. Cuthbert began to quake in terror, his neck hair standing on end.

"You!" cried Cuthbert. "You there!"

The figure seemed to have actually sprouted from the ground within the hedges, a massive yew tree dotted with angry red berries. For a moment, it spumed in all directions, chaotically, a flutter of spinning green boughs with handfuls of black soil and nightlarks and tiny owls bursting from it. A multitude of small, dark animals—they resembled hares made of shadow—poured out from its base and took off into the night air, where they dissolved. The great yew-tree figure moved toward Cuthbert, who could barely breathe, such was his dread.

"What do you want from me?" he asked.

The figure replied, "*Gagoga.*" The voice was unlike all the other animals he had been hearing. This one was familiar, yet oddly muffled. It was like code from some enormous forest, a code spoken from beneath one of its deepest, darkest brooks.

Cuthbert whispered, "Drystan?"

the depraved practitioner

CUTHBERT'S GENERAL PRACTITIONER, DR. SARB-jinder Singh Bajwa, to whom he had grown quite close in the previous months, and who had tried so hard to protect Cuthbert from himself, surely would have started tapping his middle finger on his desk the way he did if he were observing all this.

Of the small cadre of harried NHS Élite GPs who administered to the poor in the All-Indigent zone around Holloway, the locals considered Dr. Bajwa especially long-suffering and kind, and because of this, he was in mortal danger. When it came to the treatment of Indigents, the new aristocracy brutally rooted out softness. Indeed, compassion (in anyone other than King Henry) was considered a form of depravity.

But Dr. Bajwa loved on—and in so many degenerate ways—and as far as he was concerned, the regime could top itself. He was well known for his adoration of paper and his unnecessary reminders written in ink on passé sticky notes. He was always handing these to his patients, despite the dozens of Opticalls—the catchall name for audio calls, text messages, and Optispam, sent via Wiki-

Nous's neuro-optical interface—his patients automatically received with every consult. Few, apart from Cuthbert, knew that beneath the quiet, tolerant, papyrophilic surface of the doctor lurked a more swaggering personality.

Over the previous six months, and well before Cuthbert had got himself stuck beside a green phantom in the hedges, the doctor had developed feelings of both duty and bewilderment when it came to the welfare of this particular addict. Here was a tough old Flōt sot who also showed signs of depersonalization disorder as well as, perhaps, a variety of Cotard's Syndrome (a delusion in which a patient was convinced she or he is dead). He was, among other things, interesting to Dr. Bajwa. And impossible.

Cuthbert had spoken to him many times about his delusion of animal telepathy, and Dr. Bajwa, or "Baj," as friends and regulars called him, would invariably fiddle his fingers, grimace, and proffer one of his beloved English idioms. The doctor was quadralingual, with English, as he saw it, the strangest of the four tongues, but he loved how its scores of idioms put splattering city life into tidy, confident boxes. "I see you've really grasped the nettle this time," he sometimes said to Cuthbert, usually with an expansive grin.

THE REVELATIONS ABOUT Cuthbert's animals had begun one morning the previous October. He had been telling Baj about a shambling stroll he'd just taken in Regent's Park, which encased three sides of the zoo. He'd been stoned on Flōt, as usual, walking on skyscraper legs.

It was, as it happened, the day of the last performance of the season at the park's Open Air Theatre, and *The Two Gentlemen of Verona* was being hastily staged despite the outbreak of raucous protests near the theater. The protestors, who struck Cuthbert as far too obstreperous to be Heaven's Gaters, heckled the wealthy theater-goers by throwing paper balls made of crumpled pages of old mass-market paperback copies of the banned *Hamlet*. There was a live dog in the production, a badly trained mastiff with droopy flews, and it kept barking incessantly, sometimes nearly howling.

Wearing tight black garments, keeping hair long and dotted with bioluminescent pearls, and, in a few cases, marking cheeks with tiny black tattoos—like "prison tears" but actually meant to resemble the similarly shaped black warden *pears* of Worcestershire—the pro-testors frightened and repulsed Cuthbert, who revered the Crown, but he felt too wobbly to do anything about it, and the dog—those sore-throated, snappy, endless barks!—badly unsettled him.

Arf! Arf! Arf! Ar-rar-rar-arf!

"Who's torturing that wammel?" he asked the protestors, yawn-ing. They smiled and ignored him. "Doesn't anyone have one bit of respect for God's creatures?"

Just as he readied to spread himself along an empty bench for a nap, the mysterious, wild cacophony *spoke* to him.

"Eeeeeegaah raar! Zchaaag!" As he recounted to Dr. Bajwa, the noise actually knocked him onto a bench.

"Like this," he said. Cuthbert threw himself back in his chair a bit, as if to demonstrate.

The animals of the Regent's Park zoo, it seemed, didn't care for "any *Two Gentlemen*," he said.

"The dog, and the angry students and all—you see, I think all the noise sort of stirred up the animals in the zoo, you see? That's my own little theory, that. The theater's within earshot—of the zoo, right?"

"I can imagine that," said Dr. Bajwa. He was convinced, at this point, that Cuthbert was joking with him—and wasting their time.

"So, one of the otters said," Cuthbert had blurted, "*they* said, well, they said they want to be let up tha' cuts,* the ones behind Regent's, right? You know, with those pretty boats?"

"They 'said,' you say? 'Said'?"

Cuthbert glanced down, as if mildly ashamed, and added, "I might say 'yikkered,' really—that's a little more like it, actually."

"Yikkered. Otters. Cuthbert, I—"

"Exactly."

Doctor and patient sat in a consultation room at the courtyard-facing back of a Victorian office building in north London. A rusty-red and white Afshar rug with *boteh* leaf designs covered most of the floor. The space smelled of fig leaves and cedar from Dr. Bajwa's cologne, and were it not all so greatly soothing, Cuthbert might have held back more. A spray of hot green sunlight and a spring breeze trickled through the office's ancient diamond-mullioned casement windows the doctor always kept ever so slightly open. With one sweet new breeze, Dr. Bajwa's hope that Cuthbert was winding him up collapsed.

"You're *hearing* animals? In your mind?"

"What? No." He scrutinized his doctor's face for a moment. "In my ears, doc. In my lug'oles."

Soon, the particulars came out. Cuthbert claimed that thousands of animals across London—cats, dogs, rats, garden foxes, lab monkeys, hares, pet gerbils, and of course zoo animals—were trying to speak to him.

"They don't let up, doc," Cuthbert said. "It's quite difficult—to be on the receiving end, as it were." He said he tried at these moments to imagine his long-dead grandmother's kind face, with her wispy-white tendrils of hair sometimes falling in her eyes. She would have gently rued Cuthbert's whining. You didn't whine about the Wonderments—and you didn't talk about them outside the line of

---

* Canals

descent. "And you wouldn't believe how *many* cats there are in this city."

Dr. Bajwa listened, half shocked, half transfixed, and nodding more out of courtesy than acquiescence.

"There's a sort of naffed-off chimpanzee going off on me *right now*," Cuthbert had said that day. His eyes darted around the room, as though observing the black-furred words of an ape pummeling the walls. "E's warning me to leave *him* alone!"

The doctor took a deep breath and nodded his head.

"That sounds like a very sensible approach," he said, with a note of certified sternness in his voice.

Cuthbert puckered his lips and grazed his fingertips across his own forehead. "Could do," he said. "S'pose."

"And you remember, you've got help, Cuthbert. Help for you, help for your body, help for your mind." Dr. Bajwa spoke in a slow, soft cadence. "You remember all we've ever said, how I'm not going to let anything happen to you, right?"

"Ar, yam a chum," slurred Cuthbert.

reaching for the derelict heart

DR. SARBJINDER BAJWA WAS A MUSCULAR MAN
with a broad neck and great tactile power. He preferred solutions
to problems that could be applied manually, if not pharmacologi-
cally. In his spare weekends, he had, among other feats, learned
to pilot one of the new solarcopters, which could be spun through
the most theatrical, thousand-foot-high spirals with a simple
kneading motion of the hands. On his consultation desk he kept
a chromed fifteen-kilo dumbbell he liked to lift between patients.
He could be a touch boastful, but he was always warm, too, with
long, clement eyes the burned green of cardamom and a precise
beard so closely shaven it seemed more a placement mark for a
beard than the thing itself. His physical might, well known to his
friends, seemed effortless. At weddings and family celebrations,
he'd let three or four of his young nieces and nephews swing like
squirrels from his arm.

Patients would always inspect, with visible appreciation,
that gleaming dumbbell on the desk. It made them feel safe—
sheltered from disease, protected from themselves, and beside a

power more muscular, if not stronger, than King Henry and the Windsor fanatics.

ALTHOUGH CUTHBERT HAD HIS OWN Indigent block flat, or IB, as one was called, he barely occupied his assigned living-hole. The IBs were so structurally dangerous, depopulated, and crime ridden that many residents in the last twenty years had abandoned them. When he had started reporting the animal voices, he had been officially, off and on, one of Dr. Bajwa's increasing number of "no fixed address" patients, and he had indeed spent most recent years sleeping rough, mooching sofa space from strangers, moving in and out of TB-filled doss houses, missions, and cacky B&Bs. (The only family listed on his GP records was a cousin named Rebekka, a retired NHS Élite nurse listed as living in Hertfordshire. Her Wiki-Nous cryptograph was Cuthbert's last emergency contact, but she had moved voluntarily into a Calm House.)

Baj inhabited a more orderly world, but it was not without its own disjunctions and sudden partings. He was a former top sport-medicine researcher who had been stripped of access to his treasured laboratory under the resurgent monarchy; the doctor was thirty years younger than Cuthbert, but like Cuthbert, he didn't fit into his country.

Fewer and fewer did. With the introduction of the Baronetcy Alimentation Act of 2025 and Positive Disenfranchisement Act of 2028, many of Britain's most cherished social reforms passed under Victoria had been obviated. National devolution fell out of favor, and the Scottish and Welsh national assemblies lost key powers. A new Orangeman Army sprang up in Belfast. Stunningly, across Great Britain, thousands of urban laborers willingly gave up their rights to vote in exchange for secure jobs on the new soybean farms outside the cities, along with housing in family dormitories, free basic meals, and free access to mind-numbing Nexar hood treatments.

(Electroencephalographic headwear made of fibronic cloth, Nexar hoods—of a pyramidal shape and in ubiquitous NHS Élite blue—were fitted on people, often but not always voluntarily, and usually at government-operated Calm Houses, and used to send soothing signals down their neuronal axons. The signals could also be "read," monitored, and manipulated. Over the course of sessions lasting from hours to days on end, the hoods would smooth and desplinter brain activity like a kind of mental wood plane. The effects lasted for weeks.)

With the new Acts, the old National Health Service had also split into the tiny, private NHS Legacy (for hereditary or purchased peerages, certain public workers, and the thousands of hangers-on in the vast new aristocracy), and the ragged, more and more depleted free NHS Élite (for Briton's seventy million Indigents and a handful of others from the shrinking lower-middle class). Many middle-class Britons not crippled by various WikiNous distractions had already been decimated by the popular suicide cults, which attracted them in droves. Millions of the rest in the middle, having lost suffrage with the Positive Disenfranchisement Act, fell to official Indigent status during the so-called Great Reclamation of the 2020s, when trillions of pounds of value were written off financial markets.

As a physician under the Baronetcy Alimentation Act, Dr. Bajwa would normally be accorded a nonhereditary peerage, but he hadn't saved nearly enough money for even one of the new "baby-baronetcies," as they were known, and the Bajwas lacked connections. (The physician's own younger brother, Banee, a former republican activist, had overdosed on heroin years ago, despite all his family's effort to "sort Banee out," as their father put it, and this had marked the whole clan as rather dubious.) Moreover, Baj far too often spoke his mind and showed benevolence for the poor—ruinous habits under Henry IX, or "Harry9," as Indigents called him.

Baj's casual denunciations, spoken among supposed friends, of NHS Élite's emphasis on palliative neurology—in which the relief of pain supplanted research and one-on-one care—had got him assigned to an NHS Élite surgery in offices across the Holloway Road from a betting shop and a Szechuan masturbation stand. It was a far cry from the wealthier central London districts, where serene greens for spawn-ball—a slow-paced kind of tennis with genomic, hour-lifetime lagomorphic spawn-balls carefully "played" across a grassy court—art galleries, duty-reduced luxury shops, and some of the new schools for women's etiquette had all taken root.

"Your misapprehensions," he said to Cuthbert one day. "Listen. If you don't take your meds as prescribed, and you don't keep off the Flōt—Cuthbert, listen, you *listen* to me—*this* is the price. That's one thing I must say. And that's just one. You know what I mean, surely. If you do something foolish, in public, you're going to find yourself wearing a hood, my friend. Or going for a burton."*

"I don't care," said Cuthbert. "At least it's not Whittington."

"You have no idea what you mean. There is . . . nothing . . . *really* . . . wrong with Whittington," the doctor said, wincing a bit. As the last decent free hospital in London, and the only remaining NHS Élite site for addiction treatment, the Whittington Hospital, close by in Archway, was scandalously overstretched.

"Whittington doesn't work. It's hopeless. I can't understand why King Harry's let it go this way. It's not much better off than banjaxed in a Nexar hood, is it?"

"You are. The hood is . . . the end. Of everything. Whittington can be a start. There's an effort there. There's hope. A hope and a prayer."

―――――――――――

* Missing or dead

Cuthbert blinked a few times and smiled in a strange, sour way. "The most I'll ever do is get a few days past the first Flōt withdrawal. I admit they're very clever at the Whit, I s'ppose. And I feel like that lot . . . loiks me. In their way."

"See? You have friends there, thank you," said the doctor. "You go to Whittington. I'll get you in, fast-tracked. Anytime. At a moment's notice. And why worry about the second withdrawal? That's years away."

Flōt's bell-curved dual-withdrawal syndrome arose from its unique twin-cycle neurotoxic effect on the brain's serotonergic system. Unlike most abstinence-based drug recoveries, in Flōt recoveries the peril went from bad to better to lethal as years clean passed. The most recovering addicts could hope for were some comparatively peaceful years between first and second withdrawals, typically about ten to fifteen, followed by a dark time of anger, insomnia, and floridly hypomanic delirium that marked second withdrawal's arrival.

Cuthbert leaned his chair back on its hind legs for a moment, then brought it down. He tilted his head slightly, listening. He crossed his legs and gazed upward, smiling more thoroughly now, as if staring at the credits screen of a deeply gratifying film.

"I wish I could tell you more, but it's not possible," he said. "The animals, see. Again. I hear them. *Foxes* now. They want to say . . . thank you? To all the *people* in this dirty owd town." Cuthbert chuckled a bit. "Thank you! Ta! Funny, eh? 'Cheers!' What's there to thank?" Cuthbert's smile fell. His eyes glistened. "Them foxes are innocent—and foolish. Thoi've no bloody idea."

The doctor noticed a tremor in the aged man's lips as he spoke. He took a relatively small daily dose of the ancient, crude antipsychotic med Abilify, in a desultory manner, but his massive Flōt intake negated most of its benefits.

"What makes them innocent?"

"They trust us," said Cuthbert. "They oughtn't."

Dr. Bajwa started on the desk with his finger, making tiny circles. Then he began tapping powerfully—hammering, really.

"This is only your brain—and the Flōt." *Tap, tap, tap.* "You need to be careful . . . about what you say. You understand?"

"I try to be careful," said Cuthbert. "But the animals are speaking to me . . . for a reason. It's something I've waited for *my whole life*. This was supposed to happen, see?"

The doctor's knowledge of what could happen to Cuthbert in the clutches of NHS's mass psychotherapeutic division, EquiPoise, made it hard to give him the space he needed to talk freely. He feared openness. Even very casual talk therapy was considered a luxury reserved for the new aristocracy. EquiPoise's Psyalleviators, or P-levs, whose official role was to battle the era's viral cults and political radicals on behalf of the king, had convoluted the simplest rites of doctorly care among the masses.

There were smaller, new nuisances in Dr. Bajwa's life, too. Unusually, lately, he felt easily winded and kept getting bronchitis; his boyfriends kept dumping him for blue-eyed English boys; his family criticized him for not "aspiring" enough; his friends were all moving to the controversial new colonies in Antarctica. But the way Harry9's government had come between him and his patients—this, more than any other problem in his life, incensed him. Stunningly, despite all the cruelties Indigents such as Cuthbert suffered under Harry9, Cuthbert himself—and he wasn't alone among Indigents—held the monarchy in the highest regard, and he could be quite jingoistic.

"There's not one thing on earth that's not better in England," he would sometimes slur at Baj. "We've got the best cats—and best football. And good 'ole Harry's the best of all the bloody bunch."

Such statements quietly infuriated Baj, yet something about Cuthbert's blend of good-heartedness, reactionary nationalism, and almost artistic grandiosity also, despite his knowing better, mesmerized him. He wanted to understand it.

The doctor one day had looked up from his antique linen-paper notebook and smiled purposefully at Cuthbert in the consultation room.

"O-T-T-E-R-S," said Baj aloud, writing each letter with a strong hand in black ink with a big gold-plated fountain pen. The pen was inscribed with Sanskrit script that translated as, "Only action will define us." Unlike most of his colleagues, few of whom knew how to use a pen, he loathed the trendy SkinWerks digital aerosols that let one write and read on the skin.

"Why otters? Why them?"

Cuthbert looked askance. "They're . . . very godly creatures, too. Do you want to know why?"

"Yes, I do." Bajwa tried to speak in a friendly but resolved tone, but a trace of irritability crept in. "I certainly do. Now wait just a moment . . ."

He took his stethoscope from his desk drawer.

"Let me," he said, unbuttoning the top of Cuthbert's shirt and deftly, with two fingers, holding the stethoscope's diaphragm against Cuthbert's chest. He heard the tattered *hwoot-dub hwoot-dub* of his murmur. The fact was, the fat old man—six foot four and twenty-two stone—could drop dead at any moment.

"Your cardiomyopathy's not any worse," the doctor said. "But you need to take it easy." He put the stethoscope back in the top drawer of his desk. There were at least two newer cardiac Core-Mods™ available for Cuthbert's type of enlargement, but both were strictly NHS Legacy items, or one had to pay millions on the private mod market.

Thirty years before, Cuthbert had won, through the old Body-Mod™ lottery, two lower-cost mods—a cheap ventricle wall panel on his heart and a onetime infusion of pluripotent hepatocytal cells for his liver. He'd also managed, in his early eighties, to get his hands on a spool of crylon body-mesh and a used set of EverConnectors, sized 2XL, and this set had come with cartilage drugs, too, as well as free installation.

"The otters," said Cuthbert. "They have a message—for all of England."

"It's your brain," he said. "Just your brain. But if you can't stop spiring* and get through the first withdrawal—listen, Cuddy—you know, it's a *kind* place, and they're brilliant and they're discreet, Cuddy." He frowned slightly. "They'll keep you well away from EquiPoise. There's a simple and deadly health issue here, my good friend."

"Oh, Jaysus," said Cuthbert. "I should've kept my gob shut. Not Whittington. I've said too bloody much!"

It was at this point that Dr. Bajwa reached across his desk, took Cuthbert's hands in his, and gave them a firm, tender squeeze. He leaned so far forward that one of the armpits of his blue suit jacket made a little ripping sound.

Cuthbert beamed at him, although his dry lips quivered a bit.

"No, you have most certainly *not* told me too much," said the doctor. He felt as if he wanted to reach through a dark blue shell of pathology and grab the great, derelict heart before him. "You must trust me. There's nothing wrong with Whittington Hospital. But you . . . are . . . *very* . . . unwell, my friend."

"You are *very* decent, sir," Cuthbert pronounced. "But let go 'o me maulers," he said, pulling his hands back fiercely. Cuthbert couldn't remember the last time anyone had held his hands. The doctor's grip was colder than he'd imagined. Cuthbert could smell the figgy notes of his Diptyque cologne.

"I've had enough of the Whitt—I've packed it in, in *moi* mind," Cuthbert said. "I feel, I, I, I really ought to let the poor otters into

---

*   Using or being intoxicated by Flōt

the cuts. It's for England." He gave the doctor a sly look. "And the king could use my help."

"You shouldn't talk like that, my friend. I mean, Cuthbert. They are utterly merciless."

There was a long silence. After a while, the doctor wrote in his notepad.

"But, go on. Come. I'm—I'm listening carefully. And when you say otters—you do mean the sort of minky, playful things?"

"Otters," Cuthbert repeated. A gleam of aureate light radiated through the window. "I know it might sound completely barmy." It was indeed that, as far as Dr. Bajwa saw it. One surely never heard the word *otter* more than once in a career in a north London GP's office.

"You know my missing brother Dryst? I think he might have sort of become a kind of otter." Cuthbert nibbled gently at the inside of his cheek; there was a tough little ridge of flesh there that he sometimes liked to worry. "Of sorts."

Dr. Bajwa said, "I know you feel that loss. And after the challenges you've had, I'm sure you feel it all the more. And after so very many decades of . . . griefs."

"No, no, no," said Cuthbert, shaking his head. "He's back, you see? Drystan has returned. And I think 'e's in the zoo. There's more to tell. Much more, doc. But I corr."*

Dr. Bajwa thought for a moment, rubbing his short, graceful beard.

"I want you to stay away from the zoo, Cuthbert. Let's avoid things that obviously upset you. And these zoo voices—they're not your friends." The doctor coughed a few times. He was coming down with something, it seemed. He said, "You're a very clever man, so surely you grasp that?"

Cuthbert was, but he didn't, couldn't, and wouldn't.

---

* Can't

singled out for otterspaeke

SO IT WAS, AT FIRST, THAT DR. BAJWA SIMPLY advised Cuthbert to avoid Regent's Park. Anything to de-escalate Cuthbert's obsession seemed a step forward. Keep out of Regent's Park, and these "zoo voices" will fade, the doctor thought. Here was simple, sensible medicine.

"A zoo *can* be a rather intense sort of place, if you think about it," Dr. Bajwa had said to Cuthbert. "It's no place for you."

CUTHBERT RARELY MADE APPOINTMENTS; he would just show up, in all his shabby glory, with a heap of vinegary chips in his arms, or a warm purple sphere of Flōt in his coat. The frowning admins would send him back to the consultation room, holding his own file and wearing his usual shamefaced smile.

"The zoo admission's twenty-five bloody pounds," he was telling Dr. Bajwa one day. "I saw the sign at the gate." He clasped his hands together. They were filthy and mottled with white psoriasis and liver spots.

"Hardly anyone goes—that's why," Dr. Bajwa said.

A few years before, after the closings of both the Beijing and Bronx zoos, a short flurry of patriotic stories about the London Zoo had memed across WikiNous, most along the lines of "the first and last standing," although the "first" bit wasn't entirely true. Still, almost no zoo animals existed in the wild anymore, and thousands upon thousands of species were newly extinct. Polar bears, giant pandas, as well as most large marine species, wild ferrets, and cranes, survived only as genomic software that the children of the rich used to print miniature cuddle and bath toys as well as living mobiles.

Cuthbert had never been inside a zoo, even as a child, and the doctor wanted to keep it that way.

"But you're still visiting the park," the doctor noted. "You're asking for trouble. You don't realize. A drowning man isn't bothered by rain. Didn't we say we should avoid the whole of Regent's? I thought we'd got a sort of understanding, my friend."

"Ar," said Cuthbert. "But the otters—and the jackals and a few others—they've got their own little ways, haven't they? Where am I to go, if I ignore them?" He averted his gaze and looked through the window. "I nipped into the library at Finsbury Park, but I fell asleep at my table, and this skinny library bloke with one of them fuckin' Eye3 pendants 'round his neck, he said he'd hand me over to the Watch to be nicked if he saw me in there again. At least in the parks, and with the animals, I won't get nicked."

The threat of the Red Watch was real, Dr. Bajwa knew. Unlike most public spaces, the royal parks normally weren't patrolled by the Watch, but instead by the old, lenient constabulary. Being detained by the Watch could prove catastrophic for someone as powerless as Cuthbert, and the thought of ridiculous, feeble old Cuthbert getting dragged away by the red-suited Watchmen with their neuralwave pikes horrified him. Cuthbert would be warehoused with other mentally ill Indigents and shoved under a Nexar hood. He'd probably suffer cardiac arrest.

The doctor coughed a few times—a dry, barking hack that surprised him in its power. "Oh," he said, reeling a little. "This dry air." He took a deep breath and gulped. "I am just beginning to wonder," he said, recovering, his voice still croaking, "if a visit to the zoo might not actually calm you down a bit?" He coughed twice more.

"Ar," said Cuthbert, in an overplayed Black Country dialect he sometimes slipped into when feeling weary, fearful, or especially close to someone. "Now yam onto summat,* cocker. If I could just *see* the otters—just once. I'd, *loik,* discuss about a few things, roight?" He pulled out a purple sphere of Flōt and held it toward the doctor, who was coughing again. It wasn't hotted up, but it would do. "Yow alwroight, mon? Yow want a snort?"

"Stop it," said the doctor. "It's nothing. And put that away!" For a moment, he felt real anger toward Cuthbert. "Can we just get one thing sorted? If you go, can we keep in mind that the animals really aren't speaking to you? And you'll stay off your Flōt?"

Cuthbert gave him a vexed smile, the edges of his lips paled with pressure.

"And you'll have to pay for it yourself," the doctor added. "Can you do that?"

"It depends what you mean by 'pay,' " Cuthbert said. "There's more than money at stake. There's the boy." He spoke with dry matter-of-factness. His eyes, normally a Brythonic russet-brown, and as spongy as Anglesey soil, seemed newly hard and clear. "Oi've paid with my heart—for decades."

The screeching color-charge compressors of a passing bosonicabus—probably the No. 29—could be heard outside in the Holloway Road.

---

* . . . you're onto something

Cuthbert added, sounding distant: "When your brother becomes an animal, it makes you think."

"Sure, sure," said Dr. Bajwa. He felt the long blade of pity jab into him. He hated it. He despised pity's utter uselessness. But there it was—a dolor for the shredded stems of flowers never to touch the earth. Dr. Bajwa puckered his lips a bit, trying to subdue his emotions.

Cuthbert seemed to have sunk down into his chair. He was sniffling a bit.

"Why am I going to the zoo?" There were tears in Cuthbert's eyes. "What's the matter with me?" He stared dazedly at the ceiling. He said, "When my mother and father have forsaken me, the Lord will take me up." He gazed directly at Dr. Bajwa, and repeated, more frantically, "What's the matter with me?"

"I don't . . . know," said Dr. Bajwa. "Not exactly. But it seems you need these . . . voices. That's all I know." He plucked a sky-blue sticky note from his desktop and wrote his WikiNous cryptograph on it, as he had many times before, and gave it to Cuthbert. "You can message me if anything dire happens. But I really hope it won't. Just go *see* those otters. And don't do anything foolish," he said, already regretting his advice somewhat.

"I'll get the dosh," Cuthbert said, feeling atingle. "Any road up* I can."

"I know you will. I know it."

The doctor reached across the desk and squeezed Cuthbert's hand as hard as he could, and that was very hard indeed. He put a £10 coin in the dry hand—any less seemed cruel, and any more unwise.

"Just take care," the doctor said. "And at least cut back on the Flōt, you silly old fool."

---

* Any way

IN THE WEEKS THAT CAME, Cuthbert saved his dole, as best he could, panhandled a bit, and combined with Baj's tenner, he soon pulled together the £24.50 for zoo admission—enough for six liters of the economical, Dark Plume label Flōt, he ruefully noted. It had been the first time he had put anything before a drink of Flōt in years. For a few afternoons, he even stayed sober, though sobriety seemed to increase the animal voices and send his heart into wild palpitations. On one of those sober afternoons, he heard the otters again. "*Gagoga,*" they kept saying. "*Gagoga.*"

Uncharacteristically, Cuthbert had begun to avoid Dr. Bajwa a bit. He wanted to impress him with his independence. At one point, he decided to surprise Baj by *sending* an Opticall. While most Indigents received and, if literate, read dozens of Opticalls on their retinas a day, very few could afford to write them; generally, to write, you needed a quality digital epidermal aerosol such as SkinWerks and an advanced grade of access to WikiNous, things few Indigents could afford. Even emergency workers labored under strict controls and weren't normally supposed to use skin aerosols for messages.

"I want you to Opticall my GP," he was telling a street acquaintance one shaky, sober afternoon. "It's a medical issue, right?"

This wily man's name was Gadge, and he possessed a stolen case of SkinWerks, which had made him mildly noteworthy on the streets. SkinWerks was the simplest, if messiest, way to send Opticalls. A bioelectronic emollient sprayed onto the epidermis, always in high demand and pricey, it allowed wearers to read and type upon their own skin (usually, on the forearm), to exchange tactile sensations, and to display digital images on the skin—and, in limited ways, to "feel" them, too.

GADGE'S LITTLE STASH was authentic, too—and that mattered. Dangerous imitations from East Africa's new factories circulated on the black market, burning digital skin users and, at times, sparking mental illnesses, it was said.

"Yeah, medical, eh?" he asked. "Ha!"

"Tell him, 'This is Cuthbert, Baj! It's a miracle of God! I am SOBER—all caps now, that—for two hours now! Saving money for zoo! Sincerely, Cuthbert Handley.' Tell him that, right? Put exclamation points after everything, please. Please, Gadge, do your friend a favor?"

Gadge smirked and hiked up his greasy suit-jacket sleeve, throwing his head back in a floridly pompous way. He sprayed the red digital aerosol onto his own hairy forearm. He rubbed it around a bit until an ovular WikiNous portal glowed on the arm. Most people sprayed digital skins onto their own body, often for sexual thrills, but they could be applied to any flat, smooth, warm surface.

"This is a big favor I'm doing you, Cuddy," said Gadge. He had a narrow, angular face with a long, lupine jaw, and dark eyes set close together.

Cuthbert watched closely, squinting, as Gadge typed the Opticall text onto his skin, straining with every punch of a dirty finger.

"It's done," said Gadge. "I sent it. You owe me."

"Yam a fine fellow," said Cuthbert, after which Gadge released a long, rumbling fart.

WHEN DR. BAJWA got the Opticall text, he felt relief and a nervous joy. Seeing the name "Cuthbert" glide across his retinas struck him as a singular treat. There was also a sense, though much fainter, that he ought not to get enmeshed with an Indigent, but that was more for safety reasons than anything else. As a child, the egalitarianism of Sikhism and importance of *seva*, or helping the poor, were driven into him. How many *daal* dishes he'd washed at the *gurdwara*! How many golden bowls of *dahi* yogurt he had set proudly on communal tables! Nonetheless, there was also something less high-minded at work, for Baj simply liked Cuthbert. As much as any Flōt addict could be, he was honest, gentle, clever, reliable, and good—and twice the man that most Britons in Harry9's dreadful, unpredictable reign were.

ONE CHILLY SATURDAY, at the end of January, three months after the animal voices had begun, Cuthbert finally visited the zoological gardens as a paid visitor. He was, at last, going to observe living otters firsthand, paying for the privilege as other citizens had since 1828.

After passing through the turnstile at the main gate, Cuthbert began to trot feebly toward the otters in the northern part of the zoo. The exertion drove his heart into a jumble of premature contractions, and he had to stop. He stood there, gasping, beside a statue of Tony Blair that had been erected, as a diversionary tactic, during the Second Restoration. The former prime minister's aged, pinched face held a distant gaze, made all the more disconnected by the lurid bronzecast's slightly cut-price look.

"Ow am yow, Sir Tony?" asked Cuthbert. He felt he ought to be polite. "You know, I day* always vote, but I always liked your wife—so lovely." But the stiff party leader, with his hollow mind encased in bargain alloys, seemed nonetheless to look above and beyond Cuthbert.

Once at the otters' enclosure, at first Cuthbert merely watched the mustelids plunge in and out of their green-water rock pool, yinnying and playing, as he continued to catch his breath. Seeing the otters, in the flesh, wasn't so much disappointing as unnerving.

And he began to doubt, freshly, as he often did, whether he possessed the so-called Wonderments or not. It was easy to believe

---

* I didn't

that Drystan had got them. "If I'd really got them," he ruminated, "I wouldn't have ended up a sot who can't put down the bottle, would I?"

"Is that yow, trying to gab?" he asked the otters. "Or just my brain, like Baj says?"

It was right before a feeding, so they were frisky. One of the otters, a big female, as if responding to his query, regarded Cuthbert specially, standing still while another female and her whelps smashed up against her. The big female was in a delicate state of "almost pregnancy," filled with implanted sperm. Embryos would begin to gestate in a month or two. Meanwhile, the whelps kept trying to bite the other mother's neck. They wanted to nurse.

The otter habitat seemed too small, Cuthbert thought. It seemed little more than a couple of store-bought aquaria set into a mortar-and-rock faux riverbank. The otters' hair was a rich sludge color, yet iridescent, too, smoothed back by the force of a thousand dives, with light sloping off at all angles. Cuthbert had only seen such a fascinating creature once before. The female was like all the muddy moisture of England gathered into one super-muscular cat shape. She was a Sufi creature, he thought to himself, reaching back to his cannabis and acid-addled days of bad dabbling in sophomoric esoterica which began years ago at university. Neither wholly of earth nor of water, neither entirely real nor imagined, the otter occupied an eerie in-betweenness, one of the Sufi dimensions between the Absolute of the Absolute and Cuthbert's ugly life.

" 'Ello, muckers," he had said. "Am I safe now, am I? Do you remember me? From back in the *owd* days? With Drystan and what?"

He felt a sudden stab of longing for Drystan.

"Are one of you Drystan? Are you?"

No spoken word, per se, emanated from them, but Cuthbert was emotionally and mentally overwhelmed with a sense of being singled out for otterspaeke. He still felt unsure if it was the Wonderments at work, but he felt Drystan's minty presence.

"Dryst," he whispered. "Please."

His rare bout of semisobriety had intensified the experience tenfold, too. He looked into the big female otter's eyes, colored as brown-black as a river bottom. A craving seemed to concentrate in her. Or was it his craving? Who could know? There was, in any case, a desperate need in her dark eyes, from which these words emerged:

Gagoga gagoga gagoga
Miltsung miltsung miltsung

Any passing observer on the zoo's path would have noticed little more than a fat-tummied ogler of otters hunched over the display's barricade. But inside Cuthbert the worlds of nature, history, supernature, and memory had all burst and commingled.

The female otter rose upon her haunches, leaned forward toward Cuthbert, and took in the grassy-oily-boozy human scent emanating from him.

Miltsung, she said, in a squeaky mewl, then *gagoga, gagoga, gagoga.*

Cuthbert didn't know what *gagoga gagoga gagoga* was, but it was not Flōt and it wasn't the Whittington and it wasn't even the words of Dr. Bajwa; it was something new, he was sure, a guttural alphabet gurgling in his head like water off rocks. It sounded risky, too, and it sounded urgent. Above all, it sounded like "Let us out!"

And it seemed weirdly familiar to him, too, an incantation from long ago. He wondered if his vanished brother would have understood their meaning, or if he and his loss and his return *were* their meaning.

Gagoga!

Cuthbert often recalled the blue veins faintly visible on his brother's pale neck as a child, like tiny unborn rivers, dormant and perfect. He was a beautiful boy, and his loss was ugly and palpable—it roiled Cuthbert's abdomen, and over his lifetime, it had grown harder and sicker and larger, not unlike his dying liver. Lately, when he cast around his mind for more memories of the boy, he felt increasingly blank, and the unborn rivers ran dry. And yet, as he stood, leaning against the diatom-stained glass barrier, before this once most English of English beasts, there was a sure sense to him of Drystan's presence. Somewhere in the otters' dark, slick hearts, in their round tomcat heads, in their webbed claws, as a poet once wrote, "of neither water nor land," a kind of redemption lived.

There was a tap on Cuthbert's shoulder. As soon as he saw the scarlet from the corner of his eye, he knew he faced unspeakable danger.

"You don't look well, Indigent," said the Watchman coarsely, and with the usual snide undertone. He had a boxy jaw and eyes like dull blue pellets. He wore one of the less bulky mantles of the Watch, red and embroidered with gold orphreys, all with a large eye in their centers. The Eye3 devices belonged to a class of biotech barred from Indigent use. These optical devices—and several dozen glared from every Watchman's cloak—possessed the red-rimmed sclera of hound eyes. They roved. They accused. They rolled with a dim quasi intelligence. Crowded onto Watchmen cloaks, they created a grotesque effect, like draperies jeweled with eyeballs, and, along the trademark golden neuralwave pike the Watch all carried, the effect terrified the powerless.

"You paid?" the Watchman demanded.

"Ar, sir," said Cuthbert. "I did." He wasn't as high as usual on Flōt, but he wasn't sober either; the slight buzz let him speak with a touch of composure. He still possessed the illusory proprioception of long legs as well as the self-satisfaction typical of a Flōt high. But

the Red Watch were trained to watch for Ingall's Sign, the slight
stooping forward and loping gait that Flōt normally caused in longtime addicts.

"Have you noticed there aren't Indigents here? This is a place for
quality families. That's what the king wants." The Watchman ran
his hand up and down his pike. "I think it's time you went home."

"But, sir, I paid. It's a medical issue. My doctor's sent me here.
A'm a loyal subject."

The Watchman frowned at him, nodding. "You leaning forward, mate?"

"I'm just tall," said Cuthbert.

"Yeah, tall. That's a coopy* way of putting it." Then he smiled
acidly. "Oh, I'm sorry, a *medical* problem, is it? You need a hood?
Shall I put a call into the P-levs?"

"That's not right," said Cuthbert. "I hear animals. You ought
not! That's not —" Before he could get it out, the Watchman tapped
him with his pike. His knees buckled and he dropped like a sack of
onions. Cuthbert sat on the ground, an old man stunned, rubbing
his fat temples and trying to get his bearings.

"Are you thick as pig shit?" asked the Watchman, speaking in a
hushed voice. "Get the fuck up and go wash back down the urinal
you crawled from. You've no idea how miserable I could make your
life, you badger's arse. Want to spend your golden years wanking in
a Calm House? You one of them cultists?"

The Watch was recruited from other Indigents, and notoriously
sadistic, and Watchmen acted with special pitilessness toward other
Indigents. Cuthbert was in real danger, and he knew it now. It was
not uncommon to hear stories of Indigents neuralpiked to death,
especially if they were accused cultists or high on Flōt.

A small crowd, mostly milky-skinned women with small children in strollers, had gathered. They glared at Cuthbert with cu-

---

* Peculiar

riosity and contempt. There were no Indigents among them, from what Cuthbert saw.

"Leave him alone," a younger woman with a long lilac skirt said to the Watchman. "He's just a poor old man who eats too many biscuits. He's allowed at the zoo."

The Watchman quietly made a *sheeh* sound, snorting a little. "Just keeping the zoo safe, ma'am. This man was, erm, loitering. It's a tactic I associate with that Heaven's Gate lot. Or 'e's a dangerous Flōt addict."

Cuthbert picked himself up. He patted himself for the sphere of Flōt under his coat, and he felt relieved to feel it intact.

"Take it easy," he said to the Watchman. "I'll go. I'm not in any bloody cult." He glanced toward the otters for a moment, but they had disappeared, sensing a threat. He whispered to them, "Goodbye, you good creatures." He would see them again, he thought—somehow—and he would see them go free.

As Cuthbert exited through the zoo's main turnstile, an old anger erupted in him. He trudged north with heavy steps. He knew nowhere to put his ire, so he waved his arms, calling attention to himself in the streets, which was danger in itself. Like millions of others, he had tasted the wrath of an evil and reckless new monarchy's power structure. But by the time he made his way to Camden Town, halfway home, he realized his anger was gone. It was replaced with a plan: before summer, he was going to break into the zoo and free all the animals—and especially the otters.

"*Gagoga*," he had said, almost laughing. "Ga-bloody-goga!"

the secret patient

DR. BAJWA JUST HAD NO IDEA HOW DRAMATICALLY unhinged things were about to get. When he'd learned of Cuthbert's introductory debacle at the zoo, he'd merely asked Cuthbert to visit at least twice a week, "off the books," late in the day, without signing in, for Cuthbert's own protection from EquiPoise. He was perceptive enough to sense a kind of formless, escalating catastrophe on the horizon—one that seemed to have glomped onto his own life—but he felt it more as a broad-spectrum anxiety than a specific worry.

They sat in Baj's familiar consultation room, after hours. "I reckoned you'd be fed up with me by now."

Dr. Bajwa said, "I haven't minded our talks."

The long dark days of the English winter, and a worsening cough, had made the doctor morose. He found himself glad to see Cuthbert and looked forward to a resumption of their sessions, yet he sensed a subtle impatience in Cuthbert. It took him by surprise, and it seemed to mirror a mounting, recent prickliness in himself.

Cuthbert seemed especially tired and shaky this evening.

"Looks like you've been in the wars."

"Why waste your time with a wode-wode mon* as lives in doss-housen†?" asked Cuthbert, almost confrontationally.

"It's not a waste."

It was half past four o'clock, and black outside. The crack of old-tech small-arms fire outside—handguns—as well as the horrible hissing of microwave explosives filtered through the window. It all made Baj uneasy.

Cuthbert looked unfazed by the nightly sounds of north London violence. At times, he tilted his head to hear the noise outside better, then resumed conversation ebulliently.

It was said that the most prominent of the English republican terrorists, called the Army of Anonymous UK, or AA-UK for short—and engendered by the long-outlawed hacktivists, Anonymous—were amid a winter offensive in southern England, but accurate news was almost impossible to obtain these days. The flesh—the only transmitter of WikiNous—often told lies.

"Enough of this chaos for long enough, and you see why people start running to the cults," the doctor said. "Don't think I haven't thought about their promises."

Cuthbert nodded sadly and clasped his hands together, as if preparing to pray for them both.

"We're running out of options, aren't we?" the doctor said to Cuthbert. "I guess you could say that Windsors are making good health mandatory."

"Then I'm in luck," said Cuthbert, grinning. "I'm as bloody fit as a butcher's dog."

"I don't know what a butcher is, but you aren't, I'm afraid, healthy, not in the least," Baj said. He tried to speak in an ariose,

---

*   Mad man

†   Doss houses

teasing manner, not wanting to offend his charge. "If you stopped the Flōt—"

Cuthbert interrupted, "If I'm not healthy, then why don't you 'av me sign in properly?"

"I have my reasons," said Baj.

The truth was, the Ministry of Mind automatically scanned office records for what it termed "excessive support," and Dr. Bajwa's compassion had seriously endangered both of them. Hypochondriacs, Flōt addicts, and the otherwise mentally ill inevitably ended up before the Ministry's EquiPoise inquisitors, whom Dr. Bajwa considered little more than psychological versions of Red Watch thugs.

"I'm telling you," said Baj. "You've got to keep a low profile. Please, Cuthbert. Do it for your old mate." He raised his brows and tried to affect an accent from the recently declared All-Indigent zone of Bethnal Green, where he'd grown up. "Look me in me mincies, mate—I wouldn't tell you a cherry!"

Cuthbert sat puzzled, blinking. East End slang always sounded preposterous to him. It certainly wasn't yam-yammy Black Country talk, he thought, and it wasn't otterspaeke. But he did value the joviality, more than Baj realized.

"We're friends now?" asked Cuthbert.

Baj coughed a couple times. He worked to clear his throat of both phlegm and his strained Cockney. "Well . . . yes. Why not?"

"Fact is," said Cuthbert, "I'm goin' to let all the animals out of the zoo. But I dunna want to see you scragged by any Red Watch for *my* animal business."

Baj laughed. He simply did not believe Cuthbert was serious.

"No," said Baj. "You can't do that. It's quite impossible anyway. You'd have the whole bleedin' RAF bearing down on you. It's the last zoo on earth, isn't it? I've heard that underground they've thousands of complete gene-maps for every animal known. It's the ark."

"I will," he said.

"Cracking," said Baj, still not believing Cuthbert had the intention—or the means—to do so.

IN THE NEXT, final week before things turned grim for Baj, he pressed the idea of a Flōt detox at the Whittington, but gently. Cuthbert would bring in copies of old scientific journal articles, meticulously scissored out and somehow printed—and almost no one printed anything these days—onto ivory paper, a passé resource hard to come by for anyone, let alone an Indigent.

The articles all came from the sober but tiny subset of psychology researchers who studied animal cognition. "Cats Shatter Applied Rules Barrier," read one title from the 2010s. Another asked, "Do Bees Have an Imagination?"

The doctor began to wonder whether his secret patient was as crazy as he let on.

"Really, I'm not sure you're quite as ill, at the end of the day, as you may be *officially*," Dr. Bajwa found himself pronouncing at one point.

"Yes? S'that mean I oughn't worry about the otters?"

"No," said the doctor. "There's a problem there—in not worrying at all, I mean. And I've been wanting to ask you, what—er, what do they—the otters—actually say? To you?"

"Oh, they're complete sixes and sevens," said Cuthbert. "Just mad and yampy as paper tigers in the rain—ha-ha. Things like '*blah blah blah*' and so on. And let us out, or what."

"I have a feeling you're not being entirely frank now."

"I am. But as I told you before, and it didn't seem to make a difference. I told you: '*gagoga.*' That's the key."

"But you see, it's *you* who give their words meaning. The otters—or your brother, who is most likely dead—aren't actually *talking* to you, are they? It's more that you're *thinking* about them talking to you, right?"

"Ar."

"So I believe we may be getting somewhere."

"I do, too. Somewhere."

Still, each vaguely sensed that the other had a very different destination in mind.

TOWARD THE END OF JANUARY, Harry9's newly empowered Privy Council asked that Parliament study another series of social reforms, this time regarding what it called "quality of life" and "national civility" issues. It was said to be motivated by the continued spread of the most powerful of the new suicide cults—Heaven's Gate—but it sent a chill through the NHS Élite and its harried GPs. This particular cult, which practiced ritual mass suicide along with mass animal sacrifices, had begun to infiltrate the Indigent populations, who had heretofore seemed immune to its promises of human transcendence to a "Next Level." There were suspicions, too, that Heaven's Gate was secretly behind the spread of Flōt addiction, and this was beginning to panic the rising British aristocracy (and, indeed, ruling classes around the world). The voteless Indigents were, after all, Britain's new workforce par excellence.

The homeless, seen as especially vulnerable, were to be moved assertively toward controversial, unproven Nexar treatments if they wanted to keep their benefits. All provisions for any kind of free psychotherapy, except for something called "Family Integrity Counseling," were to be abolished. Among the most powerful aristocrats, only a very young former Earl of Worcester, a callow thorn in Harry9's side and distant cousin, promised to fight the proposals. Dr. Bajwa himself felt furious over the proposals, but powerless.

"I saw that Earl of Worcester on the TV," Baj was telling Cuthbert. "They've said he's secretly in deep with the Army of Anonymous, and some of the Irish Underground, but I don't know. What do you think, Cuthbert? He sure doesn't like Harry. Of course, Harry makes hatred very easy. But if it weren't for Worcestershire, they say, Harry would have taken over every mind in Europe. He's afraid. He's still afraid of going too far—thank heavens."

Cuthbert pursed his lips. "All these powerful people—none of them are really listenin'—not to me, not to anyone anymore. Not really. Not hard. If they were, they'd hear what's coming—and it's not good. But I don't mind the king. I've not much use for this Earl of Worcester bloke."

"What's coming, my friend?"

"The end."

ONE DAY, soon after this, Dr. Bajwa found himself wheezing badly after taking a run in Finsbury Park. He needed to bend over in his sky-blue training jacket and magnetic running shoes to gasp for breath. He coughed, and he noticed a few bright flecks of blood on his hand. A homeless man with an oily brown beanie hat and no upper front teeth saw him and put his hand on Baj's back.

"Easy, mate," the Indigent said. "You're awright."

"Right," he said. "Fit as a fid—" He coughed again. "Fiddle!"

The doctor had no history of asthma or bronchitis, and he had never used tobacco, so he mostly felt unworried. Still, it was strange.

A few days later, Baj visited his own NHS Legacy GP, a white-mustachioed internist on Harley Street.

Dr. Peter Bonhomme was an even-tempered pragmatist who

had survived the paroxysms of the new monarchy by feigning sentimentality when it came to politics. He always wore an old commemorative House of Windsor badge pin issued to mark Elizabeth II's death. He was short, round, and strong, and apart from his shaky hands, looked not unlike his pin's squat, stolid depiction of the Tower of Windsor. He was a kindly man, and Baj considered him a heartening presence if not quite a friend.

Dr. Bonhomme never wasted time. He drew blood, listened to Baj's chest with a mediscope, and gave him a cloudy plastic cup for urinalysis.

"Right," he said, with a characteristic firmness. "So how are you doing otherwise?" he asked.

"All is well," Baj said. He felt anxious to talk, but he couldn't bring himself to say much. An old indisposition to show weakness held him back. He almost would have felt more comfortable sharing with a social lesser—even Cuthbert.

"I'm all right," he added. "You know, 'getting on with it.' Are you well?"

"I'm glad to be working still."

"You call this work, on Harley Street?" Dr. Bajwa teased. At one time, such a quip between professionals would have seemed more amusing, he realized. "Sorry," he said. "I couldn't resist."

"No worries, Baj!" said Dr. Bonhomme, grinning, and looking at his mediscope's floating holographic readout, which plotted a colored ball—in this case red—onto a shoe box–size three-dimensional quadrangle that the doctor analyzed. "We're lucky to be working at all these days," he said.

"Yes," said Baj. Were he to say any more, he knew, the conversation would be edging toward treason. He left it there.

Dr. Bonhomme slid a white ultrasonic camera out of a small plastic case and dimmed the lights. The older doctor smiled gently at Baj for a moment, but then seemed lost in trying to work the camera.

"Hold still now," he said, "and raise your arms up." Baj complied. Four faint hums ensued—and it was over.

The aged Dr. Bonhomme could barely hold the heavy camera steady as he guided it onto a wet-titanium gooseneck base. Two lurid blue-white biometric eyes awakened above the lens. He rubbed the top of the camera for a moment, as if petting a baby white shark, and the camera instantaneously projected four-dimensional pathological extrapolations of Baj's insides on the wall.

Baj looked at white petals of a neoplasm, unfolding on the wall. There it was—a pale flower of death in the right lobe of his lung.

Dr. Bonhomme's face had fallen. He glanced nervously at Baj.

"But I don't smoke," said Baj. "This can't be."

There was a pause. Dr. Bonhomme said hoarsely, "We can do a lot these days—even with lungs." He appeared to collect himself for a moment. He stood up a little taller, then spoke confidently: "Right now. These are but 'shadows of things to come,' as they say. But you're going to need an oncologist. And you might consider a day or two of Nexar—just to destress, right?"

"I don't use the hoods," said Baj, in a tone of subdued annoyance, and Dr. Bonhomme nodded.

There was another pause. Dr. Bonhomme nodded and put his hand on his peer's shoulder.

"Look, I won't claim to understand how you feel," he said. "I'd react the same way, honestly." He switched off the ultrasonic camera, and the screen popped off with a tiny shriek. "But it's not like the twentieth century, is it? I'm sorry, Baj. But it's not a death sentence. And just thank bloody god you're in Legacy."

"God couldn't give a fuck about me," said Baj.

Dr. Bajwa had an incipient lung tumor. Treated, it wasn't necessarily terminal, he knew, but the five-year survival rate was still only 50 percent. Whole new metastasizing cancers and newly aggressive viral syndromes remained significant medical foes, even in this era of 120-year-plus life spans. The problem was, for the rich, the development of a variety of new, improved, salable BodyMods—especially CoreMods (through which most major organs, apart from brains, could be easily refurbished), and EverConnectors (synthetic, fibrous connective tissue-sleeves)—as well as new cartilage chemotherapies—had long supplanted the search for cures in terms of much research. For everyone else, and especially Indigents, Nexar hoods as well as ordinary intoxicants—even Flōt—made cancer less menacing.

As Baj left Dr. Bonhomme's office and headed toward his parking spot, he found himself silently running through part of a prayer from his childhood. *Gaavai, kotaan. Havai kisai taan*, he remembered. *Some sing of his power. Who has that power?*

An advert for Lucozade suddenly appeared on his corneas—the usual unwanted Opticalls you got walking through central London. There were dozens of grades of freedom from daytime Optispam bursts (after dark, the burst-rates fell considerably). You had to pay a huge monthly fee to keep *all* the adverts off your eyes, and even with his comparatively good income, he couldn't afford the top service (although in recent years, many brains had adapted to Optispam and begun, partially, to block it out—a neurological "anomaly" the authority's tech teams remained unable to defeat). A nude, dark-haired woman with absurdly large breasts and a startled look was shaking a Lucozade bottle in an obviously raunchy manner. "Great performance is easy to get into your hands," she cooed. The images broke Baj's attention, of course, and with that came a ferocious urge to bite out his own eyes.

And the king wonders why the suicide cults grow? he thought to himself.

He did not feel sad about the cancer—not yet. He felt unholy rage, and this, in turn, drove him to tamp down the full range of his emotions, as if intense feelings and the confusing thoughts accompanying them were cellular mutations to be understood, controlled, and dissolved. He felt a sudden, fierce urge to get to the Philip K heliport in Kent where he took, as time permitted, Saturday solar-copter lessons. If he could get above the earth, he imagined, and get strapped into a copter's fleshy bio-seats, he would shoot through Britain's raw blue air, working his thoughts and his hands at the solarcopter controls, and maybe, just maybe, he would begin to rule this new foe.

Cuthbert, on the other hand, seemed to have no interest in regulating his mind or body; Baj felt he needed to do it for them both.

For as long as he could, Baj told himself, he would try to keep Cuthbert and his bright blooms of psychosis from EquiPoise, whose psychologists showed little patience for good-hearted GPs or citizens carrying what it termed "unhygienic content," a phrase kept menacingly vague by His Majesty's Government. (Flōt *was* legal, but EquiPoise's functionaries were well known for their special hatred of Flōters, who were viewed as little more than socioeconomic parasites.)

He would not give up on this old man. Here was a chance to bring back, in some tiny measure, a simple faith in the goodness of the world that his own brother Banee's overdose and the regime had stolen.

And was Cuthbert really so far off? Everyone thinks about animals, Dr. Bajwa told himself. He himself greatly admired tigers. He still remembered a story told to him as a child about a Brahmin who spoke to jackals, buffaloes, lions, and even peepal trees. Do not half the books of little ones, he mused, contain talking animals? On any given afternoon, does Hyde Park not contain at least one old man who speaks to his terrier with verbosity, real intimacy, and even erudition?

"You aren't," the doctor was saying to Cuthbert, a few days later, "quite as mentally *off* as I think you want us all to believe, are you? You're a Flōter who likes animals. That's the overview, innit?" He'd sunk into his chummy Bethnal Green tongue.

Cuthbert smiled dejectedly. "But I'm not 'on,' at least not to you, am I?"

"You just need to stop drinking Flōt. That—and stubbornness— is ninety percent of the problem. Please, man."

Dr. Bajwa began coughing uncontrollably, this time with horrifying, papery wheezes and rales. Cuthbert toddered to his feet, trying to force himself to put his arm around this man who was, after all, his only human friend in the universe.

"I'm OK," Dr. Bajwa protested, clearly not, trying to smile in abject denial. A few tiny dots of blood spattered onto Cuthbert's forearm. "Come on, man. I've just gone for a bloody burton."

the arrest notice

IT WAS A WARM, DARK, DRIZZLY AFTERNOON IN late February, a February oddly free of the winter tornadoes that had stalked England in recent years. It was still two months before the comet Urga-Rampos appeared in the Northern Hemisphere and the zoo break-in, and Dr. Bajwa still felt he could (just) manage Cuthbert's illness. He was leaving his office in the Holloway Road for the day. He noticed the dim purple glow in his peripheral vision that indicated a new Opticall text (flashing purple signified incoming audio calls). There were two Opticalls—one with happy news, and the other devastating.

He blinked three times, and the texts began to crawl across his eyes as he walked down the pavement, wading through a red and blue sea of the rain spheres people wore.

First, he learned that the neoplasm in his right lung was, so far, isolated and "eminently treatable." The fancy Legacy oncologist he'd seen wrote with the tired, all's-well tone of one who had simply chosen white and blue instead of red and black for their new yacht spinnaker and jib sails. "Long story short: you're absolutely fine, etc. etc., and I'll see you next month for a routine follow-up. And there's a pill, as you must know." Dr. Bajwa laughed aloud at the news. He had been quite worried.

A great number of Indigent children dressed in dirty T-shirts and denims, all sopping wet (none ever wore rain spheres), seemed to be jostling around him on the pavement.

"Spare a fiver, sir," they kept asking.

As he tried to read the next Opticall, and shove his way toward the Underground entrance, he managed to pull a few pounds from his pocket.

"You're a great man," a little girl with an eye patch told him. She looked thin, with a pasty-gray pallor. "Truly, sir."

"No I'm not," he said, leaning down and scrubbling the girl's thick black hair. "But I am happy, sweet one."

When he opened the other Opticall, his happiness collapsed. As the awful words passed over his corneas, he began, instantly, to weep. It had been years since he had cried, and it strained his body. He crossed his strong arms, trying to stifle the hurt, and keep quiet. The little Indigent girl hugged his legs.

"Don't cry," she said.

His salty tears played havoc with the electro-photoreceptors in his corneal readers, turning the message script into tall, reedy, scary lettering. Nonetheless, the distressing bit was clear enough, and Dr. Bajwa scrolled it over his corneas a few times, taking it in: *NHS Élite Patient No. 87229109, Handley, Cuthbert Alfred. Arrest Notification. Offence: Drunk (Flōt) and Incapable, High Street, Camden Town. Result in Lieu of Fine and/or Detention: Compulsory Form B-810 Report, Mental Hygiene Exam, Ministry of Mind. Date: 1 March 2052 via SkinWerks Bond. Examiner: Dr. George Reece, 2nd Viscount Islington, 1st Psyalleviator (EQUIPOISE), Home Counties Region.*

It was all that Baj had been fighting to prevent, and it almost certainly meant that his elderly patient would end up institutionalized—and, soon enough, dead.

"You can come home and live with us," the little girl said. "You won't be sad with us. I've got a mother, you know."

Baj leaned down, and kissed the girl on the forehead, and walked away. He smelled the street in her hair—rain, spit, the earthy acridity of coal dust from a century ago.

He realized at that moment that he had no choice but to cooperate with EquiPoise when it came to Cuthbert, or risk his own medical registration. While the Watch might not have been unleashed on Cuthbert yet, one deviation from the Ministry of Mind's examination procedures and detention was inevitable—should he survive the arrest itself. The next day, he was able to break the news to Cuthbert, who seemed completely and rather pitifully unfazed. It was the one reaction Baj feared most.

"You need to respect EquiPoise," he pleaded with Cuthbert. "Oh god, Cuthbert. You don't understand. They will want everything from you."

"I've no worries," he answered. "There's a 'force that through the green fuse,' Baj, drives everything, and it'll never let us down. And no EquiPoise will get their grubby donnies* on my otters, I'll tell you that."

Cuthbert had just as well, the doctor thought bitterly, handed his pureed brain to EquiPoise in a disposable jar. It was over.

CUTHBERT'S FATEFUL EXAM with Dr. Reece lasted forty-five seconds, over a scent-enabled SkinWerks screen, during which Reece put a mere two questions to Cuthbert: *Do you hear voices?*

---

* Hands

and *Do you dedicate yourself to the King?* Cuthbert answered, respectively, *"Of course, don't you?"* and *"More than you'll ever know."*

Dr. Reece didn't like him. Reece's rather minor new Islington viscountcy, for which he outbid a few B-list media celebrities and paid the Windsors £130,000, hadn't quite bought him the respect he felt he deserved.

An NHS Élite First Psyalleviator who kept tabs on several thousand other destitute mental cases, Reece calibrated medications on bulk database screens and, in short, superintended thousands of unwell brains. At the start of the exam, Cuthbert's marshy smell of Flōt and old clothes so bothered him, Reece had immediately activated his high-priced olfactory CoreMods (as he often did with Indigents), an insult clearly visible to Cuthbert with the Psyalleviator's telltale swipe of his nasal septum.

Like many of the aristocracy, his face looked weird, showing signs of various rejuvenating mods with telltale "cracks" in the facade. In the Viscount Reece's case, his blue eyes had the watery, dull look of a man obviously older than 110 or so, which wasn't particularly old by today's standards, but the rest of his face belonged, cosmetically, to a twenty- or thirty-year-old man's.

Cuthbert kept staring and smiling at the man, ruffling him mightily.

Animal conversationalist that he was, he also informed Dr. Reece that "your cat told me you bore him stiff." The First Psyalleviator sniffed a little and stiffly tapped something into the SkinWerks skin-panel now glowing from the back of his officious hand.

Upon receiving Reece's report and the accompanying documentation, Dr. Bajwa was forced to code Cuthbert as "severely mentally ill" as stipulated by NHS Élite digi-form B-810, or his patient would lose all public benefits, including housing.

Reece was also insisting Cuthbert be quickly "databased," and

Cuthbert, who had ended his encounter with Reece by singing what he called "My Song to Mice," gave the Psyalleviator no reason to rethink the categorization. A databasing sanction would immediately slash his dole to £25 a week and end public transport privileges. Institutionalization, in an NHS Élite–approved Calm House, was next.

With Dr. Bajwa's help, Cuthbert could try to appeal the decision, but he would have to be off Flōt completely for at least a month or two, and he would need to shut it when it came to hearing bloody animals and toe the Ministry of Mind's lines.

It all struck Baj as impossible. Cuthbert, it seemed, was doomed.

Dr. Bajwa felt that he had betrayed his patient, too. The vile Reece, in an Opticall, indicated he could easily secure a bed for Cuthbert in the ill-famed old St. Clements Hospital in the Bow Road, in East London, and Baj didn't immediately reject the idea. What had *he* done for Cuthbert, after all?

"It's not like it used to be," Reece claimed. It was now a dedicated Grade I mental hygiene facility, and every resident wore Nexar hoods for two hours a day. Through the hoods, Dr. Reece and a small team of other First Psyalleviators from EquiPoise attended to the brains of hundreds of thousands of mental patients—a whole British sea of pathogenic alpha waves.

This use of bioelectronic stimuli had saved taxpayers millions of pounds and provided a certain comfort to the sufferers themselves. It was for this reason, ostensibly, that King Henry IX, and even the Archbishop of Canterbury, Jessica Mackenzie, were always on the broadcast news to promote Nexar treatments.

"No one in our kingdom need ever suffer again," a red-faced Harry often intoned before cameras, his eyes hard as sapphire and his neck bulging like a ripped rugby ball.

These days, the Sovereign always made such pronouncements from his bunker at Hampton Court Palace, ten miles west of central London, and far away from his psycho-dungeons like St. Clements, and surrounded by his heavily armed Yeomen of the Guard "Beefeaters."

In their updated flat black helms and glossy red body armor, all clasping red pike-like medulla wave-guns, which could stop the heart and respiration instantly, the Beefeaters typified the reconfiguring of Britain's turn-of-the-century Tourist Monarchy into a functional beast. Tudor roses, thistles, and shamrocks in gold paint decorated their breastplates and gunstocks. The Beefeaters no longer bothered to work inconspicuously. HRH Henry IX, long rumored to be responsible for the bombing of his elder brother King William's personal jet in 2028, which killed the weak ruler and all his direct heirs, was all about aggression.

"Our Realm is compassion, and it is life," the regicidal king liked to say, "and Nexar is a very clever way to dispense them both—it's that simple."

No one, including Dr. Bajwa, would question such notions openly and hope to get ahead professionally in the Britain of the 2050s, where it never paid to question the House of Windsor's love of manipulating alpha waves. The suicide cults and British republicans were openly hunted, but apart from them, just one infamously rebellious former lord, the erstwhile Earl of Worcester, only nineteen years old and reportedly hiding underground on the Welsh border (he had sent mass Opticalls against the king's power-grabs, until he was pushed off WikiNous's optical nerves), seemed willing to risk a public confrontation. The king, for his part, laughed the boy off.

"We need our earls," he liked to say plaintively. "I can't be in the business of autocracy. Worcester needs to come out to Hampton for din-dins."

It was said the young former earl, who had abdicated his ancestral seat, sent word that he would indeed accept a meal, but only "in *front* of the Banqueting House," a defiant reference, of course, to the execution site of Charles I.

(Hampton Court Palace was no longer home to flower shows and chubby Belgian tourists. The decision to turn it into the Sovereign's heavily fortified seat of residence, and to give Buckingham Palace over strictly to England's dying sightseer trade, was all based on Henry's sometimes paranoid calculations about the exercise of, and defense against, military force. The maze and real tennis court were still there, but the palace's perimeter was practically upholstered in powerful weaponry. There were advanced neural cannons, blood-gas beams, various sophisticated EMP emitters, and a rumored pièce de résistance—a dangerous, identity-wiping mobile mortar called Æthelstan's Bliss.

This device, which purportedly resembled a sort of giant sea anemone with pink tentacles and, it was said, screeched like the golden dragons of ancient Wessex, entirely dissolved all traces of one's existence, in both corporal and digital form.

ST. CLEMENTS'S REPUTATION was well known. Nexar-hooded or not, its patients almost never recovered. It was a grim, yellow-brick house of dread, built as a workhouse, and eventually one of the last Victorian asylums. A passé NHS Trust placard still appeared on its inevitable squeaking iron gate. It was, in Baj's view, a national disgrace. The last time he had visited, it had been filled exclusively with crazy Indigents.

Out of a sense of responsibility, Dr. Bajwa decided to have another look at St. Clements after receiving Dr. Reece's report. Perhaps it wasn't quite as bad as he remembered. From the outside, surrounded by lime trees and pavements heavily trod by all manner of daydream carvers, roast pigeon sellers, house-bot repairers, etc., there was a sense of happy bustle. But once past the iron gate, Baj saw a familiar awfulness he associated with decrepit buildings where Nexar patients were usually warehoused.

An old caretaker with a pinched brow smiled as Baj approached the main doors.

"Lovely day," the man said.

Baj looked up at a nearly cloudless cerulean sky, as if for the first time that year. Apart from a few cloud-doodles of elongated cats and crooked letters ("mums!") by children, the sky was a happy blank.

"Yes!" he said. "It is lovely, isn't it?"

Inside, he ambled slowly along. A few patients with simpering grins came up to him and shook his hand. The main common area of the hospital had a strange, nicotine-stained cornice molding—(yellowed) acanthus leaves and all—along the tops of the walls. Some well-intentioned staff member had allowed one of the patients, obviously, to decorate the molding. In delicate blue, yellow, and red hand-painted lines, all the way around the room, was a constellation of mathematical gibberish—direct sum-of-module symbols, various integrals, Euclidean distance marks—interspersed with the silhouettes of lions and some other, vaguer creature—a weasel or ferret or indeed *otter* or something?

How very odd, Dr. Bajwa had thought, that Cuthbert also often mentions otters, and here they are at St. Clements? The doctor tried to work out the cornice molding formulae and realized they (or it?) made utterly no sense, unless, somehow, lions and otters were ascribed mathematic value. Perhaps there was, he pondered, to people like Cuthbert, some undisclosed dimension in which $otter \sim 2.983^{11}$ or where the curves of mustelid tails followed the precise bends of timespace as they folded upon themselves?

Just then, a short, tubby orderly carrying a Nexar hood greeted Baj in a less than friendly manner.

"I wouldn't hang around here, mate. All the joy'll rub off on you."

Baj started coughing. He felt utterly breathless. He had begun a regimen of light chemotherapy. The bloody coughing had nearly vanished, but he felt weak and sick to his stomach.

Baj said, snorting a bit, "All this—it hasn't seemed to affect *you*."

"No," the man said bitterly. "I just hoods 'em, and bury 'em in pleasure. I don't like it, but it's me job, innit?" He squinted at Baj. "You poorly, man?"

"Just a little. Do they . . . ever get better?"

"Ha!" said the orderly. Then he leaned in, confidentially. There was a stench of eel and vinegar on his breath. "This is a place of where the spirit thrives. And even the ghosts live well." The man greasily chortled for a moment, then slapped Baj's shoulder.

"Right, mate," said Baj.

AS BAJ LEFT ST. CLEMENTS, the injustice of his dismissal from research hit him anew. When he passed through the gate, he turned around to see the old NHS sign bolted to a brick pillar. He glanced around to make sure no one was watching. If he wasn't careful, he'd end up struck off the medical register—or much worse, perhaps in St. Clements himself, guffawing at nothing, and planted beneath a Nexar hood.

He pulled out his old-fashioned fountain pen and wrote on the sign: "Fuck Harry." He coughed, and a few pink flecks of faintly bloody spittle landed on the sign. Then he walked away, trying not to look rushed, until breaking into a trot.

"It's going . . . to get worse . . . and then . . . it's going to get better," he said to himself, jogging along, gasping for air in gulps.

THE NEXT TIME Cuthbert came to see him, the doctor observed that, as Cuthbert saw it, the animals were vying for control over him, and the animals wanted out of their cages. He was in full, Flōt-induced hallucinosis. Walking into the consult room, he showed Ingall's Sign markedly, taking long strides and leaning forward excessively.

"I've no say in matters anymore, doc," he said.

"If you don't stop the Flōt," he told Cuthbert, "it is indeed over. And you can't go around saying you hear animals anymore, my friend. You can't."

Cuthbert had looked down at the Afshar rug with its paisley patterns. "The Flōt is one thing," he said, "but the animals, with all due respect, doctor, I could never just tell them to hush up. It's not just withdrawal. Even when I drink the Flōt, the voices come on."

"That's not a good symptom, Cuthbert. It's called hallucinosis. It will only grow worse if you don't stop."

"But their message is for everyone—for me, for you, for England, for the world. There might just be a little white pony what knows *yow*, Baj."

With that, Baj at long last lost his patience. All his professional restraint seemed to fly off like a flock of irritable starlings rousted from a tremendous, withering tree.

"Cuthbert! For fuck's sake!" he bellowed. "Can't you bloody see, you fool? It's the Flōt. The Flōt! It's standard first-Flōt-withdrawal syndrome. There are no fucking animals. There are no voices. You are delusional, my friend. It's Flōt withdrawal."

The doctor was almost weeping now, standing up from his seat, and the spectacle appalled Cuthbert, who lurched up and backed away, toward the door of the office, doddering on his old legs, his dry lips moving but nothing coming out.

"No. Stay!" cried Baj as Cuthbert opened the door. "You've got to listen to me. I don't want to lose you, my friend. The Red

Watch will be after you, you know? They'll beat the bloody fuck out of you and drag you half-dead before an EquiPoise P-Lev, and it's St. Clements after that. Please, Cuthbert. Please. Let's try the hospital—just one last time! Just one—"

But before he could finish the phrase, Cuthbert was gone.

pentecost in the trees

THUS IT CAME TO PASS THAT, ON THE LAST DAY OF
April of 2052, as an enormous comet began to smear streaks of light
above the Northern Hemisphere, the aged Cuthbert found himself
stuck in the zoo's boundary foliage beside a floaty green blob of
trouble.

For the six previous months, Baj had tried to protect him from
the Watch and from EquiPoise, but the doctor had been no match
for Cuthbert's drug addiction (nor for talking otters), and now
Cuthbert had a case of Flōt withdrawal shakes in his muscles, a bizarre plan in his head, and an arboreal phantasm beside him. He
seemed, to all appearances, beyond human aid.

The yew creature, a kind of botanical steam, was soaking into
his very skin, and Cuthbert felt himself breathing in sweet fogs tes-
sellated with long green leaves. There was still fear, but the sense
of shock had passed. His pulse puttered in his ears. There was a
minted, pennyroyal scent and a whiff of roses, and a wildness and
warmth, like an unexpected kiss from a dodgy stranger. He'd encountered, over the years, many figments in the tumbling-down

experience of Flōt withdrawal, but none that felt so intimate or so peculiar.

The closeness came with strange timing. The Red Watch was now quite actively looking for him. In the last weeks, Cuthbert had more or less abandoned his IB flat to avoid detention and gone back to his old habits of sleeping rough, panhandling, and thievery. His dole payments, of course, had stopped, as had his meetings with Baj, whose perceptions of the old man's perils had been, after all, quite accurate. Cuthbert had rarely felt so vulnerable and lonely.

But not alone. As the yew tree covered him with its sparkling emerald plasmas, Cuthbert sensed that the being (him, her, it?) knew him deeply—too deeply. He wanted to crawl away, into his grotto, but his sore limbs wouldn't budge from their integuments of age and exhaustion.

"Wha . . . what do you want?" Cuthbert asked it, his teeth a'chatter. "You want me to get caught? It ain't even dark yet, is it?" His heart began palpitating oddly—flipping over, trotting, bursting into double beats. It felt like a broken propeller in his chest. His lips and hands went numb. If he could just reach his grotto, he thought, he would get his Flōt, and all would be OK.

"You do not need to do this, Cuthbert," the being said, in a nearly melodious whistle, a sound like the breeze being inhaled by all the trees around him through mouths the size of flute holes. "You will never be the same if you do."

"Not topple the zoo, you mean? Bloody no way," Cuthbert slurred. "Oi *won't* be packing it in now. Oi'm here for the beasts. They're what's called me. And my brother."

Cuthbert squinted. He made out a kind of mouth, opening and closing in the vernal vapor, blowing lunar moths from lips as tender as a small boy's. Is this me, he wondered, from half a century ago? Was it Drystan? One of the green moths fluttered above him, then flashed into a little pentecostal flame over his head.

"*Gagoga*," he said. "*Gagoga*." He tried to touch the flame's fern-colored cloves, but they stung his hand. He jerked it away. His heart suddenly galloped a few times and settled into its normal, pulpy *hwoot-dub hwoot-dub*. The haze was beginning to thin, and the simple, pinnately veined leaves of the hedge itself were reemerging. It was nearly dark.

"Drystan?" he asked.

"No," said the creature. "But he is part of me, as are you, and you are blessed, Cuthbert. Before this night is over, you will see him. But there is great danger now . . ."

The old man's arms were beginning to shake in mild fits. He was sweating badly, and his aged Adidas weather-buffer made it worse.

"Are you . . . an *animal*, at all?" he asked. He felt starved for air. "Is you the one that's called me here?"

There was no reply, yet the breezes he'd felt before suddenly seemed to puff out from everything around him in a plangent *gaaaaaagoooooooogaaaaaaa!* The wisps of minty green vapors grew as thin as hair. When he looked for the astonishing yew tree in his midst, he saw nothing but the usual hackberry leaves.

The yew was gone.

"Jesus," he said. "Jesus fuck."

Something was jabbing his kidney now, and it wasn't the finger of common sense. It was the broken spoke of a hackberry shrub, of which there were thousands in and around the zoo.

"Shittin 'ell," he whispered. "*That* one hurts." His heart started a new round of scary, trilling beats. The Flōt half-life was only a few hours, and the withdrawal for someone as old and long-addicted as Cuthbert could be lethal.

"This is it," he said, panting. "This is how I go winkers." Darkness suddenly encroached on his peripheral vision. He felt broad, crushing chest pain, a python coiling around his chest, and the classic proprioceptive sensation of falling, literally, down from on high.

If he didn't get Flōt, he was going to die, and he could not allow that.

ROLLING TO THE side a bit, still held up by the hazel branches and a few tough hackberry boughs, Cuthbert put his hands over his eyes and bulldozered deeper yet, shoulder first. All at once, a thick mat of branches that had been impeding him came apart, and he crashed a few paces farther in. He was just a foot or two now from his grotto, but knackered. He turned again and lay with his back against a new layer of branches, allowing all his weight to be supported. He was hidden now, at rest, gazing again back out into the park. His legs ached and felt stunted—another symptom of Flōt withdrawal—and he was banged up a bit, but he felt a little better, for the moment.

I *will* stay off the Flōt, he said to himself halfheartedly, even if it kills me. But Cuthbert's body screamed for it—that purple orb of relief, concealed somewhere in sedge-grass in his grotto. Cheap enchantment. He could nearly taste its smooth, oak-charred flavor of rum and licorice, and the secret ingredient that gave it all a peppery edge: a set of alkaloids, derived from the white larvae of England's leaf-miner moth.

"Canna I have one last moment of my life without spiring?" he asked aloud. "If I'm a dead man, let me die sober with my eyes upon Drystan and animals and lovely trees that smudge* my skin."

He shook his head. "No, I won't touch it!" he cried.

Oh but yes, he thought, I bloody must. It will calm matters.

---

* Kiss

Even as he fidgeted there, caught in the hedge and vacillating about Flōt, he could hear the zoo's animals again, pulling him into their own more unruly set of traps. And while he still didn't know what they meant, he felt compelled, once again, to say aloud, in a voice as tremulous as dreams written on clouds, "*Gagoga*."

He closed his eyes. He burrowed now into this last, densest part of the shrubbery, grabbing at and deflecting branches like a blind man under attack by hornets. He ducked down to the right and felt the blunt, hard top of his liver nosing up inside him like a shark. He jerked back in agony.

"Fuck me," he said. Need to keep my back straight, he thought. He knelt down and sunk his fingers into the loose, mulchy loam.

Just then, not unexpectedly, a very familiar voice snarled at him.

"Mr. Handley!"

"No, I don't want to talk," muttered Cuthbert. "You canna see I'm bloody busy?"

It was one of the zoo's Asiatic lions, an old male, Arfur, from whom Cuthbert had been hearing quite regularly that week. Of all the zoo's denizens, the lions were without question the most articulate and provocative, especially in the last few days. They growled at Cuthbert in tones simultaneously bellicose and hard-done-by, arguing impatiently for justice, and, naturally, for release from their cages.

"You really do need to free us first," rasped Arfur. "Failing in that would be . . . well, it would be *immoral*."

"Rubbish."

"That old French writer Camus, you know he thought a man without ethics was a wild animal, 'loosed upon the world'? And if you don't let us out, you stand convicted of the gravest indifference, old Cuddy."

"But I'm not indifferent," he said. "Look at me!"

These lions could cleverly walk a line between sounding confident and subtly mistreated at the same time, thought Cuthbert. Arfur made him think back to long ago, to the pushy assurance of the once-fresh "New Labour" party chap, Tony Blair, but a version of him like the statue he'd seen during his first zoo visit—elderly, wizened, skin burnished like a body from a peat bog.

"Taking Britain forward is really the only choice, and lions simply *must* lead the way!" Arfur said to Cuthbert, groaning slightly, and goading, goading, goading. *Panthera leo* had given more to Britons than any other species, Arfur claimed, and "never once" complained or demanded reward.

Cuthbert countered: "Well, what . . . what about, say, England's field voles? They're far more common than you, these days. They're millions and millions of souls. And they're not mithering at me like dying ducks in a thunderstorm—no, not that lot. The voles 'ave no, like, *program* as you lot've got."

Arfur retorted: "You make our point, actually, Cuddy. You can't be tiny and common and very well stay regal, can you? The English aristocracy *do* things—obstinately. A field vole sounds like something from Siberia." But to Cuthbert, Arfur seemed less obstinate than pigheaded.

A few nights before, Cuthbert had admitted to the lions that he feared them. The aggrieved tone of their thoughts had unsettled him. Gravel-voiced and glottal, they were among the first creatures (perhaps *because* Cuthbert feared them most) to send messages to him, no matter where he went in London, no matter the time. They seemed to be able to reach out and finger him.

"You're really not much of a being, are you?" Arfur once observed. "We could master a whole country of Cuddies."

Cuthbert didn't like that. "You canna even master your cage. I'm the free one, aren't I?"

"Ha!" said Arfur. "Thus speaks the Solunaut. You wait. You haven't even visited us, have you? Let us out first, Cuthbert."

"I was preoccupied. There were otters . . . I . . . I needed to see."

"Nonetheless, we require immediate release, my friend. Otters! Who cares about otters?"

Cuthbert sighed. "I do."

"But mark my words, we lions are going places—you'll see." Arfur added, "I wouldn't be terribly surprised if we"—he cleared his mucky voice—"if we reclaim Alexandria someday." Arfur coughed, clearing his throat with a rumbling grunt. "Soon. And we're not really in a cage, are we? Just *undo* our enclosure. It's more a kind of moated theater of sorts."

"It's still a cage. And you're in one because you're dangerous."

"Dangerous?" Arfur whined. "We're the last lions in the last zoo on earth."

As bedraggled and amusingly haughty as Arfur could sound, lions nonetheless, as a group, still terrified Cuthbert. In childhood, he would see David Attenborough on the telly, explaining how lions used group-hunting tactics. He still recalled one program in which a lioness plunged its entire head into the open skull of an elephant. When it pulled out, Cuthbert recalled, it bore the wet-haired, sated look of a swimmer who'd just swum a dozen laps.

"You're bloody war beasts," Cuthbert said to Arfur at one point. "You're walking terror. I think it's best to let the jackals out first."

"No . . . first!" Arfur spat. "We've kept this island safe. We're 'lionhearted,' " he added with a soupçon of mockery. "Don't blame us for defending national interests."

For a moment, Cuthbert pictured his father, swilling lager in the old sitting room, raising his battered Spode mug from the queen's coronation, and belting out the words *never never never never shall be slaves* as the Proms blared on television. So much for lionhearted.

Still, Cuthbert felt a serious sympathy for the lions. Their images still ennobled pound coins, chocolate bars, passports, treacle tins. He himself knew every detail of the three Plantagenet lions *passant* on England's football jersey. Then there were Landseer's pigeon-shite-speckled quartet of bronze males at Trafalgar Square, supporting Great Britain's public imperial phallus. A thousand drainage-spigots shot through lion mouths on churches. Countless misericords, crests, hallmarks on wedding bands—the country was overrun by an animal which had not been native to its soil since the Pleistocene. Dar es Salaam, Johannesburg, and even Tehran, one might argue, held legitimate claims on the image. Rome could offer a certain logic for leophilia, perhaps. *But London?* Since Henry Plantagenet had housed his lions in Tower Menagerie, in 1235, the lions had lent England muscle it could not find in itself, at least not until the massive remilitarization under Harry9. And in the country's last zoological project, its lions lived in a cramped, bewildering terrace covered in dirt. The case for change was strong.

"In one way or another, we have been the clawed scepter of all your kings and queens, and surely, with the great King Henry, our time has come."

"Oi'm mulling it," Cuthbert had told them. "If it's good for the king and country, and all that. You do sound like you've been . . . in the wars," he said, echoing his doctor, whose ministrations seemed so far away now. It was all he knew to say. The lions just seemed too large a problem to deal with, for now.

"Where would you go, if I was, somehow, to let you lot out?"

"We'll *go* to war for you," Arfur said. "Against the republicans, against the religious fanatics, against fallen demons from the sky. We'll fight in the streets, in the hills, in the fields. We'll never surrender."

"Oh, *that's* bloody inno*vay*tive, that," said Cuthbert. "But let me think about it all. Do you think King Henry would approve?"

"We *are* King Henry, and he is us. But this is no time for ease," he answered. "It's time to dare."

"Get off my wick."

Cuthbert felt hard-pressed to make a decision, or at least to tell Arfur what he had long planned.

"I supposed I might as well say that I've mostly made up my mind. It's going to be the jackals first. They're the closest things to dogs, aren't they? And I *owe* the dogs of this world, for my evil to them as a child. I *owe* 'em. Then we'll . . . see."

"Jackals?" gasped Arfur. He guffawed showily in Cuthbert's ears. "Starting on a rather tenuous note, if you ask me. Good god, man. How will you save the English?"

"But my mind's made up, and I won't change."

With that, Arfur and the other lions let out a loud and most pained chorus.

cuthbert's grotto

CUTHBERT NOW LOWERED HIMSELF TO THE ground and moved toward his grotto, dragging his stomach over the damp soil. A foot or two more, that was all. Hazelnuts from last summer, now brown and soft like tiny rotten cabbages, rolled under his big abdomen. He stuck his head into the small cavern in the vegetation he had chosen so capably. Years of sleeping rough had given him an intuitive skill at finding hiding places in the midst of the metropolis. The city possessed countless nooks, hanging flanges, recesses in Victorian brick, but almost none went unused or uninspected, if only by other rough sleepers. You had to know what you were doing to find a quiet, safe, free place to sleep in London.

At last, his head ruptured one final net of twigs, and he poked it into his grotto. It was a perfect if messy lacuna, rounded and silent as an egg. He crawled forward on his hands and knees. He collapsed in fatigue. He was a very old man—far too old and too fat for this.

The grotto was like a zoological exhibit of its own—the parkland lair of an unhoused English urban *Homo sapiens*. There was an

air of disgrace and commercialism about it. Weathered debris—
soft-drink bottles, Flōt orbs, silvery torn-open Hula-Hoops, and
Golden Wonder and Alga-Bite bags—lay on the ground and
jammed into the branches of the shrubbery. Dark, shiny garden
snails clung to the leafy walls of the space. They were the same
sulfurous yellow-brown as the decomposing leaves on the ground
from last autumn. A slight depression in leaves and embankment,
formed only by Cuthbert's recent sometime habitation, made it look
like a one-man version of some Iron Age hill fort.

He lay still for a while. Thin strands of thought unreeled in his
head—*foamy blue grips on my bolt cutters . . . this foamy stuff, something new, isn't it?* was one bit; *my trazzies are too tight* was another.
He tried to sort one thread from another, but they diminished in
thickness the further he pursued them until they became a fine mist
of confusion.

He sat up and frantically dug out an old, enormous two-liter
orb of Dark Plume–label Flōt in the dirt of his grotto. He'd kept it
hidden beneath the back of a round-collared shirt he had found in
someone's rubbish and ripped into useful pieces. One of the hardest
things he had ever done in his life was to leave this bottle here not
completely unemptied. He popped off the cap. For all his efforts to
stop drinking Flōt, when presented with an orb, Cuthbert displayed
no resistance whatsoever. He lifted the huge bottle high and took a
few long, tense swigs. He repeated the procedure again. He lifted
the orb again, and he drank again.

"Thank bloody Jesus," he croaked. It hurt to swallow. It felt
as though something were growing in his throat, but whenever he
looked in a mirror, he saw nothing but his tongue, as well as his
slightly sunken right cheek, from an old street injury. (Up until
just a few years ago, women would still compliment him on his
high cheekbones, a feature that distinguished both him and his lost
brother Drystan.)

The old man started to feel a bit calmer, physically, and his heart slowed down. It never took much these days, such was the weakness of his heart and liver.

Apart from the animals, there was plenty else to drink about, as far as he was concerned, wasn't there? It had been a strange week, even by Cuthbert's forbearing standards. (Much of his news came by word of mouth or the lurid reports glimpsed on fast-food packaging, and the raucous public video screens around Camden Town. He only had access to WikiNous's free, advert-saturated basic Opticall service, which allowed for reception but very limited transmission of messages.)

In Los Angeles, principally, nearly sixty thousand members of one of the most infamous and oldest cults—Heaven's Gate—had poisoned themselves along with nearly a million animals in what was being called the largest mass suicide and act of animal cruelty in history. Enormous outbreaks of self-murder and animal sacrifices among the same cult members had also occurred in Britain, Germany, and Japan. With souls "released" from what they called their "vehicles," the cultists intended to travel astrally into outer space and meet a god they believed resided on the comet everyone was talking about. The animals, according to the cult's beliefs, were being helpfully "voided," as they put it, as means of travel for souls, too. It was all over the public screens. Harry9 had long ago recriminalized "self-murder" as a psychological tactic against the cults, and the Red Watch had recently begun another of its roundups of suspected cultist cells, and they weren't too particular about whom they jabbed with the neuralwave pikes.

News of the suicide cults always deeply disturbed and absorbed Cuthbert. For complicated reasons, his own views fell much in line with Harry9's virulently anticultist propaganda. He despised everything about the cults. They apparently liked to watch the antiquated 1990s program *Star Trek: The Next Generation*, a fact that ruined the show for him. They always claimed they were "transiting" between the "lower" Animal Kingdom and what they termed "the Evolutionary Kingdom Level Above Human." An enormous secret machine, built decades ago in London on two great sites, would come to life one day, and the machine, "The Gate," would begin to suck in and dissolve all the souls of animals on earth, except for those humans who suicided themselves. It terrified Cuthbert.

Behind much of his odium was a fear that he, too, could on any day be contaminated, as millions of others on earth had, with an urge to exterminate himself and to "void" as many "lower" animals as he could poison. He could not allow this. He already owed the animals his heart. And what would become of the Wonderments if he were dead? What would become of Drystan? What would become of England?

He patted his hands around in the debris. When he felt what he was looking for, he lifted up a sleeve of the ripped-up shirt and found his pair of heavy-duty, twenty-two-inch bolt cutters. He had first spotted them—they were cut-price returns—in a B&Q DIY store while ducking out of the rain, and blagged the money the same day. He poked his little finger between the hardened blades, which were concealed in a blunt plastic green housing that looked, in profile, like reptilian jaws.

He heard voices from a squawky loudspeaker. He turned toward the park. An approaching patrol from the Red Watch, out on the Broad Walk, was calling rough sleepers out of Regent's Park. They did it every night, but Cuthbert had completely forgotten. He held still, trying not to breathe. In the grotto, he was well camouflaged, but if a Watchman or his array of peripatetic Eye3's on his mantle gazed carefully in this direction, or used their infrared screeners, he might be caught.

"Watch, here! Indigents have five minutes to leave! If found in the park after this reasonable deadline, Indigents will be referred to EquiPoise." Cuthbert's hands shook with fear; finally, he could see their red and gold mantles, through the shrubbery. He held his breath.

There were two—very close. They were laughing, distracting themselves.

"Fucking beautiful, I tell you," one was saying to the other. "Really, very *loovly*."

After a few more minutes of anxiety, they ambled away. Cuthbert felt he would start crying with relief. The bolt-cutter handles were slippery with his sweat.

The cutters were in fact monsters—large, awkward, and horrifically powerful. He found himself imagining how all the small work-related apparatuses normally carried by London's dwindling middle classes—face-adjusting discs, energy satchels, Vespa hand-scooters, rain-sphere sticks—could be sliced apart by the cutters, like crepes.

The cutters seemed wonderfully industrial to him, from a fading world of huge, steaming engines and sweating, hammering men. The B&Q clerk claimed they could exert two thousand pounds of pressure onto a fine point, and handle high-tensile steel up to 9 mm thick. Cuthbert had drawn a black line on his index finger with a permanent marker, to denote 9 mm, and he meant to check it against a few different fencing gauges he might run across.

Because its space was initially fixed, the zoo's landscape architects had at first been partial to mild-steel mesh-fencing and glass rather than seminatural barriers, and the material had propagated across the zoo like a kind of mold for more than a century. The inflexible, unnatural steel mesh was one of a long list of stupidities that had hastened the zoo's decline in the twentieth and twenty-first centuries. Unlike later zoos, there were few faux rivers, moats, or invisible barriers at the London Zoo. Steel mesh bounded most of its various strolling spaces and animal enclosures. For that reason, the zoo was a bolt cutter's paradise, and Cuthbert was about to become its most faithful angel. Feigning a limp, he had taped the device to his leg a few days before and stowed it in the grotto. As an Indigent, getting caught with them would have been considered incriminating ipso facto, and the Watch would have hauled him before an EquiPoise committee. Risks aside, for Cuthbert, bringing bolt cutters to the grotto had felt like returning some arcane healing object to its rightful place, like a key brought to the door of a sacred labyrinth.

He quickly dusted off the implement. He liked it and felt competent with it, a feeling he wasn't used to.

He took a deep breath. That walking-on-silken-stilts feeling and the usual quivers in his cheeks and eyelids, all telltale signs of Flōt withdrawal, had stopped. He felt a comfortable buzz, and the wonderful elongation of his legs. How much patience and, for himself, discipline he had shown these past few days, he thought. A spark of dignity flashed inside him, and he tried to get his head around it like a child cupping a firefly with bare hands. But just as he reached for it, it fizzled out.

I can't stand much more of this, he thought to himself. He grabbed the orb again, and the Flōt glugged into his mouth violently. A wave of disgust hit him, and it wasn't because the Flōt was cold. He felt sick, instead, at himself. He should have contacted Baj, he thought. He shouldn't have come here.

"I wanted to be sober for you," he said aloud, to no one in particular.

But how tall he felt! As ever, Flōt shot you up to the stratosphere where you strode like Atlas with wings of a giant purple moth.

what the jackals said

A FEW TROPICAL GENOMIC COPIES OF EXTINCT
birds—hyacinth macaws—were now visible in blue snatches
through the bushes. Lined up in their long, grid-lattice cage, motionless and imperious on a thick perching rod, the clones seemed
devoid of wildness or even natural agitation. He felt he knew these
birds intimately; each time he'd come to his cave in the hedges he
watched them purposefully. They never spoke, never made any
sound. Their long sapphire tail feathers hung down as smooth and
poised as the Italian silk ties he saw sometimes when wandering
near Savile Row. A dozen or so London pigeons roosted atop and
around their cages, and the more Cuthbert rustled in the bushes, the
more they began to coo. But the few people he could see passing by
in the zoo—it was twenty minutes before closing—had no sense of
being watched from beyond the perimeter fence.

A single golden jackal just then trotted toward Cuthbert. They
were normally the only animals visible from outside the zoo, but
from his grotto, he was less than five or six meters from them.

"Almost time," Cuthbert said to the animal. "I am coming for you—just minutes now." Zero hour, when the zoo closed, was near. The jackals weren't otters, but they also intrigued Cuthbert, if only because they were the animals he saw most. *Our names are lie*, they would call to him, over and over. *Let us free just one just two just three just one. Lie, our names, lie, lie.* He did not understand what the jackals meant by all this, but he had a guess: they were always being told to "lie," like dogs, by a certain ilk of self-amused bystander outside the zoo, and the poor jackals had come to think of the intransitive verb as their collective name.

"You can find new names," Cuthbert had answered. "Anything you want."

We're lie, they said.

Cuthbert admired their humped, scruffly backs, angular faces, the brown swabs of tails—all tangible dog-pieces darting about a sparse pen like small rages on legs. There was a dark energy in them that made him feel stronger.

Still, he would forsake jackals in a second for a chance to visit otters. Neither he nor the public at large could get even a glimpse of otters from outside the zoo. To Cuthbert, they were the most English, most sacred, most miraculous wild animals still on earth (he didn't realize that the zoo's Asian species actually came from an annoyed flax farmer in Thailand who had grudgingly decided not to poison them).

CUTHBERT'S PLAN, IF one could call it such, was to set free a single jackal at first, then go from there. The lions and the otters could not be first, as they presented many logistical challenges. The idea of releasing other animals tantalized him, but even for Cuthbert, that also seemed, as of now, a bit crazy. He was no activist, no animal sentimentalist, no mere vandal. He was not trying to "make a statement" but to let select animals craft their own.

However things unfolded after that, the one thing Cuthbert knew he *must* accomplish, at any cost, was to free the otters. If they did know where to find Drystan, they held in their black claws, in his view, the future of all Britain—of all Earth.

He heard them then, in a susurrus of watersongs: *gagoga gagoga gagoga miltsung miltsung miltsung.*

"I am coming," he said. "You'll see."

A lone jackal was watching him, watching him talk to himself.

"Don't mind this dotty fool," he said to the jackal. "I've got otters on the brain." The jackal tilted his head to one side, then the other, puzzling over the old man.

Cuthbert imagined it running across the great dark spaces of the Regent's Park as joyfully as it might have, long ago, on the savannas of Ngorongoro. Releasing it would be a sort of ritual of atonement, of hope. He'd been able to watch these creatures all winter, as carefully as any nonpaying observer could, sizing up security issues, obtaining any necessary equipment. The jackals were by far the easiest choice, much simpler than the otters. They also struck him as oddly innocent in their messages to him. They were just dogs, he said to himself. Little ones, too. They called themselves *lies*, as though they genuinely didn't believe in their right to exist. They only want to run about the park. They had asked, calmly and without unctuousness, for a simple release. That's what any dog wants and needs, he felt.

Just one, they had said. *Just two, just three, let us free!*

AFTER HALF AN HOUR or so of dazed staring, Cuthbert took a packet of diatom-and-cinnamon chewing gum from his pocket and put a piece into his mouth. Already, he could feel a distant nervousness again, a thunder-footed jackboot of Flōt withdrawal on the far edges of his being but tramping toward him brutally with tiny, hard limbs. He got the orb back out. He took another belt off it, screwed the cap back on, and hid it beneath the shirt fragment.

The zoo's lights were beginning to pop on like an outbreak of giant orange flowers. The activity within the zoo seemed to be winding down, and finally he decided—making a woeful error— that it must be closed.

"Time now," he whispered. He wondered whether he might just not pick up a bottle again—ever. He smiled. Could it be that easy? Could he follow the otters and lions to a new life on the other side of Flōt, one in which he might see Drystan again? It was always easy to "quit" when he was kaylied.

He used his elbows and toes to shimmy forward, dragging his bolt cutters after him. Oh bloody hell, how his liver hurt, he thought.

Coated in a glossy black paint, the main zoo perimeter fence, inside and up against the hedge barrier, was a heavy iron affair with spiked pickets as well as the mild-steel mesh backing. But a few wide gaps between some of the section posts existed, and one of these fell beside Cuthbert's hiding spot, which is partly why he'd chosen it. Here, as elsewhere, only the mesh backing protected the gap, and Cuthbert had already tested the bolt cutters on this obstruction. He had been stunned by the ease with which the cutters went through steel mesh, like scissors snipping spaghetti.

He got to the place where he had fashioned an oval breach a few days before. It was time to crack on, he said to himself. As he stuck his head in, the hole seemed barely wide enough for him, and it was placed awkwardly high. Great stalks of holly entirely enveloped the other side of the fence hole, adding to the nettlesome task ahead. He first had to squeeze into the barbed gap itself, tugging his limbs while trying to keep himself above the ground. A few prongs of galvanized steel dug into his torso like fangs rising out of the ground from hell. His buffer caught, too, and its hissing rips distressed him.

But he kept pushing in. A spiny leaf of holly which had fallen to the ground got stuck into his palm and he let out a small cry. He stopped where he was, midway through the fence hole, and pulled the leaf off. He scrubbed his palm on his other arm to loosen the tiny thorns. It was all awful and he wanted to wail out for help. But he began shoving forward again. At one point, his foot seemed caught, and he thought he was trapped for good, and then, as if some iron-toothed chimera had deigned to free him from its jaws, the foot came free and Cuthbert Handley was in, bolt cutters in hand.

Even in his Flōt haze, as he stood up and surveyed this hidden area of the zoo, he could see he'd made an enormous error—the kind of stupid slipup Flōt engendered like clouds did rain. It was late in the day, but in fact, the zoo wasn't quite closed. Visitors still strolled about. He couldn't free anything yet unless he wanted to end up in a Calm House before the first animal escaped. Cuthbert thought of going back to his grotto but changed his mind, thinking it would only risk more attention. After a few seconds, he pushed the bolt cutters back through the hole in the fence. He couldn't very bloody well be seen with *them*. But why not have a look around? he thought. You're in.

"Oi'm in," he said to himself aloud. "Fuck it. I'll nip back later tonight and open the whole focking shite-stand."

Not a few people were still sauntering quite unhurriedly along the walkways and gazing at exhibits. Zoo workers scurried about—carrying boxes for restocking, sweeping, gathering rubbish bin liners—carrying out their usual closing jobs. All the people ought to have represented a huge risk for Cuthbert; a single message sent to the Red Watch, and Cuthbert would be detained. But he was now too intoxicated to grasp any of that. He only saw the silent jackals, in their enclosure, and he felt a shrieking desire to get closer to them. *We're lie*, they said to him. *Lie.*

two

a day trip to the wyre

CUTHBERT HAD SEEN AN OTTER ONCE BEFORE IN his life—or so he thought.

It happened more than eighty years before, on a scalding summer afternoon, in 1968. His family—Drystan, his mum and dad, and his maternal grandmother, Winefride, who lived with them—had driven from Birmingham to an area well west of the Black Country, not far from the Welsh Marches of Worcestershire, to visit a few elderly relatives on his father's side. It was Cuthbert and his older brother Drystan's first trip to a region their gran had told them strange tales about from their earliest years.

The visitors were first taking an early tea in their relatives' cottage, and everyone—the boys, their parents and Gran, the old Handley aunties and a great-uncle—crowded a dark sitting room. Cuthbert and Drystan were unable to sit. They kept begging to ramble off by themselves into the nearby Wyre Forest, a radiant remnant of primeval woodland near the ancient settlements of Wribbenhall and Bewdley town.

"Please, Mum, please, please, please, please, please, please, ple—"

"Enough!" scolded their mum.

Cuthbert was only six, still pronouncing his *l*'s as *w*'s, and Drystan eight, and they were city boys. Apart from the heavily trod Dartmouth Park and empty tins of Lyle's syrup, little that was green or gold grew any longer in their West Bromwich world of chemical dumps and football madness. Making matters worse, a new expressway had isolated West Brom from the park, a last salubrious leafy retreat that had been donated and laid out specifically for local factory workers a hundred years before.

"I'd like to see the deepest parts, you know, the sort of middle bits of that forest, I would. Can we have a look now?" asked Drystan. "Gran? What do—"

The boys' father, Henry Handley, interjected, "With all due respect to dear gran, she's not your gaffer, is she? Who pays for—"

But Drystan cut him off, saying boldly, "You should be better to Gran. She knows more than—"

"Huh," his father said, with an odd, taut smile. He was a dumpy, freckled man with long woolly red hair combed to the side and, at the time, muttonchop sideburns. He was often both irritable and transparent, so when he said to his aunties with clenched, stifled fury and a forced Brummie* twang, "Awww. 'E's a swait boy oo adores his gran," it sounded as false as it did spiteful. They all knew he beat the boys regularly, especially the elder one; they often had puffy pink welts on their white legs and arms, still chubby with toddler-fat in Cuthbert's case.

Their grandmother didn't react to these edgy exchanges between her eldest grandson and son-in-law, who had developed a recent mutual loathing. She waited a few moments and quietly began explaining how it was best to avoid the forest's interior, which she still remembered well.

"Things thee'll want to forget—that'll be in the middle of the

---

* From "Brum," i.e., Birmingham

Wyre," his grandmother was saying, hamming it up for the boys but not without real unease. They needed a look at the world out of West Brom, but she also sensed the Wyre might be too much for them, especially little Cuddy. "It's a tricky place, boys, but it's lovely, too. But honestly, thee const* get right lost."

Cuthbert's mother, Mary Handley, sat cramped beside Henry on a black-leather settee that looked big and misplaced in the cottage, fingering her teacup and leaning forward with a stiff, mannered face, unwilling to relax. Husband and wife each maintained, in their own miserable ways, an illusion that all was diamond-glinted good fortune in the city. Having moved themselves from the Marches to Birmingham years ago, they had barely broached the lower middle class; they kept their own ire at this state of affairs tamed with purchases of chocolate and lager and a few overworn sports jackets and perfumes, jingoism, and an abiding unctuousness toward the rich. Neither had any use for forests.

"I'd like to see it cleared, meself, except if there's any, *loik,* swans in there," said Henry. "There's loads of woodlands in Wales, and no one makes a tuppence off Wyre these days, do they? It's not like the old barking-peeling and tannin days, is it?"

Their gran, who was named Winefride after one of the local so-called miracle wells of the Marches, took a frank swallow of tea, trying to ignore the man's foolishness. Hundreds of species of birds inhabited Wyre, but no swans. She was a white-haired woman with a strong, square face; for the day trip, she'd worn a long pretty nylon dirndl skirt with gold acanthus-leaf designs and a gray Orlon sweater, both bought by catalog order from Kays.

"Of course," said Henry, sitting up a bit on the settee, and smirking. "The politics of chopping anything down is all mardy† these days. Even in Wales."

---

*   Can
†   Insane

Two plump rose-cheeked women of roughly the same vintage, the great-aunties, were scurrying in and out of the kitchen, bringing a pot of damson jam, triangles of toast, slices of Cox's Orange Pippins, and a Spode teapot.

"Bist sure thee'st stay near the big oaks, along the edges, and don't be too loud, and you'll see or hear a thing or two," their gran said to the boys, ignoring her son-in-law's last comment. "But if errun of thee go loblolling in there, all tittery and tottery, no living thing will show itself. But the Boogles will!"

"Boogles," gasped Cuthbert.

"I'll outrun any Boogles," said Drystan.

"No you won't," said Cuthbert. "You 'av to stay with me, Dryst. You're not doing a runner, roight?"

The boys had heard about Boogles, the "owd sprites," many times from their gran, but they had never been close to a place where the creatures supposedly lived.

Still restive from the car ride, they had been roving the tiny sitting room. A gold-framed photo on a wall cabinet caught Cuthbert's eye, and he scrutinized it from inches away. It showed a young, burly soldier with a brisk, proud smile. He wore the same heavy wool tunic and puttees he saw in a photograph of his dead grandfather, but this soldier looked robustly healthy.

"That's your great-uncle Tom," one of their aunties said. " 'E used to keep a pet hob-lamb e'd let run around our kitchen. E'yunt come back from Ypres."

"That's a man," said Henry.

There was a brief silence, and Cuthbert's father looked down stiffly, out of respect. He gave his whiskers a scratch.

Despite their age difference, in their blue-striped T-shirts and matching khaki camp shorts, the boys might nearly have been mistaken for twins that day. Cuthbert was very tall for his age. Unlike other Handleys, their hair was as dark brown as cloves. They both had high pale foreheads, long mahogany eyes, and small, delicate O mouths. The younger boy was only a little shorter than his brother, though he still possessed the round face and short jaw of a child.

"I'm not afraid of any Welsh forest," said Drystan. Of the two, he exuded a particularly languid self-assurance and sweet inattention, with longer hair and a slightly more prominent chin. He'd been walking around since breakfast with untied shoes. His father's quick violence toward him and lack of warmth had wrought something darker and angrier in Drystan, combined with an intense but underfed intelligence. "I promise that I'll never go mad."

Their mother, who had fairer hair but the same black-brown eyes, said, "If you don't stop your mithering, *we'll* all be mad! And it's not Wales. It's the Marches."

Winefride put down her tea and sniffed at Mary. She said, whispering loudly enough for Cuthbert to hear, "Don't be such a cruel munch. They're just lambs."

"Gran?" said Drystan. "I don't want to be any lamb. I want to be something clever—and brutal." He grabbed his little brother and scrobbled his hair, then started tickling him under his arms. Cuthbert squealed with laughter. "Someone needs to herd this little lamb."

"Dryst!" barked their father, in a severe tone that embarrassed everyone present. No one said a word for a few moments. Cuthbert's brother glared at their father with open contempt, shaking his head.

Since arriving from the city, the Handley parents had planted themselves in the murky sitting room of the great-aunties' home, a room that smelled of burned oats and damp flagstone in an eighteenth-century cottage with tiny casement windows. Their old uncle George Milburn slept in a chair.

Winefride, on the other hand, who often wore a sad expression

of declined pride, was as vivified by the trip to her "owd Wyre" as
her daughter Mary seemed querulous. She looked nearly as anxious to get outside as her grandsons, and she kept tapping her foot
and looking out the casement window. Her ongoing descriptions
of the forest could not have been more potent to Cuthbert's ears.
They seemed like the breathtaking words of some grizzled space
mercenary in his *Dan Dare* comics, not of a rheumy old woman
living in her son-in-law and daughter's cramped terrace house in
West Brom.

"Madness!" Cuthbert said, with great delight, though he had no
idea what the word meant.

"That's right," said Winefride. "And it won't go away 'til the sun
shines on both sides of the hedge."

Drystan asked his brother, quite earnestly, "What hedge? How's
that?"

Cuthbert said, "Saft head! *Whisten*, will you?"

The boys sidled up to their gran and cuddled in for stories.

of fairy kitchens and pet hares

"NO, YO'DUNNA GO TOO KEERFUL INTO THE Wyre," their gran was saying. "But ye go, just the same. 'Tis almost time, too."

She looked at her daughter, raising her eyebrows, and continued: "When I was a little badger-lass, we once found an owd broken baker's peel in there. We took it home to our dada to have it fixed. I remember him marveling, 'Why's thar a baker's peel in the middle of the forest?' Well, babbies, my granddaddy, who had the Wonderments, as thee well know, well, 'a said there were *fairy* kitchens in Wyre, where fairies and their pet hares—hares that talked, yo'know—where thay ran their coal ovens." She smiled more easily, her mouth softening, the wrinkles around her lips folding into milky pink ripples. "So once the peel was put right, we left it back in the forest, and the next day, we found in its spot the most perfect little cake we'd ever tasted, flavored with violets and juniper-berry glaze."

The boys were rapt now, kneeling beside their gran, one of their little hands on each of her chunky thighs, sitting perfectly still. Since their earliest childhood, their gran had told them various tales, notions, and advices she referred to collectively as the Wonderments. All along Welsh Marches, where Offa's Dyke once bullied the Welsh with Mercian royal might, a dwindling number of families bound "neither by rank nor nation," as their gran put it, had for centuries quietly bequeathed the Wonderments, from granddad to granddaughter, then grandmother to grandson, and so on.

"And the fairy bakers make all kinds of little cakes so *tasty* and *noice*—well, thee dunna forget it if thee 'av one."

The two aunties giggled, with bell-like happy notes, and the smaller, more vocal of the two, Bettina, said, "Er's good as gold, your gran—*you* two tiddlings, you listen. But don't let her wind you up. We've got good'n *noice* cakes here, too."

"Oh, a little winding's in my binding," said Winefride. "But your aunties' cooking is better than any fairy's." She very lightly touched her grandson's nose with her fingertip. "Do your shoes, Drystan." He slowly knelt down and tied his laces with long, sluggish movements. "Thee cosn't be foresting like that. And if thee fall down in Wyre, thee dars'na stop to get up. Thar're one or two ethers in that forest."

"Snakes," said Mary Handley, frowning. "Mum means snakes. Adders." Cuthbert looked at Drystan with a big, gap-toothed grin.

"Can't believe our luck," said Drystan, marveling, shaking his head. "Adders!"

Apart from Cuthbert's mother, the women were desperately pleased to be together—"like chicks in wool," as Bettina commented, despite an awareness of Henry and Mary's vague air of censure. When they met, which was rare, their speech silvered and gilded into the singsong, jingly bells-and-bracelets dialects of the Marches.

"More tea?" asked Bettina, standing to walk back into the kitchen. "Here goes ding-dong for a dumpling then."

Winefride chuckled. "Oh, Jack's alive," she exclaimed. "We're having fun, aren't we?"

"Yeah, Gran," said Cuthbert. "And we'll be awfully good in the wood—awfully." The brothers grinned at each other, and Cuthbert gave Drystan a little punch on the arm.

"Yeah twice," said Drystan.

"Whatever you do," said their gran, "and there's no iffing or offing in this, thee'shot stay hitched by an invisible yoke." She grabbed Drystan and sat him onto her lap, but he squirmed to get off, pedaling his legs. "Thee, little wildcat, bist sure thee'st listen and bist canny in thar, too. Thee oot hear voices, if thee'st lucky." She kissed his ear and released him.

"What?" asked Cuthbert, quite emphatically. "What did you say, Gran?"

She nodded. "Yes, yes, yes. Sometimes, in Wyre, animals talk." She tried not to look at Henry, who hated this sort of banter, and often let her know it. To him, it was an embarrassment, a sign of the peasant mentality. And he'd never had "a farthing rushlight worth of help from any Wonderment," he would say to her.

"Wike *people?*" Cuthbert asked. "They talk wike people?"

"No, not quite." She glanced at Henry, who was shaking his head at her sullenly. "It . . . rises inside thee."

"Oh, it rises all right, does it?" mocked Henry, unable to contain himself. "Why do you fill these boys' noggins with this—blether?"

Winefride looked at her daughter with an expression verging on tears.

At the age of seventy-six, Winefride Wenlock wanted nothing more than to complete a task she felt assigned; like the green drake-flies who hover for a few hours in May on the Severn then drop dead, she felt she possessed just one sparkling last moment of life to finish telling, for the boys' sakes, a set of tales as old as the river. The Wonderments, as she instructed the boys, were more than a family legacy; they flowed robustly, through the ages, sneaking beneath the Normans' noses, bursting forth from the clashing lost kingdoms and secret saints of Mercia and Arwystli and the coming of Christ to Britain. At least, that's what her grandfather had told her as he lay dying in the snowy winter of 1901. And he'd also told her something that nearly trampled her with a sense of duty, so much so that she effectively decided her sweet grandfather must have been a little mad himself: he claimed that she, Winefride Wenlock, was the very last carrier of the Wonderments, "as far as 'e knew."

Winefride once related the whole conversation to the boys.

" 'T'others are all dead,' said my gran-da. 'Our'n is the last family. After us, it's only animals and the saints as have it. And the animals will only speak to th'uns with the Wonderments.' But I said to him, 'I canna be. I canna be.' I was quite panicked, you know? And he said, 'Thee'ast heard the otters, right? From the forest and the river?' I said, 'I dunna know.' 'Well, that's a yes,' he said. Then he had cleared his throat, and he said, 'He makes the night wherein all the beasts of the forest do creep, and the lions seek their meat, but he also makes Sun ariseth.' He was very ill, poor man. Something with his poor kidneys. And he told me this: 'Look for a grandson. That's as'll have the Wonderments. Or 'e won't.' "

Cuthbert never recalled his gran, as she grew older, dashing around looking for tricky pixies or talking kingfishers. It wasn't like that, not at all. The Wonderments were deeper, palpable, more about feeling than sorcery. But she genuinely believed in her forebears' faith, even if she gave little credence to what her granddaddy had said about her own uniqueness; discounting it enabled her, it seemed, to bear its weight. As she aged, she could better shoulder psychic burdens, including her daughter's marriage to, as she often put it, "a gowkie* miser born under a threepenny planet." She felt the conviction of her ancestors as a warm jewel against her own

---

* Of weak character

dark skin, a gleam to be preserved for Britain and indeed for the world. The Wonderments chose you.

Yet it wasn't automatic. The Wonderments apparently ended if a grandparent didn't instruct the grandchild in them, and many, said Winefride, had declined to do just that, for they wanted their grandchildren to fit into the modern world.

Yet somehow, in ugly West Bromich, five decades before the Property Revolts, before the big suicide cults, before the All-Indigent zones, and before King Henry IX, two sweet grandsons in the line were born. Since Winefride's other grandchildren were girls, and the Wonderments passed from gender to gender and only every other generation, Cuthbert and Drystan represented to her—as one of her serious flaws was a habit of jumping to direst conclusions—the last of the line. But for all England knew or cared, she might be right. Winefride determined soon after Drystan's birth that she would need to work around his facile mother and abusive father to make sure the boy understood his birthright.

Her own children, along with countless other Worcestershireans and Salopeans,* had been tricked, as she saw it, by Birmingham's industry. All the Black Country and Birmingham and indeed much of the whole world lived in a state of fatal anomie, alienated from nature, and dependent on "machines," as she called all technology.

"We was going after akerns," she once told Cuthbert, "pounding 'em into flour whilst the hullocks—that's what we called people like your father—were clammed with hunger." She whispered the next words: "Your mummy and daddy, they're rawny-boughs nowadays, as far as it goes. That's the hard truth. They canna go without their satellites and tellies and Norton bikes," which was what she called all motorcycles. "But thee and I and Drystan, we can survive off the *trees*, canna we? We can always go back into the Wyre and up into the Marches and my hills of Clee."

---

* People from Shropshire

And survive Winefride had, with her green gleam. But never prospered. The truth was, even before her birth, the landscapes in and around Wyre had been chopped to bits by mining. "Despert chaps, young and owd," as she called them, sometimes by the thousands at a time, used to vie to deform the very hilltops of Clee and all the Welsh Marches with nothing but hand tools. "They was bent on steekling the hills," she said, "as if they hills 'ermselves were fattened little porkets for slaughter." With the Depression, the mining economy had collapsed. She herself, by love and by poverty, was also in time driven off the Clees, like most of her cousins. Indeed, she would go no farther east than the Wyre—a matter of a few miles—until she was forced, as an old woman, by her own petty, city-loving, money-obsessed son-in-law.

before the last photo crumbles

CUTHBERT AND DRYSTAN NOW CROWDED INTO A window, gazing out, elbowing each other.

"I dunna want to go now," said Drystan, looking toward the forest. "I corr."

Mary Handley, grimacing at Winefride, said, "Now look what you've done, Mum. You've worried that child to death."

"No," said Drystan. "I'm not afraid of the Wyre, Mum. A'm afraid I'll never want to come back."

Cuthbert said, "Well, I'm only a whittle, whittle, whittle afraid."

They gawked at a lone roan goat, grazing in a small pasture across the road. Cuthbert—whose clearest idea of animals was the moggies and birds of Birmingham and Dylan, the daisy-munching hippie rabbit on *The Magic Roundabout*—had never seen a goat before.

The animal raised its head nervously, but it kept chewing steadily.

"She's the prettiest thing I've ever seen! Is she a kind of cow?" Cuthbert asked earnestly.

"Dunno, really," said Drystan. From his pocket, he pulled out a thornless haw-tree twig with a few leaves on it, and began twirling it in his hand. He was always picking up sticks he would fiddle with for hours then toss on his dresser.

"Heard any animals lately?" Winefride suddenly asked the two aunties, as if inquiring about the latest gossip.

The big aunties nodded jovially in agreement, with occasional fixed love-stares at the two children.

"Of course—yes, yes, yes," said Auntie Bettina. "There's a Welsh *toy*ger in there now, they're saying."

"Suuuuuuuuure," said Cuthbert's father, smirking. He kicked his legs out from the sofa rather impertinently. "That's what *these* ones need," glaring at his sons.

With the proud trip out of Birmingham in his squatty new Hillman Imp, he was almost in as good a mood as he got, but he still seemed like he had, as his mother-in-law would put it, "a dog in his belly."

"Now these boys could use some scaring-up—and discipline. Especially old Cuddy." Cuthbert didn't like this nickname. His father grinned, and added, "They *could* run into a *pole*cat, mind you."

The word *discipline* from his father's lips didn't normally play well in small gatherings. It was like a hangman singing the praises of well-toned necks. His mother once told him, "Your dear old dad wouldn't give away the droppings of his nose on a frosty morning, and if he said he did, he'd be lying about it."

"Discipline? Scaring?" said Gran. "Shhhh! You inna understand at all." She spoke good-naturedly, but there was a flash of a swishing razor in her tolerance.

"That's what I said," said Henry. "These boys respect that— something they learnt from me. I don't mind giving them a little podge on their bottoms from time to time. Or with my belt."

"Stop it, Hank," said their mother.

"Give the forest its due respect, but I dunna think there's any *toy*gers anymore," said Winefride, which is what people on the Welsh Marches used to call polecats. She looked upward for a moment, as though reviewing a long-memorized taxonomy. "But there's other things, just as special as polecats. You know, we used to have lions in England and plenty o' wild cats. Tis' true. Back in the days of the barrows and stone tombs, when 'did those feet in ancient time,' as they say. You 'ad lions then, by jings. You know what I'm on about. *You* know, Hank."

"Never," said their father. "I do not know. That's all rubbish. Drink your tea, Mum." His smile was gone.

"Show some respect," said Cuthbert's mother.

"Humph," said Winefride. "It's all right."

Cuthbert's mum said to her husband, sighing with fatigue, "Aren't you capable of humoring them a bit, Hank? Can't you be decent?"

Auntie Bettina, the sharper of the two aunts, tried to change the subject. She shared most women's remarkably unswerving and politely furtive disdain for her nephew, and she felt sorry for Winefride, a Clee girl who had been dragged off to West Brom by a sore bore of a son-in-law. Winefride wasn't blood, but she felt far more a kindred spirit than Henry.

"You said you brought that camera of yours, Henry?"

Henry frowned at the woman with a harsh, instinctual alarm, and he almost ducked down in his seat. He held a flinty-eyed posture of defensiveness for a moment, as if preparing for some vast wave of other people's messy joys to wash him away.

"Yeah?" he said, with a porcine grunt so routine for him, he actually felt it as sociable noise.

"Henry!" his wife scolded. He sat up a bit, looking around with a simpering smile. His wife had a way of snapping him out of his lugubriousness.

"Sorry," he said. "Yeah, you wouldn't believe the cost of film these days. Mr. Wilson's 'pound in the pocket' is a right laugh."

"Henry, you'll be happy to take some piccies, won't you?"

"Oh, ar, of course. A'right."

After a few minutes, and much lecturing about the virtues of American manufacturing, their father produced his old Kodak Brownie 127, a small camera made of Bakelite, which Henry Handley swore by. He could coax unforgettable images in full color from it. There were three subjects—Cuthbert and Drystan or almost anyone posed in front of his or a neighbor's car; local construction projects; or mute swans at the park. The man loved white swans.

"Roight, yow scallywags—against the wall," he ordered. Cuthbert and Drystan jumped up and stood shoulder to shoulder, refusing to smile, folding their little scapulas against the dark wall like stunted bone wings. Cuthbert was actually shaking with fear; all too often, any kind of boisterousness on his father's part, especially with a lager or two, ended up with Drystan being hit, again and again, with a belt, and then him.

Drystan began spinning his hawthorn twig like a green propeller in his hand. He stuck it in his mouth, made a silly face, then a serious one.

"Smile!" their father commanded. Finally, Cuthbert started snickering, then Drystan laughed, and the magnesium flashbulb exploded.

In the white-hot actinic light, Drystan's face glowed with a robust, dark merriment. He looked different. The usual childlike fragility braced by his high cheekbones had receded. His russet-brown eyes looked smaller, harder. There was that green-leaved twig jauntily in his teeth. One could just make out something new—the forceful gaze of a man, emerging from the boy—angry, bold, honorable, and all things his father wasn't.

For years, Cuthbert kept the resulting photograph, carrying it everywhere, a stiff, white-framed square of color emulsion paper, his silver-halide talisman against oblivion. He took it onto the brownfields and doss houses and alleyways of England, until eventually, after thousands and thousands of warm orbs of Flōt, he could hardly work out why it was so important. It was the last photograph of Drystan in the universe, but when it disintegrated, soaked with urine in his pocket, he didn't even know it.

the prophecy of an animal lord

IN THE COUNTRYSIDE, IN THE ERA BETWEEN THE great world wars, and nearly a century before the death of King William, the depredations of King Harry9, and the coming of a new king, the soul of England did begin to waver. Long before the zoophobia and existential threats of Heaven's Gate, the languages of animals seldom were heard, and even among the few Britons left who still prayed to the "owd green saints," as Winefride Wenlock called them, almost no one knew enough to resist the gathering silence.

There were exceptions to the dying hush of the animals, even in Winefride's lifetime, "hidden as plain as your chops," as she'd say, most from the "golden age" of English animal stories. Countless British parents read *Peter Rabbit* to their children, she liked to claim, never grasping that the sad-eyed, dark-haired Beatrix Potter, whom Winefride had seen admiringly in one of the illustrateds, had spent much of her childhood and early adulthood speaking, secretly, to animals.

"Oh, 'tis as true as I stonds 'er! You know how little Benjamin

Bunny gathered those onions to take down into his mum's bury?" Winefride had asked Cuthbert and Drystan earlier that morning as they sat squeezed into the backseat of the Imp on the trip west from Birmingham. "And all about his and Peter's escape from that gallus cat? Well, Mrs. Potter had summut in her 'yud besides nits and lice to *wroit* all that, with these good animals acting the very moral of animals that talk —oh, Mrs. Potter knew to the tongue of rabbits and hares, be sure—probably learnt from that old Belgian buck rabbit they say she had at her house.

"Thee canna write like that about hares without lashions of the Wonderments in thee," she said.

But she said she didn't see much evidence of Wonderments anymore, not since the Great War.

"If I had the strength to clomber over to a library more often, I'd probably find I don't know what I'm mithering on about," she told Drystan and Cuthbert. The cold eyes of their mother, who sat up front, appeared in the rearview mirror. They could see her shaking her head, before turning to stare out her window with an almost predatory disinterest. Winefride continued, "But still, it's sorely hushed these days with the animals—hardly a naise!"

The notion of a great calm among animals before the arrival of a terrible messiah became a deeply felt, if eccentric, eschatology in Cuthbert's and Drystan's young psyches. Winefride would proffer the idea anytime a neighborhood spaniel stopped barking or a nightingale suddenly abandoned its song.

"My grandfather used to say that when the animals go quate, it means Jack in the Green's right 'round the corner," she once said. "Better look out! 'Tis true as christened apples on St. Swithin's Day."

"Jack in the Green?" Drystan quipped. "That some kind of pudding or bread or summut, and you put those 'oly apples on it?"

Their gran had laughed. "No, no. Jack's the same Jack as Jack's

Alive. The Green Man. The Lush One. Robin Goodfellow. Puck. The Christ of Otters."

"Otters? I don't like otters. I like tigers. Can't we have tigers?" asked Drystan.

"Or dragons?" asked Cuthbert.

"No, no," their grandmother had said. "The otter—he's the one we've got in England, and others have theirs."

The Christ of Otters was that peculiar face with ivy in its nostrils and a halo of grapevines, staring from forgotten corners of British churches, from corbels and column capitals, grave slabs and misericords, with an expression of furious fecundity. According to the legends of the Wonderments, as Cuthbert's gran described them, the Christ of Otters was to return one day to England, in the flesh, after a Great Hush in which the nation struggled then endured a deceptive ascendancy. And a risen St. Cuthbert would usher the way.

" 'A comes after we've been down on our duffs for a while," she'd once explained. "And there will be a star in the sky—in the east. Look for it, boys."

The Christ of Otters' arrival would mark the precise moment of the nadir of humankind on earth, and the beginning of the slow return of a new equilibrium.

"Now don't get me wrong," she once told Cuthbert. "I go churching for Jesus Christ our Savior, son of Joseph, son of Heli, Matthat, Levi, et cetera and whatnot." But she went on to say how those Wonderments "told your owd gran and those before for all time" that God had made a special promise to the animals of Albion.

" 'E'd given 'em souls, 'a did," she said. "And it was down to all the good things they done for all of us, especially out here in the Marches. And they would get their own saint—an animal Lord."

Souls for their service to England. That was the covenant between humans and Great Britain's animals, passed down in the
Wonderments, as Cuthbert came to understand them. Such inspired
animals of the covenant ought never be caged, or looked down upon.
"They've their own yuds," his gran always said. They possessed
animal motives and animal values; they had a few special saints
across the British Isles, their own green shoots off their own Tree
of Jesse—St. Aristobulus, St. Columba, and St. Cuthbert; they had
their own Cains and Judases. The animals of Britannia did not look
for the resurrection of the dead; they sought to live with dignity and
purpose in their ensouled eminence. So declared the Wonderments.

"God gave 'em souls, and what did the English give 'em?" she'd
once asked. "A slaughterhouse in every town—a bunch of clarty
land, dorty seas, rivers turned into gubbon holes,* and thousands of
book-learnt clish-clashers who say the bastes† are nothing but bond-
servants or jumbles of chemicals or whatnot. No wonder they went
quate!"

As Winefride remembered it, the Wyre Forest before the Second World War seemed like the last verdant haven against all this,
a place of glory and grief somewhere between Eden and Geth-
semane.

"It always 'ad a rainbow above it—the 'bow in the cloud.' A
special green and gold one, like the one God had shown Noah after
floodwaters. When I was a much younger lass, 'twas paradise to me,
and to the animals," she had said that morning, in the car. Drystan
had been plucking habitually at the end of a dark green thread in
the Hillman's springy plaid upholstery. As he began to pull it, his
gran gently took his hand in hers to stop him. "The beasts loved the

---

* Sinks for dirty water
† Beasts

forest. But they knew its end was coming, and it broke their wild hearts."

"Mother," her daughter suddenly said from the front. "These boys are gullible. You're going to worry them."

His gran had whispered into Cuthbert's ear, leaning hard against him, "I wouldn't ever lie to thee or to Drystan. Ever." He'd felt safe and happy smooshed into her warm, damp muscles; she felt like some enormous dolphin, carrying him out to sea.

the death of the wheat farmer

BEFORE THEY ARRIVED AT THE OLD HANDLEY relatives' house, his gran managed to tell Cuthbert the whole history of the region, even how she'd met his long-dead grandfather.

"Tell us, Gran."

"Ha! You're really going to suffer now," she said. "It was this one lovely day, in 1919. I had my long black hair unpinned and hovering in the wind—the villagers sometimes used to call me 'the Basque Beauty'—and I walked two pretty miles into the town of Bewdley, from the country, just beyond the Wyre, to buy a few stalks of this new fruit being sold called 'banans,' as I called them."

These "banans" had stopped appearing at the grocer during the war, their gran explained, but they were finally back, she'd heard, and she couldn't wait. They were beautiful things, soft and aromatic, "loik a kind of custard you can hold." The fish and fruit grocer, Mr. William Wood, swore they were good for heart problems and "general nutrition" (though any girl from the Clees knew you used foxglove for whatever ailed the heart).

"Eat as thee please," Mr. Wood had said. He was staring at Winefride with something just short of awe. She had long, deft fingers and that hair of hers was as shiny-black as Scottish obsidian—and blown over her one ear just so.

"I was a tall girl, and healthy, and Mr. Wood knew my family was poor, too. Back in the owd times, most of the country people had little meat to eat, but I gave it up on my own as a young lass."

Being a vegetarian at the time, Winefride said, attracted incredulity in the town, and "a kind of pity" in the country.

But that day in 1919, she stood there near a table piled with bananas, oranges, and plums, pulling the bruised skin off three bananas in a row. She dropped a skin into her purse, almost reluctantly, and plucked another small, squat cylinder off the fruit.

"I'll be making myself sick," she said. "You shanna be canting about this to everyone, oo'll be, Mr. Wood?"

Mr. Wood, a hardy man with a large belly, was amazed she could devour so much.

"Thee 'oodn't be the first," he said. "The children are mad for them. They can't get enough."

"Dack, dack, dack," she had said, using the common pig-call from her neighborhood in the hills. "Dack, dack, dack," filling her maw. "I'm a gilt-swine when it comes to banans." And just then, as she stood with her mouth stuffed with this tropical food, a young farmer, Alfred Wistan Wenlock, not long back from the Great War, walked into the shop.

" 'E wasn't much of a sight—just a thin wimbling, I thought," she recalled. "Loik summat grown in a soil of sadness. And I could see he drank too much."

A sickly veteran with roots in Northumbria and a defining talent for impracticality, Alfred came from a long line of undistinguished clerks. He'd never quite fit in at Bewdley, but having survived the war, he felt resented and guilty; so many of the town's own sons, and many of his friends, lay buried in Flanders and France among the ten thousand dead from Worcestershire. Anguish never was far from his heart, and homemade brandy never far from his lips. Occasionally, to ease his sadness, he painted harmless watercolors of town fountains and churchyards. The war depressed land prices, too, and Alfred took his paltry veteran's pay from the war and managed to buy a small cottage and plot in the hamlet of Far Forest on the western edge of Wyre.

He was going to grow wheat—an ambitious if not foolhardy crop for the district.

"Miss," he said, with a trace of a smile. "Those bananas," he said. "I had one in London. They are as lovely as anything I've ever seen." He added, peering at her carefully, "Almost."

They started talking. Alfred told her about the little plot, his plans for a farm, and Winefride, despite knowing better, found herself smitten. She lifted her hand to her mouth, trying to cover a fleck of the fruit that had emerged.

"Mmm," she said. "Oh god. Yes."

THE TWO MARRIED at St. Cuthbert's Church in Far Forest on a rainy spring day in 1921; Winefride wore a silk gown that practically her entire village had helped stitch.

"I carried a bouquet of purple saxifrage with a few straws of wheat stuck in for luck," she said. The rain, that day, had seemed providential, "a gift from the Green Man," as she put it, "from the otters."

The union brought much love and abundance, and Alfie's field became renowned around Wyre for its flavorful, nutlike, quality cereal. Yet the small holding's revenue never grew much; every year in the 1920s, it seemed wheat prices tumbled a little more. Cheap American wheat had begun pouring into England, too. Many farmers grew angry and moved to Birmingham; most who remained moved into dairy or subsidized sugar beets.

"Alfie," Winefride remembered telling her husband. "If we have a few young cows, think of all the cheese we'll sell. And they're such lovely creatures."

"But bread," he answered. "Who doesn't eat bread? Bread is everything."

"I'd rather a'kern bread, Alfie. This wheat—it worries me, my love."

"One day," Alfie said, "wheat will conquer all."

Two daughters and a son came, and in 1929, Cuthbert and Drystan's mother, Mary, was born. But 1929 also brought more rain and more and more and more of it—and then poverty.

All summer, Winefride would hear around the village the phrase "wheat loves dry feet." She grew to hate the words. Day after day, she would watch Alfie, his cheeks scarlet, trudge out to their plot with his shovel and pickaxe, struggling to carve channels and build temporary wooden sluices in mud as thick as what he'd faced at the Battle of Flers-Courcelette. He would come back, sometimes clutching evidence of what he considered his failure, torn straws of the yellow "gally wheat" that he would show to his wife and hurl down in shame.

ONE MORNING in the early autumn of 1933, Alfie drank his usual morning brandy with a raw egg in it and ate a bowl of porridge he heavily salted. On the wireless, he listened briefly to the news— Germany was withdrawing from the League of Nations, and a great drought was ravaging the American state of Oklahoma. Alfie went out to his scrubbly wheat field, hoping to salvage a bit of wheat for personal milling. The family needed food.

Later that morning, little Mary found her father, fallen in the mud, gasping for breath, his face bright red.

"Get up, Daddy!" She ran back to the house, terrified, screaming for her mum.

Alfie was carried inside by Winnie herself, and a doctor was sent for.

"It's acute lobular pneumonia," the doctor told Winefride, outside the sickroom. "It's tough, Winnie. It's the kind that gallops. You need to get the vicar over here."

"Nonsense! He was fine yesterday."

So she ran to the forest, tears in her eyes, gathering wild garlic for a tincture she made with brandy and vinegar. She tore her hands up, pulling the "crow's garlic" up through nettles and haw branches, and when she returned, her hands dripping blood, the vicar was there, praying over his body, his feet still wet with mud.

THEN CAME, Winefride told the boys, a destitution that ended the world of Merrie Worcestershire. While many of their friends fled for the city, Winefride, numb with grief, turned back to the Wyre.

She'd never lost her awe of the glimmering forest. It always resurrected itself. The disused hearths, after the Great War, quickly grew over with wild strawberry and strange fire moss with orange-tipped setae, as if the hearth's embers, centuries old, still burned beneath. Wavy hairgrass, cowslip, and valerian took over the old barking brush-piles, and these became sites of badger runs and weasel dens. The Boogles were there, yes—it was their forest, and if you crossed them, they would bedevil the mind. Your next ramble into the forest for tinder might end with an adder biting your ankle. So you must tread with respect. This is what she'd been taught by her own grandfather when she herself was a little girl. When she spoke of the "mysterious mysteries" of the Wyre to Cuthbert and Drystan, she meant it not only as a serious admonition but as a bequest, too, of what to her was sacred knowledge, the Wonderments. She loved Wyre and its creatures, and she feared them, too.

calamity at dowles brook

THIRTY-FIVE YEARS AFTER CUTHBERT'S GRAND-
daddy's death, as the family sat socializing in the dark sitting room,
Winefride found herself echoing, once again, the old sentiment
about the "Boogles," as she had with her daughter. This time she
was warning her grandchildren as they contemplated a walk into
the forest.

"Thee dunna want to hespel the Boogles," Winefride was telling them. "There bist worse things in this world, but it'll still be a
mighty good job if you taks warnin', chaps."

"*Hespel*? That's it, stop it, Mother," Cuthbert and Drystan's mum
had answered. "Speak proper to these children, or they'll grow up
to be thieves living in Dudley. And poor. Or farmers."

"An what's wrong with farmers?" Gran had asked. "They inna
any worse than the ewkins* in West Bromwich."

"I *want* to see the Boogles," Drystan had said that day. He was
jiggling the front door's knob, rocking on his heels, and nearly waking his sleeping great-uncle George. "And that magpie-sort goat."

---

* Flatlanders, i.e., people not of the Clee Hills

"Be good to that goat," Granny said. "And stay out of the forest—or be careful. They've adders in there, little noodle-like ones, but adders no less."

The two Birmingham boys obeyed their grandmother—at first. They bolted from the house but stopped almost immediately upon encountering the goat close-up. They stared in silence for a minute at the chewing, imperturbable goat. ("It's a funny old goat," Drystan kept saying. "Easily the best one I've ever seen.") They carefully clambered over hedgerows and ran across a barley field and one of Bewdley's many overgrazed pastures. They finally arrived at the sundrenched southeastern flank of the forest itself. Local children would have scampered right in, and they often did—but Cuthbert and Drystan, out of their West Brom world of street kickabouts and corner shops, dawdled. They'd just have a little look, but not enter the forest.

"Oooooooh, it's really smashing," said Drystan.

"It's all right," Cuthbert said glumly. "Can't see much, not from here."

A stand of very old oaks festooned with huge shriveled globes of gray-green mistletoe stood on the forest's edge. It had been raining hard in recent days, yet there had been no relief from the high temperatures. The flora seemed scorched, raving with energy, subtropical. Yellowish liverwort with designs as filigreed as fine necklaces hung everywhere in strands. Regal stems of pinkish purple betony and Scottish thistle grew at the feet of the ancient trees. The shiny leaves of the oaks, enmeshed in striated sunbeams and swamped in golden light, gave the forest's boundaries a kind of honeyed radiance.

Cuthbert leaned over and picked up a gnarled old black stick. For reasons one can hardly conceive, two condoms, uncurled but evidently unused, had been tied upon its end like ribbons of skin.

Neither sibling knew what they were. Cuthbert pulled one of the condoms back and let it snap back.

"This is a good stick," he said.

"Might do," said Drystan. "Let me coppit for a second?"

Cuthbert handed it to him.

Drystan crouched down and began swinging the stick at imaginary monsters. He said, in a retro-pulp TV-announcer voice: "And Dan Dare lands the *Anastasia* on northern Venus, surrounded by artificial tornadoes hatched by the Treens. He *hunches* down, gripping his Uranium Melt Sword." Cuthbert squealed with laughter, showing his gappy baby-toothed smile. "Now Dan Dare begins *slashing* at horrible gangs of dinosauroid warriors, lopping off their scaled fingers, then bashing the bulbous head of the Mekon until the evil creature spins off on his Floating Disc."

Cuthbert clapped his hands. Just turned six, he was beyond the patty-cake stage of entertainment, but Drystan could still charm him to no end with utter ease.

Drystan swung a few more times. Little hums came off the stick as the latex flapped in the air.

"Blasted," said Drystan, in a normal voice. "It's a *noice* stick." He gave it back to Cuthbert. "Coppit good, Cuddy. We may need that."

Dryst seemed to have braved himself up.

"Let's *conquer*," he said.

Then he remembered. Their granny had said "The Boogles 'as more full of nabs and tricks than Owd Nick. And by gum, thee canna be top'over-tail *maskered** an' confused at your age. Dunna stay late thar. The animals—the owd ancient animals, *thay* come out."

The forest before them looked gorgeous and intimidating; Cuthbert felt pulled in. The sun had hit its zenith, and it wouldn't be dark

---

* Rendered giddy

for hours. Drystan was generally protective of his younger brother, but he couldn't help reciting a story Gran had told him the night before in Birmingham.

"Cuddy, you know Granny said something once before, she said 'er own old aunt, Millie—she's *dead* now, roight, Cuddy?—well, she had come down off those hills where they're all from, the Clees or Clays or what, and Aunt Millie and what 'ad got *lost* in the forest. For *three days*."

"Liar," said Cuddy. "You're 'aving a go at me." He whipped the condom stick through the air.

"I'm not. When Millie finally came out, Aunt Millie, Granny said, well she was doolally—off her head or what—and she never got any different. She sat in a birch wood chair, like, for thirty years, petting her white cat. It's the truth."

Cuthbert looked down at his stick and used his thumbnail to scrape off some of its thin, green bark.

Drystan continued, "Aunt Millie would sometimes say that she was looking for leftover charcoal from the charcoal makers, but what she found was the King of Night. The King of Night. Bloody hell—that's all the reason I need to go in there. It must have been one of the prehistoric lions. Or that Welsh tiger."

"Or them Boogles," Cuthbert said sternly (his upper lip trembling).

"All right," said Drystan. "Let's nip along, then."

But they didn't move. For a while, they nervously kicked at a dead log and shouted nonsense words to hear their echoes and swatted at red damselflies and at each other.

"Googa maga waga maga!" yelled Drystan.

"Biggle flix!" screamed Cuthbert.

"Maga maga!"

"Shite!" said Cuthbert, with tingling boy-laughter ringing from him in tiny bright bells.

"Boogles!" Drystan said. Then, in a derisive, squeaky old-lady voice, he added: "*Thee* dunna want to hespel the Boogles."

It was rare for Drystan to show disrespect for their gran, but a spectral excitement combined with a prepubescent wildness had momentarily gripped him. Cuthbert frowned at him.

"Well, let's get on with it then!" said the older child a bit huffily, and started walking into the forest. "Fuck it all!"

"Wait up," said Cuthbert. "Drystan! No!" But Drystan didn't stop.

"Come on, tittybaby."

"Shut." Cuthbert didn't like naughty words, but he never threatened to tattle on his brother. The consequences were too severe.

The younger boy trotted behind, still carrying his prophylactic branch.

For a while, they combed through a sunny, flat grove of Scots pines. All these softwoods were tall as streetlamps and planted in precise, bright gaps of twelve feet or so. They weren't native to the forest but had been flash-planted in recent decades to counter vast losses of hardwoods and prevent flooding of the Severn. The smell of pine and rainy loam made Cuthbert feel secure. He and Drystan walked with sure steps over a homogeneous carpet of oranging pine needles, springing a little with each pace.

"A've had enough, Dryst," said Cuthbert. "I wanna go back." He tugged Drystan's hand with hot slippy fingers. "I dunna want to see any—you know—them Boogles. I don't need to see them."

"Oh, come on, Cuddy," said Drystan. "Just a little more. There ain't no bloody Boogles."

"Don't say 'bloody.' You'll get a smack from Mum."

Drystan said, frowning sadly, "What could I get worse than what paerstins* I've already 'ad from the Devil himself? That bastard."

---

* Beatings

Cuthbert didn't argue. He had seen Drystan treated worse than a dog by their father—hit hard with broom handles and belts and punched in the stomach. Drystan claimed their father had even once pushed him down the steps at their house, and Cuthbert, skeptical at first, eventually realized it was probably true.

The pines stopped and they found themselves wandering into a more open and varied oak and birch glade. This was the proper, ancient Wyre, before the great woodlands were turned into hunting chases. Here and there grew huge cherry trees and big-leaf limes. The air felt cooler on their faces, but it was trickier to walk. While many old footpaths traversed the forest, some of them trod for hundreds of years by locals, the two boys somehow managed to avoid them all. But it was growing darker, and Drystan seemed disorientated.

Cuthbert said, "We're lost."

"We're bloody not," said Drystan.

They were walking down into an enormous, strange furrow, about ten meters by one and another meter deep.

"It's like a giant's grave hole," said Cuthbert, fearfully.

It was filled with yellow primroses and ferns taking off in the bowled moisture at its base. It was an old saw rut from the nadir of the deforestation days; indeed, decades before, brave boys roughly the same age used to crawl below the massive circular blade to clean sawdust out. Just when Cuthbert and his brother emerged from it, Drystan hissed, "Stop! Look!" About fifty meters away through a stand of young oak seedlings was an enormous fallow buck, grazing. The two children froze. The animal's great rack spread like a huge bone map of anger, an inscape of worlds Cuthbert never knew. After a moment, a retinue of does finally appeared, sniffing carefully, nibbling leaves. The buck stared at Cuthbert with ruthless indifference, and the children were afraid and fascinated.

"Has he got a cob on* or summat?" asked Cuthbert. " 'E looks like he wants to get us."

"No," said Drystan, shoving the anxious word out of his mouth, his voice trembling. "'E's just like a sort of horse or summat. Don't be afraid."

"I'm not scared," said Cuthbert. He said then, in a rather serious tone, as if Drystan was supposed to note this for eternity in the scribbled annals of their youth, "This is the best day I've ever had."

When one of the does ran off, it leaped through the forest with a silent but powerful grace and compactness, like a great red-brown stone skipping along a lake of green. The boys remain transfixed until it vanished. The rest of the bevy held in place, still as statues, like eternity broken into dun-colored pieces shaped like deer.

"I *loik* this Wyre," said Drystan.

They took a wide circular path around the animals, crossing through painful nettles and holly patches and over several criss-crossed fallen logs. The forest grew very thick with red-berried rowan and silver-barked wild service trees. It slowed them down. Under the forest canopy spread many grotesque, splaying tree-forms caused by the intensive coppicing over the centuries by peasants cultivating cordwood. The coppiced monstrosities looked like colossal flower-heads made of spindly sticks.

As they ambled along, Drystan, at one point, stopped moving, apparently paralyzed by fear.

"I stepped on a snake!" he cried to Cuthbert. "I killed it. It's such bad luck!"

The two boys inspected the snake and buried it, but the incident obviously disturbed Drystan, and he refused to touch it. He wore an expression of real sadness. It was something Cuthbert never

---

* Angry about something

forgot—the death of the adder, before the tragedy, how it seemed to crush Drystan and how he couldn't stop crying until Cuthbert threw a juicy chunk of coal at him.

They had picked up the pace then, and tried to forget the adder. Cuthbert was having fun, whacking hairgrass and ferns down with his condom stick, as if plying a Congolese rain forest.

After a nervous, exhilarating hour, the sunlight was beginning to fade. They started frankly to run; despite Drystan's brave words, the prospect of getting caught in the Wyre after nightfall scared them. Worse, if too late, they knew there would be trouble once they got back to the cottage. The belt might come out.

As they ran through the Wyre, Drystan seemed more agile, humming to himself as he hopped over rocks and brush piles and lost antlers and the scat of badgers and stoats. "I'm a deer!" He flowed as a boy-sirocco, crunching down branches and grasses, as fast as the footwork of Roy Race on the football pitch, as dangerous as Dan Dare dashing across a Venusian no-man's-land to do battle with the green Mekon. He was giggling, couldn't seem to stop.

"It's funny this—funny, funny, funny," he cried. "Kill the Mekon, kill the Mekon!" he was yelling.

"Wait!" screamed Cuthbert, breaking into giggles that slowed him down. "Wait for me!" They charged up and up and up a worn-down red-sandstone escarpment, and dolphin-arched over it, and then they crossed to a half-dissolved railroad track that hadn't been used for a hundred years, and they roved steadily downhill now, their knees wobbly and ticklish and bending so easily. They were laughing their heads off. The trees were centuries old, taller, the ground entirely grown over with vines and maidenhair and bracken of all sizes and shapes, and everything at heights never any less than their knees, and they ran and laughed and ran and laughed and it was as if they were beating a path through a flood of green and fields of glee that would go on into the millennia.

Then, Drystan disappeared.

Cuthbert foot-planted to a stop. He sucked air in great gobs, his tiny lungs heaving, still grinning. He said, "Wha?"

Where was Dryst?

His brother had simply dropped through the floor of the forest. That's what Cuthbert saw. So overgrown was this section of the forest over the less acidic soils around Dowles Brook, that the tributary—coursing fast and wide and flush with rainwater from heavy recent storms—was completely obscured.

He ran a few steps more, and then Cuthbert was shouting out in pain and terror, smacking and rolling down a precipitous bank into a brook engorged and irate, the water pressing against him like icy stones. Neither city boy could swim. Little Cuddy grabbed at branches and grasses, but they were all too slippy or too slight or they cut into his tender boy-fingers. All at once, water rushed up his nostrils and into his mouth. It was sweet-tasting and cold but thick with flora and bugs.

He was immersed in five feet of freshwater, and he was scarcely four feet high. He tried to stand up, but he slipped and fell back, his arms winging. He could not find up. The water rushed into him in gales, in potent torrents, rotating him. His eyes opened wide. Suddenly, as Cuthbert remembered it years later, he was gazing upon a fluid face, a being of brown and white and green wearing a momentary smile, then anger, a pale hand—or a paw?—reaching toward him, desperately.

"Dryst!"

Was it Drystan, in Dowles Brook with him, drowning, or someone else? The visage let out a tremendous gurgling noise and vanished in the water. *Ga go ga maga medu,* the creature must have said. Isn't that what was remembered? Surely, that was it—the being's underwater code—the very voice of otterspaeke: *Ga go ga maga medu.*

Cuthbert had breathed deeply at that moment and felt the pain of deathly green-waters entering him—this was it. Drystan gone, and he was drowning, too, and it all felt freezing and it hurt, and darkness everywhere now—then abruptly, a force, some physical force seemed to throw him onto his knees, right-side-up, as if in prayer. Something pulled him out, and it wasn't Drystan. It was rough and animal and very strong. The boy had been pushed up to his feet by an animal. Or was it by Dryst?

But now his brother was gone. He had reached for Cuthbert, and the younger boy had tried to reach back, and he had failed.

He began coughing the water out, struggling to his feet, falling against the brook's bank. He was bleeding a bit from his lip. There were pink mallows across his forearms. Fly larvae cases made of sand grains and leaf pieces clung to his clothes like burrs.

"Drystan!"

There was no answer, and Cuthbert began to sob loudly and wetly.

The visible effects of his tumble seemed slight. Up the slick bankside was a provisional path through the hairgrass and broken reedmace where he had rolled down. A trio of white-throated dippers a bit farther downstream kept submerging their heads in and out of the water.

"Drystan!"

For many, many years after, the next few moments played time and again in Cuthbert's mind until it nearly obliterated him. As the ordinary world came back into his young consciousness, he heard the liquid snorts of Drystan coughs—a sound that still rang, unmistakably and unaltered, in his adult ears today. It was a sickening—a moaning, diaphragm-sucking, braying gurgle that was distinctly mulish and utterly Drystan.

Gugga-hurr-gugcaacaa-hurr!

Poor Cuthbert, erstwhile brave boy, believed his elder brother had been spirited away by the Boogles and was being strangled by them. He was beside himself, a six-year-old in a new world of trap-doors through which older brothers could vanish.

He cried and cried for his brother, but he couldn't see him.

And next, Cuthbert climbed the slippy bank, trying to make it fun, but he felt scared and worried about Drystan. Steaming green liverwort furred up everything, giving all the rocks and logs a cold-blooded, snaky feel.

"Don't cry, Dryst," said Cuthbert. "I'm coming. I'm all right, you sprog!" This is what he must have said. This is what he needed to think he said—again, for decades to come.

Cuthbert sensed he was lucky—even blessed. Yes, that diamond-dotted, sacred sense—that, too, became a psychic imperative, a way for Cuthbert to face so very many coming years of despair.

When Cuthbert finally emerged from the green tunnel, it was as if he were rising from the floor of the forest.

He waited for Drystan to run up to him, snorting phlegm. A dear boy in forever beauty, forever joy, and forever bluster. But Drystan never came.

"I'm not crying," Cuthbert wailed. "That was good, that. Was it—" He wiped his arm across his runny nose. "Was it fun, was it? Are you all right, you shitehead?"

He swallowed the lump building in his throat. "I saw one of them Boogles," he screamed. "I'd bet all the *mu*-nay in the world on it. It saved me!"

After an hour of waiting, Cuthbert backed away from the brook until he found the disused rail line and followed it to the right, back toward Bewdley. The line's rails were long gone, but the path was partially marked with orange strips of cloth. It was in the prelimi-nary stages of being turned into the Wyre Walk No. 3 trail by the Forest Commission.

Cuthbert was talking to himself. "It weren't bad, Drystan. The

Boogle, he was more wike an angel from God, but sort of a mardy angel." He could not comprehend that his brother had drowned, and he kept talking to him. "Is there other things here, other than Boogles? There's animals, isn't there? There's things with no names and all."

When he approached a curve in the brook, he saw a farmhouse. A couple hundred meters away or so, the rushing Dowles Brook emptied into the Severn. Cuthbert felt great relief and real exhaustion.

That's when he saw the creature again, the dark liquid swoosh of an animal flying out of the forest. It looked like a hyper little man with a chunky living rudder. It ripped through bracken fronds, low and unseen, but making the bracken wave and jerk like a hundred green pennants. It emerged again and plunged headfirst into the water.

It was a giant, Cuthbert saw, at least a meter long, with a head nearly as big as Drystan's. Cuthbert knew that face instantly: it was the good Boogle under the water wot saved him. Or was it Drystan, become a kind of giant dark cat?

The creature vanished and a few seconds later popped up on the opposite bank of the brook, where it raced angrily back and forth, glowering at him and yikkering in its odd, squeaky manner. The lush vegetation on the other side of the brook, all blue with bugle and speedwell, seemed like a special effect of the sky itself, lowered down for the otter to try flying upon.

He had not seen or heard anything like it in his short life. He was speechless, and soon Cuthbert ran off, screaming and pure doolally. It was as if all the day's events had finally rubbed the last trace of West Brom tough away.

Shadows were beginning to take over the Wyre. For ten minutes, he kept calling out and circling around.

"Where are you? Dryst!"

There was no answer. Cuthbert had cried out his loudest cries, and now he was sobbing, and then he began to settle down.

He would have to retrace his steps and bring back help. It would inconvenience the old relations and his mother. His father would kill him. He thought of his mad aunt Millie, petting her white cat, speaking of the King of Night. That seemed a kinder fate than his father's thin black belt.

He started calling as loud as he could, "Bloody hell, Drystan!"

Cuthbert kept thinking he would find him, in some brambles, gulping for air and shuddering, but West Brom tough and proud. Drystan would hug him and pat his back hard. "Chin up, Cuddy," Drystan would say to him. "You're safe now. No blarting now, Cuddy. We've got to get back."

"I saw Satan," he would tell Drystan. "Or some Head Boogle or something."

"Well, that's good, isn't it?"

"Is it?"

He could hear his brother now. "Of course. How often do you get that? Besides, you said it was more of an angel kind of thing." Drystan would push his lips out, making a kind of snout the way he did. "Must be a bit of both."

Cuthbert would smile, his pale cheeks still shiny with tears, and they would go home. And had Drystan not drowned, they would have done just that. They would have gallivanted home with wild yewsticks in their hands and otter scum in their nostrils, and God's bow in the clouds above the Wyre.

three

two kinds of triangles

CUTHBERT STOOD UP HALFWAY IN THE ZOO SHRUB-
bery and leaped forward. The process of getting in had been like
being unwound into something; he arrived dragging a spool of wet
vines and scratches with him, his head squeezed to a screaming red
bolus. He tumbleswivled through the holly, away from the perimeter fence, holding his arms over his face.

He burst into the open now, immaculately inebriated, and poised
atop a long, narrow bank where the bushes associated with the zoo's
main fence all ended and a picket of larch trees took over.

"Now that's a long popple 'round the Wrekin*," he said, panting
for breath.

He looked himself over—a mess, all torn and dirt-rubbed, bleeding underneath his clothes. He was tall and fat and befouled. If grimi-
est north London possessed an immense, snaking digestive tract,
he resembled what it would disgorge. It wasn't inconspicuous. He
slapped a greenish-yellow dirt off his old bio-mesh trousers, which
had a tendency to break down in rain, and his even older navy-blue

---

* A famous hill and landmark in east Shropshire

Adidas weather-buffer, whose heat cells had long dried out. He took
a few steps through the trees. As he moved away from the fence, an
Opticall from the zoo's own system appeared on his corneas:

> The time is now a quarter past 6:00 p.m. The London Zoo will
> close in 15 minutes. Thank you for visiting us today. Come again
> soon!

He stopped again. On second thought, he wanted to take off
the weather-buffer. It was nearly in shreds anyway, but the air was
very cool. With its three white stripes partly ripped off one arm, it
could be considered sporty only if the game were called Woe; and
more practically, a torn weather-buffer would attract attention. He
took the thing off, balled it up, tossed it down, and kicked it against
a knot of tree roots. He had a reasonably clean, maroon pullover
underneath, which he'd haggled for £12.50 at one of the back alley
markets in Holloway Road. Printed on its front was a cityscape sky-
line and the unfathomable phrase "Manhattan 3000," which apparently made sense to someone somewhere on earth.

He knew he had to mind himself. If a Watchman inside the zoo
observed him swiftly walking away from the zoo fence, he would
explain he'd needed to take a slash and couldn't find the toilets. (His
deeply wrinkled, century-old face, unsmoothed by pricey Body-
Mods, chewed by Flōt addiction, was more of a giveaway of his status than he grasped.) He was sorry, he would say, very sorry to look
suspiciously like someone who had just broken into the zoo, ha ha
ha ha! Naff, that!

He walked quickly down the rest of the bank, trying to look unruffled, but he was nearly jogging. He stepped over one of the knee-
high rails that ran beside all the footpaths in the zoo. About twenty
yards ahead, to his left, was a woman in a glowing-pink nightcape
stopped with a glide-pram—oh, a Nandroid, he saw, down from

nearby Primrose Hill. The Nandroid—she had huge, soothing violet eyes and creamy-white, skintone-adjustable digital skin—was looking at a small pack of sleeping jackals bunched together in a corner of their pen. The canine pile looked like the discarded fur coat of the god of cyclones. Since they were among the only animals you could spot from outside the zoo in the park, few paying visitors took interest in them.

The Nandroid gazed at Cuthbert and smiled with a quavering pale chin and a cooing sound, but Cuthbert averted his eyes. He couldn't see the silent baby, swaddled in its ovular glide-pram. He knew that the new aristocracy hired professional Indigent monitors who sat at desks watching dozens of infants through those purple Nandroid eyes, reporting anything suspicious to the Watch. (It was one of the highest-paid jobs an Indigent could get.)

Cuthbert felt uneasily excited. He could hear monkeys whooping, far off, from the other side of the zoo. Their aggrieved Borneo beckoning both charmed and bothered him, and he did not think he should stray far to search them out.

Suddenly the idea of letting any of the animals loose seemed nearly as idiotic to Cuthbert as it would to a normal, well-adjusted citizen. He made an audible *whew!* sound. "Natty, this is!" he said aloud. The baby began to whimper a bit, and the Nandroid started to rock the pram tenderly and sing, in Welsh. It was a song his own gran used to sing to him and Drystan: *"Holl amrantau'r sêr ddywedant, ar hyd y nos,"** and the melody almost made Cuthbert faint with wistfulness.

"A hyd y nos," Cuthbert sang quietly, with a slight slur. "Oh, Gran."

The Asiatic lion terraces with their tiered cement hillocks and lily-covered moats were right beside the jackals. He'd seen them

---

* "All the twinkling stars say, all through the night"

only once before, and he was struck now by their tranquillity. Had the lions ever, he wondered, *truly* ever spoken to him? They were nowhere in sight. The Sumatran tigers, the famous jaguar named Joseph, the black leopard, and all the birds of prey—all silent, too— were just beyond that. For several minutes, he seemed to comprehend that it wasn't normal or even good to hear animal voices.

"Jesus," he said. "I'm fucked."

When the Nandroid floated away like a great pink hot-air balloon carrying its gondola, and no one else appeared on the path, he moved in closer to the jackals. There were five, he saw, and he gave them a pained smile.

"What are your exact names, now, eh? Are you lot gonna say something now?"

He squinted at them. They were dirty and weird—real animals, and not genomic clones. They were not like the wavy-haired spaniels he saw on Sundays at the park. They had short, tawny hair and narrow skulls. Their large, sharp ears were filled with white hair. A cape of black hair spread down their backs. Their oddest trait was their lean, elongated legs. They looked like foxes on stilts. The placard on the fence read: GOLDEN JACKAL (*CANIS AUREUS*), TANZANIA.

Of course, a jackal hadn't been seen in East Africa for thirty years. Much of the region was entirely given over to colossal biomesh and "green fuel" farms.

He tapped the fence. Cuthbert said aloud, quietly, " 'Allo-allo, chaps. Don't want to talk now?"

One of the jackals rolled over and yawned. Cuthbert got out a piece of his diatom-cinnamon chewing gum. He rolled it into a hard little nut and pushed it through the cage. It fell onto the ground. Like magic, and wraithlike, the jackals all stood up and faced him. A young, lean one thrust its head forward and picked the gum off the dirt with its fore-snout, then jerked its head back to take the gum deep into its maw. The animal backed a few steps away from the other four jackals. It began to chew. It was obviously a strange, difficult food for the jackal. The movement of its jaws scared Cuthbert. It was too rapid and repetitive, and it seemed as if the jackal couldn't make the process stop. He regretted giving it. The chewing jackal's eyes stayed on the other four jackals, who looked interested and apprehensive. Cuthbert put his palms against the cage. A larger, fatter jackal gazed up at him, panting with a "happy" face. Its mouth was partially open and its glistening long tongue quivered. A sudden, lively feeling, a kind of élan, pushed up from Cuthbert's abdomen, into his neck. He felt his cheeks grow warm and tingly.

"Hi, hi," he said to the animal.

He decided to have a go at setting his marked finger on a strand of fencing, and the black 9 mm mark he'd scored, he noted, was at least five times the width of the thin fencing. It was evident that his bolt cutters could free the jackals easily—and take on much thicker-gauge fencing, too.

A yellow isosceles triangle on the fence displayed a black silhouette of a hand with an orderly half-circle cut out of its palm. It read:

These

Animals

May Bite

"Better not hold my donnies in the cage," he said to himself; but he felt that he probably could keep his finger there and no harm would come to him.

"You're only a dog, aren't you?" he said. "I've been off my head, puppy!"

After a few minutes, the jackals began to lurk around their long enclosure, except for the one still chewing the gum. They moved with an awkward grace, as if they might fall off their own legs and yet make it look purposeful. One animal held its head low to the ground, trotting around like a police sniffer dog. It seemed disturbed by something. Much of the grass inside their prison was worn away, exposing long tracts of dirt patted shiny by paws. A few coarse, raw roots sprung from the soil, like the pale elbows of underwater swimmers in a dark lupine lake.

Cuthbert knew the Red Watch was after him, but he hadn't noticed what the jackal had: one tall, unmantled Watchman striding in their direction, from near the hyacinth macaws.

Some of the jackals began barking in their high-pitched, melodious yaps.

Cuthbert realized that he hadn't moved for a long time. It was time to get going.

As he began stumbling along, he stopped to steady himself with his hand on a short brick wall, then lurched against a small elm tree. There was supposed to be a line painted on the walk somewhere for a self-guided tour, but he couldn't see it. If he tried to follow a line painted on the path, anyone with sense would see instantly that he was stewed. He began berating himself for succumbing to the impulses that had brought him here. "Fuck me," he said. "Fuck me!"

The lone Watchman bumped against him hard and scowled; he carried his golden neuralwave pike, but he seemed distracted and rushed.

"Stay the fuck to the side of the path," the Watchman hissed, stopping for a moment. "Indigent shite!"

"Ay, sir! Sorry, sir!"

"Haven't you heard? The whole bloody country's on fucking King's Alert tonight. What's the matter with you? You look like a slapped arse, mate."

The jackals snarled at the Watchman, who sneered at them, "Dirty dogs—is this your little filthy mate?"

One of the jackals, a large male, hurled itself toward the Watchman and smacked against the fence. The Watchman jumped back, reflexively.

"Shite dogs," he said, shaking his head. "Should be exterminated."

The Watchman walked away, apparently not interested in further abusing any creature for the moment. Such a painless departure was unusual and lucky, since Cuthbert was surely on the Red Watch List. At best, the Watch List meant arrest and internment; at worst, an Indigent on the list could be neuralpiked to death if she or he met the wrong Watchman. Officially, Indigents not databased or indentured had no restrictions on movement in Britain, but unofficially, the Watch sometimes beat them away, on sight, from places where the upper-middle classes and the new aristocracy congregated, and this almost always involved checking their compliance status. Whatever negligible power and dignity an Indigent ever held, the Watch List instantly crushed them.

HAVING ESCAPED THE WATCH once again, Cuthbert didn't feel relief so much as curiosity. Why was England on alert this time? Was the Army of Anonymous on the attack again? He thought, then, that he heard distant sirens, but he wasn't sure.

On the far side of the jackal enclosure, a few zoo workers in loose, pine-colored spawn-ball shirts had shown up. They were beginning to work their way through the series of chain-link fence walkways and double gates that led into the jackal enclosure. One of the keepers, a woman with a short brown ponytail, was staring at Cuthbert. He almost felt she was appraising him as a fellow animal, both absentmindedly and indulgently, like a bosonicabus passenger gazing at the face of another passenger in a passing bosonicabus, then glancing away.

Cuthbert decided that he should leave the zoo immediately. He felt certain that he was about to be found out. That last Watchman may have already put in a call. He needed to come back, but only in the deep of night. Or maybe he could get an Opticall to Dr. Bajwa, tell him he was ready for the Whittington, ready to detox.

Cuthbert strolled down footpaths. They sagged and veered with such wide egressions, and offered so few forks, they seemed designed for people easily bewildered. He felt a little more relaxed, simply moving, but this calm would wear out fast, he knew. Oh, god, he could use another good pull off that Flōt orb in the grotto.

He came to a capsule-shaped white sign that hung on black metal tubing. In black lettering, it read: GREEN LINE TRAIL: FOL-LOW THE GREEN LINE—YOU WON'T GET LOST AND YOU WON'T MISS A THING! There was an arrow pointing to the ground and a set of paws, but Cuthbert saw no green line. He suspected somehow being tricked by the zoo. The idea that the zoo had merely placed a reference sign poorly did not occur to him. He clipped along but kept pausing at footpath intersections to read cryptic signposts. A taloned claw denoting Birds of Prey; a single long-necked antelope for the Arabian Oryx's lonely zone; a crescent and stars for Moonlight World. Another sign had the zoological society's initials in animal-skin prints: ZSL—for Zoological Society of London—in zebra, snake-scales, and tiger stripes, above its long-used phrase "Living Conservation." Cuthbert did not grasp the meaning of conservation, really, but he took it as an article of faith. It had to be somewhere, in some tiny hidden cage or test tube in a back office. Unlike the rest of Britain after the Second Restoration, the fifteen-hectare scalene triangle that housed the London Zoo hadn't slid back to an almost pre-Victorian ethos where the poor, the animals, and the non-English were to be worked, caged, and subtly subju-gated. After the Property Revolts, conservation outside the zoo had ended in all but signage and laboratories, and if not for a dedicated and well-connected core of ZSL scientists, the zoo would have shuttered in the 2020s.

CUTHBERT FINALLY REACHED one of the two main exits and headed out like a satisfied punter. As he pushed the timeworn, clicking, cage-like turnstile around, a sudden lump of terror seemed to expand in his throat in that bad spot he could never see with his eyes—and just as quickly disappear.

He was out—and free to return, as long as the Watch didn't nick him. He shuffled away from the gate now, and stood there, amazed at what he had done. He savored the feeling, glancing around himself. He hadn't released any animals yet, but he'd done something rather nonpareil, and all his slipshod planning and grotto-making and crawling and Flōt-guzzling had somehow led to it.

to be worse than animals

OUTSIDE THE MAIN ENTRANCE, SEVERAL AFFLU-
ent families had begun to regroup on the pavement. The zoo was
closing, and anywhere one glanced, a fraught child yearned for
something. Cuthbert should have left then.

One red-faced toddler shook a fist for a pseudoapple-ice. A dap-
per boy in a sky-blue morning suit, surrounded by a tiny herd of holographic zebras he'd escorted from the gift shop, averred that his
sprog-juice gorilla lolly wasn't as good as last time. A little girl with
wispy blond curls damp from her own sweaty distress screeched for
an expensive "living-leather" elephant, which simulated the beast's
37.5° C body temp but retracted in chill air. Another brandished
a long, giraffe skin–design cloud-doodle pencil, a recent fad item
with which a child could scribble on the local sky. At one point, an
old-fashioned stuffed King Penguin—nothing like the zoo's own
South African birds—was hurled hopelessly toward the street in a
tantrum.

Cuthbert, an isle of relative calm, observed a fat boy next to him,
savagely ripping apart a nuplastic bag containing an owl kite and

waving its unassembled pieces through the air until a sheet with a pair of yellow eye stickers fell to the ground. The boy's mother scolded him, and Cuthbert moved to pick the eyes up for the boy, but the boy pounced on them covetously and gave him an impish grin. Several white nuplastic pieces of the old-fashioned kite assembly and its pine sticks had fallen to the ground and bounced around. Cuthbert backed off.

"Tell that gentleman thank you, Nelson," the mother said. Her pristine waffle-textured green demi-cape, her flawless blanched skin, her air of confident ease—all signified the conventions of the new aristocrats. She regarded Cuthbert with a distanced but authentic compassion. He felt exposed and didn't know quite what to do. So he waved at the woman, and she smiled at him. He and the mother then watched the boy deal with his kite mess.

Cuthbert thought of his own mother, who had died in 1994, and his father, who lived until 2014—just shy of the era of BodyMods (Cuthbert hadn't spoken to him since his mother's funeral). He felt anguish and some disgust. They were both the offspring of country people, and each had endured a kind of poverty nearly forgotten in England for almost a century, one that was now returning with grievous force.

His mother had been born in Bewdley, a pretty little medieval market town, but by age seventeen, she had moved to the larger Kidderminster, a bit closer to Birmingham. It was supposed to have been her big move out of the blighted countryside to the west. It wasn't. She lived in a noisy women's rooming house and plucked chickens at a small poultry plant. Her roommates made fun of her Wyrish dialect, her melodious accent, her love of ale and fear of hard spirits. The Black Country and Birmingham was where the real fun was—dances, cars, silk dresses, Quality Street chocolates in pink and gold cellophane. When Hitler started sending over his deadly Heinkel 111s, she ran against the refugee traffic and moved *to* bomb-targeted Brum. As she saw it, death by mustard gas or shrapnel was preferable to pulling hanks of cold feathers off hundreds of dead roasters a day. She moved to West Bromwich and got a job making bullets.

Cuthbert's father, Henry, who was a few years younger than Mary, had come to West Brom soon after the war. Like many of the new residents of the Black Country, he too hailed from the red sandstone and coal-sweetened countryside immediately to the west. He had grown up in a tiny farmhouse in Far Forest, just a few miles to the west of Bewdley, and right on the Wyre's edge. There was no running water, no electricity, no gas—only a coal stove with a big hob.

He met Mary in a dance hall, in Handsworth, in 1949. They married, and gradually turned themselves—and were turned—into Brummies of a cold, acquisitive, routine-led nature. Henry liked to think of himself as a tough "gutter Tory." He'd been a lorry driver in the Royal Army Service Corps, and eventually came to fancy himself a kind of Enoch Powell without the Cambridge degree. He had seen horrors in Egypt during the Suez emergency. He spoke of the fedayeen as "animals," and his children as one step above them, as if they were always slipping toward an ungovernableness that required a stern taking-in-hand. He had killed two Egyptians, "and enjoyed it," he would sometimes say. "It doesn't affect me as it does some blokes."

One cold day, the winter before Drystan died, he and Cuthbert were breaking icicles off the eaves of the house and licking the long dark spikes. Cuthbert remembered the bumpy-scratchy feeling of the ice on the tongue, how it tasted like rotten poplar wood.

Drystan had said that he thought that children must be considered worse than animals to parents in Birmingham—at least in their case.

"They don't care," he'd said. "The most they ever touch us is to hit us—they never give us anything nice, never give us cuddles or smiles, never kiss us, never pat our hair or say they love us. They'd put us in boxes if they could, I'm sure."

The little chubby boy Cuthbert was watching gathered up the kite pieces on all fours, then sat down on the ground, swami-style, and flattened the kite across his knees. All the kite's bits and bobs were spread around him on the pavement in front of the zoo. A few other bystanders had taken notice of the scene, and one of them, a man with a new sort of sunshades with a hovering red vapor bulbed around his eyes, now stared at Cuthbert with open suspicion.

"You," the man said to Cuthbert, who pretended to ignore him.

The boy removed the adhesive backing from the eyes, and held them as carefully by their edges as a surgeon might hold actual organs. Cuthbert wished he could help the boy, but he knew that the boy didn't want his help. So he just stayed where he was, gawping, and risking the attention of the Watch.

The boy was now smoothing the eyes onto the microthin nuplastic wings of the kite, pushing hard with his knuckles. His mother stood over him, beaming. She was a compact woman with straight red hair and an elegant waffle-cloth capelet whose loden color clashed with her hair: seen up close, she reminded Cuthbert a bit of some of the smart middle-class women he used to see getting on the train at New Street back home, back when more women worked, but her cool poise marked her out.

She said to Cuthbert, "You see, these old-fashioned toys—kites!—they're still better than all these poly-D games, don't you think?" The question was strictly rhetorical, and Cuthbert didn't dare answer.

He did nod, tentatively. He asked, shyly, "Is he going to have a go with it here and all?"

The man with the red-smoke sunshades approached the woman.

"Is this . . . man . . . is he bothering you?"

"Heavens, no," said the woman.

"So sorry—I offer ten tall tanks of apologies," the man said, sniffing at Cuthbert. The man withdrew but peered around, as if searching for a Watchman.

"Is he going to fly the kite now?" Cuthbert asked again.

The boy faced his mother scornfully, and she smiled tensely around the vicinity. The bystanders who had been paying attention to the boy turned away.

"No," she said to Cuthbert. Then she addressed the boy: "Roll it up into the bag, Nelson. Right away." The bag was already destroyed, so the boy just folded the kite into a little, puffy trapezoid and jammed it into his trouser's front pocket. The woman grabbed some of the nuplastic joints and sticks and the paper-curl of instructions off the walk, and she and the boy made to go.

She said, "He'll actually get to fly it. In Spain, next week. Hols for us—again."

"Why not just go to Hampstead Heath?"

The woman said, "Oh, that's a nice idea." She glanced around for a moment, took a pair of £5 coins from beneath her demi-cape, and forced them nervously into Cuthbert's willing, filthy hand.

"You be careful," she said. "The Watch is around. You're asking for trouble, sir."

Then the mother and son walked away, the boy still fiddling with the kite in his pocket.

Because the zoo had been unusually busy that day, a sluggish queue snaked toward a half-door set into a gate building where day-rental nuplastic strollers could be returned. The zoo was curiously authoritarian about the strollers, its staff checking in each one, sweeping an open hand underneath them, like customs officers, and creating the kind of queue one normally only saw Indigents standing in.

"Probably a neural bomb threat, from the usual suspects," a red-faced man in the queue scoffed. "Bloody last-gaspers." It was commonplace in central London for the republican terrorists to ring in phony bomb threats, except sometimes they weren't faked. They had killed civilians, all right, but their hypothetical neural devices created confusion for effect.

Cuthbert watched the families. Among them were not a few neoteric aristocrats, who looked surprisingly able to cope with a wait. It was a rare sight. He decided to stand in the line himself, just to be closer to them, even though he didn't have a stroller to return. The self-conscious, bourgeois joie de vivre he imagined them relishing engrossed him.

One lanky father behind Cuthbert lugged a ginger-haired tot on each leg. The girls seemed to be identical twins, and the man doted on them, rubbing their heads like little cats.

The bulbous, greasy-looking gray strollers were shaped like elephants, and seemed quite popular. The gate itself was a long brown-brick and stucco structure with dark Spanish tiles that reminded Cuthbert a bit of the entrance to the old Pentonville prison, but one with hanging baskets of orange and grape-colored auriculas, just like the ones at the Whittington Hospital, Cuthbert's old drying-out center, at Highgate Hill. There were geraniums on the zoo entrance, too, and polyanthuses, but it was the auriculas that fascinated him—small and exact, and intensely bright, like fairy-light bulbs.

"Allo," Cuthbert said to the little twins. He reached down for the fallen head of an auricula on the pavement. He smelled it, and he wanted to hold it out toward the girls, but he sensed that could seem creepy. "Yow 'ad some fun?" he asked them.

But the father placed a large hand on each of the twins' heads, and turned their faces away from Cuthbert. The man turned back at Cuthbert with a strained smile, as if trying to mask his apprehension.

"Girls," the father said. "Eyes forward."

Cuthbert was playing with fire, and he knew it. If the Watch saw Indigents bothering citizens, they would arrest them, beat them, or worse.

Shut yowr gaubshite mouth, he silently seethed at himself. Shut it!

becoming the moonchild

AS AN ADOLESCENT, IN THE YEARS AFTER DRYS-
tan's death, Cuthbert would whisper to a ghost-brother at night as
he lay in his narrow, creaky bed.

"You're all the good that's in our blood, Dryst—what little
there is."

Through Cuthbert's youth, in the middle 1970s, during a period
of some of the worst of the beatings, the late Drystan's tiny empty
bed had sat across from Cuthbert in the bedroom, its dark navy and
brown plaid covered in stacks of automotive part boxes from their
father and bags of undelivered clothes for Help the Aged. Around
this same period, Cuthbert began, slowly and half-secretly, first for
minutes and then for hours and days at a time, to conflate his and
his dead brother's identities. He would even call himself "Drystan"
in the third person.

Drystan can't sleep again, he might say.

Dryst just broke his shoelace.

*The orange skies of Dudley are the same color as the dirt on Drystan's
hands.*

Cuthbert also began to struggle to finish things as a teenager, struggle to get out of bed, struggle to live a single second more, and the idea of a ghost-Drystan somehow helped. Twice, he had given up a series of musical instruments after two or three lessons. At one point, his father had frogmarched him with a reluctantly rented viola back to a music shop and, slapping his head, forced him to admit he was a selfish, lazy child to a large Polish woman shop-keeper, who had seemed terrified by the scene.

"Mister, no," she'd said. "*Ty świnio!*"*

Henry Handley showed little tolerance for money spent on the arts and humanities, but to waste money on it openly—that killed him.

"But Drystan will help me, Daddy," Cuthbert would tell his father. "I promise, promise, promise."

"Leave off that gaubshite," his father had said. "You'll get taken away for being a nutter. Or a faker."

Neither parent was kind or world-wise enough to steer him to-ward either psychological counseling, which he so needed, or a good public school, where the bright boy certainly could have won a gen-erous bursary. So Cuthbert (often thinking of himself as Drystan) took his O- and A-levels two years earlier than usual, at the mediocre West Bromwich Grammar, and grew crazier and crazier. He achieved seven straight-A O's and four A-grade A-levels in the sciences and maths, leading, at age fifteen, to an unconditional place reading biol-ogy at University College, London, his first choice. It had been an as-tounding feat. The *Evening Mail* published a little profile titled "West Brom Boy Boffin off to Uni." The attention mortified Cuthbert, but another part of him, deep inside—the Drystanest part—soared.

The fragile boy seemed poised for an almost golden, if quite

---

* Polish: "You pig!"

wounded, flight away from the Black Country, to a happier place. (As an old man, Cuthbert never remembered how clever he actually was before his addictions kicked in; his main memory of grammar school chemistry was burning his finger badly while trying to form copper oxide gas with a Bunsen burner. He and his mates had been passing around and inhaling balloons of the requisite nitrous oxide under their lab tables.)

Drystan, on the other hand, *he* could be allowed in Cuthbert's blinkered mind—with its shades of dissociative disorder—to be the cleverer one, and naturally the precocious lad got into a bit of trouble at his primary and secondary schools, too, right?

In his last year of secondary school, the summer of 1977, before entering university, Cuthbert was mildly disciplined twice, by a sympathetic headmaster, Mr. Hawkes, for snogging another very lonely boy, named Ashley—Ashley had very dry, dark hands—in the school's boiler room. They had both merely wanted to try out kissing, and neither had luck with girls. But the incident attracted special enmity from Cuthbert's father.

Henry, one hot Saturday morning, used his usual black belt with the dye abraded off, and a favorite heavy-gauge wire coat hanger, to beat him for this. This time, Cuthbert felt he was fighting for his life. He struggled, defenseless as a skinned knee, to hide in the Handleys' blue eggshell kitchen, with a gray-yellow light glaring through the windows and the sound of Tommy Dorsey's "Opus No. 1" turned up loud on the phonograph to camouflage the rumpus.

"Yow'll stop this shite, yow scallywag," his father raged, raising the belt (which he folded into a rigid loop) again and bringing it down and kicking him, knocking him against the stove, and then against a pine kitchenette. "Yow bloody poof, yow bloody focking poof!"

Mary Handley howled at her husband to stop, but she did nothing else. With Winefride dead, there was nothing to mitigate the brutality.

"You'll go to hell for this, Harry. You'll go to hell," Mary yelled, but she always stayed with him, and he often went to the dirty pub afterward, where it was hellish enough, where he would paint himself as an unappreciated mentor " 'oo did wot needed done."

Cuthbert could still recall the whistle of the coat hanger in the air, the fanging bites of the belt, the squeal after squeal of "Opus No. 1" 's strangled trumpets.

Cuthbert completely depersonalized in such conditions. He would call for Drystan sometimes; he would unroll the ghost-child inside himself, like a shimmering emerald electric blanket. He would crawl beneath, panting for breath. His head that time took several bad knocks against the refrigerator, and he felt dizzy. He had tried to "defend" himself from the belt, but he only ended up woozy, with his calves whipped so hard that puffy welts rose up on them like secret budding fins. He'd wished he could use them to swim away from West Bromwich forever.

"Yam killin' Drystan!" Cuthbert once screamed when he was being attacked. "Yam killin' 'im!"

The mention of that name, in such contexts, always horrified his parents.

"Don't say that," cried Mary. "You bloody well stop that!"

"The boy's 'af-baked," Henry gasped, standing back from the boy. "He's focking mad as a box of rabbits."

Finally, during a similar life-or-death beating, the neighbors called the police, and Cuthbert—mildly concussed—was temporarily put under a protection order by Sandwell council, and he lived with a foster family near Birmingham City University. He made everyone call him "Dryst," and no one questioned him about it. He was a tall boy for age fifteen, and many overestimated his age and maturity. After a week, he was sent home. The overwhelmed social worker who'd been assigned his case had failed to transfer many of the details of the abuse discovered by the police to Cuthbert's case file. There were comments among the council authorities about how "a grown boy" had got "a bit of aggro" from his dad. In the context of Sandwell, it just wasn't a big deal. Henry, for several weeks, seemed contrite, too. He repeatedly said he was sorry ("Something's wrong with me 'yud, son. Yer dad's so sorry, son."). He even bought Cuthbert a child's phonograph that came in a sort of red suitcase. There was a David Bowie record, too, and Cuthbert would play a song called "Joe the Lion" over and over and over and over.

In a month, Henry's attitude (if not his fists and belt) was back to its old deportment. He felt hazily penitent, but the sense of public humiliation had been searing. He wouldn't risk hitting the boy again, but the emotional abuse became as caustic as ever.

"Yow'm 'aff the boy your dead brother ever was," he'd begun telling Cuthbert.

"Well, I'm *not* me—not anymore," Cuthbert would respond. "I'm something no one knows."

CUTHBERT'S PLACEMENT AT UCL never impressed Henry Handley, who still felt Cuthbert should get a trade even as he matriculated, collected his grants, and moved into Ramsay Hall.

"Yow'll give it up like everything else," his father kept telling his son. And the teenager did flounder badly at UCL, from the start. Mentally, he was completely off the rails. By 1978 or so, with London nearly at the peak of punk, Cuthbert spent most of his time thoroughly convinced he actually was his dead brother. He grew his dark brown hair unfashionably long and straight, parted on one side, and sometimes wore an absurd Native American wampum of yellow, white, and black shells as a hairband.

He skipped lectures, dropped blotter after blotter of LSD, guzzled grant money away at the pub, and found himself exquisitely alienated from every single soul he encountered.

AT UCL, his revisions eventually came to seem pointless, and he began to study noncourse books about esoteric religion and mysticism. He read *Magick—Book 4* and Sellotaped poems by Rumi and Ted Hughes to his wall beside the bed. He came to believe that Hughes was covertly trying, through his poetry, to communicate with him. Cuthbert once wrote on the wall, right beside where his head writhed nightly on its pillow, "He opened his mouth but what came out was charred black."*

He also got into kooky altercations with other UCL students.

"You keep your fucking red thoughts off me," he once screamed at an innocent sociology student as they reached for the same bowl of warm custard in the dining hall queue.

"I don't know you," the student answered.

"Arr," he said. "And I see everything you think."

Cuthbert/Drystan spent far more time reading about Sufism and obscure Middle Eastern hermeneutics than about organic chemistry. At one point, he started (then quickly abandoned) a summer Beginning Modern Standard Arabic class. He may never have been invited to join the Golden Dawn, but he became an incomprehensible moonchild to himself and to others.

It should have all caught someone's attention. Something was desperately wrong, something that went beyond the usual new-to-uni breakdown or naff religious conversion. In one letter he penned (imagining himself to be Drystan and "writing" to his brother Cuthbert in Brum) a bizarre account of gazing out a Floor Nineteen

---

* From Ted Hughes, "Crow's Fall"

window of the Senate House Library. *To the west,* he wrote, *shone the gold dome of London Central Mosque, partly green from the reflections of huge plane trees from Regent's Park.* He described the glow at that moment as "a hostile eye of sunlight," pouring out from a hole in England. He continued,

I started rocking back and forth, Cuddy, gently bumping my head upon the cold window, repeating the phrase "imagine me imagine you," quite audibly, I suppose, in my crude effort at a Sufic dhikr—*that's a sort of God-consciousness, right?—I was bumping my head, bumpiebumpiebumpie imaginemeimagineyou, bump rock bump rock bump bump bump imaginemeimagineyou—until a library aide marched over and says to me, "Do you mind, sir?" This really happened, Cuddy, all down to the Eye of God!*

Cuthbert carefully avoided his young, ambitious tutor, Mr. Daniels, who seemed only intellectually, and never emotionally, at ease with the boy's deep Brum accent and up-front manner, as well as suspicious of his exuberance for animals and religious studies. When it came to Cuthbert's signs of serious disturbance, poor Mr. Daniels, who truly stood the most chance of seeing that something was wrong, was a perfect idiot—the sort of person who liked to champion the working class as long as they did not smell up his little corner of academia a few meters from the corpse of Jeremy Bentham. Seeing in Cuthbert only a bit of sudatory kookiness, Mr. Daniels recommended the boy immerse himself in the salubrious rigors of schoolwork and contemplate his smallness in the scheme of things.

"I believe that you'll see your pleasure variables rise," Mr. Daniels said in a joking tone. "That is, if we can trust in the 'felicific calculus' of old Jeremy, right? Ha-ha!"

But for Cuthbert, grueling revision on his biology course offered no chance for self-forgetting, least not as Mr. Daniels conceived it. When he did forget himself, he drew into Drystan even more—the ghost beneath the green rushes, the otter-brother in the bosky claw-waters of long, long ago. Otters obsessed him, too; at one point, after reading Ted Hughes's "An Otter," he developed the notion that the poet was, like Drystan, a therianthropic being who crossed between the animal and human worlds, and in fact, Hughes had simply been writing about himself in his animal poems—and not metaphorically. In one meeting with Mr. Daniels, just before he abandoned the course, he tried to explain Hughes's secret to Mr. Daniels in his sour-smelling office.

"I'm stuck on Hughes, and I can't stop thinking about 'im, no matter how hard I try," he was saying. "His otter's the most profound sort of animal. It's all biology and all of the animal soul, in one little beast. 'Of neither water nor land. Seeking some world lost when first he dived . . . from water that nourishes and drowns.' See what I'm getting at?"

Mr. Daniels looked annoyed, tapping the crystal on his cheap watch. It had a black wristband, and he kept playing with it. "This isn't a literature course, is it?" He looked at Cuthbert solemnly. "Forget 'animals' and think 'cells.' Forget 'phenotype' and think 'gene.' It's liberating, I tell you, if you really think about it. Have you finished *The Selfish Gene* yet?"

"I day," answered Cuthbert. "I mean, I did not, sir."

"Too bad. See, you're born, you hitch a ride to your alleles, and you fly forward into human evolution. We really have no utter control over anything. Ha-ha."

"Ar—I mean, *yes*," he had answered. "I tried to read it, but it made me feel . . . like life's pointless."

"Not for genes it's not."

Cuthbert/Drystan survived two terms at UCL. He went straight from Ramsay Hall to a squat in Euston to the park benches. It was a terrific, if not quite classic, debauched decline. And it was during this time that the ghost-brother first went missing from Cuthbert's ambit of control. He seemed separate from Cuthbert. Indeed, Cuthbert had even begun to think of himself again, ever so slightly, as himself. For whatever reason, Cuthbert's total replacement of himself with the wiser, more intelligent, more able, more erotic figure of Drystan came to a ragged end that coincided with the failure at uni.

For now, again, Drystan was gone.

FOR A WHILE, Cuthbert "searched" all over London for his missing brother, with no success, and afterward, tried to convince his parents to report him missing to the Metropolitan Police. But this request, as one might imagine, was seen by them as a kind of antagonistic lunacy, an effort to torment them.

Soon afterward, Cuthbert himself was homeless and sleeping rough in the capital.

His parents, from whom Cuthbert concealed his living situation, were by now totally inured to his ramblings about Drystan, and normally simply repeated, when the name was mentioned, "You saw your poor brother drown in Dowles Brook in 1968, Cuddy, and you blocked it out. And that's that!"

Cuthbert didn't believe a word they said, not anymore. No matter what anyone said, he would find Drystan; around this time, in 1980 or so, Cuthbert also started a habit of visiting, unannounced, his cousin Rebekka, who lived in Hemel Hempstead and worked as a school nurse.

Rebekka didn't know how to coax Cuthbert back from his insanity.

"You look poorly," she once said to him. "That's the tragic truth."

"Hang on. Hang on. What's that?" Cuthbert once asked Rebekka. "You almost sound like you're talking about *me*, Becks. Or do you *mean* Drystan? He wasn't taking care of himself, was he?"

"Drystan? Oh, Cuddy, why are you bringing up your sweet brother?"

"Because you're talking about him!"

"No," Rebekka said. "Oh, Cuddy. I mean *you*. *You* need help, dear one. Couldn't we find someone. To talk to you?"

"Look," he said, "I'll find him!"

Rebekka would sigh despondently, but she felt nothing she said would ever get through.

Meanwhile, Cuthbert himself, while imagining Drystan's downhill slide, was of course frequently coping with his own drop into penury in central London. He was indeed looking poorly. His fingernails and teeth were gradually blackening. His clothes smelled of urine. He wore shoes with burst soles. For a while, he feared Drystan's old schoolmates from UCL would recognize him as Drystan's brother; after a year or two, he knew they wouldn't.

Cuthbert's delusions had become an unstable system. He no longer knew whether he was himself, or his brother, or someone else entirely. His flashes of lucidity often served only to confuse and to depress him more deeply, like matches lit in a pitch-black crypt.

"Was *I* the one at UCL?" he would ask himself. "Did *I* write letters to myself?"

His last complete grasp of reality in his lifetime, at around age twenty, was far more self-bewildering than what was to become his new normal—a calmer normal where Drystan, the last holder of the Wonderments on earth, was only "missing," and he, Cuthbert Handley, was leading the search for him. In his life to come, he would take, in the rarest of moments, hold of the real truth, as his gran saw it—that Drystan *was* dead, and Cuthbert himself was actually the last to carry the Wonderments. But such knowledge, in the infrequent seconds that his mind would allow for it, proved such a crushing burden that he spent his life hiding from it—in Flōt stupors, in shame, in delusions florid and incessant. But Drystan and the Black Country of childhood would not stay away forever.

CUTHBERT EVENTUALLY MOVED BACK to Birmingham for a few years, but not to his parents' house—they had told him never to come back. He loitered around the pubs in Handsworth, where his parents had met at the dance hall thirty years before. He would spend a night here and there in the local doss houses and missions.

He'd also plunged into his dreadful mysticism once again, stinking up bookstores and libraries to read about Sufism, the *Mabinogion*, the *Legenda Aurea*. He grabbed hold of a bit of Rastafarianism, too, and Navaho and Hopi myths. He started hugging other rough-sleepers when he would see them, exclaiming *"Wa'ppun, mi key?"*

One day, half-drunk, he was buying a tea in the coffee shop at the Selfridges department store in the Bullring, and something especially odd happened. Earlier, in a bin behind St. Martin's church, he had found a big purple sequined dress, a sort of fancy old formal garment, like something from the 1950s. It had made him think of something tossed out after a funeral. It was enormous in size, the garment of a woman whose heart must have exploded. The top bit looked not unlike a kind of dress-up disco shirt, so Cuthbert cut it off with some old scissors he kept, and wore it into Selfridges.

It had been a mistake to enter the store in his state. A young man about his age seemed to be following him, he noticed, a gent in a sort of New Romantic pirate costume, with sky-blue knee britches, a flouncy shirt with a lace jabot, and a cummerbund. He wore dramatic pink-and-black eye shadow and overstated cheek-lines, and he unnerved Cuthbert.

Cuthbert decided to take his tea out of the shop part of the store, but then the man hurried up to him. They ended up sitting on one of the Home Department sofas in a faux sitting room. An array of television screens blared in front of them.

"Adu?" asked the pirate, in a strong Brummie. He smiled gently. "Ow am ya? I don't mean to worry yow—yow look worried. I just, I'm new to this, and, erm, I just wanted to say 'adu.' " The man took a deep breath. "I like your top—but yow've got a face as long as Livery Street."

On the televisions, a woman presenter wearing a kind of khaki photographer's shirt with many little pockets was talking while she stood in what looked like a farm pasture.

Cuthbert didn't say anything. He didn't want to talk.

"Come on," the pirate said. He scrunched his eyes and said, "I'll flog yow at dawn, lubber. Oi's there something *rung* with me?" He seemed wholly amused with himself, but Cuthbert was oblivious, absorbed by the reporter.

The reporter said: "This remarkable coin, or bracteate, was found on Undley Common in Suffolk by a local resident out with his metal detector. Its inscription, written in Anglo-Saxon runes, is being studied by researchers at the University of Leicester. I won't try to pronounce it!"

On the telly screens was a close-up of an embossed image from the gold bracteate. There was a helmeted man in a beard above a she-wolf. Two little human figures, crouched below the animal, drank from its teats.

Cuthbert turned toward the pirate and daringly put his hand on his knee, as softly as a sparrow. He said, in his deepest Brummie, "Do yow feel like a lost bab? That's as *oi* do."

The pirate-man looked petrified for a moment, and excited, and he looked around to see if anyone was watching. When he saw that others indeed were, he at once stood up, squinting dramatically and pointing at Cuthbert, and said, "Oh, fuck off, yow . . . ya' *reek*. It just bloody hit me. You're just a *street* cunt, poncing about, aren't yow—a poof probably, yeah?" He started walking away. "God *damn* it!"

"Oh, don't do a bunk," he said to the man. "Please."

Shoppers turned to look. A man scowled at Cuthbert and pulled a little girl by the arm away from his vicinity.

Cuthbert felt humiliated at first, but also a bit pleased. This New Romantic odd-one—lashing out, fussy, wanton—had at least paid attention, had responded to his presence. It was as close to intimacy as he had been in ages. Cuthbert wondered if, given more time, he might have persuaded the man to take him to the gent's and kiss him.

A university lecturer, a gaunt-looking man with long brown hair, was now being interviewed on the telly, and Cuthbert turned his attention and thoughts back to the television. The lecturer was saying, "It reads, '*gægogæ mægæ medu.*' We don't quite grasp what it means—not just yet—but we think that it's a kind of blend of Old English and Old Frisian. It's quite fascinating, really." But Cuthbert felt he knew. Of course he knew. *Gægogæ mægæ medu* was the language of otters.

BY THE SUMMER OF '81, when the first riots started in Lozells Road, homeless Cuthbert dove right into the fray along with everyone else, blessed by Jah Creator. He tried to help (rather ineffectively) turn over a few cars, stoke up the street fires. Hundreds of young men, Caribbean, Irish and English and Bangladeshi, rampaged together, and Cuthbert felt as happy as he had ever before or since. He ended up getting truncheoned by a copper, fracturing his cheek. An almost imperceptible crushed appearance endured on the left side of his face. It was the subtlest of features, and something that still remained part of his own bloated countenance—the slightest depression on the left hemisphere of his skull, as if the gradual loss of logic from his life, over nearly a century, were physically visible.

Cuthbert remembered Rebekka showing him a news clip about the riots from the *Birmingham Mail*. He'd hitchhiked down to Hemel Hempstead to visit her at her house, which she shared with a divorced Danish woman. (Cuthbert had worked out that Rebekka probably fancied women more than men, but she couldn't seem to acknowledge it.)

"You read this," she said, pushing a nearly clipped rectangle of newsprint across her tea table set. She had given him a handful of Penguin snacks for his pockets. "Read it, Cuthbert. It's you."

He read the article. In it, he encountered the confusing sentence: "West Midlands Police are currently seeking to interview the following individuals." Near the bottom of a following long list of names was his own—and not Drystan's.

"I, in the riot?"

"You old fool," said Rebekka. "Why? You're too bloody vulnerable, Cuddy. You better go talk to the bill and sort it out."

"But where was Drystan? Where's he bloody gone?"

Rebekka looked pale and shaky. She shook her head, taking a deep breath, and she tried to embrace him.

Cuthbert jerked away.

"Cuddy, no. Don't be afraid," she said. "Your darling brother—don't you remember?"

But Cuthbert was getting out of there. He jumped to his feet quickly. He brushed dark, oily crumbs of Dundee cake from his trousers.

"I have to go, Becks," he said. "Tararabit!"* He scampered out of his weeping cousin's house. He yearned for the safety and florid possibilities of the streets—and for the next half century, it was the best home he'd ever had.

---

* Good-bye

the £10 talisman

OUTSIDE THE ZOO, WHERE CUTHBERT HAD RE-
mained, the man with the two ginger-haired daughters set them
back into their own stroller, their legs kicking all the way in. A
bobby who stood near the head of the poky stroller-return queue
held one of the stroller's handles to stabilize it. The girls sat, blinking at the officer, and one of them touched his steadying hand. The
copper, who wore the red armband of the Watch Auxiliary, looked
up and frowned at Cuthbert, who was getting closer to the head of
the queue. The Auxiliary were nowhere near as antagonistic as the
Watch, but they would not hesitate to message a Watchman if faced
with Indigents who called attention to themselves.

Cuthbert tried to picture himself, in the queue, with his own
make-believe family, but he could imagine only vague human figures with blanked-out faces like the owl kite. There was Rebekka,
but she was a little older now, at age 101, and unreachable. To
Cuthbert's despair, she'd moved prematurely into a Calm House
almost as soon as they opened, after the Property Revolts, and like
almost everyone in them, she received no visitors and neither sent

nor acknowledged messages. She lived shut away, Nexar-hooded for hours on end.

That last time he'd seen Rebekka, in the mid-2020s, before she'd gone to the Calm House, he'd taken a rare train trip up from London to her former home in Hemel Hempstead. In the early 1980s, he had moved back to London, telling everyone he was going to "have a look for my brother," but by that time he was out of his mind so often, he scarcely understood how, when, or why he'd even come back to the Big Smoke.* He had brought Rebekka a strange gift from the British Museum gift shop.

He considered the museum a hallowed ground so overstuffed with charmed talismans, angel-made objets d'art, and consecrated monuments that one in need could not help but be aided by all those healing powers. During one of his many visits, he'd spotted in the gift shop a silly old £10 zinc-nickel rendering of the Undley Bracteate. The reproduction was authentic-looking enough for tourists and fashioned into a handy key chain. He'd rubbed his thumb over the image of Constantine the Great on the obverse, and then the she-wolf suckling the two boys. He eventually wrapped it in a huge leaf from a plane tree, dropped it in his pocket, and, on a relatively halcyon summer day in 2024, brought it with him to Hemel Hempstead for Rebekka.

At the time, Rebekka shared a semidetached twin condominium with a chubby middle-aged school headmistress from Scotland named Louise.

He, Rebekka, and Louise sat for an awkward tea in the women's sitting room. Cuthbert, who smelled of urine and sour Flōt, gulped his tea and ate one handful after another of thick wedges of a sticky Dundee cake; the two women asked him if he needed new clothes and shoes and handed him an envelope with £150 collected from

* London

their church. In the context of the 2020s—the Great Reclamation had just eliminated the Bank of England, and the violent Property Revolts were in full effect—it was an almost unthinkable act of big-heartedness, and Cuthbert felt unworthy. He was inebriated enough to fend off withdrawal symptoms, but comparably lucid.

"I don't *need* this," he'd said.

Louise rolled her eyes. "Yes you do!" she said to Cuthbert. He didn't know Louise well, but he appreciated her robust, youthful personality. At least twenty years Rebekka's junior, she had a short graying Afro and a pair of the new golden cloud-earrings hovering on either side of her neck.

"She's right," said Rebekka. "Don't be a silly gorbie."

When Rebekka hugged him, he didn't want her to let go. Normally, he couldn't deal with hugs. She was only in her seventies at the time, and remained quite attractive, with a petite frame, drowsy blue eyes, and pretty almond freckles on her arms and neck. Her voice was exceptionally breathy, almost hyperfeminized. She had never married, nor was she out as gay, and she exuded a delicate, muted sexuality that, for Cuthbert, came across as simple human tenderness.

"I don't need a thing," he said. But he kept the envelope without looking inside it.

He pulled the Undley Bracteate key chain from his pocket and unfolded the plane-tree leaf he'd wrapped the talisman in. He handed it over to Rebekka, who examined it almost too politely. He explained how he had heard about it, years ago, on a news program.

"Oh, it's quite special, I can see that."

Louise raised her eyebrows. "Is this some kind—something made out to look ancient or whatnot? It's lovely."

"It'll keep you safe," he said. "You keep it." He looked at Louise's cloud-earrings.

"Can I . . . touch one?"

"You can try," said Louise. "But they're illusions. It's light. Pure light."

Cuthbert reached beneath Louise's ears, and indeed, nothing was there.

"Bostin!"* he said.

Rebekka asked, "You say you heard about this bracteate on a TV broadcast, in the 1980s, whilst you were living in Handsworth?"

"Arr. It's all to do with Drystan, you know."

"Drystan?" asked Rebekka. She looked at Louise, who smiled at Cuthbert with apprehension.

"Are you all right, Cuddy?" asked Rebekka.

"Read it. The inscription. It says, '*gægogæ mægæ medu*.' That's how—that's how," he said, his arms tremoring badly. "That's how otters speak. Them's the words I heard in Dowles Brook—when Drystan and meself almost drowned, roight? I heard it from this animal underwater, right? You say those words—*gægogæ mægæ medu*—and every time, animals hear you."

Rebekka held her cousin's shaky hand as he told her all this.

"What's the matter, Becks?" he asked.

"Nothing, you. Just having a little sigh." She looked at the Undley Bracteate in her palm, sniffing a little. "Now, Cuddy, what's this all about really, now? What's the matter, dear one? Have you got a place to sleep, in London?"

"Nothing. It's for good luck. It'll help us find Drystan. 'E's somewhere in London, I'm convinced."

"Oh, Cuddy. Listen, your brother, he passed away, I'm afraid." Rebekka's hand was taken up gently by Louise. Rebekka had tried, so hopelessly, so many times, to explain to her cousin, gently, what had happened to Drystan at Dowles Brook, she now relied on simple repetition.

---

* Awesome!

" 'E's not," said Cuthbert. "You shouldn't talk that way. 'E's gone to UCL, you know. 'E's brilliant, he is."

"Cuddy," said Rebekka. "You're the one that's brilliant. You're the one that went to London on that clever-clogs grant. You keep imagining your brother's around, and we don't always have the heart to say it otherwise, but you need to know, my dearest love. You need to know. *Please,* Cuddy. The poor boy—he died—in 1968, Cuddy—we all loved him. Any Drystan you imagine after that—it's just *you*. It's *you*, love. You're the one you keep calling Dryst."

"No one loved him—no one but Granny and me—and maybe you."

"I'm sure your mum and dad tried to love him."

"Bollocks," he had said to Rebekka. "You're a great girl and all that, but you're wrong, Becks. I'll find him."

Rebekka insisted that Cuthbert keep the commemorative Undley Bracteate. He refused, but she finally pushed it into his trouser pocket, and he relented.

"You need it more than we do," said Rebekka.

"But I have one—in my heart," he said.

He learned a few months later that Rebekka and Louise had ended their relationship, partly because Rebekka couldn't reconcile her own sexuality and her devotion to the Church, and she'd absconded in a matter of days to a Calm House. Cuthbert never saw either one again, but he liked to imagine her holding the bracteate in her hand even as a Nexar hood leeched away her soul.

Now he carried it in his pocket wherever he went. Apart from his mental illness, it was his only permanent possession.

CUTHBERT JUMPED OUT of the queue outside the zoo and stood awkwardly to the side. He was attracting serious unwelcome attention now. A single Eye3 scan of his face by a Watchman, and his life would be effectively over. He knew *that* much, if not as clearly as he ought. But it had fully dawned on him that he must leave the entire area or risk imprisonment and virtual lobotomization.

A man who had been behind him in the queue, with very old-fashioned, rectangular OHMD* glasses, the precursor to corneal readers, seemed reluctant to move into the gap where Cuthbert had been standing, and so Cuthbert moved away farther. The man raised his eyebrows and stepped into the spot.

"Thanks, Indigent," the man said. "Ha!"

The red-arm-banded Watch Auxiliary officer from earlier began walking toward him, rubbing his fingers together. Cuthbert looked away from his stare, as if it were fire.

"Please, no, no, no," Cuthbert whispered to himself. "I've got to bloody go."

There was a bawling boy with leopard face paint among the families and other middle-class strangers. The paint was so ingeniously delicate that the boy did indeed look like a bipedal cat-child. He was punching a man's knee—his father? uncle?—with a solemn effort. His tears made the yellow and black makeup runny below his eyes, drawing his humanness out, against his will. The boy's fist was fat and soft and the man took little notice, except for a passing smirk. Cuthbert felt an urge to accost this heedless man, to show him what violence could mean. The compulsion animated him, and he wove deftly through all the people, and away from the bobby. He felt unnoticed, too, in a familiar way—as if he had not just left the zoo after undertaking the first part of his scheme, as if the copper only recognized a common vagabond hanging about children and good parents.

But the animals noticed him—especially the lions. They were beginning to speak at him again, imploring him to stay.

---

* Optical head-mounted display, e.g., Google Glass

"You can't delay your solemn duty any longer," Arfur the lion moaned. "You can't—unless you *want* to look weak. You can't go now."

"I'll return tonight—I promise," he answered. "A promise is a promise."

The lions roared angrily in reply. And there were monkeys crying, antelope nickering, and bobcats screeching miserably, threatening to escape the zoo themselves if left behind.

Stay! they all begged.

"Leave off now!" he pleaded, so loud that everyone around him looked at him, this man with dirty hands, this irritating Indigent, talking to himself.

He left the area quickly, trotting toward Camden Town station. After a while, he turned around and he saw that the Watch Auxiliary was back near the same queue. The hovering officer irked him, but Cuthbert also felt a new, feral kind of satisfaction, too, something he could not recall ever feeling so intensely.

He said aloud, to all the beasts, "Ta-rah, animals, ta-rah!"

Will you come back? many of the creatures asked.

"Oh, will I," he gasped. "And soon. And this time, the true prince of England will come again, in all his furry glory."

the words of a wise chihuahua

CUTHBERT DECIDED TO HEAD TOWARD HIS ABAN-
doned IB. It was a dicey move, to hide there until night, but by
now, he reckoned, the Red Watch would already have tossed his
IB and departed. The IB grounds and hallways always offered one
certainty: apart from the occasional mugger, rapist, or psychopath,
no one cared about you.

Using one of the £5 coins from the kind wealthy woman outside
the zoo, he took the No. 29 bosonicabus from Camden Town, just
north of the zoo, to Finsbury Park—a district that had remained
resistant to gentrification for three centuries—and from there, he
walked from Finsbury Park's raucous station to the Indigent estate
where he'd last lived.

A few teenage Indigent boys loitered in front of IB Building 3,
the great pillar of reinforced concrete ignominy he'd once inhabited, and as usual, the boys were trading insults and venting bluster.
Cuthbert felt uneasy.

One skinny-faced kid with a sharp chin, who wore a prepos-
terously tall sky-blue speedfin on his back (such fins worked with

glider-discs, a mode of transport the boy would almost certainly never be able to afford), was hurling a hardened hurtball at his mates, over and over, aiming below the neck (yet holding back a bit on his pitches, too). In the fading light, the glowing ball marked the air in red gashes. The game, a dangerous pastime often played in stairwells and lifts, was popular among Indigents in their towering IBs. The object was to throw the pointillion-cored, steel-studded ball at one another with the full intention of causing bodily injury. One normally went for the head in hurtball, and games often devolved into out-and-out fights. Cuts and blood were commonplace, concussions never unexpected, and deaths from cranial hematomas frighteningly common.

As Cuthbert approached, he took a deep breath. He wanted to get away from the boys, and he feared they could perceive this. Just as he passed, the sharp-chinned kid fired the ball very hard, its glowing neowool rasping the air. A red blot whooshed past Cuthbert's face. The ball glanced off the back of a boy who had skin colored like burned sugar and a very round face with dark freckles.

"Just look at the cunt," the victim said, rolling his eyes and wagging a finger at the ball-tosser, but obviously in some pain. "He couldn't hurt shite."

"Fuck off," said the thrower. "You're a tosser, mate."

For a second, Cuthbert felt he was also being addressed. He wanted to seem neither too interested nor too aloof—either might irritate them. He tried to step past them fast. Even these boys probably feared causing any trouble that might bring the Red Watch down on them all.

" 'Allo, boys," he said.

There was swapped between the boys, only half-secretly, a snicker, then a girlish tittering, and a showy punch on the arm. But the moment Cuthbert started to turn around to look, the giggling stopped. He could feel his heart thumping, his chin trembling. A kid with huge, watery eyes stepped into his way. "You're not allowed out here, now are you, fat man?" he said to Cuthbert.

Cuthbert said nothing and kept walking.

"Give us a pound." The wet-eyed boy ran in front of Cuthbert and stood there.

Cuthbert leaned in close to the boy and reached to put a hand on each of his shoulders but stopped short. "Now beware, child. The tigers are coming, and lions and bears. They'll be all over the estate by tomorrow—you'll see."

The boy's lips formed an oval, then he pulled back and grinned furiously. " 'E's off his fucking chump!" The others laughed at the remark. "Off his fucking chump! Off it! I bet e's the one the Watch was 'round for to have a pop at. A facking scrote!"

The skinny-faced boy thrust himself in front of the other, with a trace of fear on his face, and said to Cuthbert:

"Excuse me fucking dicksplat, gent. 'E's sorry, isn't he?" The skinny-face punched the other boy in the side, who screwed up his face in agony.

Cuthbert started to tug on his own earlobes and fumble with his hands. He sidled around the boys, rubbing sweaty fingers together and trudging forward. He imagined what it would feel like to be hit on the back of the head by their hurtball. What if he found himself on his knees on the pavement, dizzy? He would kneel as placidly as a churchgoer, blinking his eyes, watching bits of light swarm like flies across the IB.

Finally, a spiral of whispers unwrapped itself behind him as he moved along, keeping his eyes closed.

"Why'd you do that?" he heard. "You stupid cunt! You stupid cunt! Why'd you do it? You want the fucking Watch here?"

He heard the sound of scampering feet, and finally silence. He opened his eyes, steadied himself, and opened the battered front door of the IB, entering the murky atrium. Voices, supple and slippy, suddenly came into his head again: *Remeowbrooow, Cuthber-yeow*. It was otterspaeke—weird, dunked language. *Remember St. Cuthbert*. That's what it really meant. He took a deep breath. His heart was pounding. He whispered, "I hear, I do." There was a malfunction in the lift to his flat—it did not stop at the eleventh floor. It had not for the past year, as far as he knew. A note from the parish, in a special Plexiglas wall-slot, assured residents that the conveyance was "perfectly safe." He did not doubt this. But still, he did not like having to go to the tenth or the twelfth floor, then taking the stairs. He was, after all, a nonagenarian—and even his EverConnectors didn't change that. He could not escape a feeling that he and the other dwellers of the eleventh had been singled out for isolation.

He hit "12." There was a delay before the poorly lit compartment lurched up. There were 144 IBs in Building 3. Most of the other floors' main hallways appeared worse than his, yet all were sunless shafts that stank of mammalian urine and cigarettes. The floors were littered with an excreta of Wimpy Burger papers and KFC*hwa* boxes, flattened milk cartons, shattered bottles. He frequently thought about how the dirt of the place would have been unbearable to his mother, who had considered filth and religion low-class, despite her own soiled and fey peasant pedigree. Cuthbert had once dragged his fingernail along a wall for a few feet, just to see what would happen; it came back furred with a brown gluey grime, and he did not mind it. It was a new kind of English soil. On walks through the building he discovered other Indigent wanderers. There was an old man from the north who liked to tell nasty jokes and who suffered fainting spells. There was another, round-cheeked man who always wanted Cuthbert to come into his flat for a curry. He encountered people who did not appear to see him.

On Friday nights, many young Muslim Indigent men laughed

and talked in their long, moon-white prayer shirts in the hallways after service at the venerable nearby North London Central Mosque, now managed by a group of Aga Khanian Fatimids called The Life, or Al-Haya. The mosque, its radicalism long softened yet under close scrutiny for decades, remained open under King Henry's reign only as a cynical exhibit of Windsor tolerance. The Privy Council felt it had its royal plate full with English republicans and suicide cultists, and it couldn't be bothered to persecute a harmless religious minority.

Cuthbert often saw children, of course, chasing each other, kicking hurtballs and flying on speedfins down the sticky floor tiles. Some were the offspring of refugees; some came from poor, ignorant locals who distrusted foreigners, who were vulnerable to hatred. They all lived together and, somehow, muddled on.

A gaggle of older women and young children were walking down the hall, about to go past him, carrying baskets of flowers.

One of the girls carried a tiny black and brown Chihuahua closely in her arms. The dog looked used to cuddling.

It gazed at Cuthbert and said, in a docile voice: *We are waiting for you, St. Cuthbert.*

"We?" he said aloud.

The animals, the dog said, sounding slightly weary. *Listen for us.*

Another Indigent girl, who was missing an eye, thrust a spray of pink and purple campanula flowers into his hand. He felt dizzy with shock. He took the campanulas, and held them to his nose, but there was no smell.

"Take," said the girl, tugging his sleeve.

The old women stopped in the hallway and grinned at him. Between Buildings 3 and 4, several older Indigent women—English, Chinese, Pakistani—had cultivated a small flower and herb garden in a disused sandbox. Hyacinth and gold whisper blooms grew in tall, proud stalks.

"I've hardly any money," he said. He pointed at the Chihuahua. "Your little dog. She speaks."

"Yes," one of the youngest of the old women said. "You are so funny." With her black hair and Middle Eastern features—and her poverty—he guessed she was Kurdish. "It's a he. His name is Osman."

"Osman," he said. " 'E's a good dog, I can tell. What can I give you for the flowers?"

"We don't take money!" the woman said, still smiling. "Keep money."

"Isn't there something?" he asked.

"Just be careful," the woman said. "The Watch is around."

She's right, said Osman. *Be careful, St. Cuthbert.*

Why do you call me that? he asked the dog. Why?

Because you have almost reached the bottom, and it has almost reached you. Do you not acknowledge your own sins against the animal world? You must, or the Otter Prince will not come.

the evils of rotten park

IN THE DISORDERED, UNHOLY TIMES IMMEDIATELY before and forever after Granny died of a stroke, in 1974, the Handley household's last ties to the Wyre and its folkways—and the Wonderments—dissolved. His father's beatings and punch-ups had long moved from the vaguely disciplinary, but they lacked the pure, chaotic malice of Cuthbert's last year at home. At grammar school, three or four boys saw the bruises, but no one said a thing to anyone.

A few months before she died, Winefride had started setting food out for a brindled mog named Sally who lived in their neighborhood. She was always feeding local cats, but she especially loved this mog, and eventually, Sally grew enormous. Soon, Winefride found a clowder of kittens with Sally in the back garden, behind a plastic bucket. Winefride seemed especially captivated by the lot, but she warned Cuthbert to stay away from them and let Sally tend to them and, above all, not allow her son-in-law to find out about them.

When Henry Handley finally did find out about the kittens, they and Sally disappeared.

Almost anything could set Henry off, but petty acts of rebellion or inattention—slamming a door too hard, loudly slurping at tea, kicking a football into the kitchen—seemed especially to goad him.

A few weeks later, this time on Sunday, after the pub's afternoon closing, Cuthbert's gran was plastering the leg of a new tuxedo moggy kitten she'd found limping in the garden. She expertly wrapped its paw onto an ice-lolly stick that still smelled of black currant.

Cuthbert watched closely for a while, but he grew bored, and just as his father stumbled into the kitchen, drunk, Cuthbert flicked another lolly stick across the kitchen table.

"What the fock is that then? 'Oos brought this dirty thing into the kitchen, and why did yow throw that stick?"

"It's just a kitten, Daddy."

"We're almost done here," said his gran sternly. "This kit will be gone soon enough."

"Why did yow throw that focking stick?"

"You're drunk as a mop," said Gran. "Let us be. Please, Hank."

"I day mean to, Daddy."

"Yow useless focking yam-yam*!" he screamed. He started kicking at his son, then unhitched his belt and began whipping him. "Yow're focking off your focking chump!"

His grandmother set the kitten aside and tried, pathetically, to soothe her son-in-law, as a diversion, placing her fat hands on his shoulders, but Henry simply stepped around her and continued.

It was, of course, perfectly legal for a father to whip his children. Before the Children Act of 1989, abusers more easily slipped detection. Winefride had rung the police seven times, and each time was

---

* A person from the Black Country; can be contemptuous

told no crime had occurred, but if someone was injured she should call back.

"I'm calling the police again," she said. She did, once again, but this time the authorities sent a very young social worker who wore a brown suit and a white shirt with a stained collar. That Monday afternoon, he talked to Henry for about twenty minutes. Henry, badly hungover, made a show of apologizing to everyone. But nothing seemed likely to change soon, partly because Cuthbert was too terrified to tell the truth. And he even defended Henry.

"My dad's alroight," he said to the man from the council. "And I ain't the best."

The next night, on a Tuesday, Winefride Wenlock died in her sleep of a massive ruptured aneurysm.

THE MOST EVIL beatings came after his gran died, in the years before Cuthbert left home for uni. He endured criminal abuse. (The timing of everything had become unclear as Cuthbert aged, and at age ninety with a brain half-pickled, what he remembered most was his own shame and self-hatred—and his undying worship of his dead brother.)

Cuthbert became just as spiteful as all the Black Country boys he knew. His worst injuries, of course, weren't visible; but his mind was gradually being thrashed into the early stages of a dark syndrome that had no name.

He grew to loathe himself and the world and everything in it, and an almost continual guilt assaulted his heart. Eventually, the guilt turned outward. In agony, he would throw stones at old men and smack small children who supported the Baggies or Wolves.* (Cuthbert supported Aston Villa.) He once threw a baby gerbil into

---

* Nicknames for West Bromwich Albion and Wolverhampton football clubs

a goldfish bowl and watched it drown. He helped a small gang of boys kill a stray spaniel under a canal bridge he came to call Otter Bridge. He and the boys buried the animal under a blanket of gorse yanked from the canalside.

When he was twelve, he put his hand into one of these boys' pants, and he invited him to put his mouth on his thing, but the boy only punched him in the stomach and began laughing at him. "I don't want your ugly cock," he said, squealing. Once, Cuthbert tore an electric blanket apart in his bedroom and spread the curly, cotton-stuck wires over his bedroom floor, trying to work out a system to electrocute himself. But he got scared. It seemed too industrial a way to top yourself. It would be like getting snagged on his father's metal lathe and spun to death. Later, there was a phase of vexed strolling near an old iron bridge along the Birmingham Canal near Rotten Park, a sad walk up from his parents' neighborhood, and toward the heart of the Black Country. He would spit on the bridge's walkway and attempt to summon the icy will to kick one leg, then another, over the rails. The wrought handrails groaned and screeched and cars shoomed past. In the distance, grassy fields and lawns were still broken here and there with the black patches of scoria, which used to cover the region. Emptied of its natural resources, the land was still recovering. He could look down into the dark water and dream of death. However, even in this most deserving place, he could not kill himself.

Like so many abused children, his fundamental frame of mind was one of ghastly shame and self-contempt. At one point, he gave the canal beneath this bridge of his failed suicides a new name, the Otter River. Trying to work up the nerve to kill himself became compulsive; he would also try, when he remembered, to "beg forgiveness" from a Christ of Otters. He forced himself to picture this robed messiah of all murdered animals, a gimlet-eyed and long-whiskered Jesus with a long pearly claw upon each soft finger. He made himself say, "My sin has offended you." Once, praying the words *Christ forgive me,* over and over without stop, he had walked far up the canal walks, away from West Brom, out toward Dudley, then beyond, eventually reaching branches of the disused canal system he had never seen. Once beyond the brownfields and blighted elm trees and ruined foundries near West Brom, the dark motor-oil water of the canal became more and more green, bright as grass and greener still. As he had walked, Cuthbert kept thinking that if he prayed hard enough and long enough, he would see another otter, as he had seen at the Wyre Forest after he and Drystan went into Dowles Brook. This otter would uncurl itself from the mossy water, turn a few spirals, and, with St. Cuthbert's blessing, save him from drowning, this time from despair.

He remembered this as he made his way through the clattering hallways of his old IB. When he was younger, it had simply been too early for him to learn the language of animals—and too early in Britain's national life, since it hadn't yet hit its prophesied bottom. And not until Dr. Bajwa had sent him to the London Zoo had he begun, really, to know that something new was afoot, and to believe he would find Drystan again, and to act, despite great peril, to welcome the Christ of Otters.

"Christ, forgive me," whispered Cuthbert. "I've my own heart of a demon."

But we take you back, he could hear the dog Osman say. *Without condition.*

the death cult strikes

CUTHBERT OPENED THE DOOR AND LUMBERED
into his old IB, No. 1102. The locks were gone, but it didn't look
as if the Watch had tossed the flat. It was stark—dark and va-
cant, mostly, just the brown-stained tiling on floors and walls and
hundreds of empty containers. If the Watch had been here, they
hadn't taken anything, and miraculously—probably out of fear of
the Watch—it seemed as if none of the IB's resident thieves had
touched a thing.

"Fuck me," said Cuthbert. "I don't bloody believe it."

He plopped down in a white butterfly chair placed before a
small, ancient Philips TV that picked up digital signals from old
"relic" transmitters left in place for Indigents, normally beamed
straight to WikiNous. This was a familiar vessel he sailed upon
to visit various continents of despair. Dozens of empty two-liter
bottles of cheap cider, bitter, and lager encircled the chair like limpid, amber buoys, along with countless drained orbs of Flōt. The
remote was in the chair's pouch-like seat, and Cuthbert had to dig
under his rump for it. He was too big for the chair, and one of its

splaying metal rods pressed into his kidneys, but the chair comforted him, and he wanted its bad pleasures to take him over. He switched on the TV. He waved his hand across the tops of the various bottles around the chair until he found an old, cold Flōt orb with weight in it; he grabbed it and guzzled hard.

There were fresh animal voices then, and they said, *Remember, St. Cuthbert.*

Cuthbert sat up in his chair, and shook his bottle at the air. He said, angrily: "Take this away, St. Cuthbert, will you?" He took another great swig and hurled the bottle across the room. He closed his eyes. He began to weep as he felt his legs grow long.

"Cuthbert—Drystan," he said. "Someone." After a while, the Flōt settled him a bit. He felt calmer, almost able to judge matters.

The news was on. For all his disorder, Cuthbert actually enjoyed watching the news, and especially the royally imprimatured BBC/WikiNous. Once the dull election coverage was over (it was obvious Harry9's hand-chosen new LabouraTory man, in this case one of the former prime minister Tony Blair's sons, would be elected as his prime minister), he began to watch more carefully.

"The enemies of humanity have struck again," read the presenter. "What may be one of the worst mass suicides in history has occurred, once again, in the American state of California, coordinated with at least a few thousand self-murders—and animal killings—in Britain, as well as, once again, in India, in Korea Hana, and the Nigerian Federation."

On the screen was raw video footage—the crude automated news-reporting so popular on WikiNous—of the aftermath of a mass self-murder by the most diabolical of the cults, Heaven's Gate. A camera was being toggle-driven through a sort of dormitory. Lying neatly in bunk beds, on stiff-looking backs, were dead people with purple cloth triangles covering their faces. Beside every bed was a large nuplastic set of drawers on wheels. In the video, the drawers were opened slowly, revealing horrifying contents: inside each were all manner of small, freshly poisoned "voided" animals. There was a black toy poodle, a set of roan cavies, countless cats and kittens, robins, an iguana, hamsters large and small.

As the footage continued, Cuthbert felt almost dizzy with rage and sadness, and a sense of guilt—but he could not stop watching.

This latest Heaven's Gate affair, which was all over WikiNous, had thrown Cuthbert off his usual dolorous paths; it not only disturbed and obsessed him, but it also seemed somehow *directed* at him.

Yet the BBC/WikiNous's coverage was contemptuous, and Cuthbert ate up every morsel. Suicide was considered, in general, degenerate and disloyal to the king, and despite his own history and addictions, Cuthbert felt no love or compassion for suicides; indeed, he felt compelled, as a citizen, to keep abreast whenever these cults hit hard.

A stocky reporter with a Welsh accent spoke in a mocking tone: "Michael, the victims have now been identified by American investigators but their names are being withheld pending"—the reporter rolled his eyes—"family notifications. We're looking at an appalling sixty to seventy thousand victims this time, mostly in Southern California, with a total of more than five thousand deaths in other locations—including one in Hampshire. Crucially, the cult's reputed current leader, Marshall Applewhite III, does not seem to be among the dead.

"It's standard Heaven's Gate," the reporter continued, "a typical, cowardly operation—coinciding this time with the comet's appearance in the night skies. We have no figures on the animals, but with Heaven's Gate, one normally sees a couple dozen animal corpses along with each human body. It's . . . *reprehensible*. As per usual, the self-murderers are identically clad in long-sleeve white shirts, white trousers, and white Nike trainers. A second videotape, apparently shot just before the killings began, depicts the members in these outfits with HEAVEN'S GATE AWAY TEAM patches being sewn on their sleeves as they smilingly accept their fate. It's the same horrific modus operandi we've seen from the Gate since they first struck, way back in 1997. The king's spokesman has already released a statement condemning the action."

"Appalling," the presenter said to the reporter, who nodded.

Cuthbert said aloud, "I hope 'ole Harry gets them!"

The fact that the king's own Red Watch were also trying to hunt *him* down did not mitigate his feeling of loyalty to the Crown or its policies. Cuthbert was many things, but despite the protests of his youth, he was never a revolutionary.

He jabbed the remote's power button so hard with his thumb that there was a slight cracking sound from the device. He stood up but lost his balance and fell down onto a cluster of empty nuplastic bottles. He lay there for a long time, moaning softly. His feeling of anger soon evaporated, and he couldn't work out why he was on the floor in his old flat, trapped.

The dark orange light of evening splashed through his curtainless windows. It was an awful, coarse flush of illumination, and he felt unprotected from it. Then there was a strange sound. For a moment, he swore someone was knocking on the flat's door, softly, shyly, like a lost child. It stopped. After several minutes, it began again, *knof . . . knof . . . knof,* and he hoisted himself up.

"Drystan?" he asked aloud, his voice shaky. "That . . . you? YOU? Dryst?"

His heart pounding, he trudged to the door and yanked it open. He felt dizzy, blind with fear. It was the skinny-faced boy from outside the IB, earlier. The child's pale lower lip trembled. The scalp below his cropped ginger-brown hair showed delicate blue veins. All the bravado of the group and his speedfin were gone. He was about the same age as Drystan when he vanished, Cuthbert realized.

"You," Cuthbert said. "You?"

"I'm sorry, sir, I'm sorry. But I wanted to say don't mind my mates, right? They're gonk-bags, right? We just wanted to tell you that, right? You won't Opticall the Watch, will you, for, like, harassing you? Sorry, sir."

"No," said Cuthbert. "Never."

"Thanks, mister. And I hope your lions and tigers all come here. I really do." The child dashed down the dark hall, and Cuthbert closed the door.

Cuthbert went to the kitchen for some instant coffee. He shook some freeze-dried crystals right from a jar into his mouth and chewed them up. Then he vomited into the kitchen sink. The coffee trick worked, as always. He felt awake. And a little mardy, too. He kept ruminating about the poor animals killed by Heaven's Gate, but then he was just as blameworthy as the cultists, too, wasn't he?

Cuthbert had read excerpts of "belief statements" reprinted from the cult's notorious WikiNous stalk. This Marshall Applewhite III fellow—by all accounts a gentle, but sexually tortured son of a Presbyterian minister—had with an uncharacteristic ruthlessness demanded that his followers not only look down upon animals, as Cuthbert's father had, but also divorce themselves from *all* that was animal within and without them.

That genuinely puzzled Cuthbert.

"We really need to be moving away from stinky little sad animals, my fellow travelers," said Applewhite in one video. He spoke in a cloying, singsongy tone that Cuthbert found off-putting. "You'll see! When our great 'Gate' awakens, in merry olde England, you will all see. Right here in London, my friends!"

Animals were on the very lowest level of a deteriorating "assembly line" that produced souls like cartons of solar plugs or bosonicabus engines, according to Applewhite. Household pets such as Osman were crude, aspiring demi-souls trapped at a lower level of

existence, and waiting in anguish to join the higher level. Beasts
of burden and wildlife were less worthy yet. When a human died,
professed Applewhite, sometimes a conniving animal soul would
take over the human "container" and win its slim chance to grow.
Animals were, at best, disposable objects, at worst, organic "ves-
sels" loaded with damaging demi-souls.

The cult members, Applewhite claimed, were on much more
august metaphysical footing than either humans or animals, naturally. They were neutered—many cultists chemically sterilized
themselves—members of a faraway alien race called the Luciferians. They occupied the top of Earth's production cycle, evolv-
ing far beyond all other beings. They were not killing themselves
but merely shedding their "containers." Ideas of ecosystem or an
interconnected biosphere were hopelessly terrestrial illusions—
"scams," as Applewhite put it—and once the cult's "Level Above
Human" had finally left Earth with the "comet's" arrival, the planet
would merely be a dangerous spawning mechanism.

"We're going to be getting out of here?" Applewhite said, ending nearly every sentence with a rising-question tone. "We're going
home and it's wonderful?"

Applewhite's words rattled Cuthbert and prompted a flurry of
febrile questions in him. What if the cultists went after the zoo animals before he had the chance to free them? And what if this Applewhite scoundrel hurt the otters? Then he might not see Drystan
again.

If Urga-Rampos, reaching perihelion for the first time in four
thousand years, had been the cult's signal to move to the "higher
level" and to join their alien brethren from outer space, if the comet
was *still*, days after the mass suicide, supposed to be visible even to
the naked eye in bright London, if all these things were true, and
England was ending and Earth a broken soul-machine—well, then,
his time for action was short.

Perhaps the great comet had already landed, in London? Where would anyone find it? Near the embassies?

"Oh, who focking knows?" he said aloud, almost huffing for air.

But the otters, he knew where to find *them*. The average British citizen didn't know it, but otters were the sacred mascots of Albion, as precious as cattle to certain Hindus. If nothing else, he must release them; and, yes, along the way, he would also release as many other creatures as possible, of course, opportunistically or methodically—it didn't matter. The more free animals to face the coming attack of the death cult, the better, he reckoned.

It was all, of course, a florid delusion. But there it was, for better or worse: Cuthbert Handley, a working-class Flōt sot from Birmingham, had to save the animals.

the scent of a wounded elephant

HE FELT FAMISHED; HE WAS TREMBLING. VOMIT-
ing had made him hungry. He got out a Fray Bentos steak and
kidney pie he had been saving, as well as a leftover block of Golden
Syrup cake from the cupboard. For the past few days, he had been
eating nothing but vacuum-sealed mackerels and instant treacle
cake—and drinking cheap supermarket swills such as Longbow
cider. He liked to eat at least a pie a week, but he still considered
meat pies a luxury, since each cost seven and a half pounds at Tesco.

To preserve their traditional image, the Fray Bentos pies still came
in old-fashioned, flat tins. Cuthbert opened the tin with a can opener
whose nuplastic handle was melted badly on one side. He put the
oily lid in the sink. He touched the rubbery surface of the uncooked
pastry with his fingertips. There was a red-orange film of grease on
the pastry. He licked this off his fingers, and got the lid from the sink
and licked that, too. It was salty and metallic, and this reminded him
of the blood he tasted if he brushed his teeth too harshly.

He pinched off a corner of the manufactured treacle cake, and
chawed on that. It was beautiful, he thought, really beautiful stuff.

Count on McVitie's! The thousands of dead frugal members of Heaven's Gate apparently frowned upon the enjoyment of food. For their last meal they had "splurged," he read, and ordered thousands of turkey pot pies at a particular chain restaurant in America. They stacked their plates for the busboys. Cuthbert loathed turkey. A beef kidney—that was a feast. He carefully placed the pie in the oven. He could hardly wait for it to puff up.

When the pie was cooked and he'd finished it, he rooted through all his drawers and closets looking for dark clothes and something dark to rub on his face. He located the electric torch he kept underneath his bed; its solar-cells had run down, and it offered only a meager glow, but he still thought he should take it.

He could find no shoe polish. He did find an old case of dark brown eye shadow; the nuplastic cover was dusty and smeared with something sticky, but the makeup itself looked perfectly untouched. It was something from the days, years ago, when women and sometimes men would still touch him, perhaps even stay in his bed. He stood in front of the mirror and dabbed a little of the substance on his chin, then wiped it off with his sleeve. He leaned toward the mirror and stuck out his tongue. It seemed pale and thick, like a cod fillet. He still couldn't see any lump in his throat, but he remained convinced something was in there.

He'd thrown a pile of suitable clothes on the toilet seat. Cuthbert undressed. He did not like to see his naked body in the mirror. It was bruised and veiny and his stomach was distended beyond mere mild obesity. The doctor had explained that his liver was in, as he put it, "not great" condition, and he wasn't clearing fluids as well as he should. There was a red patch the size of an apple beneath one of his breasts. He hadn't the faintest idea what it was or what it meant, and he gratefully yanked a black jumper over himself. Trousers were another problem. He didn't own simple dark ones, and many plausible pairs that used to fit had grown too tight in the last few years. He ended up pulling on some old, dark gray pajama trousers that didn't really look like pajamas; they were "loungewear," he said to himself, and though loose and saggy, they had two big pockets.

It was well past dusk when Cuthbert put on a black training cagoule he hadn't worn since the 2010s (it had an Aston Villa patch on its lapel, with a lion and the word PREPARED in claret on a field of blue—and he feared, for good reason, wearing it around Finsbury Park's Gunner fans). He left his IB in a hurry. Just as he walked out of the IB's atrium, he saw a flash squad of the Red Watch pull up to the estate in two red-and-gold gliders. The Watchmen scampered into the building, neuralpikes held high. They were so focused on rushing the IB building, or perhaps because of Cuthbert's disguise, they completely missed him. It was, to the say the least, a whisker-close call.

He took the No. 29 back down to Camden Town. No one had looked at him askance on the bus, of course, but that's not saying much—he was in Camden, an Indigent zone, and the pubs were just closing. He saw a haggard couple he knew from a mental health drop-in center he used to visit in Kentish Town when such services still existed. They sat on a blanket outside Camden New Tube station with a small ratty dog, a border collie of some kind, but from the border of a very morose nation; they were selling carnations whose stems had been wrapped in faux-palladium foil. No one was buying, naturally, and Cuthbert kept getting jostled.

The flower sellers were thoroughly cabbaged, as far as Cuthbert could see. He waved at them and leaned down and looked at the sad pink carnations, but they didn't recognize him. He remembered the woman, who had long ginger hair—they'd played Master Mind Air a few times at the center and had a tea. But she was off her box, that's for sure, and Cuthbert felt a bit jealous of it. For a moment, he felt a sense of being very different from the lost souls he saw on the blanket. The public were not looking at him with pity and contempt. Did they sense who he was? Could they see the Wonderments in him?

"Maybe I can stop all this bloody business," he said to himself. He could go home, pour all his Flōt down the toilet. He would pick up around the flat and clean himself up. He would put on his old silver-flecked necktie and go see Dr. Bajwa and tell him he was ready to be healthy now. He would throw himself at the king's mercy, which he fervently wanted to believe in.

He was beginning to sense that this king and his Watch had no mercy.

"Don't you two remember me?" he asked the two. They held carnations toward him but seemed to look straight through him. It was clear to Cuthbert that Nexar hoods or Flōt had melted his old acquaintances' brains.

A drunk bloke, a guy in one of the new Burberry "frilly polos"—probably some commodities trader of rapeseed futures, out with the mates among the Indigents—put his hand on Cuthbert's shoulder. "Hell-loo!" he said, in a Scottish accent. "You're a real bamstick!"

Cuthbert ran.

"Waitsch!" the yob was calling. "Just waitsch! Bam! Bam!"

CUTHBERT WAS GLAD to escape the ruckus around the New Tube station. He quickly made his way down the wide pavement of Parkway toward Regent's Park. The night air was cold for the eve of May Day, but it felt fleetingly balmy as he came upon the big old oak and sweet chestnut trees—once part of the vanished Marylebone chase of Henry VIII—that signaled the edge of Regent's district. A crisp breeze stirred and he shivered. He was near his beloved zoo.

WITH THE RIGHT TOOLS, it was easy to get into the park itself at night, if not the zoo. It wasn't Buckingham Palace—no spinning spike-wheels or crenellated walls capped with broken bottles pushed into mortar. He threw his leg over a low ironwork fence, well concealed between two bushes, and that was that. He made his way through a strange, manufactured, medievalesque playground, and past a famous sculpture called *Wounded Elephant,* which looked like a granite boulder melted. He'd seen it in the day and not been impressed, but he found himself stopping now. It was some kind of save-the-whales propaganda art. He sniffed it.

The smell—ancient, like frankincense, like lost time itself—reminded him of a cellar; he thought of the crypts of the old parish church in Worcestershire, in whose soil his grandfather, Alfred Wenlock, the wheat farmer, was supposed to have been buried. Cuthbert had never met the man, of course—he'd died when his mother was a mere four years old from the flash pneumonia traceable to a gas attack at Ypres. Henry had never met his father-in-law Alfie either, but he was the only human being he had ever truly spoken of with an odd respect, and Cuthbert wondered if his own father would have been more humane had the wheat farmer not always been, essentially, a ghost.

It was rare—too rare—that Cuthbert could feel self-pity, but he momentarily sensed the depth of his own unfair treatment, profoundly, and felt a righteous anger whenever he thought of the dead grandfather he had never met.

"Why didn't you protect us?" he said aloud just then. "Why not? All we had was an old woman—and the otters."

Cuthbert began to sob, but he soon stuffed the red ropes of pain back down his throat and made himself stop.

green st. cuthbert the wonderworker

CUTHBERT SAW HIS MONSTROUS FATHER WEEP FOR the second and last time in his life when the family—father, mother, and himself—took a harrowing trip to visit his grandfather's grave, which his parents hadn't visited for two decades. It was around 1970 or so—two years after Drystan's vanishing during the trip to the aunties' cottage, two years after he fell into Dowles Brook and was "saved" by the otter. Granny had been bedridden often at that time, he remembered, and he'd had to swear to his father not to tell Granny about the excursion. It was a rare moment of sensitivity on the part of his father.

"It would break her 'art," his mother had explained. "She's buried this part of the past and it *shouldna* be opened again."

The Handleys had driven southwest from West Bromwich in their aquamarine Hillman Imp, through Dudley, Netherton, Quarry Bank, and Lye, to the other side of the Black Country, past Stourbridge and Kiddy, and once again to the narrow, jobless old lanes of the Wyre Forest.

Even though Alfie was his father-in-law, Harry Handley had

revered the man he imagined—the soldier, the self-starting farmer, the morning drinker—far more than his own father, in fact, who still lived, in a caravan senior community, in Stafford, where he was curiously renowned for his excellent orange-peel rock cakes.

"If yow end up as 'af the bloke as Alfie Wenlock," Henry was telling his son, "yow'll make the old man proud."

"But he wasn't yowr father, was he?" Cuthbert remembered asking that day. "And Gran says he was gentle. He was very sweet. He was a sweet and gentle man."

"Ha," said his father. "He was a right hard man."

CUTHBERT RECALLED how they careered up to an ancient Norman church, St. Cuthbert's, his namesake, parking in a gravel semicircular drive. They were less than a kilometer from the Wyre Forest. There was the greenest grass he'd ever seen in the driveway's center. The day was blue and clement, with splashy sunlight and swifts circling the square belltower like hot, torn electrons.

"Yow're going to learn a thing or two," his father told them, smiling, almost skipping up to the church. He was in a rare good mood. "Your granddaddy's in the oldest church in this part of England!"

The sexton, a very thin man with white hair and thick white eyebrows, had showed them a jumble of misshapen stones mortared into an inside wall, stones, he said, from the "ode times church" the Normans had built St. Cuthbert's above. An elaborate oak chancel screen, near the altar, was covered by the faces of men with foliage growing around their heads like halos. Oak and ivy leaves poured from their mouths. Some of the faces cried leaves.

Eventually, he took them into the crypt to examine a book of burial records. The "book," as he called it, was kept in a modern steel strongbox in a desk that seemed unused and dusty. It took a long time to get the volume out and placed solidly upon the desk. There was a smell of frankincense.

"It's Alfred Wistan Wenlock, you say?"

"Arr, died 1933," answered his father.

The sexton began looking through the pages. "Handley . . . Handley . . . Handley," he said. He settled on one page, and ran his thumb down a long column. He peered close, putting his face nearly against the paper. But he suddenly pulled away, almost jumping back. He scrutinized Cuthbert's father. He seemed boldly nervous, shaking his head, frowning. He began flapping through the large, grid-covered pages again, but he hardly was looking—it was strictly for manners. Then he stopped.

"There's a matter," he said, and Cuthbert to this day remembered him repeating the exact phrase: "A matter."

"Your relative's plot cannot be located precisely," he had said. "The ode lane, see?" He licked his lips and looked down. Cuthbert's father was still smiling gently, and blinking. "The ode lane," the sexton said, "the one that runs beside the churchyard—where there's that stone wall, see? It was dangerous, it was so narrow, see?" The face of Cuthbert's father was reddening and his smile had gone. "The council had to widen it and we sadly 'ad to move a few of the unmarked graves."

"Cannot be located!" Cuthbert's father bellowed. "What?"

The sexton took off his green plaid cap and kneaded it with his fingers. "Uh, we only moved them as we *found* them, but where we *could* find them, mind you. I'm afraid a few of the sites—quite a few—there was a mishap with the backhoe and the builders. They . . . they removed some soil they shouldn't have, see? We just didn't know where the plots were afterward, not anymore. It's always the poor who suffers, isn't it?"

Cuthbert's mother had said, "We're not poor."

The sexton continued: "Of course not. But the graves that

got moved, they was the ones under the statue of St. Cuthbert the Wonderworker—the graves of people who didn't have much money, and abandoned people, and the paupers' graves and such. Half of them . . . are still under the statue, we suspect, and half of them, see, are under the new road pavement, I'm sad to say. No one ever visited, see?"

The sexton turned his cap over and over in his hands. He set it down and sorrowfully set the book back into the strongbox, and clasped the lock. He looked aggrieved, but not ashamed. There was a flat look on Cuthbert's father's face; then he screwed up his eyes and started to weep.

"You bloody bet I'll complain about this," his father said, snorting, waving his arms around.

"Hank," Cuthbert's mother said.

"I'll go see the focking Archbishop of Canterbury!" Henry continued. "I will." The sexton nodded, as if he thought this was a plausible idea.

"And I don't blame you, sir. I couldn't," said the sexton. "I just couldn't."

Eventually, without saying a word, the family had trudged outside to the churchyard, and walked over to have a look at the statue. The sexton trailed behind them, standing at a respectful distance. He stepped forward at one point and ushered the four of them toward a neat, plain, pretty corner section of the churchyard—the remainder of the paupers' graveyard. White and pink campion flowered on the grassy mounds. On a thick pedestal, plated with bright green copper, stood the weathered figure of Cuthbert.

Over the years, acid rain from the Black Country had given the statue its green patina of copper sulfate. The saint was represented in flowing bishop's vestments and a miter, bending over to lift a hank of marble cloth up from his leg to let a sea otter comfort him. Two short-haired otters (which looked oddly like fox terriers) stretched at Cuthbert's feet. The otters were of a brown-painted bronze, the same color as the soil, and the same that he had seen near the Wyre Forest on the day Drystan went away. The forelegs of one of the otters were off the ground, clasped angelically, its paws holding a small cross. Cuthbert had nearly frozen himself to death while standing in the North Sea to pray, and God had sent the otters to warm and dry his legs.

Henry Handley gave the statue a tortured look.

At the time, it had seemed quite clear to Cuthbert that both otters and the saint had come straight from heaven. The animal, the human, and the divine were all part of the same. He recalled Granny saying that, long ago, her own father had trained an otter to fish for eels and roach on the Stour and Severn near Kidderminster, and it made many of the townspeople jealous. Cuthbert's father and mother both claimed it was impossible, but to Cuthbert it did not seem impossible at all.

"Grandad's watched by a Green Man," Cuthbert had said. "Just like Drystan."

"Oh, Jesus," said his father. "If only the focking vicar would have watched."

"Hank," said Cuthbert's mum, grimacing at her husband. "The boy. Please. Not here."

His parents looked destroyed that day, but Cuthbert, bruised inside and out, actually felt very proud. He still recalled how he had rubbed one of the otters' heads and said, "Magic." To Cuthbert, his ghostly granddaddy was as well marked as he could possibly be. His lost body, folded into deep England, was being both guarded and marked by St. Cuthbert and two otters that traveled between dimensions. This was far better than any headstone, better than religion, better than his parents, better nearly than England.

a brother to jackals

CUTHBERT, STANDING IN REGENT'S PARK, FEEL-
ing ready to wake up the world, leaned close to the *Wounded Elephant* and kissed the granite as if it were some blarney stone. He
wished it would kiss back, warming him inside, licking him like an
otter into its own sacred self, into warm animal sainthood, into its
strong, hot, brown mind of bronze.

"St. Cuthbert," he said. "I will not drink Flōt again. Here I will
stop. I will really give it a go!" It was his own distraught form of
"taking the pledge," perhaps. He'd have a go at stopping tonight,
with all his heart. As he freed them, he would ask the animals
for help.

CUTHBERT WAS EXCITED NOW, and he trotted along toward the
zoo. He crossed the Broad Walk. Far away south, on the other side
of a big, ornate fountain, he thought for a moment that he saw a
light flash that would have to be inside the park itself. He ran to his
little nest in the shrubs beside the zoo's fence. Just as he crawled

in, an astonishingly long and tightly focused beam of light shot across the playground. It raked across a tubular slide and an aerial ropeway. There were four little wood-plank towers with red saddle roofs in the middle of the playground, and the searchlight lingered on the towers, as if waiting for dome-helmed archers to rise from the fortress cupolas.

Cuthbert sat as still as he could. A Royal Parks Constabulary glider, a Vauxhall Paladin, drove right up the Broad Walk and parked about thirty meters from him. It was a bright white police pandaglider with yellow-green decals and reflective strips, and it stood out in the darkness as if it were radioactive. Cuthbert couldn't believe his bad luck.

He pressed himself as close to the ground as possible, and rifled through the junk in his jacket pocket for the eye shadow.

He opened the case while it was still in his jacket and clawed out as much makeup as he could with his fingernails and then, with his face down, rubbed the stuff all over his cheeks and forehead. It smelled odd to him, like clovers burned in oil, and for a moment he began to retch. He figured that there must have been some trouble reported—perhaps an argy-bargy between two street people. Or had someone seen him come in?

Eventually, Cuthbert managed to get his hands on the old Flōt orb left from his last visit.

"Just once more," he said quietly. He drank. The Flōt soothed his muscles quickly, but it didn't take away the dread. He drank all that was left, but it just didn't help.

"Now, it's really over," he said, burping. "It's all over. Never again. I'll never drink again."

After what seemed hours to him, the glider's engine stopped and the headlamps snapped off. A little while later, the searchlight, which had remained aimed at the playground, was extinguished. Cuthbert felt a little less afraid, but not relaxed, not by a long shot.

He could just make out the hot cherry of a cigarette glowing where the officer would be sitting. He felt a spell of relief. The officer lowered the driver-side window of the glider. Its electric, churning hum was weird in the greenish black silence of the park, as if a tiny section of the natural night had become motorized. He could make out a dim outline, a gentle shape—a female constable, by herself. She seemed to be fussing with something in the car he could not see.

He didn't know what time it was, but he guessed around midnight. He was sick of waiting and watching, and finally he shimmied himself around, grabbed his bolt cutters, and squeezed through the hole he'd made in the zoo's fence earlier in the month. Once inside, he stood up clumsily, and sidestepped, half-hunched, to the Golden Jackal exhibit. There were no sounds in their pen, no "voices" in the air. They had all stopped. Cuthbert wished, so dearly wished, that he could hear words now. The foolishness of his actions tonight had brought with them a barren, icy sanity. And the Flōt had put a nice little glow above the ice, and allowed him to gaze down on it from purple clouds.

Something's going to happen now, he thought.

Indeed, it did. The second he stepped onto one of the paved paths, a small overhead light clicked on. Motion detectors. Cuthbert knew that much. He hopped off the path and crouched down. After a few minutes, the light went off, again with a click. The night could turn into a great disaster, he sensed. Yet he felt no anxiety. Indeed, part of him hoped for catastrophe.

The jackals were stowed in their guillotine-gated kennels at night, yet this made Cuthbert's task easy because each kennel's back wall was formed by the main fence of the exhibit. He only needed to cut through one flimsy fence and the jackals would be free, at least to roam the paths of the zoo. They weren't otters, and nothing sacred, but they were a start, surely.

He got down on his knees and began snipping through the fence.

He worked quickly and handily, moving right to left, one kennel to the next. The fence gauge was so light, and his cutters so powerful, he could not feel the slightest resistance.

There were three cages total, with five jackals. On each cage he ended up making three arm-length cuts, creating little flaps, which he pulled back with considerable strain. The fencing seemed easier to cut than to bend. The animals were keyed up, roving in fast ovals in the cages. One of the jackals barked at him with a high, compressed *Yip! Yip!* It stopped barking and approached him warily and he stopped. He was so terrified he could not move; three of his fingers were still latched into a fencing. The jackal began to lick his fingers. He began to cry. "Soz,* mates," he said. He pictured the dead stray beside the canal, its blank black eye staring at him, the prickles on his hands as he and his friends gathered furze to hide their crime. "I was evil, evil, evil. Please forgive me, puppies." Don't care if the jackal takes off me arm, he told himself. I'm doing what I set out to. So he kept snipping and tugging at the fence, and when he worked each flap open, one or two at a time, the yellow-haired creatures bolted out of their cages, took a few long-legged lopes, and halted. One of the jackals brushed against his hand, and he was surprised by the softness of the hair and the lightness of its frame.

We're lies, they said to Cuthbert. *Lie and lie and lie and lie and lie.*

"No," Cuthbert said. "Now you're out, aren't you? You can have all the names you want, see? You can go out into England, you can. We have otters, you know."

They said *lie down lie down lie lie lie sit stay lie down lie lie lie.*

Cuthbert felt a bond with the dogs, "a brother to jackals," like Job, with an anxious, despairing pride in his actions.

He wanted the jackals to keep moving, and for the most part,

---

* Sorry

they did—and seemed to know exactly where they were going, as if they'd done this for years but merely fallen out of practice recently. Each of the jackals traipsed over to an especially flouncy line of daffodils planted along the main path. They sniffed and dug at the flowers, and to Cuthbert they looked both obsessive and surprisingly gentle. A few yellow cups and long leaves flew into the air behind them. Their backs would hump way up, accentuating the shaggy black mane between their shoulders. The daffodils were planted directly across from the sign that described the Golden Jackal exhibit. Cuthbert sat back, delighted. The last jackal urinated on the flowers, and darted off with the others. They were, if nothing else, staying together.

Cuthbert set down his cutters. He pressed one of the fence-flaps back to its original position as best as he could. The repair appeared crude, like an old tin of kippers with its pull-lid breached. He decided not to bother with the other openings. Maybe the jackals will want to return, he thought. He retrieved the cutters and stood.

Cuthbert walked over to the path in an awkward manner. A huge array of lights blazed on with a sound of metal unlatching. It was as if the whole zoo had been opened for night visitors.

"That bloody copper," he slurred. "Bloody git." His head was spinning and he could barely balance, such was the perceived length of his legs. He was still spiring on Flōt, a little more than he had expected to be. He collected himself as best he could, holding on to his own jumper's front for balance, and he staggered ahead, trying not to tumble forward. He felt both vengeful and scared. He would find some monkeys—yes, they needed to be freed next. They were smart creatures, and England needed them to defend it and themselves against the death cult. Then the giraffes. Tall, useful sentinels of the layer of Britain located between ten and twenty feet above the ground. Arr. Any animal he could free—why not?

But above all else, of course, the otters—they must be released into the canal!

He heard a stir of animal grunts and screeches, rising steadily around him—the jackals were making their presence known in the world. Cuthbert Handley was going to make his presence known, too.

four

the jackals' first kills

A FAILING SCREAM ROSE FROM SOMEWHERE BE-
hind Cuthbert in the zoo. It was distant and plangent, the sound
of a creature losing everything. A series of gross barks cavorted
around it. Listening, rubbing his thumb across the foam handle of
his bolt cutters, Cuthbert felt a tiny, ugly maggot of grief, weak but
true, squirming beneath his Flōter's stupor. He prayed the otters
were not the victims. A swell of mammalian cries mounted for a
moment, as if in response to his feeling, and faded. He wondered if
Drystan was hearing this, too.

"Drystan? Are yow here?"

Cuthbert thought, for a moment, that he heard a man's voice,
but then the sounds of other animals flooded in.

Eeeealllhhhhhhh! some sorry animal yawled. *Eeeealllhhhhhhh!*

The jackals' bloodcurdling enterprise had begun. It is a jour-
nalistic cliché that when even the fiercest wild animal escapes from
a sanctuary, or a circus, or from some foolish Floridian's roadside
zoo, these fugitives seldom show aggression or shrewdness. A loose
puma's dispassion near children, or the chimp found asleep on a

park swing—all proof of the softening effects of captivity, it will be noted in the news, and with a firm touch of bathos.

But the jackals were not following clichés. They were obeying scent. From southwest of their broken pen had floated the intoxicating reek of the Children's Zoo—sweet loafs of mule manure, oats, damp poplar, and yesterday's spilled Mars chocolate drinks. The Children's Zoo was the oldest of its kind in the world. It had in the 1930s caused a ruckus among the fellows of the Zoological Society of London, who were aghast that the public might be *too amused*. As far as they were concerned, the hoi-polloi's most advanced questions of zoology involved matters such as the number of lemon Jelly Babies a given animal could eat consecutively. But as often happened during the experimental postwar period, the zoo's uncommonly arty secretary, Julian Huxley, was adamant: amusement was intriguing, and it sold tickets. It was Huxley's idea of safe, direct access to benign animals that made it the most unguarded of all the exhibits.

The Children's Zoo was meant to look like an old-fashioned, working twentieth-century farm. It contained a half-size red barn with white accents, a miniature sty for the hogs, and a bank of wire rabbit hutches. Near the barn, a colorful set of panels posed questions for children. *Is it true that goats will eat anything?* The display was supposed to look like a set of stables, and you lifted little wooden "barn" doors to view the answers. *Actually, goats are fussy! At the London Zoo, they are offered a blend of oats, barley, linseed and soya . . .*

The jackals were not fussy. Two young bitches leaped over the picket fence and barreled toward the barn. Outside, in the corral, the llama let out a high, pulsing set of orgles. These caught the attention of the jackals, who paused and gazed at this Peruvian oddity for a moment, then roved toward a three-sided oak shelter where the llama stood.

It was a young, ungelded male, piebald with a black "mask" over its eyes. It bucked forward, darting and kicking. The jackals tried to nip at its cloven toes. They barked maniacally. The llama emitted piercing screams. Every time the jackals tried to get beneath it, it dribbled them back. Soon, a third, male jackal appeared. It scrambled into the fight with a fresh energy and tried to climb up the haunches of the llama, gnashing its teeth, frantically pulling up hanks of woolen hair like a boy who'd dropped all his pocket change on the ground and was trying to grab every last coin. But when the llama spun around and began to cough, it seemed to startle the jackals.

A bolt of dark slime shot from the llama's mouth onto the male jackal. The substance was greenish and plentiful, at least a pint. It hit the jackal like an angry smack, spattering over its head and neck. There was a strong, sour stench. The dog whimpered like a puppy, and began circling pathetically, chomping at its own back like a dog chasing its tail. The bitches broke off the fight, and crossed the barnyard, away from the llama. They sniffed at their unlucky brother, and tended to him, but the stench was powerful and disturbing.

The pack members preened themselves for a full ten minutes, stopping to howl in ragged chorus, and to bite tenderly at one another. Soon, the two other male jackals released by Cuthbert appeared. There was a general refrain of pack-joy, a violent merriment.

We catch we kill we eat we live!

The llama, which had calmed down, watched them stiffly. It had defeated the canines, but they could find easier prey.

The jackals howled again, in furious bliss, and trotted along the edges of the corral, sniffing at a sun-blanched Ribena sip-bag and a tiny green butterfly hairclip and a lost £10 coin. Two stopped to lick at the glistening snails that crept up the fence posts at night like darkness's very jewels.

Eventually the pack began ducking into the barn, one by one, stalking, then as a pack. With the spring, the keepers left the main door open in the evening. The mule, especially, enjoyed the cool air. Sometimes, a starling or mockingbird would fly in and perch on its hay feeder.

When the mule finally perceived the jackals, she neighed stridently. She was a strong, old creature, a retired draft animal whose mother was a Clydesdale and father a favorite beach donkey from Anglesey. She started kicking at the stable walls. It sounded like she would beat the place down.

One by one, the jackals slipped beneath one of the stable doors. Behind it, they found the two poor, tethered goat brothers. They were sweet, blond billies who were fawned over by children. Aside from the occasional cruel boy, they had never seen a predator in their lives. Now they faced their most ancient enemy, the same species who had chased their wild ancestors in the Zagros foothills of Persia.

The jackals set upon one of the goats all at once. Within a few seconds, the pack had managed to wedge part of its liver out. The other goat bleated in horror, kicking repeatedly from the stall's corner, until the jackals massed upon it and brought it, too, to the hay-strewn floor. Each of the goats, conscious and in shock, choking, could feel the dogs rooting in their insides, the snouts digging for their meek, soft hearts. In their caprine minds, there were picture-thoughts amid the agony: a grassy meadowland; buckthorn berries on sugary twigs; a range of granite massifs climbing to ever higher playgrounds of stone. And then the pictures stopped.

The mule, in the opposite stable stall, who thought of the goats as small, equine associates, brayed without end. Soon, the llama began screaming again, too, and from there another wave of anxiety washed across the entire southern end of the zoo.

Cuthbert could not see any of this, but he could hear it. It was clear something ghastly and heartbreaking had happened. Neither inebriation, delusions, nor hepatic brain-fog could screen the shock of it. He did not want to guess at the details, what harmless being was being torn to pieces. What had he caused?

"Damn, damn, damn," he said to himself.

Soon, another new set of cries rose. There were feral chitters and dumb groans. So many animals, in an uproar again. It seemed to Cuthbert that, perhaps, his great plan to free as many animals as possible was causing only universal torment.

He stood still, taking it all in, angling his head to hear every detail.

"Bugger," he said. After a full minute or so, the noises abruptly stopped.

He remained on the path near the jackal kennels, not sure where to go next.

"Blessed bloody Jesus."

He started swinging his bolt cutters with one hand, back and forth, until the loose handle scraped against the ground. The security lamps blazed like daylight. Everything had seemed so straightforward moments before. There was an existential danger to all Britain's—and the entire earth's—animals, a threat posed by the Heaven's Gate cult, by social disorder, and by widespread apathy toward the animal kingdom. His solution had seemed magnificently simple: *just let the animals out—all of them*. He had not seriously considered that the freed animals presented any danger to the caged ones. What am I doing, then? Stop me, God, help me! He tried to visualize St. Cuthbert, a living statue, the ice on his legs getting licked by an otter's tongue, his flesh scoured with the enzymes of miracles.

"I pray to you, St. Cuthbert," he said, quite earnestly. "For help and for comfort. I pray to you—please!"

A man screamed, far to the north in the zoo, where Cuthbert

had not yet ventured. Cuthbert was sure about it—it was a man. He could not make out the words. It sounded like "No!" or "Wolf!" Cuthbert remembered that the otters were in the north section of the zoo.

Then, for nearly the last time, Cuthbert was able to step back from everything inside him for a moment. He could see how enormous and real this trouble had grown. While any experienced zookeeper knows that zoos normally echo at night with unhuman sounds, Cuthbert didn't. To him it was as if something bigger than anything he knew was booming in his head. He did not know how to drive it from his brain, into the world, to expose it. The animals were grabbing it and running with it all by themselves.

A garbled thought came to him: he could still stop everything, he believed, if he only Opticalled Dr. Bajwa. There was the Opticall address in his wallet. He'd seen a few of the venerable red phone boxes in the zoo, all fitted with passé neuro-optical matrices, but functional enough if you didn't have any SkinWerks handy. He imagined Baj in his surgery, frowning at him, but not without kindness. Baj would wrap a long linen healing cloth around his skull. The fabric would suck away the sickness like a great swab. Baj would press an iron bracelet into Cuthbert's palm, and place a curved knife with square emeralds in its handle before him as a gift. "There is your *kirpan*. You are very Sikh now!" he would tell Cuthbert. "I am certain!"

But Cuthbert was plenty Sikh already.

A STRONG BREEZE AROSE, cooling Cuthbert's face. He held still in it for a moment; he could feel his trouser legs, rippling. The wind made him feel a bit better. He closed his eyes—the easiest way for most Indigents to turn nighttime Optispam bursts completely off—and he watched glowing shapes and swirls on his eyelids, all shadows of optical adverts and headlines that would normally light up if he opened his eyes (though Cuthbert's brain had learned to bypass much Optispam "noise").

Keep your hair on, he thought to himself. Play it cool, now. Such self-therapy, he knew, was hopeless: he might as well have been fire, telling itself to become orange gummy worms.

He squeezed his eyes shut tighter. He saw floating gray crescents that stretched into scimitars. Drifting discs metamorphosed into skulls. The longer he watched the patterns on his eyelids, the more ornate and creepy they grew. There were tiny scrimshaw designs now, needle-etched in marine bones, with dead sailor faces painted in tobacco juice, afloat in his head. He snapped his eyes open. Was it a siren he heard? Was that the otterspaeke *gagoga maga medu*? Was that the song of St. Cuthbert, the otter song of exoneration, or the sound of seawaters smashing into this island nation? Were his prayers being answered, in an otter-language peculiarly well suited to the middle of the twenty-first century? If that was so, he mused, he had gained a wonderful ally against the false Heaven's Gate. He would gain absolution for his childhood evil. And perhaps, yes, a cure for his Flōt addiction. There would be much to be happy about, really. When the otters slipped into the Regent's Canal, a great greenness would explode over Britain, a verdant bubble-shield against the death cult. And would he see his brother? Would he get to give Drystan a kiss and a cuddle, and tell him how sorry he was to have failed to save him, so many, many, many years ago?

For a moment, Cuthbert felt a bit of plain, golden-green delight. No state of mind would seem less appropriate for a well-adjusted human being in Cuthbert's circumstances; it was another bad sign. Were his EEG available at that moment, the high spikes and shallow valleys of euphoria would be unmistakable: it was Flōt withdrawal—a very bad case. The feeling of joy jarred him to the soul, but it soon passed.

"Don't feel like meself," he said aloud. "Where's Cuthbert?"

Where indeed. He did not even resemble himself—he was standing tall, and sucking in his stomach. Instead of his usual fearful, parted lips, his weak, wrinkled, nonagenarian grimace, he glared ahead and scowled. He felt strong and anguished and ready to act. If madness and sanity sat upon opposite ends of a seesaw in Cuthbert's head, madness could be lifted no longer, and the old Cuthbert was gone, launched into the lunatic sky.

a way out for animals

CUTHBERT NOW FELT, WITH A CERTAINTY ONLY A psychotic, withdrawing Flōter could muster, that he *would* get the jackals out of the zoo. But he also understood, if hazily, that unless the animals found the comparably small and well-concealed hole he'd earlier cut in the perimeter fence, which seemed unlikely, they would be stuck. He hadn't considered this detail, and he felt irritated, and worried—though not nearly as worried as he ought to have been.

To Cuthbert, the problem of his personal safety with jackals on the loose seemed minor, though it was far more real than he knew. (As late as the 2030s, in Cyprus—where the last wild population had lived—jackals still dragged the occasional child or old woman off to her death.) A defenseless Flōter, shaky on his illusory stilt-legs, would pose little challenge to a few of them. In any case, he needed a safe way to guide the jackals, and all the animals, out into the city. Meanwhile, the jackals had dissolved, gone liquid brown, and the night had drunk them in. They seemed not just part of the dark now; they were darkness itself, tearing blue flesh from the day and secreting it in their bodies with howls. The vistas around Cuthbert were dominated by canid colors and crass shadows that concealed all light and all graceful things. He felt he had undoubtedly done right to liberate as many of them as possible. Yet he could not expunge the sounds—murderous, gash-filled, so close by—from his head, and in this they were like all things that gnashed his soul.

He began walking south, toward the main glow of central London. It was a kind of dirty aurora, and it seemed more distinct because of the park's expanse of darkened sports pitches sandwiched between the zoo and the city outside. As he proceeded, he tripped more and more of the motion detectors, switching on more arrays of lights. They followed him like camera flashes. Every few moments, he would also see lights from others parts of the zoo snap on. The jackals were on the move, too.

In a few minutes, he came to the southernmost point of the zoo's interior. It was the place where, on the other side of the main fence, the Broad Walk in Regent's Park and another footpath intersected, forming the tip of a great pointer directed toward Marylebone, and beyond it busy Oxford Circus and Centre Point. During opening hours, it was one of the spots in the zoo where all visitors turned around.

There was a maintenance shed and a little white Cushman electroglider. In the bed of the Cushman were a few big peat moss bags, a safety cone, a pitchfork, and a couple of metal buckets. An orange electrical cord was plugged into a socket above its bumper—its molten salt batteries were charging. Cuthbert sat on the white vinyl bench-style cushion of the microlorry and touched the steering wheel with his fingertips. Then he slammed his fist into the horn. *Berp!* He hit it again. *Berp!* He got up and walked over to the shed. He jiggled the doorknob—locked. He circled around the shed and realized it had no windows.

While behind the shed, Cuthbert saw something quite interesting. The zoo's perimeter fence, in this concealed section of the zoo, comprised just two short panels. These panels formed the squared-off tip of the entire zoo enclosure.

Open this "tip," open the zoo.

Cuthbert worked his way through a bramble toward the fence; he tangled his foot. He pulled up half the underbrush behind the shed, revealing bare ground covered with snails and glistening black mealworm beetles.

Near the fence were a few old, thin tree branches he broke off. It had the effect of opening an enormous vista of Regent's Park.

Directly in front of him, on the other side of the fence, was the ornate Readymoney Fountain, that Zoroastrian fantasy of marble and pink granite. As a frequent rough-sleeper in Regent's, Cuthbert had long known that it readily offered neither money nor water. But it did, reputedly, offer something he valued: luck. At least, that's what many of the homeless Indigents who slept in the park believed, and they often bedded down near the pavilion-like Victorian structure, for security.

Cuthbert set down his bolt cutters and pushed against one of the sections of the fence. It was loose. Heavy wrought iron, painted black, it had sharp, barbless spikes on offset shafts. An animal could easily be deterred, if not killed, trying to cross it; yet though substantial, the fence was ill secured. He surveyed the damp ground into which the fence was planted. He went back to the Cushman and grabbed the pitchfork.

It took him only a few minutes to chop away and expose the fence's staking bars. The soil came away effortlessly, like chocolate cake. Cuthbert could not believe how easy it was.

He stopped to rest and looked up. He plunged the pitchfork into the ground and let it stand. Where was Urga-Rampos? Where would the comet stop, precisely? (Clouds still veiled it a bit.) Soon, the sky started spinning and Cuthbert grew dizzy and lost his balance. He crashed sideways, tumbling onto another dreaded holly switch. The fall was made more treacherous by a short, young stand of ornamental bamboo. But Cuthbert's bulk simply crushed it all. He felt prickles from the holly along the side of his leg. A little slit came open on his trousers at the groin. Though he had fallen hard, he felt no pain whatsoever, only the slight prickles. He no longer registered stings the way normal bodies do. In fact, he felt grotesquely amused.

"I'm coming apart," he said. "Damn me trazzies!" He lay there for a minute or two. He thought he heard the squawk of a loudspeaker, and voices. He clambered to his feet. Was it the Watch? Or the Heaven's Gate cultists, coming for the animals?

Within a few minutes, he was able to push the fence down far enough that he could get his feet onto it. With his considerable weight, the old man simply "walked" up the fence and flattened it. He fell again, forward this time, onto the soft, grassy turf of Regent's Park proper. He staggered back to his feet. He looked at his handiwork. Pressed into the ground, the fence's line of spikes all pointed out, to the open park, like a road sign.

The London Zoo now had a twenty-five-foot hole in it. It was big enough for an elephant to shamble through. And the location of the breach—at a tip of the triangular zoo—could not have been more favorable for a freed wild beast looking for a way out of the zoo. A single clever, brave person—or a clever, psychotic one—would be able to flush any wandering creatures toward the tip of a natural funnel.

Cuthbert did not think of these tactics quite so logistically, of course; he didn't yet grasp how effective his idea might prove. There was more than a passing blip of joy in openly destroying part of the perimeter fence. It was the elation of a vandal—fleeting and culpable. And something was wrong, too. His euphoria, and some of the decisiveness that attended it, were fading. He was beginning to feel sullen and shaky and irritated and close to the ground, whose gravity felt as strong as Jupiter's. His Flōt spire was wearing thin, his psychosis plateauing.

He thought to himself, Where are the bloody saints now? I've been handed a pitchfork, but no other directions.

He wiped sweat roughly from his forehead with his arm. He grabbed his bolt cutters from the grass.

He started back to the zoo's path, feeling its gravity acutely. He kept rubbing his tongue against a bit of loose skin on the inside of his cheek. It wouldn't stay in place. It was as if every strand and filament in his body were drooping away, post-Flōt. He stopped at one point until he could scrape the tiny piece away; he rolled it against the roof of his mouth, then swallowed it. He began walking again, stiffly, with the short-legged proprioceptive illusion one often felt in withdrawal. At the path, he tried to orientate himself in the way sloshed people do, cocking his head to the side and squinting through one eye. He only vaguely understood the zoo's layout, but he could sense that the location and vastness of the breach in the fence held possibilities.

The zoo seemed far larger than he had remembered it. Outside, in the park, it had always looked compact, like a secret animal-holding cell set behind a hedge or two. Inside it felt bigger than England. He felt a stab of impatience in his stomach. He started to hurry, in a leaning, stiff-legged manner. He decided he might just as well flit from exhibit to exhibit for a while, "regrouping" before the night's larger, onerous undertakings.

Again, he heard a voice shouting out, now more distinctly: "Help me!" It was hard to tell if it was a man or a woman. The voice sounded very old, however, and weak. It couldn't have been Drystan—he knew that much.

Cuthbert thought for a moment of calling back. But what was there to say?

The idea that a human being, the night watchman, for instance, could be standing, terrified, atop a picnic table, begging for help, or trying to find a tree to climb—nothing even close crossed Cuthbert's mind.

He followed one of the paths and ambled north, past the Bactrian camels. On the path he came upon part of a carcass. It was a hoofed leg, but its thigh and haunch had been shorn away neatly around a bloodied bone. Cuthbert knelt down; he felt he would weep, but didn't. There was only a stinging rigidity in his throat that soon passed.

He touched the cloven hoof. Its halves reminded him of a tiny pair of beaten ballerina slippers. He rubbed the pastern and, pinching the hock, he turned the leg over. It felt cool and sticky with blood. He pulled his hand away in a jerk. He could not work out what sort of animal the leg belonged to, but he guessed a deer. He thought momentarily of the roe deer he would sometimes see grazing in the lawns of a ruined castle in Dudley the family had sometimes visited on the way to Worcestershire and the Wyre. But they had short, reddish-brown hair, and this animal's was blond and long, and as soft as a girl's.

When he stood up, he checked around the ground for any other parts of the unfortunate creature. He did not see anything obvious.

He walked along, using his foot to push aside shrubs that edged the path. He soon came to a place that looked ravaged. There were long smears of red on the pavement, streaking into the grass like the lamb's blood signs of Passover. In a spray of new grass he spotted something odd. At first, he thought it was a watering jug with a strange pink spout, left by some forgetful gardener. Only when he looked much closer did he see it was an animal head—a goat's. Its eyes and the sockets around looked vigorously chewed out. The whole muzzle and lips had been removed, giving the skull a teeth-gritting mien.

"Fuck me," said Cuthbert.

He grabbed the head by a horn—it was surprisingly heavy, as heavy as a four-pack of Flōt orbs. He went back and got the goat's leg and tucked it under his arm.

He made his way back to the maintenance shed area and the broken-open main fence. Every half dozen yards, he knelt down and daubed the pavement with the carcass remains. A few times, he bashed the head down, splattering bits of blood and brain matter on the walk. He did it calmly and meticulously, like someone trying to get ketchup from a bottle. When he finished marking a spot, he would move on another half dozen meters or so. He used his foot to mush the pieces of goat into the pavement until he could see a distinct mark. When he got to the maintenance shed, he threw the head toward the spot where the fence had been brought down, but it bounced and rolled horribly several yards to the left, its one remaining long ear whipping like a tiny bloody pennant. He was trying to create a system of blood-splattered signposts. He hoped the animals might follow the trail out, like Hansel and Gretel's trail of bread crumbs. It seemed an astute plan to him, based not in wheat flour, but in gore and death and insanity—things that lasted.

Heading north again, toward the majority of the animal enclosures, including the otters', Cuthbert felt more buoyant. The blotches of the goat's blood did not strike him as morbid or gory, but momentous. They marked the beginning of the end of a great threat to Kingdom Animalia.

song of the penguins

SOON CUTHBERT CAME UPON THE LONDON ZOO'S once-famous Penguin Pool, adjacent to the Children's Zoo. He gazed at the stark DNA-like double-helix of ramps at its center, which many an architecture student in the previous century had observed with an unruffled enchantment. Cuthbert gave a satisfied little chuckle.

"Bostin, that is!" he said.

The birds were not visible.

"Penguin muckers," he called in his most singsongy Black Country accent. "I'm *heeee-earrrrr*. I can help *yew-oo* . . . es*cape*, eh—from your *noyce* little clink."

There was no response. At that moment, the zoo's relic collection of black-footed African species—their joints arthritic, their instincts to dive and swim cramped by the unnaturally shallow pool, their hatcheries incorrectly placed—were dozing miserably, slightly offstage, in a High Modernist rookery of iceberg-white cement attached to the main pool and facing into it. These "Jackass" penguins, as they were called in their homeland, had lived up until their extinction in the wild on the softest of sands, not on icebergs, and certainly not on reinforced concrete.

THE LEGENDARY POOL had been designed in the early 1930s by a young Jewish émigré from Russia. Berthold Lubetkin and his team of Bauhausers, all of whom ate great quantities of a new white food called yoghurt, had studied the penguins very carefully and very earnestly. Unfortunately, what they mostly kept discovering were artistic-politico devices rather than birds. (This was the politically explosive 1930s, after all.) At the time, this approach excited the zoo authorities terribly, stoking up their worst paternalistic impulses. As absurd as it sounds, it actually seemed to them that the zoo might lead the nation not merely in life sciences, but also in social architecture: if penguins could appear happy in a clean, hygienic, artful domicile, and given proper care and food, it would set a great example for what to do with England's poor in their flea-infested, crumbling slums. Tuberculosis would vanish. Joy would appear. One of the greatest of the zoo secretaries, Chalmers Mitchell, brought in unemployed Welsh miners as laborers to dig out the pool—all part of the example.

"More light!" Mr. Mitchell was to have exclaimed one day while the pool was under construction in 1933. He had stood at the edge of the lovely new hole. It was the happiest day of his life. He had brought a pewter tray of teacups for the workers. They were all full of yoghurt. Personally, he found the stuff nauseating, but it was supposed to be very healthful, according to one of Lubetkin's Bauhauser friends who was selling and promoting it on the side.

"More light! Here's a bit of refreshment—free, of course!"

The pool was completed in seven weeks and the laborers were let go. When all was said and done, the public cared little for the pool. They liked the penguins all right, but they did not properly rise to the challenge of the pool's Art. In time, various naysayers in the papers began to opine on the pool. It was, among other things, they said, a fantastic failure from a zoological perspective—the penguins would not or could not multiply in it. How, they asked, had Chalmers Mitchell missed this flaw? They declared the pool, literally, sterile architecture, and while its beauty amused champions of High Modernism, the penguins truly suffered.

Cuthbert read the small, polished brass plaque, placed by the Royal Institute of British Architects, that was riveted beside the penguin's information sign: BERTHOLD LUBETKIN (TECTON), 1901–1990, RIBA GOLD MEDAL. He rubbed his fingertip across, down, and then up the tiny engraved *e* in *Tecton*. "There, like a little penguin, up the walk," he said.

DOLOR HUNG OVER the pool like faint, gray-green mist, but Cuthbert saw hope there, too.

In his opinion, the pool was certainly a symbol for something, or a sort of trick process, he reckoned, but he needed time to work it out. He felt a vague sanguinity, a feeling that the structure might offer a kind of release of both personal and national power of some sort, a splitting of spiritual atoms. It was often this way when he first gazed at extraordinary public art and architecture in the city: the Centre Point skyscraper seemed a sleek, wafer-windowed version of his own tower block. The half-century-old Westminster Tube station, with its glistening grays and massive grids of escalator chutes and support beams, was a breathing machinery he could inhabit and taste the power of. Even its perforated silver steel claddings, with a trillion dimple holes, made it seem as if the station itself exhaled air from mathematical lungs. But Cuthbert's feelings of awe and inclusion always faded; the red nuplastic half-benches at Westminster seemed cynically designed to keep vagrants—and he was one, sometimes—from getting too comfortable.

And yet, the Penguin Pool seemed of a different, higher order. It wasn't mere urban infrastructure. It flabbergasted Cuthbert, more than anything he had ever encountered in the city. It seemed to be trying to delight him personally, like some enormous, fragile toy tied with a white bow. He read the plaque again. He wondered if the pool might "work correctly" if he stopped to eat a bowl of yoghurt. He said the word "Tecton" aloud. He acquired the erroneous idea that it served not as the name of Lubetkin's architectural practice, but as his professional nom de guerre, as with the forgotten artist Christo or the new "Dead Pixel" sculptor, Pointe.

"Tecton," he said, several times. "There's a clever clogs. Tec. Ton. Tec. Ton. Tec. Ton."

He leaned over the rail. He spoke down toward the rippling ovular pool of water. In the day, this water looked blue and aesthetically ingenious; at night, it glowed a sick, radioactive yellow.

"Hello?" he called. A few squeaky chirps and one morose honk arose from the hidden huddle, somewhere below, but nothing else. Cuthbert wondered if he was irritating the penguins.

He spoke again, rather nervously: "Hello, you! Come on now, right?" He suspected the birds had been moved, or that they were protesting his presence. He felt frustrated.

"Say something, geezers!" he blurted.

What occurred next was important, an unmistakable indication of the new, ever more florid stage of Cuthbert's Flōter's hallucinosis. While not dissimilar to schizophrenia, Flōter's hallucinosis is oddly uniform in how it attacks the mind when it does take root. Nearly always, victims encounter something that is not supposed to talk talking up a storm. It may be a pineapple on a table that grows a face and recites the Book of Revelation. It may be a hundred wicked homunculi hiding in the drunk's bedroom walls, jabbering about the merits of infant stew. It may be a tree whose wind-blown leaves are calling for better child glider-seat designs. And it may be a jackal or otters at the London Zoo, or the souls of lost brothers. Or a huddle of penguins.

In any case, if what happened to Cuthbert comes across as too far-fetched, rest assured, it was all too true for him: after he had demanded, in so many words, that the penguins answer him, they finally obliged. The nearly extinct Jackasses, none of whom had ever seen their dinette-size home isles off the Cape of Good Hope, who slept stuck inside a twenty-ton objet d'art, sang these bizarre words:

> *Seagulls of Imago, your song shall make us free,*
> *From Cornwall to Orkney, we dine on irony,*
> *Along with lovely kippers from the Irish Sea.*
>
> *Seagulls of Imago, your song shall make us free,*
> *Until that day we'll wait, and watch French art movies,*
> *Your avant-garde near saved the twentieth century,*
>
> *Along with lovely kippers from the Irish Sea,*
> *We'll take our daily fill of anguished poetry,*
> *'Til the world becomes zoologically arty.*
>
> *Seagulls of Imago, your song shall make us free,*
> *Seagulls of Imago, your song shall make us free,*
> *Make it new! Things not ideas! Ambiguity!*
> *And endless lovely kippers from the Irish Sea.*

Whatever did it mean? If all the Nobel laureates in the world parsed such a grandiloquent, rambling statement, they would surely have remained befuddled. It was the essence of obscurity.

Yet this case could be no plainer to one man, yoghurt in his tummy or no.

Cuthbert said, "You're all stuck up, you lot." He felt piqued by the villanelle the penguins had recited. What he wanted to talk with them about was helping them to escape the zoo, not the mysteries of Imago. Who the bloody hell were the Seagulls of Imago anyhow? He wondered how Drystan might view all this—far more sensibly and clearly than he, Cuthbert guessed. He'd sort these penguins. He'd handle 'em.

a broken art, a broken neck

"COME OUT THEN," CUTHBERT SAID. HE FELT SUR-
prised that the penguins *still* refused to show themselves, even
after their paean to seagulls and all. There were unnatural noises
elsewhere in the zoo again, and he knew his time to free them was
quickly running out.

"If yow don't come *now*," he slurred. " 'A corr come back."

Unlike most enclosures, the Penguin Pool, sunken about twenty
feet down in its Modernist pit, could not simply be sliced open with
wire cutters. He could not throw a rope down or wedge open a door
or gate. Indeed, he could not determine how the penguins had been
put into the pool. The only approach he felt might work was to find
a long, flat plank of some sort to tilt down onto one of the pool's helical ramps. But then what? Short of walking across the plank himself and grabbing a penguin in each arm, he would need to employ
persuasion. What would he use to lure the penguins out? He had no
kippers, from the Irish Sea or anywhere.

He examined the little information sign. It read: "The only natural home of the endangered jackass penguin was off the coast of

South Africa. Harvesting and eating of penguin eggs by humans was the greatest reason for the species' extinction in the wild."

Penguins from South Africa, he thought. What a marvel!

Cuthbert had an idea. He felt he knew these arty types well enough to make the plan work. It was luminously simple: he would shame the penguins into action by accusing them of snobbery.

He said, "Bloody elitist birds!"

No, answered the penguins. *Never. We are . . . artists.*

"Artists? Oh-ho-ho! That's quite *particular*, innit?" He mouthed the word like a filthy, oily slur. Gazing into their quiet pool, with its dull green blanket of vapor trapped in white, stiff walls, he could not resist grinning. The birds had got a cob on all right. Surely, they'd come out any second.

He waited a moment and added: "So come along then. Defend yourselves. Show yourselves—*artistes!*"

Nothing. Not the faintest echo of a stirring.

"You're going to let the world be destroyed if you don't come out, little poshies."

Seagulls of Imago, your song shall make us free.

The poetry startled Cuthbert from his thoughts. He looked at one of the ramps. Penguins! He was amazed to see, as instantly apparent as something switched on, a sort of conga line of half a dozen penguins. They looked different than he had imagined—they weren't robust, tall creatures colored in neat tuxedo panels of black and white. They possessed mottled bellies, very small, delicate frames, and hooked banded beaks.

"Bostin!" he said. "Oh, I knew you'd come. Some of you, anyway." He jumped higher upon the wide, shelf-like edge of the pool—the edge with a notorious flaw of being too high for most children—and balanced on his stomach. His feet were off the ground. He could see, from this perspective, that he could, perhaps, drop himself onto a set of service stairs, to his right. The stairs led down to the lowest level of the pool platforms, where the nesting boxes were. From there, conceivably, he would pluck the birds out and toss them (gently) over the wall.

But would it hurt the penguins? They seemed so vulnerable, so diminutive. More of the penguins had appeared on the ramps. They seemed to be engaged in a kind of preliminary procession. It was as if some critical mass of discomfort had ejected them from their nests, and now, once stirred, they all had to leave their nests and prepare for—what? Cuthbert had no idea. Some confrontation between bird and drunkard, sculpture and dissolution?

"Come along, come now," he said.

He felt newly disheartened as well as indecisive. He'd tried so hard to lure the penguins out, and his effort had seemed to pay off, but what did it add up to?

He saw only one solution. He put his wire cutters on the ground and climbed up upon the Penguin Pool's wall. He had to heave himself up with a brutal lurch that almost threw him over the edge into the pool itself. He rose for a second, reeling side to side, trying to recover balance, then sunk down on all fours like some drunk, acrophobic infant on a rooftop. He crawled to the service stairs.

Do not try to touch us, the penguins suddenly said. *We go nowhere without the gulls of Imago.*

Cuthbert felt annoyed by all this. Perhaps the penguins were, in fact, snobs.

He kicked his legs back, dangling them down, feeling for the stairs with his feet, and dropped down onto a small, square landing.

Leave us, said the penguins. *We perform by secret schedule, and not without the gulls of Imago.*

Cuthbert sucked a bit of mucus from the walls of his mouth, and spat down into the pool.

"Bollocks," he said.

The gesture had an immediate effect, causing a streak of chittering up the conga line. He noticed for the first time a few little wooden hutches, like red taxiglider shacks, set poolside, a few feet from the water. They didn't match the crisp style of the Penguin Pool in any way. They looked like hovels, sloppily nailed together.

"What's in there?" he said aloud.

He took a few steps down, but all at once began to fall forward. He reeled back, and nearly tumbled straight down the stairs. He grabbed hold of the edge of one of the wide, spiraling ramps and flumped in its direction with his whole body. Almost falling against it, he felt the ramp's corners jab hard into his side.

"Oi, Christ," he said. "Ow!" He needed to get onto the ramp. With great difficulty, he managed to get one fat leg, then his fat middle, then his other fat leg up on the ramp. At first, he didn't try to stand up. He could feel that the ramp was slick with fish-slime, and at this point, it was crowded with little penguins. He thought, If I let go, I'll slide right down to Penguin Hell. And a slip might knock a dozen penguins down, he thought, like bowling pins. So he edged down, carefully, first one butt cheek, then a foot, then the heel of his hand, then the other butt cheek, and so on. The closest penguins, no more than a meter away, turned around and began waddling away from him, crowding each other. Suddenly, first individually, then in twos and threes, gaggles of them started sliding down the ramp, zipping along expertly. A few birds made stiff little leaps off the ramp and plummeted down into the pool water with plunking splashes.

Cuthbert said, "Oh, damn it, wait now then. I'll find your blunky gulls." He commenced to shimmy forward hastily. He approached the place where one ramp crossed the other—if he didn't mind himself, he was going to slam into the other incline. As often was the case with Cuthbert, he was the last person whom he protected.

"I'll find them, all right! I'll promise you that much. I'll get my clever brother, Drystan, too, and 'e'll get to the bottom of all this.

You need to get moving now, out of the zoo, see? This American chap, Applewhite, he aims to obliterate you, see?"

When the Gulls of Imago return.

"You're yampy, you lot!"

Cuthbert asked: "What have these fucking Imago chaps done for you? For fuck's sake!" He felt frustrations cutting through his chest like an opening and closing fan of blades.

So he tried to stand—a huge mistake. Not more than a few seconds passed before, unable to grip the slick concrete ramp, his feet flipped out from under him, and he was swiftly the very description of the term "arse over tits." He seemed to rise up a few inches before all twenty-two stones of him crashed hard. A deep-reaching, snapping noise sounded out. Cuthbert bounced up, and when he hit the ramp again, he knew something strange had occurred. He was still plunging toward the water, almost flying.

The force of his tumble had been so severe it broke one of the two ramps off. Down went Cuthbert and ramp. In a matter of seconds, Lubetkin's fanciful "DNA strand" was forever unstrung, and a new mutation born. It was as if a new epoch, when all art was to be broken and imperfect and free, had been signaled, and Cuthbert was playing the role of unknowing situationist. After he smacked the water and sank, he felt, perhaps for an entire half minute, fixed in serene suspension. He was unable to breathe, lost to time, place, direction. He felt euphoric. I can die now, he thought, and I'm not afraid. He recalled thirty years before, submerged in Dowles Brook, where an otter had looked him in the face and spoken to him. *Ga go ga maga medu.* The otterspaeke sang in this head, a lovely death hymn. The animals will leave the zoo on their own. But what of the aliens and their Californian proxies? He shook his head, underwater, and said, "nooooooo" with a burbling seriousness. The salty, bitter birdwater finally flooded his nostrils and mouth, and he panicked. He threw his head back and arched out of the water. He swam, coughing, to the poolside and flopped up onto a sort of performance platform. He lay there for a few minutes, recovering, but blankly staring at the penguins.

The penguins were terrified. They had crowded by now on the opposite side of the pool to guard the red nesting boxes, those huge eyesores of rough-daubed wood that had been added to the architectural masterpiece to make it more livable. Indeed, there were four live eggs in the boxes (and two infertile ones).

Cuthbert pulled himself up and sat forward and stretched his legs out, letting the water run out of his trousers and shoes. He felt more sober than he had in months. He wanted to stand up and cheer. It was all a big laugh—the busted pool, the penguins stirred from their torpor.

Then he noticed a dark object floating on the water. What's that, eh? With a rising horror, he realized it was a penguin, floating grotesquely with beak down in the water, a corona of pink water around it. The animal had been unlucky—smacked unconscious by the falling ramp.

Cuthbert dove into the water and got his hands on the bird.

"Oh bloody Jesus!" he cried. "Oh fuck me, fuck me, fuck me!" With one windmilling arm, he paddled frantically; in the other arm he held the wounded bird—it was lighter and warmer than he expected. He scampered back onto the pool's apron and lay the penguin down gently. Blood covered his arm. The penguin's neck was completely slack, its head at a severe, obtuse angle from his body. Its beak was parted open.

"Oh sweet Jesus," Cuthbert said. He touched the animal. It was already dead, he believed. "A'm a bastard," he said. He backed away from the bird and fell down on his hands and knees, gnashing his teeth. He started to stand up, then sat down, kicking his heels. He thrust his face into his hands and he wept wildly, his arms flailing, scratching at himself with cold fingers. He reached up crookedly and cried in screeching jags. He was like an old tree scraping its own bark off.

"It was a mistake!" he blubbered. "I'm sorry, chaps!"

The penguins now formed a mottled black and white phalanx around the boxes of their makeshift rookery. Some of them rocked their heads back and forth with taut, beaky aggression. Cuthbert stood up. He said, "I'll find the Gulls of Imago, muckers. I'll find them for you, you'll see."

The penguins began a furious, rhythmic song—it was a noise unlike any Cuthbert had ever heard, like a tone collage of rusty, clicky kazoos, all insisting on the same note, a note that was equal parts buzziness and sweetness, rancor and innocence. Among their thistly lament was a quiet layer of something far more melodious and soft, a little reedlike slip of music. Cuthbert could see now, inside the middle nesting box, a tiny, fuzzy form that could only be a penguin chick. It was as small as a sparrow and colored a solid, sticky gray.

"Oh god," said Cuthbert. "Oh bless you all."

Find the Gulls of Imago, they said to Cuthbert. *Find our friends. But you will never be forgiven.*

Cuthbert cleared his throat with a harrumph. "I know, I know. I deserve to die." He wouldn't mind it at the moment, so awful did he feel. He must help the penguins though, if he could. He owed them that.

"I'll find a way to get your gulls." He raised his index finger and gave it a good wag, like some little Mussolini. He said, "Blunky, munky gulls!"

But he didn't feel very confident.

Never forgiven, they repeated. *You are an enemy of penguins. Forever.*

"That's OK," he said. "I'll still help you. And I'm certain Dryst will muck in, too. You'll see."

Oh, Cuthbert may not have recognized these Imago gulls personally, not off the top of his head, but he could make inquiries.

"I've a few notions where to start looking, boys," he said.

Through the high windows of his flat in Finsbury Park, for instance, he occasionally noted gray-mantled mew gulls. They would float at eye level, on the eastern winds that blew all the way up from the Thames Estuary. These gulls were excellent spotters of discarded chip cones, he had observed, and with so many chippies in Finsbury Park, they were eternally busy. But not too busy to be put a question or two from a certain psychotic fellow.

"I'll ask 'em when I see them next," he said to himself. "Which of you knows where I might find your Imago comrades?"

A few times, he had seen his gulls swoop down audaciously and, he believed, snag a hot chip from an Indigent child or lady's wooden chip-fork. Cuthbert felt that this *seemed* a kind of torment, did it not? But no, the Gulls of Imago had to be something quite grander. They would not fly in the airspace of north London.

And would they ever appear at night? He had never seen a seagull at night—their whiteness seemed a sort of violation of it. But he determined to keep his eyes peeled. If the penguins seemed to honor them so, surely, from somewhere, they were watching, from above, right now.

Then Cuthbert took a few steps back up the pool stairway and slapped the side of his thigh: "Saft man!" The obvious solution to the problem of the gulls was right under his nose. The long-dead architect, this Tecton fellow, like a great heap of white concrete pushed off the cliffs of Dover, had shattered into a thousand, flying pieces—seagulls. Here were the Gulls of Imago—the "father" of the penguins. They had risen from the scraps of rubbish magazine spreads. They had risen from unbuilt dream cities, from the sad spirit of the man whose greatest architectural success had not been for workers, as he wanted, but for a few displaced, bravely appreciative penguins. If Tecton could not create a comfortable place for the birds, he had at least tried to please the public, truly and deeply and incompetently.

Cuthbert said, to the dark sky above the zoo, "I'll find them—or him!"

So he left the pool, a guilty servant, a criminal, and a man enthralled to flightless telepathic birds imprisoned in the wrong hemisphere.

popcorn for the lions

AS CUTHBERT HANDLEY TRIED TO DECIDE HOW and where to find the storied Gulls of Imago, and at the same time accomplish his most consecrated task—the freeing of the otters— he got himself rather seriously diverted once again, this time by a religious development among the zoo's felines.

Cats have a way of drawing people into their worlds. Penguin dreams and holy otters, gory jackals and creepy cults, King Henry's Red Watch and the very white seagulls—all would have to wait. A set of needle-clawed gauntlets, with fur licked clean to a sheen, were about to be thrown down.

Cuthbert found himself in the big cats district of the zoo, passing a series of semicircular windows intended to give glimpses of large felines in their separate enclosures: tigers, a black leopard, a jaguar, and the Asiatic lions, but from that side of the complex, none of the cats were visible at the time. He wondered whether the cats were quartered in secret night quarters, and whether a tube connected them somehow to the penguins' clandestine night-holes. Can't imagine what the penguins and the tigers would have to say to each other, Cuthbert thought. But you never knew, did you?

He quietly sidled around to the front of the cat compound, to a gift kiosk called the Cat's Curiosity Shop, across from the lion enclosure. There's something happening here, he thought. There was a red sign fastened to the kiosk that read (in handpainted, gold, metal-flake script, which was incongruously ornate):

ALARM BELL

IN EMERGENCY BREAK GLASS

Below the sign was a small red box. It was designed for the lion enclosure specifically, but Cuthbert didn't see that. Instinctively, he started to reach for the box, then hesitated. He took a deep breath and rubbed his wrist across his eyebrow. There was certainly an emergency of some kind in England, he felt.

He gawked into the darkened shop. It nauseated him, looking in. There was a shelf crammed with old-fashioned, twentieth-century-style stuffed leopards and pumas. On another shelf, several holographic jaguars and tigers waved their glowing heads back and forth, but the projections were jumbled up and growing grotesquely through one another like a spotted and striped cancer of catness. He tried a window, and, surprisingly, it opened. There were, right beside the window, bags of popcorn and algae crisps on sale, too, and Cuthbert grabbed a few and stuffed them into his shirt. Close to the locked door, the blue-light numerals on a till could be seen displaying a huge sum from earlier in the day: £80,044.50. Was it possible, he wondered, that a zoo visitor had purchased a lion?

He closed the window, turned around, and stepped toward the lions, who had come out from wherever they were hiding. They appeared wide awake, scrutinizing him, but sat crouched and motionless, their forelegs extended like furry golden cudgels. To be watched in this way by wild animals, as the sole human of interest, was the rarest of occurrences in England, a phenomenon daytime zoo visitors seldom experienced or would even notice. Cuthbert took it for granted. One of the lions' tails rose like a brown-headed cobra, then fell. There were five of the creatures, the famous old maned male, Arfur, fronted by four females. One of the females, Chandani, suddenly stood up and strutted a few meters to the right; she climbed up into a grassy cubbyhole, and turned around to face Cuthbert again.

Gregarious and greater in number than all the other big cats, the lions held prime position in their enclosure. Theirs was one of the more sensitive, animal-friendly enclosures in the zoo, but it still offered little more space than a studio flat gives a human. It comprised a widely moated jumble of ledges and tall pillars made of concrete. Tall grass, overgrown by design, spewed from every cranny and obscured the concrete's geometric motif of rhomboids and sly cambers. To their credit, the zoo managers were trying especially hard to make the lion exhibit seem less artificial, less self-conscious, less "boundary driven" than so many others at the zoo—it was all part of a "new" thinking that had flowered for a while with the millennium celebrations fifty years ago.

But sentimentality, scientific stuffiness, a lack of funds, little space, and three persistent fetishes—for art, architecture, and horticulture—had stymied the new thinking elsewhere in the zoo, and when the social upheavals and rapid extinctions of the 2020s came along, the zoo management had its hands full simply keeping one of a quickly dwindling number of zoos open. The lion terraces seemed gracelessly situated. The organic wholesomeness of the weeds often looked a lot like simple laxity: bright algae blanketed the moat water so thickly it resembled some green variety of the reinforced cement with a few lily pads set on top, like table doilies. Mud splattered every flat surface.

The lions themselves looked grubby and somnolent, and their flaccid musculature betrayed years of confinement. The algae stains all over the concrete gave the terraces an abandoned quality, too.

Toward the center of the den stood a Chinese tree of heaven with its beckoning thousands of paired, shiny leaves. Beside it was a three-tiered play-shack built of logs. It was as if children had taken up residence in a Mesopotamian temple ruin. The whole enclosure impressed and disturbed Cuthbert greatly.

"Come over here, Cuthbert," Chandani said, in a gravelly, richly self-pitying voice. "Come forward, not back. We don't want to die like this, as slaves, in cages."

Cuthbert said, "Not sure. Not yet. Do you know the penguins?"

"They are good animals," she said. "But they are fooling themselves. They are waiting for something that will never happen. Now, Cuthbert, step closer."

"Not yet," he said. "You're the end of me, you lot. I can see it."

He still felt terribly nervous about approaching the huge felids themselves—their communications to him had been characterized by an immaculate righteousness. No other animal unnerved him as much. He felt that the lions were trying to keep something from him—they represented a kind of authority that had never welcomed him, an official power. It smelled much like Harry9 and the Windsorite radicals. And yet, the lions were also victims of that power, even as they symbolized it. Cuthbert was not sure why this should all bother him particularly. But he decided to put the lions on hold, again, and he crept around the back of the terraces and there came upon an often-missed nook in the rockery where the sand cats lived.

"You cannot ignore us," the lions in unison called. "You will come back here."

"I will," Cuthbert said, strolling away. "Maybe." He pulled the bags of "butter-flavored" popcorn and algae crisps from his shirt and, one by one, ripped each open and hurled it into the lion enclosure, the contents flying out. One of the lions sniffed at the popcorn and licked up a few pieces, then slunk away.

Chandani roared, and said, "At the end of time, you will always come back to the lions. You will see. When we are consulted, saints arise, angels sing, and flags unfurl. We are the only animals with the power to make empires."

Cuthbert said, "I'm building an empire of otters. But I won't forget you."

"Right," said Chandani. "What matters more, sir, is that we shan't forget you."

a cat from the caliphate

THE SAND CATS, *FELIS MARGARITA*, INHABITED A deep, semicylindrical chamber built at waist height into the rear of the terraces. Their floor was spread with coarse sand and pebbles that looked suspiciously like what covered the beaches of South-ampton. A complex set of dehumidifiers in the roof kept the chamber more arid than any other spot in England. A few bone-dry pieces of acacia and, of all things, a dried sponge were illuminated with an orange halide heat lamp. Though unintended, the sand cats' narrow cattery came across as a kind of tidy accessory to their enormous cousins' weedy cement heap, plugged into the same mass of mud-spattered, unnaturally smooth concrete. The orange light glowed like the inside of an old bread toaster.

Cuthbert started to bend close to look into the orange-glowing pocket but was distracted. He turned around. He felt a presence near, something low and smutty and ancient. He searched the nearby hedges with his eyes. There was a tremble in a certain holly branch, and dark shapes, the size of footballs, scurrying beneath it.

Something was rustling in there. The wind, he thought. Or a little field vole? Or his eyes playing tricks.

He rotated back around abstractedly. He read part of the short description of the animals printed on a black rectangle. *The sand cat's specialized urinary system allows it to survive long without drinking. It derives nearly all the moisture it needs from food.* He tapped on the window of the cat enclosure. A single golden paw extended spectacularly from the shadows. He could not help but smile.

"Wakie, wakie!" Cuthbert said.

Three of the animals came into focus in the dark. They stood up, their backs rising into huge, awakening arches. Their keepers had petted and touched them assiduously since their arrival from Chad, and they were unafraid of humans. They were among the few animals in the zoo not yet extinct in the wild, but they were far from safe.

"Hello, you lot," he said. "Yam beautiful, yow am."

Cuthbert liked them immediately. The docile animals' gold-green eyes were jeweled and soothing. One of them, whose keeper had named it Muezza (after the Prophet's pet, according to the sign), gazed at Cuthbert. It bucked to the side and puffed its ringed tail. It was accustomed to human contact, but not totally at ease with strangers, and never at this hour.

The sand cats were smaller and stretchier-looking than the mogs Cuthbert saw on the streets of London, but their faces were wide and their ears immense—huge golden triangles that could hear the bellies of desert vipers and the feet of jerboas in the Sahara. The cats seemed wide awake in their glass case; they were pawing the window now, looking into Cuthbert's eyes.

Come, Seeker, Cuthbert thought he heard Muezza say. *Come, Saliq.* The cat's head inclined slightly sideways when it mewled. The attention engrossed Cuthbert greatly. Was *saliq* a word of blame, or a warm assignation? It seemed a bit of both.

Cuthbert felt he didn't have time to bother with the fine points of a cat greeting. He still wanted to solve the conundrum of the Gulls of Imago. To him the Penguin Pool remained the most obvious mechanism of an unfathomable, and perhaps good (and perhaps not) sort of power, and he wanted to turn it on.

"Ow bist?* Have you seen any seagulls in the area?" he asked the cats.

If there was one thing Cuthbert knew about the moggies of London, it was that they watched birds gingerly. He touched his forehead against the glass. The cats circled around one another, taking turns rubbing against the pane. There was no other response.

Cuthbert decided to change tack. "If a'm a 'saliq,' mates, perhaps you would be willing to lend a hand—I'm officially seeking otters," he said. "That's my immediate business. And seagulls—oi'suppose. They're important . . . to help these penguins out, see? And I'm looking for a sort of ghost—or two ghosts, in a manner of speaking. There's this fellow, this Tecton—e's split into a million living bitties. 'E's a load of gulls these days. And my older brother—Drystan. 'E's the most important, mind you. I say 'ghost,' but it's only as 'e's missing. He ain't jedded."†

Muezza squeezed his way past the other cats, and as he did, he also seemed to squeeze subtly past Cuthbert's world of prayers and madness and dreams, and to speak with familiarity and directness: "You free us, brother, and I *can* tell you about many, many, many small living pests, and perhaps about other things, too."

---

* How are you?
† Dead

"I don't see how it's possible, cat. I only have these bolt cutters, right?" He held them up by one handle, and shook it around, as though gripping a great swan or goose by the neck.

"Oh, brother seeker—and 'brother-seeker'—surely you know that I would also take you, of all creatures, to the sacred path. I am here to tell you that the path leads eventually to the Shayk of Night. Don't be afraid. I know your purpose. The Shayk has been waiting for you. But I get ahead of myself."

"That so," Cuthbert said. He wondered what to make of the cat's strange ideas. They struck him as no less inscrutable than the penguins', but this animal had at least alluded to a plan, as well as a quid pro quo arrangement of genuine promise. Given the fact that he'd made a sort of promise to the penguins, he felt inclined to work with this creature.

"Can you help me free the otters into the cut? This is my most important task."

"Yes, I can help. All things are possible," said the cat.

"Really?"

"Oh, so much," said the cat.

Cuthbert thought for a moment. There was no little red emergency box here; there was merely glass. How dangerous could a little cat be? He tried to weigh pros and cons, and it did not take him long to reach a decision.

"Mind now," said Cuthbert.

There was a heavy garden hose and squirter looped around its portable, wheeled spool a few feet away, propped against the back wall of the lion terraces. The apparatus was made of a heavy, galvanized alloy. He heaved up the entire assemblage, took a few steps back, and ran forward, ramming it into the glass. As he ran, he began to think of his brother, as if Drystan himself were helping him to push forward. There was a loud knock, oddly attenuated and resonant, as if the blow had come from beneath the sea. The force of the impact threw Cuthbert back. He toppled over. He was in great pain.

He screamed, "Drystaaaaaaaaan!" What he would give to see him tonight, even under these embarrassing circumstances. How he missed Dryst!

He sat on his arse for a few seconds, catching his breath.

"Drystan," he groaned. "Jesus, help me. Jesus Drystan. Jesus Drystan. Help me, help me, help me, help me. Don't I have a mucker somewhere? St. Cuthbert? Christ of Otters? Someone?"

The air had grown colder and he was shivering, his teeth chattering occasionally. He lurched up onto his knees and steadied himself. He felt dizzy and self-conscious. "I'm really doing it," he whispered to himself. Kneeling made him think of prayer, but he felt unsure of what to do about it just then. "Bloody help me, someone," he said. Here he was, a first-class social disaster on one hand, and on the other a supplicant to Family Felidae of Order Carnivora—all he needed was a rosary of fangs.

A huge triangle of the glass pane, half the size of a newspaper page, had broken off and tilted into the tank. Cuthbert got up and approached the opening—there were the three cats, lumped into a little cave made of artificial, flat rocks; their ears were pulled back in terror. After a little while, seeing Cuthbert and hearing a few soothing words he remembered his granny using ("Kitty-kyloe! Kitty-kyloe!"), their giant ears pricked up. The one named Muezza stepped forward first. *Felis margarita* are known for their gentleness, their sweetness of temper—provided you aren't a snake, chicken, or rodent. Cuthbert simply pulled them out, like free kittens, and dropped them onto the pavement.

the green line to allah

THE SAND CATS STARTED TO KEEN AWAY, STRETCH-ing their legs into grand, picky steps, then pushing themselves into low, predatory crawls. This, evidently, is what a little imprisoned meat-eater does when it suddenly takes its place at the top of the local food chain. The killing of natural prey, which the zoo hadn't allowed for decades, had to be eased into; it was like crawling beneath a tender belly—the animal looks for teats, and failing that, goes for the heart.

Watching them, Cuthbert was rapt. He felt that cats were healing, almost magical, and in a funny way, a force stronger than Flōtism.

His grandmother Winefride, among other things, was one of those great cat-loving women one encounters in the world, from Alabama to Zanzibar, the sort who, if given the opportunity, would keep a dozen in the house and feed a dozen more strays under the back porch. Removed from her Clee and Wyre environs to West Bromwich, she had turned to cats and birds as signs of wildness.

In her later years, Cuthbert's father forbade all pets, but Winefride always talked as though cats were, apart from otters, the most perfect of God's creatures. If otters brought miracles to the dying and to saints, cats helped the living. She often employed the word *useful* to describe them, though Cuthbert never understood just what that implied. She was always putting out saucers of milk and the occasional kipper for the moggies in the neighborhood.

"They deserve it," she would say.

In his mind, he could still hear her calling "Kitty-kyloe! Kitty-kyloe!"

Cuthbert watched the sand cats begin to relax and stand taller. In London, a cat could command a certain respect. He remembered the prancing cat logo one saw when visiting the A&E at the Whittington Hospital, up the Holloway Road, where he had regularly shown up in recent years for neulibrium and a hot meal and Flōt detox.

You again, Cuthbert? his favorite nurses would say. *After your jabs again?* Going to hospital used to be a relief for Cuthbert; he had been welcomed at Whittington for a long time, and the staff never minced words: *Keep it up, Cuthbert, and you'll be dead before you're a hundred.* He had been placed in the hospital's large psychiatric unit seven times for chronic Flōtism, with stays from three days to nine weeks, typically signed off by Dr. Bajwa. He never stayed away from Flōt more than a few hours after his discharges, but he felt a temporary relief—he saw that, in theory at least, it was possible to stop drinking.

And this sense of a reprieve was what he associated with Whittington and felines. He always felt charmed by the hospital's logo of a black silhouette of a cat standing upon a *W*. It reminded him of his grandmother and her earthy strength, a power he tried misguidedly to tap by going to the hospital, where decisions, it turned out, were made for you. But he had trusted the Whittington deeply, and now, he was sure, the Red Watch would be all over it, hunting for him.

In the days before Calm Houses and the Red Watch, he'd known friends from the streets or marginal housing who would, every few years, deliberately smash a storefront, or give some stranger a bad lampin', solely for the privilege of being arrested and sent to the Whittington. Cuthbert especially loved how you could look out many psych ward windows at the Whittington and see, in the distance, the bright beech trees and glowing stonework of Highgate Cemetery, where a few blokes he knew from panhandling and sleeping rough sometimes slept at night in the company of Douglas Adams and Karl Marx, both of whom, one imagines, would sympathize.

CUTHBERT FELT MESMERIZED as the sand cats made themselves, second by second, freer before his eyes. He felt a strong urge to cuddle one, and he stepped closer to Muezza. Unlike the jackals, the cats did not mark their new territory, but there was a pause. The other cats seemed reluctant to part from one another, but at the same time instinctually compelled to do just that, their noses thrusting ahead. They each gradually slipped into tentative stalks, in three different directions. They were solitary at last, but nearly flattened by a flood of need to stalk blood.

What Cuthbert did not perceive was that the sand cats were also enormously preoccupied with Norway rats. These were the "pests" Muezza spoke of. The cats had heard, smelled, and sometimes seen these rodents near their enclosure since their arrival. Now they could perceive them directly, rustling in innumerable shrubs, in service drains, in zoo stores where dingo kibbles and bolts of dehydrated bananas for the monkeys were kept. Aside from human beings, the rats were the most common free animals in the zoo. And now something beautiful was out to devour them.

One of the cats scrammed madly up a very tall plane tree and disappeared. Another was tooling around inside a black plastic bucket that stood near the door of an adjacent maintenance shed.

Muezza rolled onto his back, right in the middle of the path that led, eventually, toward the monkeys. Although Muezza was real, Cuthbert's hallucinosis enriched the cat's movements, giving each paw a winged grace and fluidity. The cat, freed by a mentally ill man's delusions, was still acting a cat, but even more utterly so than the lions; he seemed a being more animate and sentient than anything Cuthbert had seen in the animal world. Cuthbert's hallucinations were growing more elaborate, and the animals more garrulous and complex: he was imagining versions of the very "souls" that Heaven's Gate claimed all animals possessed. But whereas the death cult saw these souls as crude, infantile demi-spirits, Cuthbert saw whole, mature psyches. He felt deep wonder before Muezza.

Perhaps this Muezza, he thought, if he couldn't help find Drystan or the Gulls of Imago or the Christ of Otters, could at least absolve him, somehow, of his lifetime of guilt and shame.

The cat froze for a moment, upside down, and extended his pudgy legs to a startling degree. It was as if he were trying to make himself as long as a leopard.

Cuthbert had never seen a cat so desperate to be larger. Muezza sprung back together, a recoiling bungee cord. Then he did something Cuthbert had never seen a cat do: he ran around and around in a tight circle, around and around, chasing his tail, almost ecstatically, until he fell and rolled and stopped himself. The cat turned his head toward Cuthbert as warmly as a fellow sleeper in bed. Cuthbert saw something very odd; it seemed to him that the cat was smiling at him. The expression didn't last long—it was not sewn to his muzzle. The cat stood up, shook its golden ears, and gazed at Cuthbert circumspectly.

"Shukran!" said Muezza. "As-salamu alaykum!" The cat trotted up to Cuthbert, and peered into his face with what appeared to him utter sentience. "Whoever is kind to the creatures of God is kind to God also. Whoever imprisons a cat will imprison himself."

"Oh," Cuthbert said. He had to think about that one. It was a daunting notion, implying that a controlling relationship with animals was like trying to control God. He'd certainly been evil toward animals as a child. But did he ever want to control God?

"I've wandered the world like a dead creature for many years," he told the cat. "When I was young, even after being blessed by the otters, even after my gran's Learning, even after I knew the truth, after Gran died, I *was* wicked to other animals—and to dogs, in particular. It has spoiled me. It has destroyed my soul, and damned me to alcoholism, then to Flōtism. I thought that by letting the jackals out and whatnot, and then you, too, it might help. Just a little bit of help."

Muezza began to sniff at a hessian mulch mat set along a trail to protect grass seedlings, then at a long, outstretched hornbeam limb.

"So good, so moral, *saliq*," said Muezza. "What you fail to understand, perhaps because you are too English, is that all are welcome on the Green Path. We say, 'Come, come, whoever you are, no matter how many times you've broken your vows.' The blessing of the otters—oh, you will see. It never ends."

"I did not take vows, Muezza."

"No need to complicate matters, *saliq*. What I mean to tell you is that there are no restrictions now, not even past sins. You've been forgiven long ago. But you must take the sacred path, the Tariqat. This, *this* is the great beginning. You do not understand who you are, do you?" He spoke with an abstracted air, and without looking away from his plant explorations.

"I don't feel forgiven," said Cuthbert. "I need help."

Muezza said: "No one can help you now if you are truly ready.

We cannot make you *more* ready. Your 'help' is the droppings of depraved sand mice beside my golden, jeweled '*This.*' The Tariqat awaits you."

Then the cat added: "Yet, I must say, if you don't mind, that though you may follow the Green Line to Allah, the *dogs* you have mentioned, *saliq,* I do not understand how you could *not* see that they are of little importance anyway, in the scheme of things. To kill a dog is no great sin—you know that, don't you? They are not allowed to set a single paw on the Green Line. And most dogs are dirty idolaters, you may have noticed. They *worship* lowly human beings. Forget your jackals. Or are you a dog? Of course not!"

Cuthbert didn't understand Muezza fully, but he knew he didn't like the cat's slerting on about dogs or people. His own guilt—for his childhood abuse of a dog, for hurting the penguin tonight, but mostly for nothing at all—stung him hard, goading his indignation into something quite ferocious.

"Are you a dog?" the cat asked again, needling.

He said: "Oh, shut it. That's ronk, you, and quite hateful, really. To injure a dog is cruelty, plain and simple." The image of the injured penguin came to mind. "To injure *any* animal," he said. He felt angry and charmed and abashed by the cat. "Why don't you look at me when we're having a word?"

"I smell you." Muezza laughed. The cat pushed his snout deeper into the grassy weeds. "Regardless of what you say, it is very bad that the jackals have been released. They are ruthless. The Shayk of Night, I have heard, has had to end the lives of many of them in the old land. But if you released them, that must be correct, brother."

"Are you just saying that, then?"

Muezza didn't answer.

Cuthbert felt baffled—and impatient to go. It seemed to him that the cat was either barmy or ill behaved. He stammered, "I don't know about any Shakey-Fakey-Half-Bakey of Night. But you're getting on my pip, cat," said Cuthbert. "I said, it's rude not to look at someone when they're speaking. I've got to go. The otters— they've got to be let out of here. Soon."

The cat seemed to ignore him—like, in fact, a cat.

Then he said, "*Saliq*, let me accompany you, for as long as I can. If you will have me? I can show you, as I said, the Green Line, the One True Path, that leads to the Shayk of Night, and from the Shayk you can find the way to . . . a cure, before Allah. If you really want the cure."

A feeling of sadness pushed up from Cuthbert's belly, into his throat.

"I think I am beyond a cure. A'm the worst on earth. If it weren't for my brother, Dryst—and 'e's gone missing, as I said—I wouldn't exist at all to any being, apart from my GP a bit." At that moment, he felt for the first time sure that he would not survive the next twenty-four hours. He had not wanted this, not tonight, not death.

He said, "The soul-grabbers, they are coming to destroy us all. I've failed miserably, cat. I was thinking—was it thinking or was it something else?—that if I could let you all out, there might be a way to prevent the cult freaks from wiping out all the animals."

Muezza paused for a moment, twitching his ears and glancing at Cuthbert, then returning his attention to the weeds.

The cat continued, "Enough of your self-pity, Cuthbert. There is always hope. You, *saliq*, are carrying the Wonderments. You do not feel it, but you have them, my *Al-Madhi*."

"You mean my brother, cat. I am not gifted in the least."

"I do not. I mean you, *Cuthbert*—the last holder of the sacred knowledge of animal speech."

" 'A corr do this," he said.

The cat pointed at his bolt cutters.

"But you are doing it, *saliq*," said Muezza, "and you *must* do it. The world of cats depends on it."

A siren sounded in the distance. Behind the cat, fringing his golden fur, the strong yellow and blue lights from the edge of the zoo popped open like flowers hungry for night. It was clear to Cuthbert now that someone—police officers? the Watch?—outside the zoo had arrived. His time was running out.

britain's true cats

"YET FOCUS ON YOUR INSIDES, NOT ON THE COMET infidels," Muezza was saying. It was as if Cuthbert ought simply to ignore the perturbing lights. "You *are* the one who will save us, *saliq*. They are coming soon—be sure—the 'Neuters,' as they call themselves, one of the arrogant Luciferian species. But look to your Shayk for help. Forget the dangers of the night. The Shayk may feel like a knife on your neck, but he is truly the sweet finger of the Almighty within. It is *good* to feel him, brother. He will give you the strength you need. Feel it, *saliq*. Fear not. It *is* the end of Self."

"All I feel right now," said Cuthbert, "is torment. And impatience. And cravings for Flōt. I wish I did *fear* something."

"Oh-ho, no, *saliq*. There is much to fear ahead tonight. When the white Altar of Lost Chances awakes," the cat continued, "and when all its dead dreams come to slake the thirst of dead souls, and clouds of white seabirds swoop for cheap lures, when the Altar's machinery of lies bursts open, like a fatal ghost flower, and it begins sucking in the souls of all—*that* is when *he* will come, as we always hear and as it is written, like 'a thief in the night,' and he *will* attack without mercy, and he *will* sort the good and the evil. And because he is a cat, he *will* rip away the veils on all hearts—and on your cat heart, especially."

Muezza's little chest, with its yellow-sapphire center, puffed out. He popped up to the balls of his paws, and all his hair stood up. After a minute of stiff, anxious silence, his tawny body deflated a bit, his hairs relaxed, and he intoned, with the greatest of gravity: "Thus, we shall have a decent look at the *thing*—the heart of hearts. It is the whole reason why all cats play with sharp claws. They are always reaching for a thing so very precious, something that must not be let go once it's grasped—the *heart*, brother. Do not forget that. In the same way the platinum prongs of a ring need a ruby, the cat's claws need a human heart."

Cuthbert considered all that Muezza said. He felt impressed less by the cat's lucidity than by his fey fervor. He nodded for a moment. He took a deep breath, and an answering flutter of arrhythmias tickled inside him. Dr. Bajwa had tried to teach him to get used to his early beats, but they ever vexed him.

He asked darkly, "The Altar of Lost Chances? That's this bloody entire island, according to my gran." He squinted at the animal. "But let me put this to you, Cat of Wonder, since you seem to know so much: do you know what the otterspaeke phrase '*gagoga maga medu*' means?"

Muezza shook his head. "Oh my friend, my *new* friend, I am no expert in languages. You may actually have overestimated my extensive feline powers. But I am sure this '*gaga-maga-baba-boo*' means something good and important, *saliq*. I am sure it is something to do with cats, and nothing to do with dogs."

"You're really on a line* about dogs, little cocker—and that wants no translation," said Cuthbert. "Now what about that? S'that Islam proper? And it's '*gagoga . . . maga . . . medu*.' It ain't to do with dogs

---

* Annoyed by

or cats. It's the words your otters, *your* London Zoo otters, send me."

"Otters?" asked Muezza. "*Most* sacred creatures, *saliq*."

The cat disappeared into the vegetation. Cuthbert could see the black-ringed tip of its tail sticking up from a carpet of ivy. It waved drowsily.

"Yes, brother. You have me. Perhaps I'm not a perfect scribe.* But I respect otters—and all living creatures. I don't like dogs, it is true. And rats. You see my weakness. I want to destroy rats."

There was a pause and the tail stopped cold and stood straight as a reed. "Oh, I smell them everywhere here!" Muezza emitted a short, pained growl. The strange sound was as diminutive and precise as his face. "Rats, brother. Can you hear them?"

"No, I do not," said Cuthbert. "For some reason, I don't hear rodents. And now I need to go."

"Ah, see? They are beneath you, too, brother."

"Oi, no. Nothing's below me. And I'm not your brother. Please don't call me that." Cuthbert felt a sudden surge of self-loathing, with his West Bromwich childhood on him like piss on chips. "You wouldn't want me anyway, if you knew me. I'm not like you. I'm a Flōt sot is all. And 'a've a brother, and 'e's more of a gent than me, believe you me. 'E's really my better half, see? 'E's the one what's supposed to carry the Wonderments, but I couldn't save him, see? I couldn't. But if I can free the otters . . ."

An old, very sane bitterness was beginning to engorge his mind. "I'm the monster. I'm worse than human, as my 'dear old dad' used to say. I'm not even sure if I'm alive. I can't seem to live in this country, see? How can I save a single animal? I couldn't even save my brother."

Cuthbert felt his heart doubling beats rapidly, and a slight numbness in his lips that always came with his worst arrhythmias. He felt angry.

---

* In this case, translator

He coughed. He asked, "I'm dying, cat. I'm ninety years old, and I've been in the wars, as they say. Why don't you just run away and take your freedom, like your mates? I've come to help you. It will help me to help you, you see, if you'd only just run away. Please?"

"Gladly," said Muezza. "But I am fated to assist you, my elder *saliq*. There are greater concerns than me, and even you, that await us. But you released me—that's a bell that cannot be unrung. So I must help you. And I am also fated to devour rats. We must consume the things we can, the things that are good for us, even if they are dirty and *haram* to the mullahs. The rats are all looking for each other, and since they are so stupid—and they can't even bother to address such wise creatures as you—all they usually find are miles of garden walls between themselves. Yet, let us not forget that even these dirty beasts have love for one another. They are continually trying to cross boundaries, not to write them. It is not their fault that they are disgusting sisterfuckers. And regardless of how I feel about them, they offer nourishment to cats everywhere. What could be more important?"

The cat nodded yes for several seconds, then continued: "But the Salafists and the suicide cults and the doomy ultrasonic neural-missile traders—and even your king, Henry—they—"

"Don't cank on my king!" Cuthbert said. "You leave Harry out of your feline philosophizing."

The cat grinned, but nervously. "Of course," he said. "I meant some of these—other . . . leaders? I forget my place, *saliq*. Not the illustrious and powerful king, not His Human Highness. But his Red Watch and his bureaucracy of bullying, and all these new human princes and barons and viscounts—they cannot survive without their cruel apartness. And that is truly death, *saliq*, as you have found yourself. The love of death—it binds them to your Luciferian Neuters in outer space, you see. They want to control. They do not see how joined we are to one another. Fools!"

"Arr," Cuthbert said. "For most of my life, I've been looking for a touch of someone or something lost long ago. I think I understand you a bit, cat."

Muezza nodded his huge, bat-eared head—he was gesticulating with enormous melodrama. "But even with the infidels, their time of empowered apartness is ending."

Then Muezza almost spat: "You will see, brother!" The cat began to chase his own tail. He seemed intent on creating his own tiny tornado of golden fur as he spun out of the hedge, yanking a few ivy vines with him, and dancing and tapping his paws on the walk almost brutally.

"What's the matter with you, cat?" asked Cuthbert. He was beginning to think the cat was more than a few sultanas short of a fruitcake.

"Stop that *cat dance*," he said. "Please, listen now."

But Muezza kept spinning, and finally, as though whirling off an invisible axis, the cat fell over with dizziness. He lay there, panting hard, half-covered in ivy leaves.

"You daft muppet," said Cuthbert. "You silly beast."

He found it very hard to sustain ill feeling for the cat. He fought off a big urge to pet the animal's golden hair, which nearly sparkled with luminescence.

The cat jumped onto its paws. It slanted its head to the side a bit and blinked slowly. Then it began again to scamper around in a frantic circle, spinning again and again and again until it finally somersaulted.

"Forgive me, *saliq*!" cried the cat, sitting up with a dazed look. "I . . . I say . . . I began to feel Allah in me. I do go on sometimes! Even the Shayk has said so. He says I am too emotional. I am a drunk Sufi. Understand: there has been much destruction in my world, in the *secret Islam*. My brothers and my sisters, we used to range from the Hindu Kush to the Caspian Sea to Morocco and everywhere between. But the Salafists, and the Wahhabis, and all their tyrants, with their nerve-bombs and fatwas and self-righteousness, they too, *saliq,* are part of the death cult, the Heaven's Gate. And they are all part of a larger Luciferian invasion. We must stop them."

Muezza pointed toward the sky, extending a little pale-pink claw to the east of the zoo, and for the first time, Cuthbert saw the comet Urga-Rampos. It was vast—a glistening spill of cream rubbed fuzzy, but twice as bright as Sirius. It had two great arms on either side, like an airplane with swept wings and a huge contrail. And it was suddenly all too clear (to his spiring brain, at least). *No* question. That's an alien spacecraft.

"Oh, bloody Jay-*sus,*" said Cuthbert. "It's really there! I must go. You're right, about the comet at least."

"Yes," the cat said. "It's a sign. A new dark age is upon us—a long night of evil, ruled by Luciferian hands—and there will be no one trustworthy to bear the news. They are coming to London—but where? That I know not. I have heard that their death machines, made of living concrete, are already here, disguised as buildings. And we cats, of the Inner Way, we must hide in the hills—even the nomads, our old friends, will imprison and sell us to certain deaths, things have become so bad."

"It's clear that this new world, well, it won't be one I can cope with," Cuthbert said sadly.

Muezza said, "There is a way, *saliq.* In this England of tomorrow, it's true: you will need your wits. You will need intelligence. You will need claws. You will need grace. You will, in short, need to be, erm—you will need to be a cat. So you have nothing to worry about, do you?"

The cat chuckled a little, and added: "But I am your fated friend. That's the difference. I know things. You could learn much from me, brother. For example, I get all my moisture from kills. Impressive, eh? It's all the liquid I need. Does that make you realize something?"

The cat took on a shy and unctuous expression, and looked down. "I *do not drink*. Because I have been removed, by you, from the care of my keeper—and praise Allah for that—I can only survive if I kill rats. They are abundant in London—praise Allah, again. But I *do* not drink, *saliq*. You could learn from me. I am like a camel, only I am not stupid and ugly and malodorous."

Cuthbert said, "You're a sober Sufi."

"I am the Truth, brother," said the cat. "And you are, too. You, al-Mahdi of beasts, the green saint, the herald, will save us from captivity and destroy the Enemy, and through you will come a new Messiah—the Otter Messiah. We are together this night because all the animals of the earth depend upon it. Your brother, this emir you love, he depends on it, too, I suspect. We are in the Animal Moment. My mythology is your mythology. My green eyes, they belong to this Green Man of England. And in the desert, where we call him al-Khidr—the Green One. Al-Khidr, the one who helps the Sufi wanderer, who carries our desert secrets, just as you carry your forest Wonderments. You have been praying to your Green Man, the saint of the otters, of seabirds, of the holy island. He is your only true British saint—so, but follow the clues. Don't you see them? Your otters—what are they? They are Britain's cats! Nothing more, nothing less. The Green Man looks at you, he sees you, even now. He will *take you over* if you open your heart. You will see. Light will slash across the night sky, and you will see your destiny. Wait until you visit your Shayk!"

Muezza's eyes were in fact gold-green, Cuthbert saw when he looked carefully. A careless observer would call them gold.

"I don't think your eyes are quite what you think," Cuthbert said, unswayed by Muezza's metaphysical blandishments. "And aren't Britain's true cats . . . its *cats*? We have thousands of them, you know. Millions, maybe."

"Yes, yes, you're right—no cat should be overlooked. It's just that the otter in England, the otter is *most noteworthy*—and most excellent. The otter is truly sacred. I swear to you: on the soul of your St. Cuthbert, the soul of your grandmother, the souls of all the good people who have ever died on this island, and—"

"Yow're right barmy!" Cuthbert interrupted, laughing a bit. "Yow're silly as a pie-can."

Yet he had to admit that he felt quietly moved by Muezza's words. He was drinking himself to death, and now, if nothing else, a considerate kitty was looking in on him, trying to help. And he felt responsible for making sure Muezza got some food. He said, "Yes, well, I suppose you must chobble a few rats then. If it's your fittle and all. But I don't want to see it, right?"

"If you would not mind terribly, brother. Time, my *saliq,* is short. The end is near. Still, you see, there are certain absolutes one cannot avoid. Al-Khidr or not, I must on English soil eat rats. And I would like to pay my respects to the Shayk, and you must, you really *must,* too. And I want to take you there. We must go now."

two rats for every londoner

BUT CUTHBERT FELT A NEED TO REST. THE CRAWL into the zoo, the gap-making in the fence, the catastrophic tumble in the Penguin Pool, the freeing of the cats—it was all knackering him. And now more strange lights were appearing outside the zoo, along with sirens and faint human voices. Was there something in the sky, besides children's cloud-doodles? Had the suicided cultists completely gathered in their comet ship? Had their California cocktails of death "released" them from their bodily "vehicles," and soon their hordes would be in London?

As much as Cuthbert felt affection for Muezza, along with no small dose of bewilderment, he wondered how much more he could take. He leaned against a rubbish receptacle meant to resemble a hippopotamus with a gaping, dust-devouring maw. Wasn't he already spoken for? The poor penguins had already tasked him with helping them find their Gulls of Imago, and he was failing them.

Cuthbert said to Muezza, "If I go with you to see your 'shayk,' I'll lose more time. I've already promised meself to these blunky penguins, see?"

"The penguins?" gasped the cat. "Oh, *saliq*! Why waste time with them? Don't you know that their pool is the Altar of Lost Chances? They cannot be harmed or helped, nor can the prophecies surrounding them be changed: the Altar *will* stir."

"Well, I wouldn't know about *that*, would I?"

"You will. It is beyond us," said Muezza. "Only Allah understands it. But the Altar, no single thing could be more dangerous to animals. It is a contraption of promises not kept. You watch—your Luciferians, oh, they will admire the Altar, you will see. It is part of their technology."

"But it's a lovely thing, it is. This Tecton chap, he won a big award for it."

"It's white cement. No one ever asked the penguins what *they* thought of their yoghurt-colored house of amusement. And it wouldn't have been so hard. But now, the penguins are brainwashed. They are ciphers of design. They are waiting to perform for someone who will never come. They wait every night, in their secret chambers, singing their verses to the Gulls of Imago."

"Well, what's so terrible about that?"

"I'm surprised at you, wise brother," said the cat. "The poor penguins are merely very clever decor, and when the aliens bring the Altar to life, the little jackarses will also perish. Don't you see? The Altar is a monument to what *should* be but never quite *will* be? The penguins wait to perform a ballet of collectivist magnificence that can be danced nowhere else but in the mind of an architect."

Cuthbert said: "You said—you *promised*—to tell me about the gulls, then. They're important, to me, and to the penguin muckers. I'm in a real palaver with all this penguin stuff. There's this Tecton fellow—'e's been ghosted into birds. But I distinctly heard you say you would help me if I got you out of your—your cat capsule. You did say that, didn't you?"

"If that is what you say, if you must say it, I will believe it," said Muezza. "But that is not what I said."

"Ah, cat!"

"Calm your heart, *saliq*. Listen: I suppose you have already done what is necessary to bring the 'Imago gulls' upon you; we will see—in time. But, really, how can you bother with these"—he spoke as though a bolt of dead worms had gushed into his mouth—"these *birds*? Birds eat garbage, not good, warm, beautiful blood, as cats do. When I am talking to you about the True Path, to Allah, you want to talk about a socialist museum piece. Did you not hear me? You are about to meet the Shayk of Night."

"I heard it, cat! Now what about the thing I said?"

"Yes, of course. I do believe I said I would tell you about *many small living pests*. And I have!" Muezza sighed. "You do not always act like a cat, brother."

Cuthbert wished he could gently clasp the fur between Muezza's ears and hold it until the cat began talking a bit of sense. Clearly, Cuthbert's idea of "a bit of sense"—locating a brilliant architect's ghost, which had morphed into white birds—wasn't straight-forward. But Cuthbert *was* losing his mind, after all. He leaned down and reached for Muezza, and the cat leaped back violently, hissing and growling, puffing its tail.

"Don't touch me! That is where the Prophet pets cats," said Muezza. "You see the *M* mark on my forehead? Where his finger painted all small cats?"

The sand cat ventured a few steps closer to Cuthbert, but he looked frankly scared.

The mark was apparent enough, Cuthbert saw. Like on any old tabby cat, there was indeed an *M* in dark fur. It astounded Cuthbert.

"The sign of Mohammed," said the sand cat.

Cuthbert said, a little nervously, "But that could just as well stand for Mary the Virgin, or some Saxon war god whose name starts with *M*—Mugnor or Muglund or some such. Or what about Muezza?"

"Yes, brother, you may be right. But I doubt it. You should be careful not to jump to conclusions. And since you're not able to stop drinking, it is probably best for you to turn my *M* upside down, and make it a *W*. Consider: all things bright and green and strong to you—Worcestershire, Wyre, the Whittington, and your granny Winefride—are also on my face, and merely inverted. I have it all. The *M* is the version of the *W* which can walk upright."

"I can walk," Cuthbert slurred.

"You shamble, brother. You do not walk."

Finally, Cuthbert mumbled: "I don't think *M* or *W* has much to do with anything." He bit his lip, then spoke more confidently: "I think you're a bit too clever for your own good, cat. And for the last time, I'm not your brother! My brother is Drystan. 'E's a real boffin, believe you me!" He sighed, and said: "Now, what about the gulls?"

"I never said *gulls* specifically. All that I meant were *rats*," said the cat.

"Gerrout!" Cuthbert screamed, his frustration peaking. The sound was as loud as that of any of the animals in the zoo. The cat seemed puzzled, but unfazed.

"Do you hear them?" said Muezza. "They are everywhere. Squeaking and squeaking and gnawing all of bad Britain. *Squeak, squeak, squeak.* I have been freed by you so that I and my friends can kill them. *Squeak, squeak, squeak.*"

"The seagulls?"

"No, the rats," said Muezza. "*Squeak, squeak, squeak.*"

"Cat, you're trouble, yow am. I hear no such thing."

It dawned on him that Muezza was acting no different from any small cat he had ever encountered in Britain. Cats were, after all, famously intractable. He suddenly felt, quite unwillingly, tender toward the myopic, rodent-obsessed cat. He felt that he wanted to rock the animal like a baby, but he knew Muezza would wriggle out from his arms, and possibly scratch or bite him badly.

"Oh, I wish I could touch you, Muezza, and hold you, and carry you 'round the zoo. You're a perfect cat. A'm sure that every person who comes to the zoo thinks the same."

"Not everyone," said Muezza. "Many visitors—and many other animals here—would like to strangle me. Your comet cult, well, you know what they want to do to me! No, I will walk by myself. I don't like to be mollycoddled, if you don't mind, brother."

The cat circled around Cuthbert's legs, his tail quivering. "Besides, I am famished. The zookeepers, they pretend to know Africa, but they out-starve even the Magreb. They are fanatical about weighing us and keeping us trim. They do nothing to stop the rats from getting into the zoo, but they have never given us even *one* skinny one. They torture us with them, I tell you. And the rats, they're everywhere, you know. Millions of them. Two for every human in London. Do you smell them?"

Cuthbert gazed around. He had indeed seen dirty little shadows moving in a holly bush. And there was that rustling noise.

"Doesn't the scent make you thirsty?" asked Muezza.

Cuthbert said, "I don't smell anything. And a'av no interest in rats. I want seagulls, a'do. And I'm losing my marbles 'cause of it." He took a deep breath but reeled backward, almost falling. "Or maybe it's because I'm not drinking Flōt. That. And if I could only make it a few days off the sauce, you know, I would be past the difficult bit. It's actually something I planned to bring up with you, though I don't see the point now. I had the naff idea that *you* might be able to help me to stop drinking, with your Allah and shayks and whatnot."

"Don't lose hope, brother!" Muezza rolled onto his back, and again stretched out his short, stout legs. He whispered, "You are the correct one always. You *will* be forgiven tonight in a way that you'll feel, and you *will* stop drinking, and you *will* free the animals, and your brother, too, your wondrous emir—Drystan, is his name?—he *will* be brought forth into the land of the living. And . . . he may be. Drystan *could* be . . ."

"What? Who?"

"The Otter Christ."

"Oh, please," slurred Cuthbert. "He is my brother, not the world's. I do want to see him. Just once. It has been so many, many years."

"And since all is hope and happiness now, would you like, first, to hunt a rat with me?" asked the cat.

Cuthbert shook his head, rolling his eyes.

"No, of course not, *saliq*. Though if you do not want to hunt for rats, I am surprised once again, I have to say."

"You shouldn't be."

"Yet, we have so much else in common, brother."

"No."

"But where was I? Yes, yes, yes—I still must show you the Sacred Trail to the Shayk of Night. You are my brother, but he is my sovereign. He is one who may be able to help you to stop drinking your fermented insect drink, that refreshment of thieves and the memory of prisoners."

"You mean the tipple?" asked Cuthbert. "You say 'booze,' awlright? Flōt."

"The Flōt *jinn*," said Muezza.

"Gin is fine, too."

The cat trotted away toward one of the main zoo paths, and stopped and turned around to face Cuthbert. When Cuthbert got to where he was standing on the path, he saw for the first time one of the Green Line markers, painted on the path, which he'd seen on the sign during his day visit. It was the same flat, broccoli green as the animal-group signs, the shirts of the zoo staff, and any of the cafés' serviettes.

Muezza said: "I should tell you: this is an incomparable night for me, too. It is just as all the cats of the zoo have always said, brother. There is the line painted the sacred color, and if we follow it from here, it takes us to the Shayk. I also believe this line, if you follow it farther, will take you to the otter friends you wish to free, and, *in-shallah,* to the Gulls of Imago, and ultimately to your wondrous lost Drystan. Naturally, because of my entrapment, I have never seen these things or the line myself. I never thought this night would come!"

Cuthbert did not know what to think. He said: "Let's see this Shayk then. He offers a cure, for my—condition?"

"The Shayk can do many things. I can make no promises."

"Well, on then, anyhow. A rat or two for you, and a cat for me."

Cuthbert knew he would see this Shayk, one way or another, no matter what he did. So he would go with Muezza. He would seek out the otters, and help them get into the Regent's Canal. Perhaps the otters would know where to find the Gulls of Imago. He thought of the disused canals of the Black Country, how the water turned green and luminous as one passed through the abandoned industrial landscapes toward the rural west. He did not mind following green lines—for a while, anyway. At the very least, it was somewhere to go. It was away from the aliens, away from the Black Country, and away from the Red Watch. Most of all, it was away from himself.

freeing the black panther

WITH THE SAND CAT TRAILING, CUTHBERT—STILL spiring, still in a state of Flōter's hallucinosis—paced west and then north, and ended up passing the flamingos. The birds were all sleeping on little islands. They looked like he felt on Flōt—leggy, sleepy, solitary, needing nothing. Cuthbert thought they were shaped like beans, and he kept repeating a phrase, in his head, "Them's like beans, they are. Them's like beans. Them's like beans." For a moment, he waved his bolt cutters back and forth like a giant pair of conductor's wands. Oh, he liked those concrete islets. "Them's like beans!" he sang aloud.

Muezza looked at him and shrugged.

"You are funny sometimes, brother. You act *human*."

The flamingos' necks curled back like shepherds' staffs, and their beaks rested upon nests made of their own pink-feathered backs. Cuthbert did not see how they could be so peaceful, nor why they stayed on their islands (there was no cage or netting anywhere), but he resisted his urge to awaken them. He did not often care for birds, especially the genomic clones people often thought of as posh. Pigeons, magpies, seagulls, and starlings—dowdy city birds were what he liked best. But he liked these things.

"How do you talk to a flamingo?" he said aloud, half-hoping that Muezza would offer some animal-world answer. The cat was watching the sleeping birds charily. The question seemed a critical matter to Muezza.

The cat answered: "I would not bother, really. These are ugly, self-important creatures. I have heard that lawn-worshippers in America, the kind of people who poison neighborhood cats, put effigies of them on their lawns. Blasphemous!" He paused, and looked down, speculatively. "When I was a kitten, I saw them in the reeds, near a great dying lake, but they stopped coming. But the nomads never liked them, nor did the camels or cattle or foxes. And then all the water dried up. My grandfather said thousands used to come, long ago—but no more." Muezza snapped out of his contemplation and gave a little chirping laugh. He said: "It is said they are pink because they are so vain, and they are already beginning to burn in hell, at the command of Allah."

Cuthbert did not like to think of them this way. This strain of moralism in Muezza was a challenge. He said, "I find them rather sprucy, myself. But I agree, there is something wrong with flamingos. They've got 'em in Birmingham, too, you know. Genomic clones, of course."

"But these birds, they are real. Among the last on earth," said Muezza. "Still, they *are* not a blessed color. As I said. Let's move along now, and you will thank me eternally for taking you to the great angel of all animals. I believe he is going to end all your problems."

Cuthbert did not like the sound of that.

"I don't know," he said. "I feel you're not telling me something. And I still need to find the otters, and the Gulls of Imago."

The cat said, "As for these birds you keep harping on about, dear *saliq*, you might just ask another bird. Try one of the local herons or mandarin ducks. And be faithful, Kitten-Man. *You* mustn't fear the Shayk. Through the Shayk, and through you, all things are possible now."

"Kitten what?"

"Oh, never mind," hissed Muezza, aggravation splintering his voice. "Brother."

THE TWO OF THEM walked a bit faster now along the Green Line trail. It curved back from the flamingo pond past a big, open plaza and then toward the other big cats. The plaza, with its potted junipers, precision-cut rows of yellow and pink peonies, and abstract bronze-cast of two baboons (with trapezoids meant to resemble ears) stood in contrast to the steel mesh, dirty cement, and scratchy glass of the big cat enclosures. The paws painted on either side of the Green Line, every few meters and as large as footballs, seemed distinctly feline now to Cuthbert. It was almost as if the London Zoo management's contrivance to help guests "not miss a thing!" was in fact designed to appeal especially to an escaped sand cat with the soul of a ninth-century Islamic warrior. The thought disturbed Cuthbert. At one point, as they walked, Muezza encountered the paws and skipped from one to the other, as though playing hopscotch. The cat seemed not merely happy, but full of a *hajji*'s ecstasy.

The Green Line took Cuthbert and the sand cat past the angular enclosures of Joseph the jaguar, who had been born in the zoo, and who, for a time, garnered much publicity, and also the tragic Sumatran tigers.

The tigers were long-waisted, potent creatures who spent much of their time circling back and forth in a corner, over and over, demonstrating the captive animal reflex known as stereotypy.

These big felids lived their lives out in convoluted, shelf-life residences with low ceilings. There were no impressive moats or ha-has, no tiered daises, no lion-head bollards, no geometrical points of interest. Cuthbert tried to get a glimpse of a tiger or Joseph and saw only the empty, concrete-and-dirt slots they inhabited in the day.

"Where are they?" he asked Muezza, tapping his bolt cutters against his open palm.

"We zoo cats all ask that, too. The keepers used to put these wonder-beings away at night, but they stopped that, years ago. Nonetheless, the cats—hunters of the night—now *sleep* at night. It's unholy."

"Yow'd bloody think they'd get better digs, wouldn't you?"

"Such cruelties remind people of their own power all the better."

At last they arrived at the exhibit of the black leopard. Like all the big cat areas where the enclosure lay close to the footpath, a steel fence of a meter high stood between the trail and the caging. This existed for no other reason than to keep guests at arm's length from the cages. It would have been too easy, otherwise, for an aristocratic hand to be bitten off. Almost no light shone in this section of the zoo at night, and Cuthbert could not easily read the brief description of the leopard on the sign, though he made out something about genetic mutations and pigmentation.

"We are here!" said Muezza, and immediately rolled onto his back and drew in his paws. "You must crawl!"

"I won't," said Cuthbert. "I don't do that for anyone."

The sand cat said, "You really must, brother. The mercy of the Shayk of Night is not boundless. He is not Allah!"

Cuthbert looked into the cage, but it was impossible to see a thing. He did not understand what the "Shayk of Night" meant precisely, but he felt now a need to meet the animal that, if nothing else, held his little friend's spirit in thrall. (In fact, the zookeepers had made a point recently of allowing their big cats to wander their exhibits at night instead of keeping them in old-fashioned night rooms. Somewhere, an ebony mutation of *Panthera pardus* watched.)

Muezza said: "It's written that the Night, *Al Layl*, holds the glory of Allah in it, somewhere within it, always, like a bright star. If you let the Shayk free, he *will* be the harbinger of the Judgment Day, you *will* see. He is part of the preparation period. As are you."

Cuthbert felt shaken by the cat's words, and the hairs on his neck stood up. What Muezza said was just the sort of eschatological banter that could pick up Cuthbert like a scrawny lamb on Armageddon's Valley of Jezreel, and lurch him away to utter craziness.

Cuthbert asked, in a wavering whisper, "Can he help me to abstain from the Flōt?"

The cat said: "In his way, yes. There is no question."

Cuthbert felt encouraged, but the cat's vagueness, again, concerned him.

"But I don't see him, Muezza," he said, still speaking quietly, his voice going husky. "I don't see any star either, for that matter. Just the comet-craft. I don't like all this Judgment Day talk. Do not forget: y'am a cat."

"I? Forget *that?*" asked Muezza. "I see him as clearly as I see you. What do you think you are? And the star—it's just a comparison, *saliq*." That Muezza could suddenly talk as if metaphors could be metaphors and nothing else, as if their long discussion was not a figurative exploration, had the effect of calming Cuthbert. It was as though a creature in a Flōt dream had said to him, "I'm here because you're smashed, bloke, and that's that."

"A'm sorry," said Cuthbert. "I'm . . . having mind trouble."

"That is a most excellent way of saying it, brother. You have nothing to be sorry about, not tonight. You possess the same fatal grace our kind all do. Why wouldn't you?"

With that, he finally realized that Muezza, from the moment

they met, actually considered him feline. He did not see the point of disabusing him of the notion; he wondered whether, perhaps, on some level, he had indeed become cat.

Cuthbert grasped his bolt cutters with both hands and stepped over the steel fence. He cut open the leopard enclosure. As far as he could tell, there was no leopard there anyway.

"You think a'm a cat, don't you?"

"Funny, *saliq*. You are blessed. And whatever else would you be? You are not just any cat. You are the Mahdi. You will soon meet your Shayk."

"A'm scared, Muezza. I don't believe I'll be hurt. But I don't like this feeling of fear—it tears you apart. Why can't I hear him? Perhaps it is better if you take me to the otters. I know about otterspaeke—*that* I can grasp, at least a bit. *Gagoga maga medu* and all that."

"The Shayk is silent," said the sand cat. "Forget about your zoo otters for a while. We are *cats*. The Shayk is more vital, for the moment, to us all. However, he may not need, perhaps, to *speak* with you, not here, not now. He is here to take you, in ways you need not imagine, to Allah. What could there possibly be to say, even with someone as capitally important as you?"

In the deep murk of the enclosure, several shadows seemed to burst to life for a second or two. It was as if little dark doors were swinging open to reveal silhouettes of lost souls.

"Oh, now I see something!" said Cuthbert. There was a kind of sirocco of dark heat that stole past him. "That something? That it? Am I seeing it?"

"I do not know, *saliq*. It's not so simple. But something is wrong, I sense. This is not how I expected this to go. The Shayk, he is disturbed, I fear. We must leave now. You will see him, I promise, before the night ends."

"The *darkness*—it's fucking roasting, like boiling oil." Cuthbert stuck his head into the gap in the enclosure, ignoring Muezza. He slurred, "A'm ready, ready, ready. To stop killing myself. With booze, right? Help me, Shayk."

Muezza said, in a severe tone, "We really must leave. He can kill you, *saliq*. He is not . . . easy to predict."

"I don't care," said Cuthbert. "Not really."

"Your insect juice speaks now. We do not want to anger him, and you are too important to endanger. You—you caged Kitten-Man—you are more to Allah than even the Shayk. He prepares to stalk upon endless fields of urban darkness, to tear great secrecies, flesh from bone, and we must accept that. It is a powerful thing to be blessed to behold, but we don't want to behold it now."

"Why is he angry?"

"I don't know," said Muezza. "Perhaps because of the invasion of the comet cult. Something is wrong. He left before we could talk with him. That is sometimes . . . his way."

"But I don't 'behold' anything! I want to stop. To stop the Flōt!" Cuthbert beseeched. "I want my fucking otters. And my brother! For England's sake, they really must be found."

The cat didn't seem to hear him. "We must go," said the cat. "This is how Allah's will has worked! If you wish to find Drystan, let's go."

Muezza began running ahead in the direction he wanted Cuthbert to follow, then trotting back to goad him on when Cuthbert hesitated, craning his head around to look back at the opened cage, several times, like Lot's wife. He felt bitterly disappointed in the failure of the meeting to lead to a sense of imminent hope over his Flōtism, or even to get him closer to finding the Gulls. He stumbled after the cat, not knowing where precisely to put his feet, reeling a bit.

"I don't believe you!" said Cuthbert. "Look at your Shayk. When we came to pay our respects, he offers nothing. No sounds. Noth-

ing. I still will drink, won't I? Just glimpses of something dark—
and possibly asleep?—moving inside its box? This is the end of your
Green Line, your One True Path? D'yow think I'm saft?"

Muezza stopped trotting along in his fussy cat prance, and shook
his head. He said, "So narrow, so ephemeral, so small is this way of
thinking! Surely you are in pain and suffering, because this could
not be our Mahdi talking. This is your Flōtism, poor one. It wants
you to want everything now, now, now. I will tell you once more,
the Shayk will take you to Allah. He is your ally. He will have a part
in grave future events, but you, not he, are the key. And Drystan,
too—he *will* appear. Do you not understand what just happened?"

Cuthbert said, "Oh, I understand too well now. You have
tricked me into doing something very very stupid. I understand it
perfectly."

"I did not trick you, most assuredly I say to you. But stay on the
Green Line. I warn you."

"Ha! Let's not talk, OK?"

For a while, they did not. Then Muezza said, "Cuthbert, my
saliq, you have just released the Shayk. He is without question the
most important one of our kind on the earth, except for you, of
course. The moment we stepped away from his sight, I assure you,
he left his prison. A new era has arrived! The Dajjal will perish, in
a pool of fire. Don't you comprehend the consequence of this occasion?"

The cat lay on its side for a moment and looked up at Cuthbert,
with a sort of smile on its muzzle. "I do not know precisely how he
will get you off Satan's milk, but it will come about, just as surely
as the day follows the night. He is the Shayk of Night. He controls
all things of the dark. He will prise you away from your Flōt orbs,
somehow."

"Well," said Cuthbert. "I'll believe it when it 'appens."

It was not exactly "the moment we stepped away," but when the spiring man and his ghost cat staggered from the rough slash in the fencing, the zoo's melanistic leopard specimen—and his name actually was Montgomery—did exit his cage and slink silently into the night. Old Monty, as his keepers called him, was a larger example of *Panthera pardus*—twelve stone, twenty-eight inches at the shoulder, and massive, muscular skull. He did not care about Sufism, or green lines, or Cuthbert's spiring madness, or Anglo-Saxon saints.

Nor was he very hungry, not yet. He was something much more dangerous than that: he was outside a routine he had been habituated to for the nine years of his life in captivity, and he was both terrified and curious.

the autonewsmedia rolls in

CUTHBERT WAS SEVERAL DOZEN YARDS FROM THE
big cats area when he was sure that he heard sirens. He could
swear, too, there was the man's voice again, a man calling out. His
head was playing tricks on him again, it seemed. He wondered
what had happened to the jackals. He feared they would come after
the sand cats. And how would he himself handle an encounter with
them?

He told Muezza of his concern about the jackals, but Muezza
only gave a chirpy chuckle.

"I *know* jackals," said Muezza finally, and rather pompously.
"They are really just East African foxes. They are harmless to me,
inshallah, and thus to you. We can kill them all. But I don't smell
them, not anywhere close. I smell monkeys."

"I don't see how that could be true," said Cuthbert. "I found
jackal handiwork close to here. Bit of a scene, really. "

Muezza shook his head, knowingly. "It's kill-play, brother. Just
kill-play." He swatted out with a splayed paw, as if to demonstrate.

Cuthbert realized he was being preached to in terms that applied strictly to the feline universe. It was as if he were getting swim lessons from a shark. Try as he might, he would always lack gills, fins, and a requisite shark brain.

The cat continued: "It's the *fel,* the elephant, you must be careful with. This is known to every animal in the zoo. The jackal is only dangerous if you are young, or sick, or old, and there are more than one of them."

Cuthbert said, "Is that right? How would you know about elephants?"

"How!" the cat hissed. "All the creatures in the zoo know the elephants. I am surprised you would doubt this!"

"I'm still surprised that you're talking. So we're even. I don't even know if you are real."

Muezza said, "There are three in the paddock—Layang, Dilberta, and Mahmoud. The one called Mahmoud killed his keeper last year. The zoo tried to say it was an accident, but it was not. It was not, after all, Mahmoud who stepped on his keeper's head, it was Allah. And that reminds me, it should be said, too, that the *maimum,* the apes, also, are bad, bad ones. Allah has punished certain men by making them apes and monkeys. They are more a spiritual warning to humans than a physical peril."

"You like to gab a bit, don't you?" said Cuthbert. "What's all this cantin' business? You should be more careful."

"Thank you, brother. There is our gossip, of a sort," said the cat. "We—we imprisoned animals—have little else to do, you see."

A terrible, high-pitched howl went up, followed by another, then a series of barks.

"That's them!" said Cuthbert.

"Those are not jackals, I tell you," said Muezza. "They are monkeys—and they are terrifying. The jackals—I sense they are no longer in the zoo at all. They would have left to enter the city. There is news to spread, after all: you are here."

The cat raised his snout up, somewhat pridefully. He said, "It may surprise you to learn that we chordates *all* knew you were coming. I did, and I have been telling all the other creatures. I am the one who asked them all to communicate with you—because you are the green cat-saint of England. It is no mere accident you have come to me, by the way." He was silent for a moment, looking all around himself, slowly, as though something might be spying on them. He added, with a hissy sigh: "It is in their best interests."

Cuthbert felt a chill run up his spine. He was starting to feel as though he needed a drink, frantically. He said, "But others have heard you, too, right?"

Muezza said, "You are the only one. *You.* I think you know the reason."

The cat put his two front paws on Cuthbert's shin and looked up at Cuthbert. "Among the Christians, the animals spoke on the night of their messiah's birth. This I do not believe. There would, after all, be nothing to discuss. In the Holy Qur'an, it says that not since the days of Solomon have human beings known the speech of animals—'*O people! We have been taught the speech of birds!*' But now you are here—the Mahdi—to save us from Dajjal."

"A'm the what? I'm to save us from what?"

"From the Antichrist."

Muezza coiled tightly around Cuthbert's foot. "You believed in the Christ of Otters, correct? Well, what is the Christ of Otters, brother, but the Redeemer of all, the bringer of the end of days? And who is His harbinger? There is only the Mahdi—that is who. And *you* are him—and you and I and everything and everyone tonight are inside you, *saliq*—that is also true. We may call you the John the Baptist or Cuthbert or something else—but it is the same. They are all the Mahdi. On the authority of Abu Huyrayrah the Kitten-Man, I say to you: Allah will make the night long until the Mahdi comes!"

"No," said Cuthbert. "I must be *dead*—that's what's happening here. A'm gone—jedded, mate. And *yow* are not real."

Muezza, standing in front of Cuthbert, blocked his way down the path. "Yes, brother. I am not real, as you say. I am from the dimension of the *jinna*—the subtle universe beneath the one where men live."

"Oh, that's helpful," Cuthbert said.

The pair moved on.

He felt baffled and irritated by Muezza's latest claims for him, but he also found it hard not to indulge the idea of saving all the animals.

Cuthbert didn't understand why he hadn't run into the jackals. He wondered if they had indeed escaped into the park and therefore into London. Yet the growling, bleating, baying cacophony stirring around them had increased, especially from the northern areas of the park, where the main entrance lay. And although he mistook them for the vanguard of an alien attack, one autonewsmedia flying drone and a Red Watch frightcopter were already beginning to hum in the sky above Regent's Park, searching for the sources of the disturbance at the zoo.

Muezza fixated on a tall Opticall dish and transmitter from ITN/WikiNous that had spoked high into the air. Cuthbert and the cat could easily see it from inside the zoo.

"It is an abomination," he said. "Satan's big white spoon!"

It was actually part of an automated news-reporting vehicle, no doubt attracted to the zoo by police Opticall activity. A camera operator and half-literate producer from ITN sometimes rode inside these automatic-news gliders, but human staff weren't strictly necessary—"raw" footage, usually posted with a vocalized caption or two: "OK, coopy-coo friends of WikiNous, we got buck-chuck troubles at the London Zoo"—was very popular on the open reaches of WikiNous, even among aristocrats.

For his part, Muezza instantly recognized, in his own way, the tall white stick with a lozenge-shaped dish on its top.

"It's definitely the soul-killing infidel device of Baphomet," the cat said. "This is a tool from outside the desert, I am sure. This kind of thing is surely what destroyed the Hittites—old friends of the cat. The Luciferians have brought the machines of the great demon, Baphomet."

It made all too perfect sense to Cuthbert, yet it was the agitated animals *inside* the zoo that concerned him more. Something, if not jackals, or someone, was upsetting them.

Above the din, there also now floated a siren-like, glissando duet. Cuthbert had never heard such a song. It emitted from a pair of crested gibbons, who, like so many of the zoo's specimens, were the only of their kind on earth who had ever lived in the wild. The melodies rose up and up and vibrated in the wind like red paper streamers. They were not far from Cuthbert, it seemed, and he felt excited, but puzzled, too.

"Do you know that wonderful sound?" he asked Muezza.

The cat said, with rich condescension, "It is an unpleasant noise. I have heard it in the zoo, but never seen its origin. Yet I know the sound: some kind of *apes*. These monsters are upset because the Shayk of Night now moves around the zoo. They are warning other apes. They despise cats, so they despise you, too, Kitten-Man, my Mahdi."

"It is impossible for them to be against me. They don't know me from Adam. And I don't look like you or the Shayk or the lions or any cat."

"But you are not part of their stinking monkey race," the cat said.

"Are they—the apes—against the otters, too?"

"Yes, of course. I told you: otters are Britain's *natural* cats. They are more *cat* than your stray moggies of Hackney."

"Of course, you're wrong on this bit, I'm sure. You're barmy and absurd and I won't listen to another word," said Cuthbert. "That monkey, erm, monkey madrigal sort of thing, well, it's the most beautiful sound I've ever heard, it is. It's bostin."

The cat said, "Yes. You are right, about its beauty. But it does not honor the Shayk, or you, or Allah. Apes do not love God. They don't even love other apes. They love violence and anger. But what you say, I will believe. You are the correct one always and—"

"You're talking bloody flannel now," said Cuthbert. "I'm a kind of ape, you know."

Muezza laughed so hard he had to roll onto his back. His fat golden paws stuck up, quivering.

"The Mahdi, he jokes now. It's very funny. This is 'dark' humor."

"I'm a human bloke," said Cuthbert. "I am a primate form."

"This is very humorous," said Muezza. "But it is time for me to leave. I have many deserts to cross, to spread the news, that salvation has come to all the cats of the world."

This upset Cuthbert. He felt he was beginning to love this mixed-up sand cat. He felt that a connection between human and feline had been wrought, even if clouded by the cat's messianism. In the loneliness of his Flōtism, creatures who approved of him were rare.

"Please," Cuthbert said, "don't go. I will be your Mahdi."

"Of course you will," said Muezza. "But go I must. The end-times are upon us, and I have hundreds of rodents to slaughter. I say, thank you, Abu Hurayrah, thank you, Kitten-Man, thank you, al-Mahdi, thank you, O Lord of the Wonderments. I will see you again, someday. You shall see!"

"Ridiculous cat," he muttered.

CUTHBERT FLOUNDERED FOR a few moments, searching for the Green Line. He heard the apes singing again and turned toward them. He felt he might as well locate the ape singers and ask *them* what they meant. He tripped several more motion detectors as he stumbled on. Bunch after bunch of lights snapped on. From a distance, near the edge of Regent's Park, the switching on of the lights looked eerily floral, full of glimmering white-pinks and white-greens, like the aurora borealis. But up close, on the other side of the zoo fence, where authorities were assembling, the lights appeared harsh, as if some rough wedge of white was being hammered into the aged zoo, spuming out from its southeastern corner and into its sternum.

For a while, Muezza and Cuthbert walked together toward the pretty notes, and then the cat slunk away to his ivy-covered secrecies of Sufi dreams.

"I'm not any savior," Cuthbert slurred aloud, thinking the cat was still beside him. A hideous self-pity filled him. "I'm not al-Mahdi. I don't know why my gran had to tell me about any focking Wonderments. I'm a Black Country fool, and I've accomplished nothing."

But he had achieved something: five jackals, three sand cats, and one black leopard were now free.

five

alarm at the seamen's rest

WHEN THE ORANGE-FREQ ALERT WENT OFF IN IN-
spector Astrid Sullivan's eyes that night, it was just about the last
thing in the world she felt able to cope with. After years of a relatively happy recovery from Flōt addiction in Flōters Anonymō,
Astrid was one of the few Britons to make it to the agonizing
second-withdrawal from Flōt, which typically occurred around a
dozen years after first withdrawal. She hadn't been able to get over
to Highbury's public pool that day for her usual soothing, salutary
swim, and she felt especially bonkers. As a senior constabulary
officer, she was allowed to set Optispam and adverts to "off," but
she couldn't stop King Henry's official bulletins (no British subject
could)—and she couldn't stop a fucking bloody orange-freq.

The freq's flame animations lashed across her corneas. The
alerts were meant to shock officers to attention, and they worked.
A steady accompanying pair of *eeps* and *ʒungas* screamed and clan-
gored into the auditory ganglia, so directly they turned eardrums
into minuscule audio speakers. If one stood beside a recipient of
such orange-freqs, one could *hear* the victim's ears. The sensate

assault on Astrid's skull could hardly clash more with the familiar
damp basement kitchen of the old Seamen's Rest, where she was
making—*trying to make*—her famously vile tea for her Flōters
Anonymō meeting.

Eep, eep, eep, eep! Zunga-gunga-gunga!

"Can't," she said, nearly whimpering. "Can fucking not. Not
now."

She put her fingertips up to her eyes and flicked off the alert's text
without reading it. She could get fired for that, but she just didn't
care. The digital fire in her eyes stopped, but the noise wouldn't
until she read the bloody thing, and soon it would transform into a
steady chittering shriek. Should she read it? No, no—not yet.

Eep, eep, eep, eep! Zunga-gunga-gunga!

The basement had a badly cracked cement floor painted the
color of rotten oysters. A small SkinWerks panel squawked with
SkyNews/WikiNous in the background. A seaweedy, salty smell
hung in the air.

Eeeeeeeeeeeeeeeeeeeeep! Eeeeeeeeeeeeeeeeeeeeeep!

"Fuck!" she gasped, trying to tune the noise out. It was a skill
she was growing fairly adept at, along with her newly acquired
compulsion to swim laps at Highbury pool, which often seemed
to be the only way she could settle her mind and body. She got on
her knees to reach two enormous steel teapots on a lower shelf, ancient pots, greasy things with decades and decades of orange-black
flame marks up their sides and their Bakelite handles in spidery
cracks.

THAT THE POLICE OFFICER tasked with after-hours alarms at
the London Zoo was herself a Flōter might seem a mordant coincidence. But so pervasive was the desire to "get up," few institutions
lacked their share of active addicts, and the Royal Parks Constabu-

lary was no different. If you were Indigent or middle class, and not yet living under a Nexar hood at a Calm House or in soybean-farm serfdom, the defining Scylla-or-Charybdis quandary of the mid-twenty-first century was how to survive the attractions of Flōt versus the milky-sweet promises of the suicide cults.

What made Astrid special was that she was one of a few hundred Flōters in the country who had managed, for now, to break the addiction.

But only just. After eleven years dormant in FA, the dragon of second withdrawal was upon her. Astrid felt incensed it had come to this. She'd done what was suggested. Despite attending meetings semiweekly, volunteering often for tea duties, working with newcomers, relapse and death genuinely threatened her. She couldn't sleep, her muscles hurt, and she endured a daily yearning to push her thumbs into her eyes and gouge out her prefrontal cortex. There were the Flōt cravings, too, of course—cravings that hooked up from the belly like a long silver claw.

THE SEAMEN'S REST, operated by Methodists, was in a forgotten All-Indigent corner of the Isle of Dogs. It was a place she felt she'd consciously condemned herself to in London's struggling Flōters Anonymō community.

She heaved the two pots onto the steel sink counter.

"One last time," she said to the teapots. "Up there, you." She was awake, and alive, and she hadn't evidently topped herself yet. But she wasn't doing tea-making duties again—ever.

The FA meeting merely rented its space at the old Queen Victoria Seamen's Rest, commonly called "the Queen Vic." It was the biggest hostel for Indigent seafarers in Britain, but now it served more as an anachronism from the days when nonautomated ships deposited crews in the Docklands for shore leaves where brothels, barrooms, or the Queen Vic were the only alternatives for accommodation. It was a great, ramshackle pile of Portland stone and brick. Atop the Rest perched a three-foot-high statue of an eagle with a noble hooked beak and indomitable steel eyes. The figure was a little weird, but Astrid associated it with recovery. Eagles protected things, she'd think to herself.

Astrid had left work for the evening a few hours before, and a sickening heaviness now squatted in her stomach. She was getting her bearings, and the continuous *eeeeep!* screech had receded in its power to annoy. "Can't I get one night without an alert?" she said, a whine battling her low, thick voice.

Her two orange-freqs that week had been about young aristocrats having sex at night in the Inner Circle rose garden at Regent's Park, which struck Astrid as rather romantic, really. But couldn't the constables deal with that by themselves?

Taking a long breath, she tapped her eyebrow and called up the dismissed alert text: *Hello Insp Sullivan! Possible to pls. Opticall me? Lamps on @zoo. Sorry! PC JL Atwell.*

The screaming stopped.

The zoo. *What?*

The new probationer—Jasmine Atwell. She was canny, too canny, thought Astrid. PC Atwell did everything by the book, and the upshot was extra work for everyone—at least until her regular sergeant came back from his latest weeklong sickie.

Lights on at zoo? What did that mean? *At the zoo?* False alarms and security-lamp trips were nightly annoyances in the royal parks because of the homeless Indigents who used them to sleep rough. The constables on call at night were unofficially encouraged to pay little heed to the alarms until they invariably stopped. But one at the zoo? A bit odd, that, thought Astrid.

Astrid was more dutiful than many of her colleagues, but she wanted to wait, this time, just a few minutes, before responding.

She needed to calm herself. Her Flōt withdrawal hurt, and it made her feel bonkers. She felt stuck in a sort of cramped, curvilinear awareness with her mind as bare and dark and rubbery as the inside of a cracked tennis ball. Her heart pounded. The zoo! It wasn't the English republicans shooting Mark 66 rockets at Hampton Court, right? It wasn't even a purse snatch. Besides, she was also busy saving her own life, wasn't she? To do that meant finishing two enormous, miserable pots of tea. That's how FA worked. *Serve and recover.* A dozen fellow recovering Flōters, several drug addicts, an old-school alkie or two, and a few plain old psychic bomb-outs—nearly all Indigents—would be showing up within minutes, whinging about tea. Everyone, it seemed to her, complained that her tea was not made early enough, then complained about the tea itself.

Tea done? Tea done? Ooooh, good girl, loovly, loovly—but it's a bit thin, innit?

a chest of drawers filled with tears

ASTRID TRIED TO HURRY UP, AND A METAL POT lid slipped from her hand and clattered on the floor. She made a big point of rinsing it off. Sykes, the Rest's caretaker, was in his room, watching her every move, tonight as every night she was tea-maker.

She knew that her guv at the constabulary, Chief Inspector Bobby Omotoso, wouldn't mind if she needed a few extra minutes to respond to this sort of freq. To her guv, Astrid's being an abstinent, reformed Flōter suggested a noble destiny hard to find at the outmoded constabulary, and he tended to indulge her. She'd once spent a few years working at the Houston Police Department to boot, as part of an Interpol Prime exchange program. The experience put a bright Texas star above Astrid's name in the guv's mind.

"You will be something big someday," he once opined, answering a question Astrid hadn't asked, and sounding as if *he* ought to know its answer. "But how am I supposed to know what? How?"

A stout, overburdened Anglo-Nigerian from a family that practiced Yoruba religion, the guv was also fascinated by American policing methodologies and their implied moralistic bents. He felt Astrid's Texas experience made the whole constabulary look better.

"*Hugh-Stone, Texas*, I'm sure, is London's future," he'd once said to a quietly chagrined Astrid. "There's not all this English *depression*. And you *know* I've an uncle in Houston. And now, can you tell me how many officers would be scheduled to neuralzinger-range practice at once? I am trying to picture these astonishing training days in my head."

"I think, erm, about ten per subdistrict. And there were about five subdistricts having a go at once, guv."

"Impressive. That's firepower! We send, what . . . two at a time? How are we going to win against the republicans, like that?"

Astrid glanced behind her and looked at the door where the caretaker was pretending to watch a tiny SkinWerks screen—god knows how he, as an Indigent, could afford it—he'd sprayed over his tremoring, skinny forearm. Astrid knew his telly-watching was partly an act. He was just waiting for her to try to pocket one of the church's own teaspoons, or to burn the place down. They went through the same thing every week. The sobriety of FA members meant nothing to the suspicious Sykes, who may well have been a Red Watch informant. Henry IX, it was said, generally tolerated FA and other older self-help fellowships, but that didn't mean he trusted them. If they kept English souls out of the suicide cults, and cost no Treasure, he would endure them. Meanwhile, people like Sykes stood ready to inform on them for the slightest sign of sedition.

Sykes shook his head, pretending to be outraged at whatever rubbish he was watching on his stingy-small screen; he met Astrid's eyes with his own for an awkward second, then turned back to his flesh-telly.

"Lights," she whispered to herself. It was surely not a big problem.

It was an odd one, however. But what if it was a B&E?* Then what?

She realized that she'd forgotten to get out the artificial sweetener, a product called Smile invented in the 2030s. It came in tiny dissolving sheets you pulled from a pastel-green dispenser, and it tasted like bitter orange-blossom honey. The Flōtheads loved it. She bent down and reached far back into the cupboard, but there was something in the way.

She had to slide out a small, obstructing wooden box. It was a strange old thing she'd noticed before, designed to resemble a ship—the HMS *Victory*—with a profile of the famous yellow and black vessel painted on each side. She looked at it more closely. There was a tiny, rusty little padlock on it. The lock unclasped when she instinctively pulled on it. Broken, she thought. Figures. She threw open the box.

There was a miniature bottle of Bacardi rum—half-empty. There was a likely unplayable, century-old audiocassette tape with BOB MARLEY scrawled in pink on its label. There was also a large bag of Bassetts Jelly Babies, torn opened. Someone had eaten all but the black currant jellies, and those were smashed and decomposing. The Smile was there, too, in the wrong place, its minty-green dispenser pried open, with only a few sheets left.

"Weird fucks," she said. "Who does this shit?" She picked up the bottle and turned it in her fingers. It was tempting, but she knew it was far too little to do anything but torture her. Only Flōt would scratch the itch she felt. (And Sykes was watching, of course.) She grabbed the Smile, closed the box, and shoved the HMS *Victory* back into its cupboard.

Astrid knew she would not be able to relax now. The zoo was normally the single bit in the royal parks that the constabulary never worried about, especially at night. Being on call for the zoo

---

* Breaking and entering

was normally tantamount to a free night. The zoo staff did safety drills, of course, semiannually—but these posited daylight emergencies. There was already a built-in guard, of sorts, an Indigent night keeper with a small apartment fashioned into the old Reptile House. Astrid had met him once, long ago. Dawkins. A strange, very fat young gent with a narrow head and obsessed with a passé steampunk magazine called *Hiss*. He was, she'd heard, weirdly possessive of the Reptile House.

And now this. *Lights on at the zoo?*

She counted out ten Typhoo tea-spheres and set them aside on the counter. They were about half the spheres needed for a pot, but tea's price was up to £20 a box. She touched her fingertips to her brow again—an Opticall-related tick many experienced. Before FA, she had been getting sloppy on the job, she remembered, and not handling her Flōt too well. And there had been a sexy man in Houston, too, a topiary shop manager with full lips and long thighs, a man who was as cleverly tidy about pouring an orb of Flōt as he was with fica shrubs. Astrid had wanted to impress him—and look what happened. She'd disgraced herself in Texas. So here she was, several years into a second chance, back in Blighty. Was she getting sloppy again?

If Astrid knew that Omotoso thought well of her, and even took advantage of that a bit, she also knew he was under pressure this year from the constabulary's overly promoted and overtaxed senior commander, Derek Brown, who was in turn being monitored carefully by the Royal Parks Advisory Board and the Red Watch, and even, it was said, by Harry9's secretive Privy Council. In the past year, ministerial scrutiny had trained upon what it considered the Royal Parks Constabulary's general obsolescence and Commander Brown's poor leadership.

The luminous Jasmine Atwell, on the other hand, had an ambition and intelligence that forced her supervisors to pay attention and work the details, and she was exactly the kind of earnest, whip smart PC the constabulary needed. The trouble was, no one like Atwell ever wanted to stay with the "Parkies." From the paddle-boats at Hyde to the cardinal click beetles at Richmond to the pelicans at St. James, there was little drama and not one iota of policing glamour. If a constable was lucky, she might one day get to arrest a molester of the swans. (Through the twenty-first century, most of the smaller regional and specialist British police forces had been absorbed by London's Met or obviated by the Red Watch—"national policing," all the rage in America, had become the order of the day in the UK, too, with an added Windsor crest.) There was much talk of shuttering the parks constabulary. With half the officers pulling sickies half the time, and the Home Office police forces and the upper echelons of the Red Watch picking off new, freshly trained probationers, it was in trouble, and every day a little more isolated from mainstream policing.

All this accentuated Astrid's own feeling of being cut off from any connections, human, animal, or otherwise, with second withdrawal's anger searing nearly every thought. She hadn't been touched by any lover in at least a year, and she suffered almost nightly insomnia, typically waking at 5:00 A.M. and finding herself unable to sleep again.

Among FA members, second withdrawal was often simply called, like the last minute in a football match, "The Death," and it was always suffered in isolation because no one could handle it, and users inevitably went back to Flōt.

Or killed themselves.

But Astrid knew isolation, and it hadn't killed her yet, had it? She'd grown up in Bermondsey with a single parent, somewhat overprotected, her mum her only source of kisses, hugs, or real love as a child. The two had remained profoundly attached until recently (her mother suffered from an Alzheimer's-like syndrome, caused by a virus called Bruta7). But long before the neurodegenerative disorder, their relationship felt, as Astrid grew older, increasingly musty, restrictive. During Astrid's time in Houston, she felt as if she were, in this universe, wretchedly sui generis—a freak of aloneness. She'd spent thousands of dollars on international calls to her mum, and on Flōt.

The aloneness almost felt genealogical to Astrid. Her mum was herself the product of a one-night stand between an Indigent barmaid and a mysterious man who came from somewhere up north. She never met her grandfather, but like so many of the men in her family—like so many men of the twenty-first century, really—he was said to have been ravaged by alcohol and Flōt. She never met her own father, either, and her mother would say almost nothing about him. "He's not worth the air it takes to verbalize what I'm saying now," she once told a young Astrid. "But your grandfather—he was special."

"What do you mean, Mum?"

"He knew things. He was from some deeper England—deeper and wilder and a bit scarier."

"Couldn't be scarier than now," Astrid had answered.

Her clever mum had read literature at Durham, worked as a freelance subeditor at a WikiNous research office in Islington, struggling against ghastly odds to prevent herself and her only child from getting reclassified Indigent. Unlike almost everyone they knew, they went to church, Catholic church, no less, every Sunday morning, to the nearly empty black-bricked Our Lady of La Salette & St. Joseph, in Melior Street. She prayed hard as a child, too, crunched into the pew, clutching the cultured-pearl rosary from her gran in Galway.

Once, as a teenager, her mother had caught her rummaging through the chest of drawers in her bedroom. The thing that devastated Astrid more than anything about that day, as she grabbed at pillowcases and rectangles of cedar, was what she *couldn't* find in her mum's chest. There were no old photographs, no documents, no locks of hair. All she located of interest was her gran's rosary and a brittle old paperback titled *Flow My Tears, the Policeman Said*. And nothing else. Just pants and socks and wood and torment.

"Tell me," she had screamed at her mum, tears streaming. "Tell me! Where the fuck is he? Who is he?"

Her mother's face screwed up. "He was a drunk, my love. Your dad was, and your granddaddy was, too. That's it, unvarnished."

Her mother sat down on the bed. She softly wept.

"I'm sorry, my lamb," she said, her voice muffled. She sat back up, wiping away a string of snot, and she clasped both of her daughter's long, cold hands. "But your grandfather—he wasn't *just* a sot. He was quality, Astrid. An uncommon one. I . . . er . . . I don't know where he was from, exactly—Shropshire? Something north of the Thames, anyway. And I don't even . . . I don't *even* know his name. But he was charming, said Grandma, and crazy."

Instead of her father, it was the excruciatingly delivered image of her "north of the Thames" *grandfather*—as a kind of paranormal, benighted inamorato, half an aged poet, half a mental patient—that stuck with Astrid. She could hardly have been more primed to meet a certain night visitor to the zoo.

the grumpy caretaker

ASTRID PULLED THE SPIGOTS WIDE OPEN ON THE faucets. The noise of the water splashing into the empty sink was stupendous, like a tropical storm on a tin roof in Bali.

She noticed that Sykes had stood up now in his "office," as he called it, and begun watching her again.

"Something the matter?" Astrid asked. It was an aggressive thing to say, and she immediately regretted it.

Sykes was a dispirited-looking, head-wagging Indigent with a yellowish complexion. He rarely uttered a word, but he watched that SkinWerks panel in his room with the door left partially open. He was always there when Astrid showed, but if Astrid so much as glanced at him, he averted his eyes and pushed the door closed an inch or two, often using the arm with the panel blaring off it. A few minutes later, Astrid would notice that the office door was opened even farther.

"I heard a noise," Sykes said, almost snarling. The fact that he said anything at all took Astrid by surprise.

She spluttered, "Oh, well, the sinks? You mean the sinks?"

Sykes shook his head, his nostrils flaring ever so subtly. "No, it sounded like a little bird."

"That's my orange-freq. They're very loud. That's all." Astrid hesitated. "I'm a kind of a police inspector, believe it or not. I'm 'on call' tonight—sort of. It's my eyes—and my ears—right? That's all."

"An inspector!" Sykes sat back down and pushed the door to, almost shutting it. "Tsh. Inspector!"

Through the window on the door, he gave Astrid one of his especially opprobrious looks. He possessed a few of them—a don't-waste-our-water stare, don't-make-excessive-noise, don't-burn-down-the-Rest-with-your-fellow-solunauts'-noxious-cigarettes, don't-keep-secret-birds. And above all, there was a don't-lie-about-your-job glower.

Sykes turned up the volume on his telly, so loud the sound from the SkinWerks panel distorted a bit.

The grumpy Sykes had a thing against FA, it seemed—after all, the fellowship comprised people who were, by definition, admitted misfits, colonizing the "community rooms" of half London's churches and missions, messing up their kitchens, fiddling with their stoves, borrowing and occasionally stealing (Astrid felt sure he believed this) their limited supply of old, crooked, stained teaspoons, ad nauseam. She wondered if Sykes had a problem with the tipple himself, and was sublimating his self-hatred, or with women.

She started sloshing old tea sediment out of the pots. She turned the pots upside down in the sink and looked at the thousands of dark dots that formed a layer on the sink bottom.

Sykes's telly was broadcasting the news. Astrid found it hard not to listen. A homemade video of the cult leader Marshall Applewhite was being discussed. Astrid turned off the spigots and stepped closer. She found the Heaven's Gate business compelling, but in a detached, academic way. She felt a bit jealous of police who got to deal with the suicide cults. She pushed the caretaker's door open gently.

"Mind if I watch?"

Sykes glared at her, fuming, but then he said, "Of course not."

A woman with long, widely set eyes was being interviewed. A caption read that she was a cult expert who worked for one of King Harry9's new mental health institutes. She was saying, with visible anger, "People get drawn into these thought systems a step at a time. The person is never told at the outset what the bottom line is going to be." One of the cult's infamous videos came on. Applewhite was dressed in a sparkly silver tunic of sorts, hair shaved short, with a shimmering purple pleated curtain behind him. Total freakstyle, Astrid thought. Her practical-minded mum—who had nonetheless moved earth and sky to send Astrid to independent schools as a child—would have called him a tosser.

Applewhite was saying, in a silky, unctuous voice: "I feel that we are at the end of the age. Now, I don't want to sound like a prophet, but my gut says that it's going to come in the next year or two. I could be off a few years, too."

Astrid had read in yesterday's paper that Applewhite a few years back had gone to Mexico, paid a fee, and been castrated. She found herself respecting the sheer physical courage of the man.

Applewhite and his cohorts apparently kept an American five-dollar bill in their pockets at all times for some reason. All the cult members did. This seemed like an intriguing fact to Astrid. She watched with Sykes for a few more seconds, then went back to the big stainless sink and jerked the cold water spigot back on. That was the downside of America, the violence bit, with a few people like Applewhite—cloying in their amiableness and yet murderous to the core. But you had them in England these days, too, didn't you?

Astrid decided to say something conversational to Sykes, some-thing to demonstrate that she wasn't insensitive to the spectacle of a mass, stupid suicide, wasn't below vapid, even prurient interest in it, provided a certain perspective held. She turned two of the stove gas burners on, and they whispered on with a faint "pa" sound. She said to Sykes, gamely, "Never join a religion less than a thousand years old, I say." She felt a slight pinch in her tummy. "I believe in Buddha, myself."

Sykes didn't say a word or look. He pulled his office door closed. Astrid felt like an idiot. She said, not very loudly, "I don't mean I believe *in* him." But Sykes wouldn't have heard a thing.

When the water boiled, Astrid dropped five tea spheres in each pot. She enjoyed watching them float like little scalding suns as the pekoe orange color bloomed around them. She gave each pot a stir with a wooden spoon. It was 7:45—the recovering Flōters of the meeting, mostly first-withdrawal survivors, would be upstairs hem-ming and hawing by now, asking the same faintly critical question they already knew the answer to: "Who's the tea-maker this week?" They bloody well knew who the tea-maker was.

But try to get one of *them* to volunteer and make tea.

Astrid felt modicums of pleasure and pride as she delivered the pots of tea. She forgot about the zoo and Atwell's Opticall text. *Serve and recover.* She marched each pot upstairs, one at a time, to the room where the meeting was held. When she walked in, a few of the regulars smiled her way.

"Ah, Astrid, my dream love," said a homeless man, Burt, speak-ing in a wry tone made spitty and wet by his missing teeth. "You are one I want to marry."

"Hello, Burt," she said.

It usually didn't bug her that the other addicts would do nothing to help her, but today their inaction seemed churlish. Everyone in her FA group knew she was on the cusp of second Flōt withdrawal, a trial few recovering Flōters survived.

And Astrid made things difficult for those who tried to help her. She would have been bothered had they attempted it, and she would have tried to co-opt every task herself. And by god, if there were lamps on at the zoo, Atwell or no Atwell, she knew now she was going to have to turn them off herself. I'll do that, as usual. Sure. I always do the bit that needs done.

Need help, Astrid?

No, she always said.

I can do this. I can do almost anything.

the problem with people like marcus

ASTRID CLUNKED EACH POT ON A HEAVY TABLE. She put out the sugar and Smile and milk. She quickly dealt out a couple cylinders of Jaffa Cakes, organizing them in two concentric circles on a pretty, ancient piece of Wedgwood she had found in the basement. In the center of the plate was a bucolic scene of a shepherd and shepherdess cuddling by a brook-side while a dairy cow and two lambs looked on. On the rim of the plate were wildflowers—a light purple marsh-mallow, a butter-colored primrose, tight white coils of Irish lady's tresses.

Next, she put out a small plastic tray with a pink and yellow Battenberg. One of the Indigent fellows who still slept rough, Ed, who'd come to London from Galway in the early '20s and claimed that the homeless were suffering from a contemporary, secret holocaust in London ("the Watch are killing thousands of us, I tell you!"), almost immediately cleared half the plate of Jaffa Cakes, stuffing more than a few into his reeking coat pocket. Astrid said nothing.

Then she remembered her orange-freq. She'd better find out

exactly what Atwell wanted. Must be more than zoo lights. Later though—the moment the meeting ends. The guv wouldn't mind that.

THE SUBJECT OF THE MEETING was "honesty," a standard FA meeting topic. Astrid was glad for the meeting's start because she actually wanted to tell people about how much pain she was in as the crisis of second withdrawal deepened. Here was one last chance to describe her sense of hollow loneliness, her shameful feeling of not fitting at Indigent-dominated FA meetings, her new cravings. If I let it out, she thought, the monsters would be out and free and down to size. A problem shared is half a problem, promised the old twelve-step adage.

She found her mind wandering, to the water. How she loved to plunge into the lapping lanes at Highbury, with something nearing desperation. The marks of stress would wash off her back like wet bandages. She swam with power, a salubrious self-centeredness, and a kind of aggression that was very different in tone from anything anyone ever saw at Highbury. She was thirty-two years old, and her arms and legs looked more robust than those of many of the men in the constabulary.

About a dozen Flōters and addicts were at the meeting now, and most were people Astrid actually felt deep affection for: there was Gerard, the ex–economics professor with a thick accent who had been banned, literally and, somehow, legally, from his hometown in the obscure farmlands of Alsace. The lovely pensioner, Tom P.— the one second-withdrawal survivor she'd met—was on hand, too. He seemed educated, but he wore the torn clothes typical of Indigents. He also claimed to be a former Dominican brother from County Kerry who, having slept in cemeteries during his homelessness, said he pined for graveyards even yet: "They're the only quiet in London," he would say, "like gifts from God, and larger by the day." Astrid liked Tom—loved him even. As with many of the people at the meetings in East London, Tom had little money. But he was no skiver. When he first got sober, years before, he had worked his way up the ladder at a Catholic social services agency. He was handy with wood. He built intricate dollhouses for his granddaughters, and he had one expression he had become locally famous for in FA: "The best is yet to come." Because he was the only addict at the Seamen's Rest past second Flōt withdrawal, the adage was freighted with irony.

An irate Irish single mother named Louisa, whom Astrid felt unaccountably intimidated by, was taking her turn to rave about how she wanted to stab a man at another FA meeting who had told her to "work the steps." With her thick, curly blond hair and freckled skin, she was dreadfully gorgeous. Like Astrid, Flōt-recovery anger was strangling her, too, but unlike Astrid, Louisa was nowhere near second withdrawal, and sometimes Astrid wished she knew what she was in for—an anger that would crush rubies like grapes and stab more than a few errant Flōtheads.

Louisa said, in a mock ladylike tone, "Oh, I just need to examine myself. That's right, how could I be so thick?" Then she said, "I'm being honest: I wanted to top this prat." Louisa was always right up front about people who bothered her, whom she placed in the ignominious categories of "gits" and "prats." She scared the bejesus out of Astrid, but she often felt she shared her rage, and was comforted that so many others accepted her. Louisa gave her a sense of hope. She wished she would be so open.

When Louisa finished, Astrid tried to speak up. She wanted to start in with the orange-freqs driving her crazy that week— yes, fucking *bloody* lights on at the *fucking* bloody zoo, for fuck's sake—and the stupid useless constabulary wouldn't know a terrorist from a hippofuckingpotamus, and the filthy teapots, and

Sykes watching her, and his spiteful little skin-screen, and how none of you cunts know a fucking *thing* about withdrawal because you stupid *twats* always *use* before you get within a decade of it, you *fucking cunts*!

But it suddenly seemed awkward to talk at all, and Louisa had just sounded so confident, and then Astrid, at that moment, couldn't see how her thoughts even *vaguely* related to "Honesty."

"I feel a bit off at my job," she began, "and I've these wicked new cravings for the stuff. And I've got this naff alarm tonight, again, another naff, time-wasting alarm, and this time it's at the zoo, right?" She hesitated. "I'm just trying to be honest, right?" It was a moronic beginning, she felt.

She continued: "See, it's a bit of a bore, really. I actually feel like I understand why so many people are killing themselves in those cults and all. I'm not doing that, but I understand, right? Again, I'm trying to be honest, right?" She paused and noticed that all the friendly chatter in the room had stopped; when others spoke, people still felt free to carry on a bit in whispers. But Astrid, in second withdrawal, after all, was *so serious*. It was oppressive.

"Let me offer a bit of . . . context, first?" she said.

She heard Burt whisper moistly, "What's that mean? What's 'con-tex'?"

Right beside her was Tom P., who had been carefully dropping bits of tobacco into his old Golden Virginia rolling machine. Tom put the device on his knee and sat up, as if he had been misbehaving while a schoolmarm intoned facts. Astrid was swept with stomach-churning self-consciousness. Why did she always have to sound so stiff at FA meetings? she asked herself miserably. But she went on, she had to: "Oh dammit, how do I put this? You all know I work for the Royal Parks Police. I have a staff of twelve PCs and three sergeants who cover the Hyde and Regent's parks. Well, my Opticall panels are going off even tonight and I just can't answer this time, and I don't think I'll ever go back to work again—I'm packing it in. I feel as though I want to act out, if you understand?" She looked down into her hands, and opened and closed them into limps fists. "There are lights on—at the fucking zoo. The zoo! I need to tell you about that. Does that make sense?"

Tom leaned forward in his chair, and twisted to one side. He looked directly at Astrid with a strange expression, raising his eyes and gritting his teeth, and then it struck: a magnificent, darkly pneumonic, arse-splitting fart. It was loud and proud, though poor Tom instantly turned crimson.

"Oh, I'm sorry."

The whole room exploded. A few people stood up, slapping their legs and doubling over. The chairperson of the meeting, a wintry-souled Glaswegian named Fred, started banging a tiny wooden gavel. "Oooo-kay! Oooo-kay!" he kept saying. "Let the laaaaaaaay-dee have her say." But then Fred's face broke into a helpless grin. He still banged the gavel, but no one, least of all himself, was able to pay attention to anything other than the complete hilarity of the situation.

Just then, a small, tightly built Indigent named Marcus, whom she didn't care for, goaded, "Keep talking, Astrid. Keep it up!"

Astrid was mortified. She pretended to laugh, too, but the impulse had to be entirely, and not easily, faked. Here she had been trying to discuss an important issue in her life, one that involved economic security and moral impropriety and the society of peers and madness and depression, and she had lost the floor to juvenile crudeness. It seemed to her that with the stink had also come a total disillusionment with this meeting. She instinctively blamed people like Marcus—but part of her knew this wasn't the problem. She was the problem. The zoo was the problem.

Fred said, "Go ahead, Astrid. You finish what you were saying, lassy." A rivulet of milky tea had spiked out from beneath her chair;

someone had knocked over a cup. She heard Louisa say, "Fuck! Get a tea towel! Get that stuff sopped up now!"

Astrid said, "I think that's it. I said what I needed to say."

"No it's not, out with it," someone said. "Please, Astrid."

"Shouldn't a copper be answering her Opticalls," another person cracked.

"Hey, listen," Astrid said, irritably.

The silence came on again. All the snickering ended—it was as if Astrid Sullivan was a scythe of sternness, mowing down every sign of good humor in the room. By the time she felt, after a long silence, that she might start in again about her job, and perhaps broach the more important subject of her deadened emotional life, Marcus jumped in, not even waiting for the traditional "thank you" FA members said after another member spoke.

Marcus said, "Me ex-wife is trying to keep me from seeing my kid, in little, sneaky ways." Shaking his long brown hair mullet, and sniffing, he gazed around to see if anyone was paying attention.

Astrid could almost physically feel the room lighten up and take earnest interest in Marcus's plight. "I bought the boy a bicycle, a three-wheeler trainer thing, and—I'm just going to say it—the two-bone bitch sold the bicycle on that OpticAuctions business!"

Everyone seemed stilled by the intensity of Marcus's words; many bowed their heads.

"I'm sorry," Marcus said, his Dublin brogue coming in. "I'm just angry. I know it's not good but I *hate* her." Several listeners nodded. Louisa put her hand on Marcus's shoulder.

Astrid felt envious and sad about the Seamen's Rest lot's embracing of the hotheaded Marcus over her, then felt angry at herself for her jealousy.

Tom leaned close to her. He said, in a kind, low voice, "Astrid, I'm so sorry. Don't mind us. You *know* an open meeting at the Seamen's Rest isn't necessarily the best place to bring up anything too personal; they'll chew you up here. We *love* you, Astrid, we do. Let's go have a chat after the meeting, OK?"

Astrid usually felt great affection for Tom, but at that moment she wanted to grab one of the pots of tea and dump it on his head. Instead, she smiled. Of course she smiled, and said distantly, "Thanks for the input."

Never had she felt so convinced that she was ready to stop attending FA meetings, something she had never dared do since her first meeting in Houston in 2041.

"Arseholes," she said quietly, tearing up.

Tom nodded, and said, "You're right. But there are other meetings that are much more—you know—civilized and just, er, *intelligent*."

She felt that, at last and unforeseeably, she understood something that had escaped her since 2041: FA's problem is that it's full of Flōters.

"where's my miracle?"

ASTRID LEFT THE MEETING EARLY. ASTOUND-
ingly, it was the first time she had ever done this in eleven years
of FA meetings. She was going to let the others clean up the tea.
Fuck 'em! She heard old Tom calling after her as she walked outside; it was as though he knew something quite awful was happening to Astrid.

"Can I have a word, Astrid?" Tom was saying. "Wait up, girl!"

She pretended she didn't hear and walked toward the wobbly old
Docklands Light Railway station at Poplar. The rotting elevated
walkways toward the crumbling skyscrapers of Canary Wharf,
covered in 3D graffiti and louche adverts, always confused her,
but apart from Canary Wharf itself—where half the offices were
shuttered or tee-hee 5-5* dens—the DLR station was the one place
within half a mile where one could find a quiet nook to make a private audio Opticall. An orange-freq's flames were again whipping
across her eyes, and new shrieking had begun. She felt an odd sen-

---

* An addictive and dangerous recreational drug of the future that causes a
characteristic snicker

sation, something new, as if the zoo itself were sucking her in, swallowing.

The area near the station displayed the usual roaring ugliness of a late midweek evening. Cartons of unsold market produce—brownish clementines, scores of lychees spanned with white mold—overstuffed the rubbish bins along with the day's discarded food wrappers. She felt compelled to duck beneath a giant, purple holographic penis jutting from the station wall along with scads of other obscene 3D images and tags and Army of Anonymous–UK slogans. Spread around the entrances were splayed drink boxes of Ribena, Cokelager orbs, and Lucozade bags.

She found a disused, old phone box with broken windows, across from a train ticket window, and she ducked inside and Opticalled PC Atwell, ignoring the video option and sticking to audio only.

"Hello?" asked Atwell.

Astrid cleared her throat. "Sullivan here. Hope you don't mind if I kill the camera."

"Oh, no, thank you, ma'am," said Atwell. "I actually appreciate it. I smoked a cigarette, and I feel like my head's on Neptune. I can't believe I did that—a stupid git, I am." She gave a little cough. "I'm sorry to disturb you, ma'am. Very sorry. Are you all right, guv? It took awhile. You sound . . ."

"No worries, Atwell," she said, trying to sound weary (but not too weary).

"Well, ma'am, at first I was thinking it's probably nothing, yeah? But now I think it's—a something. A potential emergency."

"I'm sorry? What?"

Atwell continued, "I'm parked on the Broad Walk, in the pandaglider, of course—I'm not getting out alone—and several sets of lights have come *on* at the zoo and—are you sure you're OK, ma'am? And there's an occupied autonews glider here, with its dish set up, and at least one solar-frightcopter."

"A frightcopter?" said Astrid. "Bloody hell. Probably triggered by the autoreporters. That's how these things go—lights trigger autonews, autonews triggers Watch, Watch sends up frightcopters, then we beg Watch to go home, and the bastards blame us for everything." She needed to put a stop to this nonsense. It was rarely good to draw scrutiny from the Watch. You never knew how it would end up—with a demotion, a new title, reclassification, or a Nexar hood, or dinner with the king. "Did you call the night keeper? That's protocol."

"Night keeper, ma'am?"

"At the *zoo*, Atwell. There's this legendary weirdo. He's in the old Reptile House—name's Dawkins." Astrid knew every centimeter of the three thousand hectares in the royal parks, and especially those she was charged with policing—Hyde, Kensington Gardens, and Regent's. Directional details were a point of pride. She could explain every curve of the Serpentine, or navigate blindfolded through the fifty thousand roses of Queen Mary's Garden. But the zoo. Now that was a bit of a blank for Astrid. It was part of the royal parks, but not, too. It was in her constabulary's domain, but not *really*. The police ignored it. It wasn't even wholly London, not when she thought about it.

New Parkies were required to attend zoo crisis drills, but no one took them seriously. Astrid recalled her own training sessions on the zoo several years back when she hired on; and three years ago (through a special arrangement with the Metropolitan Police), she herself had been allowed to help train the keepers to use their neuralzingers, which were kept in a locked case at the security office. The guns were effective against even the largest mammals, but no keeper had ever used one that she recalled.

Like the Open Air Theatre, the zoo was fenced in and required a fee, and generally, you didn't worry about it from a policing perspective. Jurisdictionally, it wasn't parkland, and constables normally would have required explicit permission to enter the zoo, even if in hot pursuit. In fact, the zoo had developed its own security squad, sanctioned by Royal Parks bylaws, and this included an animal recovery team. The team members were all very specialized but very relaxed. One man wore dreadlocks, another a beard as puffy and long as Karl Marx's. But they knew how to coax a lion, how to calm a zebra, or call to an escaped eagle, and now how to kill one of these animals if necessary.

Dubbed the AnimalSafe Squad, it was headed by a very tall, passionate man named David Beauchamp. Astrid didn't particularly like him. Beauchamp didn't fit in with the others, who could have passed for hemp farmers or festival-following crusties. He talked a great, great deal. And he seemed to have zero respect for the constabulary. Chief Inspector Omotoso described him to Astrid as "self-serving, pompous, manipulative, and hostile." Omotoso claimed that Beauchamp secretly wanted to see the parks police taken over by the Watch.

"My team are pros," he once said to Astrid, his voice entirely gravied-over with a rich, thick condescension. "We take our roles seriously. We're not some PC Plods force arresting litterers. Not that the RPC is that—of course not." The not-so-subtle dig at the constabulary was stinging, but Astrid could only wince and get on with work.

The AnimalSafe Squad had had their firearms training, and they now trained their own. Few in the constabulary seriously contemplated any one of the AnimalSafers ever gunning anything down.

"Inspector?"

Astrid stared through the phone box window onto the walk.

"Inspector, you were saying . . . about the night keeper?"

"Right, yes, Atwell, let the standard zoo staff—not their security detail, mind you—handle this one. They've got their own way of doing things. They're animal-friendly. And see that the Watch knows *we* know. They'll blow up the whole zoo if we don't stop them."

"I'm sorry, ma'am, but I think—you with me?—the problem *is* actually an emergency—of some sort, yeah?" She was sounding exasperated, and Astrid felt her guidance wasn't proving genius. She said, "The thing is, the second time that I freq'd you, it wasn't simply the light. It was the bizarre sounds, ma'am."

Astrid was genuinely perplexed by Atwell's alarm.

"It is a zoo, Atwell, right? I don't mean to be funny, but . . . and who said it wasn't an emergency?"

"I appreciate that, ma'am, but it sounded beyond *that*—Inspector—I mean, past what a zoo *should* sound like." Atwell spoke now in a snappish, annoyed tone.

"Maybe it's because it's the night before the General Election," Astrid said. "Animals are constitutionally liberal—and the polls don't look good."

Atwell groaned. "Right. Ma'am. Damn it. With respect, and I know it's not my place, but I feel you're not taking it seriously. You should. It sounded like murder. Then a man half-dressed came sprinting past the car. He looked crazy, with hair all sticking up, and a head that looked—it looked *compressed*. He was pounding my window, ma'am, then he ran off, toward Albany Street. He was saying the *jackals* were loose. He said he was the night watchman but . . . I don't know . . . for some reason, I didn't believe him, to be frank, guv. He said there was someone in the zoo. He wanted into the pandaglider, but I wouldn't do it, ma'am. I wasn't scared, ma'am. It just didn't seem advisable, yeah? But, well, I believe we have an incident here that goes beyond my regular training, ma'am."

Astrid felt a chill on her neck. She said, "Jackals loose—that's new." No wonder the autonews was on the prowl. "Stone the crows. I'm sorry. I didn't mean to put you off, Jasmine, but you can surely understand . . . this is all . . . it's just . . . never before, not in my time." She scratched her nose. "What did the man look like? I've met the night watchman—he's the night keeper, too—Dawkins. Odd fellow. He's quite a fat biffa."

There was a pause. "This man wasn't fat at all, ma'am. He was a string bean." Atwell didn't say anything for a moment. "I don't know now. I'm actually hearing something new now. I'm staying where I am, ma'am. Something's making a terrible row over the fence, ma'am. You know—GBH of the earhole*, yeah? It sounds like a *thousand* jackals. I've not seen one, however. But ma'am, I don't know what a bleeding jackal looks like anyway."

"I'm sure they're all bark," said Astrid. It still seemed likely that some drunk or Flōter sleeping rough in Regent's had spotted Atwell patrolling by herself and decided to lark about. Atwell was an attractive young woman, second-generation English (her mother and father were from New British Guyana's modest middle class, a schoolteacher and a chemist, respectively), with lovely very dark green eyes and dark, clear skin the color of burnt honey. No doubt such a man would enjoy any sort of attention she would deign to offer him.

"There's one other thing, ma'am," said Atwell. "The man said his *mother* was still in the zoo. His mother! That took the prize, Inspector. Honestly, I felt nearly desperate. I wanted to open the glider—I felt desperate to—but I would have been defenseless, yeah?"

Astrid turned with a jerk of annoyance in the old phone booth, and noticed that old Tom was standing next to her, looking sad and concerned. He must have followed her from the meeting. Astrid felt embarrassed.

"Atwell, I'll come down, OK? I'm certain you've been had is all,

---

* Grievous bodily harm of the earhole, i.e., something painful to hear

and if it's not that, it's nothing to worry about. You're on the Broad Walk?"

"Yes, ma'am. But ma'am, I think something *is* actually wrong. I have a feeling this is rather serious, ma'am."

At the best of times, certain young probationers occasionally got on Astrid's Flōt-frazzled nerves, but she found herself now feeling an ugly, confusing irritation toward Atwell, and she hated it.

"Well, perhaps," said Astrid. "I've got some feelings, too, PC. We've had—what?—a dozen 'spectacular nothing' alarms at night this week? Right. Of course something's wrong, of course it's possibly *serious* . . . Jasmine. I'm afraid I'm sounding condescending, PC. Sorry. But stay there. I'll take a cab. Give me twenty-five minutes or so." She looked at Tom directly and raised her eyebrows. She pointed at her eyes to indicate she was on an Opticall. She shook her head, as if she were talking to an insane person. "Make that thirty."

"Good, Inspector. Thank you, Inspector. And Inspector?"

"Yes?"

"Should I make sure the chief inspector is aware of all this?"

"Oh, no. Let Omotoso sleep."

There was a pause. She said, "Are you quite sure I shouldn't at least *notify* the zoo's security team? Mr. Beauchamp and all?"

Astrid shook her head. "Oh, for fuck's sake, no, Atwell. Not Beauchamp, no. I'd like to assess things, with you, before we proceed."

"Right, ma'am. Number thirty-two out."

Astrid blinked off, and turned toward her fellow FA member.

"Oh, Tom, I'm sorry I didn't clean up the tea," said Astrid. "I'm having some troubles, Tom. Work. It's this orange-freq, see?" She pointed to her eyes. "I've been a right cunt with my colleague."

Tom gazed at her eyes carefully and frowned, then looked into them anew, scrutinizing. "That's a demeaning expression. It only degrades you." Gone was the tobacco-scrounging farter; arrived was the Dominican brother who had slept with London's dead.

"Who cares about cleaning up tea? Are you all right, Astrid? I'm worried about you."

"I'm all right, Tom, really. I won't drink. I promise."

The tightened skin around Tom's eyes and mouth slackened a bit. He said, "I didn't mean to be offensive, at the meeting and all. I'm just a grubby street Flōter, Astrid. That's my bottom line."

"No, Tom, you're all right."

"We don't want to lose you, love."

Tom scratched his neck, where he had a sort of soft-whiskered dewlap. "I've never seen you walk out of a meeting. We're just teasing you a bit, you know. This isn't some King's Road meeting. We're on the front lines. It don't make us better or worse, but we're what we are, aren't we?" He looked down. A loud group of young West Ham United supporters, fresh-shaved and dressed in ironed vintage Ben Shermans, reeking of bergamot cologne, came storming around a building at the corner, across the street.

"Astrid, the pool—in Highbury. Didn't I say you would feel better if you swam? It's how I made it past second withdrawal. I'd see liquid ghosts, shining in the water beside me—water angels." Tom had been the one who'd turned her on to swimming.

"Oh, I wish I could. You don't know how badly." It was true. In the pool at Highbury, she would melt away and still be herself, sort of, and sort of not, a creature not quite of the water and not quite terrestrial—and transcendently powerful. Whatever the sensations of Flōting and withdrawal were, swimming was their opposite.

The group of louts headed toward the stairway that led up to the railway platforms with angular panels of frosted glass and steel supports; they were slapping each other and jumping and laughing, like a pack of plump, pink terriers yanking against their leash to get out the door. They were off to what was left of the West End club scene. Tom began watching them quizzically.

"I'm not like those lot," said Tom, pointing at the jack-the-lads. "And you're not, either. We're weaker than that. And that's what makes us able to survive." He seemed abstracted for a moment. "I don't want to 'take your inventory,' " he said, referring to an FA phrase meaning, roughly, unbidden moral examination, "but, Astrid, I think you're close, you're *too close*, to the Flōt again."

Astrid winced at Tom's words. They seemed bottomless in their paternalism—and she couldn't get beyond that.

"Oh, piss off!" she said. "You old fucking sot."

There were DLR passengers coming down the steps now, and a few slowed down and glanced at Astrid. Rather than looking embarrassed or hurt, Tom appeared interested. He smiled gently. "I'm sorry, Astrid. I've put a spanner in the works all right." He backed away even more, giving Astrid a full two or three meters of breathing space. "Let it out, Astrid, let it out. This is good."

Astrid said, almost spitting, "I've got work to do."

Tom rubbed his hands together. He gave a tight, overwrought smile of sympathy, showing his dark teeth. He said, "Yes, but let's talk later, right?"

Astrid said nothing, and Tom turned away. Tom's smile had collapsed, and he hunched over as he walked in a way Astrid had never seen before.

Tom stopped across the street, and with a nervous grin shouted an FA slogan: "Don't leave five minutes before the miracle!"

Astrid frowned and stood there. She had heard the expression for eleven years. But it wasn't enough any longer. "Where's my miracle?" she asked herself. She felt as if she wanted to smash herself in the face.

The sky was slightly darker on this older side of London, despite the old skyscrapers and glimmering wine bars above the Thames's water-condos, and you could see a few stars. The comet was supposed to be quite visible in the wee hours of the night, Astrid had heard. She wouldn't mind seeing it, not at all. It wouldn't be coming back, after all, until the forty-fourth century A.D., it was said, and by then England might be gone.

After a few seconds, she saw, to the east, a white splotch with a kind of smear beside it, but it didn't impress her much, such was the city's light pollution. Very strange, thought Astrid, if that's it—like a celestial mistake. It was as if an old pencil rubber had been taken to a dark, glossy magazine page in a careless way, leaving a straggling blemish. Nothing special there, she thought. Maybe you had to be somewhere else in the world to see the comet truly, somewhere like California.

Astrid stayed where she was for a while, feeling righteous and cold and drowning in anger. She watched Tom walk across the street to a Tesco mini-grocery that had a few petrol pumps out front. Through the windows she could see Tom grab a blue handbasket and go to the little produce section. Tom lifted up a bunch of bananas and put them into his basket. A dark-haired store clerk who was arranging cantaloupes started pointing at Tom and telling him something and Tom looked befuddled. The clerk looked irate. Is this what happens? Astrid wondered. You stay sober for years and end up not being able to manage bananas? She did not want this life any longer.

She said aloud, "Tom, I am sorry, Tom."

six

uniformity and its comforts

ASTRID SCAMPERED UP THE WHITE, REINFORCED cement stairs of her building. She owned an older ex-council flat in Haggerston, on a little street between the Regent's Canal and a pocket park.

She wanted to put her kit on before venturing to the zoo, and Haggerston was more or less on the way west from the Isle of Dogs. Even if the constabulary's responsibility code let her wear civvies for off-hours emergencies, she took comfort in the potent ornaments of the uniform. She scrabbled the locks open, pushed the door wide, and flipped on a powerful, standing twin-uplighter. She had nipped a couple three-boson color-charge bulbs into the lamp—Astrid liked things very bright. She felt safe in the bland room, a kind of safety she would rarely allow any guest to invade; even her closest friends in FA were kept away from her flat.

Astrid ran into her bedroom, the site of so much sexual frustration and insomnia, and didn't bother closing the flat's main door. Her bed, with its duvet cover and pillowcases of multicolored harlequin diamonds, was made as tidily and tight as a birthday box.

A private taxiglider, or cabcab, as they were called, was still idling outside with its "path-manager" onboard. (Path-managers usually controlled several satellite cabcabs at once while driving "control" cabcabs themselves capable of transporting passengers.)

Astrid's bedroom, crassly lit, also reeking of paint solvents, possessed none of the contemporary furniture of the sitting room. There was the old pine double bed with large blond posts and a battered oak dresser she'd had since she was fifteen. On the dresser was a small shrine of fotolives of her mum, mostly as a child, and her old five-decade rosary, curled and dead as a crushed snake. She picked it up, rubbed a pearl a few times, and slipped it into her pocket.

She opened her closet to a neat array of pressed, white regulation shirts, each still in its plastic sleeve from the cleaner's. She chose one randomly and carefully slipped the shirt out of the plastic protector. I'm going too slow, she said to herself. Too slow! She began to strip as fast as she could then, kicking her shoes and trousers off, hopping around on one leg. She changed into a more comfortable, M&S "living support" bra (its cultured bio-fibers gently tightened with exertion or softened with rest). She jerked her police uniform on in less than a minute and gave herself a quick look. She often felt vulnerable before the mirror, but not now. She raised her heavy, dark brows and smiled sympathetically, as if trying to encourage someone trying something new without a hope of pulling it off.

Shoes! She sat on her bed and tugged on an old but still polished pair of black service shoes. She brushed a few filaments of lint off her black trousers. She set her women's police trilby on her head and then took it off—being an inspector gave her the privilege of not needing to wear it. She brushed her long black hair and put it back in its tie. Then she put her silly trilby back on, feeling a fool. During regular hours, outside the office she was supposed to wear a protective vest with Kevlar4 inserts, but like other officers, she kept hers at the "ranch," which is what her colleagues called the RPC police station in Old Police House at Hyde Park. She put on a slick black jacket and stood at attention.

She faced the mirror again, arms akimbo, putting on a haughty little slouch. She looked sharp, she knew, about as sharp as she ever got. Her high cheekbones, her brunette sleekness, her nearly black-brown eyes—they all gave her a mink-like appearance, hard and gorgeous, washed for years by the fast icy rivers of Mount Bitch.

It's still good, this, she thought. In the kit, Flōter or not, she was It. She felt safe from relapse, at least for a while.

"You need more uniforms," she said to the mirror. She already owned two dozen identical shirts, but she could never have too many. "And *fuck* what anyone else says," she whispered.

Lastly, she went back to her dresser and pulled out the top drawer. Her neuralzinger rested on a neat stack of black silk panties. In Texas, she'd had a single triangular rhinestone jewelered onto the stock, just on one side. It gleamed with icy sadism. She flipped open the chamber. Loaded with living gangliatoxic nets—the most dangerous rounds allowed by nonfirearm specialists in Britain. She slipped the gun into her trouser pocket.

jackals in the headlamps

WHEN ASTRID SCUTTLED BACK TO THE TAXI-glider, the path-manager said, through the video panel on a bulletproof clear divider, "No charge, free ride, all the way." The path-manager was smiling, craning his head around at Astrid, then looking back at something on his monitors, moving his long fingers over holo-controls with a flurrying grace. He seemed nervous, with something that went beyond even the stress of his Indigent job. Astrid hadn't looked at him very closely before but now took him in. He wore a navy down puffy vest over an old wool jumper with ragged cuffs. His eyes were almond-shaped and close together, and he had thick eyebrows and bushy hair.

"I need to go fast," said Astrid.

She wanted to make small talk with the path-manager, but she thought this would make the man more tense. He faded from the video screen. Unlike some officers, Parkies possessed no policing powers outside the parks, but Indigents always saw the law as an extension of the hated Red Watch. Astrid wished she could explain this, perhaps put the man at ease. But she felt uneasy. As a woman officer, she'd had her share of being called a "plonk" or worse by colleagues, and a little part of her didn't mind feeling the man's deference.

"It's a quiet night," said Astrid.

The path-manager faded back on-screen and said, "Yes." He looked at Astrid more closely, but not impertinently. "Too little business, I think, so far, if you notice," said the path-manager. "It's OK to me if it is not too quiet."

Astrid said, "Good luck." She cleared her throat. "With your fares and all." The cab was speeding somewhat, and Astrid grabbed the safety handle above the window. It was flimsy, cool, nuplastic— a toy door knocker without a door.

She tried to roll down the window, but it only came down a few inches—broken.

The cabcab was barreling forward now, bucking Astrid from side to side. It somehow careened around a rough-looking Indigent pushing a cart in the street.

"Oh!" Astrid said.

"Sorry!" said the path-manager, blinking back on the screen.

"It's fine," she said.

The driver's recklessness seemed part of a larger wildness in her life.

The cabcab shook and its bosonic color-charge engines shrieked as the glider encountered a bit of LST, or low-speed turbulence, a mysterious phenomenon that occurred with gliders in parts of the old City.

"Right," Astrid said. "I'm in no absolutely life-or-death rush." It was her subtlest way of saying "slow down."

AT GREAT PORTLAND STREET STATION, Astrid asked the path-manager to turn right and get onto Regent Park's Outer Circle road.

She saw at least two solarcopters quietly warbling in the sky above the zoo area, their spotlights roving irritably. One was indeed a Red Watch frightcopter. Its rotors were made of living black feather-like blades that gave off a distinctive hornet whir. (They retracted in overlapping layers on the ground, where the rarely seen frightcopters could reputedly be driven as easily as gliders.) Its two powerful neural-cannons, spiking off its nose, could turn—and had turned—a crowd of people's brains to gray soup in a matter of seconds. The other solarcopter was a small autonewsmedia drone. She also saw the towering white dish of an autonewsmedia glider truck Atwell had mentioned. She hadn't quite believed it could all be possible.

"Dagenham,"* she said.

At that moment, two things happened: first, Astrid felt a mild, unexpected easing of second withdrawal. Simply being *close* to the zoo had done something. Her muscles and tendons were weirdly freer of tightness. She could think again. Even the taloned craves ripping in her gut had softened a bit.

The other thing was that she understood that lives, possibly even her own, were in peril. She wasn't sure how or why. Am I going to top meself? she wondered. No—I won't do that. That the Watch and autonews might arrive at an incident in advance of the police wasn't in itself all that unusual in 2052, such was the feral alacrity of the WikiNous rumor mill. Unfortunately, because of this, it also wasn't uncommon for ride-along autonewsmedia producers and camera operators—often not the sharpest blades on the fan—to get injured and worse at incidents along with gawking rubberneckers. Autonews solarcopter drones regularly scanned for photo-anomalies from the skies of London, and they darted instantly to the scene of anything unusual. And if the Watch were on

---

* "Out there," crazy, etc.

hand, well, anything could happen. The Watch always neuralpiked first and asked questions later.

"Make us go faster, but careful," she said. "Please."

They drove north for a minute or two until they came upon, to the left, lavish Chester Gate. It was a Victorian shambles of ornate wrought iron painted glossy black and metallic gold. The gate itself was open, as usual, and they drove into the park a few meters, into the two-lane thoroughfare called Chester Road, paved with the characteristic pink asphalt of the park's interior byways.

"Right here," said Astrid.

"Yes," said the path-manager. "We're off the operating grid now, ma'am. You may notice."

"I know. It's OK, right?"

"It is no problem for *you*, ma'am."

Immediately, on the right, appeared the locked gate to the Broad Walk, through which one could access all the interior of the northern part of the park. Virtually all the gates and locks of Regent's Park were little more than psychological deterrence, meant not just to keep vagrants and kids out at night, but also to suggest forcefully that something of worth stood beyond reach. The truth was, except for the zoo itself, and the park's Inner Circle, Regent's was a perfect sieve.

Chester Road led to the Inner Circle, which in turn held the rose gardens and the furtive nests of mute swans and Egyptian geese. The Inner Circle was all locked down tight for the night, per usual procedure. It was the Broad Walk Astrid needed to open. Unless in hot pursuit, PC Atwell would have followed procedure and locked it after herself. How the autonews got in was anyone's guess, but it didn't surprise Astrid.

Atwell was supposed to be parked a quarter mile or so up the path, beside the zoo.

Astrid said, "We're going in there, but I need to unlock it."

She jumped out of the cabcab. The loose turbine-cover noise was much louder outside the glider—it sounded like a bean tin steadily rapped with a spoon. She also heard animals—loads of them—bawling, braying, whooping, and yinnying, and all clearly very upset.

As soon as Astrid approached the gate, she could see something was very wrong in the zoo, too. Looking north from where she stood, the lights from inside the zoo raged. She heard more animals screaming. She could barely fathom it. It was as though a missile had hit Noah's Ark.

"Oh god," she said.

Her hands shook as she yanked out her master key and rolled the black fence back. She felt wound up tight, buzzing, like a coil of plutonium. It wasn't exhilaration, but more a sparkling disquiet, both radiant and distressing. 'Bout time we have a bit of action, she thought. No, don't wish for it, that's naff. *Stay professional.*

The gate was indeed locked, as it turned out. Atwell's good, Astrid thought. Most veteran men on the constabulary just let a detail like that go these days. And that's precisely why they're still Parkies.

Astrid sprinted back to the cabcab and explained to the path-manager, breathing hard in the backseat, that they needed to proceed up the Broad Walk as fast as safely possible.

"We possibly have an intruder in the zoo," Astrid said. "Someone could get hurt in there, feasibly." There was the faintest sense of a deeper conscientiousness creeping into her mind. "You see, I've been off duty, and was called here by my colleague. But it's all a bit odd, really."

The path-manager gave a high, slightly wheezy giggle. "I didn't know there was a zoo here," said the path-manager. "Very, very hard to see, if you notice. You hear me before? I said there's no glider path. I drive on my own, OK?"

It was rare and often illegal for a cabcab to be switched to manual controls.

"I know," said Astrid, trying to stay polite. "Please. Go. You can drive without the glider path, right? Your eyes will adjust. This would be a great benefit to the police."

"I'm not good in dark," said the path-manager. "I try."

"Yes," said Astrid. "Now."

The path-manager said, "These animals, they maybe want to play around with you."

"Mmm. Maybe." Astrid chuckled in a rather fake way.

The cab's path-manager looked straight ahead. He had begun to slouch into the path-manager's side door a bit, like he was preparing for a long night, but he'd sat up straight. Up to now he had been working his holo-controls, obviously taking care of other riders on other routes, but he dropped that now.

The path-manager was speeding, the headlamps gathering great, moving bowls of green park scenery as the glider shot along. The pale patches on plane trees along the Broad Walk shone white, despite the darkness of the park, and became an oscillating flash in Astrid's periphery. She felt disorientated and dizzy. She hunched forward on the seat, looking out for the signs of Atwell's Paladin pandaglider.

"Sorry, friend, please, slow down, please," said Astrid. She spoke in a stern tone she had not used before. The path-manager slammed on the brakes. Astrid bucked forward. The path-manager gave one of his funny laughs again.

She said, "Thanks."

As they were sitting there, the glider's small color-charge engines ticking with heat, Astrid spotted the taillamps of the Paladin, just a hundred meters or so in front of them on the walk. If the path-manager hadn't stopped when he had, they might have rear-ended Atwell.

"Just a little farther," said Astrid. "Please, slowly." The cabcab started gliding forward, and the path-manager banged the brakes again.

"What the devil's wrong?" said Astrid.

"Wawi!" the path-manager said. "Wawi!"

Astrid looked out, saw the creatures, and nearly hit the ceiling of the cabcab. There were five of them, right in front of the Citroën. They just stood there, stock-still apart from the flicking of the great triangles of tawny fur that was their ears. Their snouts weren't as pointy as those of the foxes she'd see sometimes at night on her back garden wall in Haggerston, and they stood taller, yet they looked similar. The main difference was an unnervingly adorable, sloe-eyed expression on all their faces that was pure jackal.

"Wawi!"

"What's *wawi?*" asked Astrid. "What do you mean?"

The headlamps had made the jackals' eyes glow a hellish phosphorous yellow-white.

The path-manager seemed not to hear her and honked the horn several times. The peculiar animals backed off a bit, tails curled under. These *wawi* would fade back, stop for a moment, then mince forward again, each dog following a sort of ragged orbit around the area in front of the vehicle. Astrid watched, speechless. The pack structure seemed to disperse and re-form in a shaggy cadence, contracting, expanding, contracting, expanding, breathing out England's air through equatorial lungs.

"I don't know about *wawi,*" said the path-manager. "Don't know English word." He sounded irritated. Astrid had got him into something over his head.

"Please, keep driving," said Astrid. She could see Atwell's dim form poised in her glider. Atwell wasn't visibly reacting to the horn or the headlamps, and this by itself alarmed Astrid.

She said to the path-manager, "Don't stop here, if you don't mind, sir. Pull up a bit, please."

The path-manager, sounding far away, said, "I don't like *wawi*. They are trouble. That's problem." The path-manager eased the cab forward slowly, and the animals roved around it for a moment or two, then passed into the night, busy muscles pulling along their dog skeletons like restless little hate-cages on paws.

Astrid got out of the cab. She felt very nervous again. She unlocked two fresh £50 Optimatrix holograms for the path-manager, twice the fare—but it didn't seem much to her, considering. The man frowned upon seeing the floaty red holograms. He pinched them up from Astrid's hand and muttered a few words in a language Astrid didn't recognize, much less understand. For a moment, he sniffed at Astrid's hand (the old counterfeit holograms left a distinctive tomato-leaf scent on the skin), and said, "I like OptiCredits—the holograms cost two pounds in fees, ma'am." The path-manager pushed the swirling red holograms into his OptiCredit reader. "But I take." His window popped shut.

He motored away in reverse, the broken-fan sound audible even after the cabcab's headlamps vanished into the city.

oliver cromwell's got a jumbie, too

WHEN ASTRID GOT TO PC ATWELL, THE YOUNGER constable hesitated a bit before switching off the pandaglider's imagiglass windows. This peeved Astrid, a little more than it ought.

"Come on, Atwell. We haven't all bloody night, have we?"

Astrid knew she was being cruel and highhanded, especially since she'd so delayed responding to the initial orange-freq, but there was a prowling anger in her again after the brief respite in the cab. Cigarette smoke and the scent of crushed almonds poured from the pandaglider. Atwell wore a dazed expression that suggested to Astrid she'd had a tough time waiting alone. A sheen of perspiration covered her forehead. Atwell didn't say anything, and she wouldn't look at Astrid. She merely held her arms crossed, rubbing them as if cold.

"Didn't you see us? Behind you? *Smoking,* Atwell?"

"I know," said Atwell. "I just, I—"

"I saw your little jackal dogs," Astrid interjected. "You called them in?"

"Yes, ma'am. At least half a dozen different units, on their way."

The younger constable leaned forward in her seat for a moment, took a deep, fretful breath.

"Jesus, I'm sorry, Atwell. I am sorry. I'm . . . well, I've been. Things aren't good. You all right?"

"Yes, ma'am."

She found herself feeling worried about Atwell, and about her own apparent incapacity to help. She wondered whether one of the new viruses might have Atwell.

"You'd said there were some people about, too, right?" asked Astrid. "They're always the most difficult animals, aren't they?"

"Yes, some autoreporters—I've left them alone, ma'am." Atwell was finally looking up at her. There remained an odd languor in how she moved, with liquidy arms and a heavy-necked torpor, and she coughed a few times.

"Are you ill?"

"Maybe," said Atwell.

She wondered whether Atwell herself might be Flōting, though she didn't have quite the right signs of that.

Atwell said, "Two souls—inside the autonewsmedia glider-truck."

"Good. They're safe in there." Astrid stood on tiptoes for a moment and peered across the glider's roof. Powerful limbs of plane trees, festooned with bunches of white blossoms, bowered the area where she and the constable spoke. Distant city lights twinkled through the branches. "I would have thought you've done just about all you can. All right?"

"Yes, ma'am. I do hope. And there was that strange man I mentioned." She hacked in a wheezy cough again; she was careful to turn away and cover her mouth. "But I—I had to decide on my own what to do—and I decided not to give chase."

"Never," said Astrid. "That wouldn't have been too clever, I would've thought."

"That's what I thought."

Astrid asked, "What did this . . . this funny chap . . . what did he look like?"

"I don't know. It was dark, ma'am. Like a crazy man. A long face. He had ginger hair sticking up all over, like his head was going in twenty different directions at once."

"These rough-sleepers," said Astrid, "and I don't say this in judgment, but they can be quite, well, tricky, god bless 'em. Trust me—this man's OK, as much as any Indigent can be these days. And the jackals—the fact is, they seem, PC Atwell, . . . they're *small*. We'll sort this."

Atwell, taking a breath, looked as if she wanted to interrupt Astrid, whose patronizing tone had made things awkward.

"The man," said Atwell, "he was quite distressed. Really, ma'am, I don't think he was sleeping rough. Like I said before, he says his mother's in—"

"Yes, his mother. I heard you the first time."

"Yes, ma'am."

There was a hesitation, and then Atwell looked straight at Astrid. "Guv . . . it's not my place to say, but we all admire you, guv. What's the matter? What's got you? You seem . . . frustrated. We're on the same team, yeah? And I really like you. What's wrong?"

Astrid began working her mouth, slowly. Her lips were quivering a bit, but no words came out. After a few more seconds, she said, in a husky whisper: "I can't say." She couldn't very well list the litany of second withdrawal's horrors to the officer she supervised.

Frustrated—that was a funny word for it.

"Inspector, I hear you. All is well."

But nothing was "well," Astrid thought. Indeed, she might at that moment half enjoy some errant tiger burning bright, in the park's forest of the night, springing upon her, thrashing her withdrawal apart like a dirty pangolin. For if being near the zoo had initially eased the horrors inside her, new anxieties now seemed to be unhatching, and fast. And she felt sure of a terrible fact: she was going to end up drinking Flōt that night. Her life of sobriety was ending. FA could fuck itself. She'd had enough of being strong.

Just one orb, Astrid tried to tell herself, ruefully. She knew that even a mouthful of Flōt would restart her addiction in all its ugly fury. A drink of Flōt would be the beginning of the end of her life. She couldn't escape that reality.

From across the zoo's fence, at a distance, the two women suddenly heard a pair of African wild asses, among the most endangered animals on earth, bray heinously.

"Is that so?" Astrid pretended to answer, with a clownish voice. "Well. Good luck to you, then!"

Atwell laughed.

Astrid asked, "And are you OK, Constable?"

Atwell seemed not to hear, and now she was looking above the zoo, toward the mackerel-striped sky. She said, abstractedly, "I feel terrible about locking that man out. Physically." She was grinning eerily. "Crikey. I'm feverish. My head hurts. Oh, I don't feel well, I really don't, guv." She shook her head, looking away from Astrid. She said, "I just want to do a good job, yeah?"

"I understand," said Astrid.

"Do you?" Atwell glanced at her and good-naturedly scoffed. "Maybe 'a good job' seems like a piddling ambition, but it's not to me, yeah? You know, my mother and father, from Guyana, they think law enforcement is, you know, povvy.* But I love it—I just do. They say they didn't come to England so their children could work as coppers. Ha! Big ambitions, everyone had—before the reclassifications. They thought I should be a barrister. They still think I may yet, yeah?"

---

* Of poor quality

"Why not?"

"You know why. England's going backward. Oliver Cromwell's jumbie must be crying. Fucking King Hen—"

"Don't, Jasmine," she whispered. "Don't say it. Not here. It's good to fear the Watch. They're everywhere."

"Sorry, guv," she whispered. "You're so fucking right. Ma'am."

"For once."

Atwell said, "Should we call Mr. Beauchamp?" She looked a little more awake now, and tense. She began picking expertly at a cuticle with her fingernail.

"Yes," Astrid said. "Sadly." She didn't want to wake the zoo director, but she recognized the necessity of getting specialists on scene. "I suppose we can't just shout, 'Come along, Trixie!' and just pick up a jackal like a lost cocker spaniel."

It was Atwell who used the police glider's old-but-secure comm-port for a few minutes to contact Beauchamp. Astrid could hear Beauchamp's needly voice, whining in the background, taking up far too much of Atwell's time. But she was glad *she* hadn't had to deal with him. Atwell kept blinking during the call, as if trying to stay ready for the moment when the mountain that was Beau-champ's grandiosity collapsed on her head.

"All set?" Astrid asked Atwell when the call ended. "Did he say anything useful?"

"Yes, guv. He said a lot. He said we needed to 'get a perimeter.' I asked about the jackals and he begged us, please, to leave them alone. He doesn't think there's much we can do about them any-way, since we lack proper training, for now, right? But *I* want to find that man."

"Yes, the night keeper, Dawkins. Yes, we must. And anyone else in trouble. Have we heard anything from the Watch? Did Beau-champ say anything about them?"

"No, ma'am."

"So typical. The Watch do things their way, and so does Beau-champ. No bleedin' coordination—ever. Anyway, we should get moving."

"That makes sense, Inspector," said Atwell. She hesitated for a second. "Inspector, I feel the chills and I'm knackered and woozy."

"You want to leave off?"

"Oh, no, no, no. I'm just . . . not myself, OK? I'm very sorry if I seem . . . odd. I've been hearing such terrible noises. And this zoo—I don't know how to put it. Something about it just gives me gippy tummy to the core. I feel somehow extra soul-tired, just being near this bleeding place, guv. Like I'm part of something awful being born, and it's not just the lost jackals. It's more. It's worse."

"I feel it, too," said Astrid. "It's like something bigger than the biggest animal, fighting . . . for its life."

"Yes. I think. Or we're mad."

"Could very well be."

Astrid put her palm over Atwell's forehead. It was damp and febrile and oh so vulnerable, like a sick child's. She did look a little bluish somehow, and slightly awestruck, Astrid saw. Her eyes appeared poorly focused. They were greenish-brown eyes of a huge size she sometimes associated with people of Scottish ancestry. Her black, penciled-up eyebrows angled slightly into peaks, giving her a puckish expression that Astrid normally found winsome.

"Yes, you're warm. Jeez. Very warm."

"Right," Atwell said. "But I can work, I tell you. 'I be *iree*,'* as they say."

Astrid said, "It's also fine if you're not fine, too. If you need to go home . . ."

"I'll be OK, yeah?" Atwell chuckled a little, in the throaty, sniffly way someone does when she's just been weeping. "That was funny,

---

* All right

how you talked back to that animal. Right funny, that. Right." She took a breath. "Shall we find this man now?" She started to get out of the car.

When she cracked the pandaglider's door open, Astrid could smell her more completely. Atwell didn't wear any kind of perfume—regulation discouraged strong fragrances—but for reasons she could not guess, Atwell possessed an agreeable scent, aromatic but bright, like almonds and watercress crushed along with something strong and rough, a tropical grass—*vetiver?*—that she could not name.

"Can I . . . ask you something . . . Inspector?" Atwell nodded once and squinted slightly, as if uttering a credo. She wore a serious expression. "God, I feel odd. I . . . I don't want to show you any sort of eye-pass.* But you—I *heard* that you're in what they call recovery—from Flōt? Is it true?"

The question was very rarely asked in Astrid's experience; it shocked her. "It is, for now."

"And I've heard that . . . you know, Flōtism?" Astrid could hear miles and miles of Guyana in Atwell's accent. "It's *wicked* impossible to kill off, yeah? What with two withdrawals and all. And you end up trapped in the devil's own torture chambers, and you're pure anta banta if you go *chronic*. There's no way out then. And almost everyone dies. That's what I hear. You become a prisoner, for life, and everyone looks at you and troubles you and gives you the minute of your doom on a paper dog-horn, and then you're dead." Atwell cleared her throat and gazed directly at Astrid. She even leaned in a bit. "You tell me: Is that the truth?"

"Yes," she said. "I think."

"OK. But ma'am, here's *my* perspective, right? See, I think you

---

* Disrespect. Guyanese slang.

can make it. And that's what I wanted to say. I think you're different. I just do, and I know it's kind of weird . . . but I felt I needed to tell you that. I don't know much about recovery, like I said. But still."

"Thanks, Atwell. Thank you, Jasmine. There's some paracetamol back at the nick, by the way. For your fever."

"Good. All right," she said. She opened the door of the panda-glider and jumped out. "I'm glad you're here, guv." She slammed the door shut with surprising strength. "To work!" she said.

Astrid felt a wobbly sense of normalcy returning. She said, turning toward the zoo, "So, what do you think's happening in there?"

Just as she spoke, an elephant trumpeted distantly. It was so loud Astrid could feel it in her chest.

"Unbelievable," said Astrid. "I wonder whether things are worse in there than they seem."

"I've been thinking that for the last hour, ma'am. We don't really have situational awareness here. I wish we could talk to those frightcopters."

"Don't even think it! You know the Watch. They don't share info. They try to dismantle you. God, but listen. Why does the zoo *sound* so much worse than it looks?"

Although a few of the security light arrays in the interior of the zoo still raged, after several minutes they had begun to shut down. It was an almost comically worthless energy-saving aspect of the system of motion detectors. Why, after all, would a detector at the zoo ever be triggered in the middle of the night unless a dire occasion had arisen, in which case there could not possibly be a valid reason for such a light, once triggered, to turn off again. Perhaps the zoo's own security team, run by David Beauchamp, was primarily concerned with theft and vandalism deterrence. (A few of the animals, such as okapi, were reportedly worth hundreds of thousands of pounds, though precisely what a burglar would do in England with a two-hundred-pound extinct-in-the-wild forest ungulate from Central Africa seemed hard to fathom.)

Atwell bit her lower lip; she seemed to consider Astrid's question grave. She said, "I just don't know. Whatever's in there—this *jumbie* or whatever it is—it's still there."

"Jumbie?" She giggled. "What's that then? Oliver Cromwell's got one, too?"

"Oh, sorry. I mean, 'evil spirit'—or ghost. Guyanese, ma'am. You know—creole."

"Mmm," said Astrid. "Island lore?"

"Ha! Guyana's no island. That's Britain." Atwell grinned. "And this zoo, this island of almost-extinct pets in cages. Either a very intelligent animal has broken loose, and let the jackals out, or a very foolish person has broken in. How long for Beauchamp, you suppose?"

"Who knows?" said Astrid. "Oh, how I loathe that man. Sorry to say that, but he really gets on my knob."

In the firearm training sessions Astrid had helped lead for the zoo team, Beauchamp had rushed her along and acted as if the constabulary's onetime involvement with the zoo practically contaminated his staff. Beauchamp seemed to have neither particular respect for, nor desire to be addled with, schooling in safety or crisis management.

One of Astrid's few friends in the zoo reported that he occupied his important job unhappily, with the impatient but apparently plausible hope that he might obtain some administrative position on the ZSL board, which would have carried with it a title of nobility. He scorned the ZSL's own public relations team and craved WikiNous attention, so much so that the ZSL's spokespeople steered visiting reporters away from him. Once, during a grim morning training session on the topic of what would happen if an animal needed to be shot, Astrid had tried to lighten things up. She pointed to an anteater in the Moonlight World exhibit, and made a wisecrack about the dangers an escaping "bull aardvark" could pose. Many of the zoo staff members laughed.

"That's a Bolivian anteater," Beauchamp had said, seething from the back, wagging his finger. "It's an important distinction. And it's a female specimen. And her name is Dinah." With that, Beauchamp peered into the glass and said with a straight face, "Right, Dinah?"

He was what Astrid considered an animal fanatic. She adored animals—but she wasn't a nut. Still, Atwell's point was procedurally correct, she knew. The man knew his specimens.

"I've heard he's difficult," said Atwell.

"Yes," said Astrid. "The zoo's *his* babs to take care of. But he's not going to be right chuffed about tonight."

"I've heard he takes the animals very seriously and all."

There were two torches in the boot of the pandaglider, along with muscle-slowing batons and extra sets of invisible handcuffs (they weren't actually invisible, but used magnetic force to impel hands or feet together).

Astrid rummaged through them while Atwell used the comm to make sure Beauchamp and his small team were en route. For a moment, Astrid set the cuffs to reverse polarity and "floated" one cuff piece a few inches above her hand, amusing herself. She kept the torches and batons, and put back the cuffs—what was she going to do, lock up the jackals?

When Atwell came around to the back, she said, "I actually spoke to him. He's coming. He sounded, erm, whipped up. He said we need to move quickly."

"He's whipped up all right, I'm sure."

"He wants to seal off the zoo. He was beside himself, actually, guv. I told him about the man who claimed to be the watchman and he scarcely seemed to hear me. He wanted to know if we'd established a perimeter. He said it was 'dead urgent.' He was rather definite about that. I quote, 'It's the last line of defense against tragedy.' "

Astrid gritted her teeth. Had things really progressed into such a grand arena as that—*tragedy?* Wasn't this more a mishap?

A few new scattered animal noises began coming from the zoo. This time, they sounded like monkeys or apes shrieking hellishly. It unnerved Astrid badly.

"Jesus fuck," she said. "OK, let's do our best to find out what's going on. We sure as hell can't establish a perimeter with two officers, can we? We'll do what we can."

She handed a torch and a baton to Atwell, and Atwell reminded her about the terribly distressed man who claimed to be the night watchman, whose mother was somehow still in the zoo—they wouldn't forget about him, would they? She assured her they would look for them, but she thought it a waste of time. The real danger lay in Beauchamp's appearing. He was such a fool. Then Astrid realized something.

"Oh Jesus, Atwell. We're in for it tonight. I tell you, mark my words. I'd forgot something—you know Beauchamp's going to have us at *his* disposal? That's the reg. Crown property and whatnot."

"Maybe it won't be *so* bad, ma'am," said Atwell. "Least it's not the Watch as gaffer."

"True."

Atwell flipped the torch on and it shone up into her face. It gave her a sinister look with a moonglow brow and icy-looking cheeks.

They decided to walk down toward the place where the jackals had been. Astrid felt charged. Here she was in the midst of interesting police work. It was rare for Parkies. But there was something more and more frightening about the night, too, a sense of things flying out in broken pieces she could neither catch nor fix without getting hurt. The feeling back at the FA meeting, and Atwell's jumbie, and the terrifying sounds in the zoo—there was something baleful afoot.

"You know," said Astrid. "I think we'd better freq Omotoso. But I can't imagine the old man's going to be happy."

Astrid waited as Atwell glanced down to prepare a new orange-freq.

"It's done," she said. "Omotoso knows a thing or two now."

finding the head of satan

THEY WOULD FIRST CIRCUMNAVIGATE THE ZOO, Astrid decided, and inspect the fence. Meanwhile, they would also keep on the lookout for the alleged watchman—and, perhaps, of all people, his poor mother.

The two officers—one an addict in extremis, the other an unwell rookie—stayed on the Broad Walk, which, in the constricting darkness, hardly lived up to its name. The beams from their torches waved back and forth over the edges of the pink pavement like the antennae of a giant, blind beetle, and the night seemed to have grown unusually murky; Astrid thought this was due to some trick of the torches on her digitalized retinas, or perhaps because of the security lamps jumping on and off and on inside the zoo, to their right, as they patrolled forward. They passed a small tea kiosk, little more than a whitewashed hut built around a big gas-operated kettle. Beside it was a folding chair, apparently forgotten after closing. The chair had been knocked onto its side.

Atwell seemed rapt by the strange, melted-looking granite of the contemporary statues in the large children's field to their left.

They were all elephants. "See that, Inspector?" she said. "They sort of come to life in the night. They're like hearts, folded up on themselves and all gone gray. I don't know if I see *elephants*, per se. But I see loads of feeling. It's nice, ma'am, yeah?"

"Yes, yes," she said. "I suppose you're right."

In truth, Astrid didn't see indrawn hearts—she saw insufficiency, the grayness of indecision, an ingrownness of old dreams. This art didn't move her. They walked on.

But there was that comet somewhere, Astrid thought, the one all over the WikiNous. Something brighter and more cutting than this world—now *that* would speak to her. The "most widely observed comet in human history" visible and she was stuck chasing wild dogs down. Urga-Rampos—*it* would *really* be something to see.

Ironically, the comet was actually more luminous in southern Britain at that time than almost anywhere else on Earth, but it was blocked, in north London, by a very southern English formation of stratus clouds. The cloud cover was beginning to push off.

Astrid thought about Atwell's apparently heartfelt conviction that she could do what almost no one else had—withstand second withdrawal. It was touching, but wasn't it misplaced? Oh, she hoped not. Could she beat Death? She was so close, after all, wasn't she? Or was she? *For if she could drink just one orb of Flōt— and no more—and walk sober thereafter—and never again after that. If, if, if. Just one orb. One and only one and never again on this debased Earth.*

"Inspector!" Atwell was scurrying ahead of her. She had her torch trained on a red and black shape. "There's something wrong up there." She pointed toward a shadowy misplacement.

"Wait, Jasmine. Wait!" But she kept bustling along, well in front now.

Now she shined her torch over the thing. It was a small, chawed-out head of some kind. Atwell reeled backward.

"Jesus!" she said, her hand over her mouth. "I'm going to be sick."

Astrid caught up and shined her light down. "My god," she said.

Her first flare of thought was that she was looking down at the lean, masticated head of Satan. Smudged with dark, bloody fingerprints, to Astrid the ribbed horns appeared to have been curled not by eons of genetic adaptation, but by murderous demons. There was a sense, too, that the appalling object had come to meet her. It was out of the zoo, ready to swallow her with its skinny skull and one wet ear. For a moment, she even thought she heard a faint voice calling her, but she put that down to withdrawal.

"It's a goat," Astrid heard herself whisper hoarsely. "I'm fairly certain of that."

"I don't want to look," said Atwell.

"Don't," Astrid said. She used her baton to roll the head over. There were no maggots or flies, no fetid smell. "This is part of the whole lights business," she said. "Whatever did this did it tonight. Nothing to be worried about. It's not a person that's done it. People don't chew goat snouts off." People did much worse, she thought.

She turned to face Atwell, who seemed to be recovering, standing taller. Atwell finally glanced at it again.

"It's just my stomach, ma'am—it's been bothering me. Crikey! It's horrible." She turned her face away again. "I can't look or I'm going to chunder. Don't—look—at me—yeah, if I lose it, Inspector? It's humiliating, guv, in front of you, yeah?"

Atwell bent over and vomited. Astrid gently placed her hand on her colleague's back. It was hot and damp and muscular. "OK, I'm OK," Atwell said. "OK, it's passing. Good." She breathed in thickly, then spat. "Fuck!"

"Easy," said Astrid.

"This head, guv, it does fright me just a bit. I mean, I don't want to go like this goat. Who did this?"

"Easy," she said. She rubbed Atwell's back. "Easy." She said, "It's *what* did it. This bit, it's animals on animals. That's precisely what we're looking at." Squinty faced and tilting her head, she held her hand up for quiet.

Then she was sure she heard a voice—a peculiar, persecuted one, quietly whinging from thin air.

Umm, kay-kay, femaleans! You're flarking me out, kay-kay! It was high-pitched but distinctly male, and it came from above. There was no one in sight.

"Fuck all," said Atwell.

"Now *that* is right crooked by half-fives," said Astrid.

Atwell nodded and said, "Couldn't *be* more. Do you think we . . . well, should keep walking, around the 'perimeter'?"

"Oh—Beauchamp's bloody perimeter. For fuck's sake. No." Astrid bit her lower lip. There was that anger. A rage before the Death. If she just held on. It was passing, wasn't it? "Actually, yes. Sorry. Beauchamp's right. We can walk, of course, we'll get around, but I want to investigate that person who's having a lark at our expense. It's back toward the pandaglider. It may be the joker who tried to give you a scare, earlier." She looked up at the sky. A cool night-breeze was blowing. She said, "It came from up. Up is a funny place for a person." She pointed at the field beyond the grove of plane trees that lined the Broad Walk. She said, "Maybe in that direction?"

So they left the goat head and walked back toward the glider.

Had they made it around the southern tip of the zoo, just a few yards beyond the goat head, they would have encountered Cuthbert's notable handiwork with the fence. They would have been able to raise the section of heavy ironwork fencing Cuthbert had pushed down into the turf, and plug up the only hole in the zoo in its two centuries.

up a tree like zacchaeus

THE JACKALS WERE ALREADY LONG GONE. THE five of them had scurried out of Regent's Park and managed safely to cross the Marylebone Road. A young group of True Conservative politicos, drinking themselves silly at a local public house over Election Eve polls (LabouraTory was crushing them), had seen the jackals outside the window and mistook them for large bizarre cats (cats that lived, mysteriously, in packs).

"It's a good sign—animals," one of them slurred. "A jolly good one. As long as we've got our cats, England will *dure*."

"*Dure?* Steady, Michael."

"*Yath!*" Michael answered, quite definitively.

When Astrid and Atwell got back to the pandaglider, the sound of the high-pitched man whinging started up again, but it sounded even closer.

Femaleans, help me—kay-kay?

"Who's there?" shouted Astrid.

"Up here. *Here!*"

Astrid and Atwell started jogging across a small pitch that

fanned into the northeastern quadrant of the park, against Camden Town. They soon made it to another stand of young plane trees.

"Jesus suffering Christ!" the man rasped, in a lower, raspier, gravedigger's voice. "Worthless!"

For a moment, no one responded. Then the man spoke again: "It's Dawkins—the night keeper. Up bloody here." They looked up, and there in one of the smallest trees in the group, caught like a horrible fly in a spiderweb of branches, dangled a lanky young man. "No one fucking respects the night keepers!"

Astrid and Atwell trained their torches on the figure, and Astrid immediately recognized the face, and so did Atwell. He looked very different than Astrid recalled. He was much thinner. He wasn't so much a bag of bones as a ripped-open turnip sack of them. He was wearing a saggy set of boxers, thick knit socks slipped around his ankles, and a pair of very old weatherbeaten Reebok hovershoes, which clearly were missing their hover-cell, or he would have floated back home. But it was Dawkins all right, the eccentric Indigent the powers that be allowed to watch the zoo at night from the inside, the latest in a two-hundred-year line of eerie, solitary, and terminally irascible nocturnals who kept the London Zoo at night.

"Dawkins? You've lost several stone, right?"

"Who wants to know?"

The fellow looked worse for it. The blotchy skin of his face stretched over a narrow skull and deep-sunk eyeholes. His lips were a pair of dead leeches—gray but very full (of what, one daren't ask). His ginger-colored hair stood up in a stiff patch like corroded steel wool. Astrid had met him only once, when she first started working for the constabulary (she was introduced then to most of the zoo's key personnel), but the guy gave one such a creepy feeling, he was impossible to forget.

Dawkins had quite the reputation, too. Astrid had heard that so protective and secretive was he about his tiny apartment in the old Reptile House (at night, he was the only soul—unless one believes animals have souls—in the zoo), he was mostly kept on due to kindly administrators who did not want to confront him. That he had abandoned his snake pit tonight was remarkable. Astrid recalled a more filled-out Dawkins, wearing riveted glass-goggles, a ridiculous red toy-soldier jacket with epaulets, and a brass-cast antique respirator. She remembered him asking her if she'd read the long-passé steampunk magazine *Hiss* (its heyday must have been around 2014, if she recalled).

"It's all I read," he had once boasted to Astrid. "It's the only bit of truly *high* culture that's not tat, at least in England. On real paper, you know."

"Oh yeah. They do paper. That's their little thing," she'd replied.

Dawkins's main duty, Astrid knew, was to turn the zoo's security system on and off each night and, above all else, notify others if some emergency arose. This night he seemed to have failed magnificently in his only real charge. This bone-spur of a man had been jostled out of his hole, and all he wanted was to get back in it safely. To hell with the rest of humankind.

"You don't remember me?" Astrid asked. "It's Inspector Sullivan? We've met, Dawkins."

"I might do," he said glumly.

"Well, I remember you. Do you need help, getting down?"

"I don't need any help."

"Well come down then, please."

"I remember your partner, the cow," Dawkins said, repositioning his feet, as if preparing for a long stay in the tree. "She piggin' abandoned me to the animals. I can't bloody believe it." He jabbed a skinny finger toward Atwell. He said, "You're duff, you, you're a wanky excuse for a copper."

Atwell looked deservedly angry, puffing air out between her lips. She started tapping her toe. She said to Astrid, almost inaudibly, "Shall I get him down?"

Dawkins wouldn't shut up for a moment, it seemed. "The Parks Police! Ha! The anti-litter Gestapo is more like it! And she's a duffer, a —"

Suddenly, Astrid screamed, her anger as big as Dawkins's tree, "Gerrout! Shut your cake-hole and come down, sir. You're getting on my wick now, *you are,* damn it. You stupid *son* of a bitch—you *two*-bone dox!" The deadly ire of second withdrawal was out again, this time for all to see. And it felt like righteousness. It felt like bliss on fire.

"Tell him," said Atwell. "Tell him."

Astrid took hold of herself. She grabbed the little thread of fury spinning out from her heart and she reeled it back in.

"This is inexcusable, sir," she said, coughing a little. "I'm sorry. I didn't mean . . . I . . . but you're an employee of the royal parks, right? There's no need for all these insults. But Mr. Dawkins, that is. You come down now. You must be cold and tired, mustn't you?"

"No, mammy, I will not," he said. "There's bloody dangerous animals loose. No can do, officer." He gave them a scandalous, bony-cheeked grin. "Why should I come down now with tigers still birdy-fly-fly free?" He pointed again at Atwell, wagging his finger. "I wasn't enough of a victim before, was I? I was all ballsed up and you did nothing, and that's wot's really got me up a tree."

Atwell shook her head. She looked at Astrid with a momentary confusion, her big eyes like almonds suddenly cracked open. She said to Astrid, "I didn't know who he was, ma'am. He was screaming—I was alone. You know that, yeah? You know I needed assistance. That's the reg."

Atwell turned back to Dawkins and said with an affected confidence (which Astrid found a little off-putting), "You can't have everything you want, just the way you want it, on your schedule, Mr. Dawkins. That is life, my friend." She whispered to Astrid, "Look at him, up a tree like Zacchaeus. He's *strange*. Remember: he said his mother was in the zoo."

Astrid whispered back, "I say we just make as though we're going to leave him. He's an . . . obscure gent, isn't he?"

Then Astrid said to Dawkins, "Mr. Dawkins, what's this about your mother, in the zoo?"

Dawkins startled, raised his arms as though defending himself against something, then looked into his lap. He said, "She's not exactly me mother. She's my sister. She's visiting. Except . . ."

"Wha?" said Atwell.

Astrid said: "I need the facts here, Dawkins. I'm warning you. I won't be bothered with nonsense at this point. You don't want to be arrested for obstructing the course of justice, do you? Let's get this straight: your *sis*ter is at your flat, in the Reptile House?"

Dawkins glared at her, nodding his narrow head in anguished fury.

"She's my best friend. Her name's Una. She's really not supposed to be there, in the apartment. I hain't allowed to have visitors. She's Indigent, of course, but she don't have the special status wot I've got. But I thought, if I just tell people she's my mother, right, they won't press. It's not what you think. It's not *abnormal*," he said, pronouncing each syllable. "See, she's a bit thick, all right? I take care of her, sort of like. We have our own pet snake, too. She's all white—perfectly. Una doesn't go anywhere without our snake. People don't understand it, you see? She has brain damage. When she was nineteen, she was run over. A glider-lorry full of Bronze Age artifacts, from one of the unis—a student driving it. In Dagenham."

Atwell and Astrid looked at each other, and Atwell said, "Dagenham—just past Barking, of course."

"Ha-ha," said Dawkins. "If the Watch comes, they'll put her in a Calm House, and I'll never see her again. You can't tell them."

Astrid said, "Mr. Dawkins, I'm very sorry, sir. I think we'll just need to make sure Una is safe is all. I'm not worried about anything else. I won't tell the Watch. But will you please come down?"

Dawkins said, "Can you get me a soft drink?"

"Uh, well," said Astrid. "I suppose we—could? Can't you just climb down? You're going to hurt yourself."

"I'll need a Diet Vanilla Coca-Cola?" he said, a bit shyly. "Then I'll come down."

Atwell turned to Astrid, her lips parted, with a perplexed expression. "Where do we get that, sir? That's from fifty years ago." Astrid shook her head, and quietly said, "We don't."

She said to Dawkins, "Listen, we'll see if we can get someone to get you a . . . Coke . . . back at the nick, but you really need to come down."

"*Diet. Vanilla.* Coke. There's a special edition."

"Yes, well," said Astrid. "You're going to feel the fool if you stay there, aren't you? What would Una think? Aren't you worried about her? And Mr. Beauchamp is on the way. Do you know Mr. Beauchamp? David Beauchamp? Is he your . . . gaffer, or something?"

"Beauchamp? Oh, f-allin' bugger us all," said Dawkins, looking crestfallen. "He'll give me the sack if he hears about Una." He shook his head. "Poor girl! She's not well—physically. She's got the stomach flu's goin' round. And I'm . . . not well. We need each other very badly, Inspector. I told her to stay in the Reptile House when I saw the lights start to go on around the zoo. She's a bit done up tonight. I blagged a kind of fancy explorer's outfit, right, with lots of pockets and all, yeah? But when I saw the jackals, I panicked, and I nipped off, and I don't know where Una is now. Oh blood and sand! I'm an 'orrible thing!"

Astrid sighed. She said, "You're making this out to be more than it is. Really, Mr. Dawkins. Come down. Beauchamp doesn't need to know anything."

"You all can take the mick out of me if you like, and so can Mr. Beauchamp, but I'll report it to the King's Employment Tribunal, I will. I'm not going to be forced to endanger myself. And there's a crazy man in the zoo, too—I saw him. Mad as a box of frogs. Talking to himself."

"You saw someone *else?*" This new fact blindsided Astrid. She looked toward the zoo for a moment. "A man? Another man?"

"From a distance. I think. I think. Yes, I thought I did. I was too terrified to get close. He looked rather desperate. He—this is *odd*—he—"

"Take your time, sweet pea," said Atwell.

Dawkins smiled at her, blinking. "I *am* a sweet pea, to be honest. But a fucking cold one!" He starting hugging himself with his arms, but could not, in his exhaustion, muster much vigor. "Well," he continued. "Here's something funny." He rubbed his hand on his thigh and looked at Astrid. "I could have sworn the man, well, he weren't at all the spit of you, no, Inspector, and he'd be a minging, plug-ugly version of you. But he *sort* of 'ad your cheekbones, like, *vaguely* mind you, and a *sort* of similar something about his face, though he did look badly battered—and drunk. Typical Flōt sot, I should think. Do you know him?"

"Of course not," she said.

"You ain't some . . . type of . . . cousin?"

Dawkins's claim disturbed Astrid, and her heart began racing. She said, "Ha! Now you're off your chump." But her anxiety hadn't gone. The idea of her drunken doppelgänger, in the zoo, created an instant sense of unreality that signaled, for her, the last gasp of her own sanity. The travails of second withdrawal were far worse than she'd imagined, it seemed.

Nonetheless, she decided to try an old FA trick—to "act as if," that is, to pretend she wasn't really crazy. She said, "Now, will you come down from the tree? Or will we need to send something up to get you?"

"Yes, a Flōt sot!" Dawkins repeated. He seemed pleased to be able to condescend to anyone.

He didn't say anything for a while, and then, with an agility that took Astrid and Atwell by surprise, he started to lower himself to the ground, unfurling one arm, taking hold of a branch, and so on, again and again, with balletic grace.

"I've been getting more fit," he said. "It's more attractive. I'm going to be sex on a stick someday."

"Yes you are, love," said Atwell. She put her hand on Dawkins's back and gave him a few puppy-pats. At first, he jumped forward, then he leaned back into her hand. "Let's get you warm now," she was saying.

Just as Atwell said that, several huge sets of headlamps exploded onto the Broad Walk and on all the area around them. It was not illumination; it was the national autonewsmedia, or a leading edge of it—a white squarish satellite truck from ITN/WikiNous, a tired, slightly shit-faced reporter from the *Sun*/WikiNous, and some kind of European woman freelancer in a Lancia glider with a smashed-in front end. This little trio alone had the power to do lasting damage, or bring great approbation, to almost any public figure or institution in Britain, provided the target wasn't one of the king's favorites. How they got wind of the zoo occurrences seemed beside the point, but Astrid felt she knew whose long-fingered hand had given the media's naughty bits a throttle in the night.

"Unbelievable," said Atwell, stating the obvious.

Dawkins looked newly terrified. "I want to hide," he said. "If they put me on TV, I'll sue the bastards."

a cry in the night

YES, THE MASTURBATORY STAGECRAFT OF DAVID Beauchamp was unmistakable. An ugly blue hatchback glider was zooming up behind the others. It was he, long and sallow and perfectly humorless. He wanted the nation to see how the zoo handled a crisis—and perhaps position himself better for the zoo director's role.

Before Astrid and Atwell had got Dawkins back to the pandaglider, Beauchamp was waving his arms around, gathering the reporters, and starting an ersatz, melodramatic "press briefing."

"And I emphasize," Beauchamp was saying. He was got up in some purple shiny-tie-and-powerwool-shirt combo from Burton Menswear and trendy, loose, star-pleated trousers. On top, he appeared to be two parts Chillcreem to hair.

"The London Zoo will recover from this calamity," he was saying.

One of the ITV autonews producers, a muscular woman with a green and yellow trainer jacket, slipped away from Beauchamp and approached Astrid as soon as she saw her. With her tidy uniform and shiny baton, Astrid did seem to know what she was doing, at least more than the meretricious bigmouth in Chillcreem.

"What's he on about—a calamity? I don't see any calamity."

"There are some little jackal dogs out," said Astrid. "Bloody knows how it happened. But that's off the record, mind you. You'll have to call the constabulary's headquarters in the morning if you want it official, right? You guys have been played, you have. This is overkill."

"Would you agree to being paraphrased as 'an official source'? Or how about just 'a police source'? No direct quotes, I promise."

Astrid said, "No, sorry, I have to insist that you contact the constabulary. I can't be quoted. Please. Talk to the governor—Chief Inspector Omotoso."

"Have you or anyone contacted him yet?"

"He will be there, soon enough."

The producer began waving to a cameraman, clearly trying to get the man to come over toward her. A double-ponytailed cameraman nodded, jogged away from the ITN van, and switched his on-camera ultralight on. Suddenly Astrid was in blinding irradiance.

"Jackals?" the producer asked Astrid.

Then she spoke in a lower voice, looking down, turning away from Astrid, and speaking to someone obviously appearing by Opticall on her corneas. "Molly—they're telling me there are jackals loose. What do you think?" She hunched protectively away from the bright lights, speaking quietly. "Yeah, it's great stuff. Yeah. Let's put something together on this. It's great. I mean RTS-award-great."

While the producer began planning her coverage with her team, and the cameraman switched off his on-camera light—he looked terribly bored—Astrid tried to steal away. She wanted to stand off to the side with Atwell until she could talk with Beauchamp and work out what to do. The night was starting to seem utter lunacy to her. The world seemed to be going crazy over a few African dogs.

But Beauchamp ran over to her before she could make it out of earshot of the pompous press briefing. Beauchamp was smiling with his thin, quavering lips, and it looked forced.

"Inspector," he said with a barely veiled derision. "How are you?"

"I've been better. This is all a bit much, isn't it?"

Beauchamp's smile fell. Sneering slightly, he said, "Listen: to be brief, did you seal the perimeter, as I requested?"

"Erm, well, we never quite made it all the way around—"

Beauchamp grimaced. "Oh, that's ace! You're a dab hand for a copper, aren't you? That was the most important thing—the *only* bit that mattered!"

"There's two of us. More park police are on the way."

Astrid felt furious. She brushed her hand against the gun in her trousers, just for the feeling of calm power it afforded her.

"We did our best," she said. "We—"

"Do you know what that means? Do you?" demanded Beauchamp, nearly shouting.

As far as Astrid was concerned, it mostly meant that Beauchamp was making life harder for her.

She said to him, in a loud voice, "The Royal Parks Constabulary's full resources are at your pleasure, sir. If you want to get snarky, that's your business. What's done is done. We'll cover the perimeter, or go into the zoo and investigate the trouble. There's apparently a man in there, perhaps some kind of vagrant in there. But I don't understand how animals could have escaped."

The producer and cameraman began walking toward them, attracted by the tense exchange. The big camera light snapped on, and Astrid immediately regretted being shrill.

"You don't need to understand, do you?" asked Beauchamp.

With that ill-judged remark, Beauchamp looked pompous and

self-conscious for a fleeting moment; he began rubbing his hands together and nodding. He said, "I just think we need to get inside the zoo as soon as possible, Inspector. A vagrant molesting the animals is worse than anyone could have possibly imagined."

"Mmm," said Astrid. "It may be that, but I doubt it."

"Did you alert the Met? And the Watch?"

"Of course. The Met. We don't call the Watch. They come— you know that. That's their ridiculous frightcopter up there." She pointed straight up without looking.

"Are you *really* trying hard enough?" Beauchamp snapped.

There was silence for a moment. Astrid tried to work out how she could explain her delays that night. She said, "Of course, we'll get support." She felt flustered now. She needed to get to the commport, fast, and make as many Opticalls as she could manage.

"At bloody least the entire AnimalSafe team is on the way," said Beauchamp. "They should be here straightaways now." He blew into his hands. The park did seem to have grown colder, Astrid thought. There was rime forming on the grass.

Beauchamp said, "Inspector, you know there's also Dawkins. He's the night—"

"Yes, we've already conferred with Mr. Dawkins. He's discussing matters with my colleague now. In the pandaglider."

"I warn you," said Beauchamp, leaning in close and confidentially. Astrid was struck by the unnatural luster and taut look of his hair. "That Dawkins, he's . . . shady. Occasionally, you know, his mother visits him at his apartment—very much against regulations—and she could be in there tonight. I wouldn't be surprised if Dawkins is at the bottom of *all* this nonsense."

"I don't think so," said Astrid, trying to interrupt before Beauchamp forced her to make life more difficult for Dawkins than it already was.

"Mr. Beauchamp, I don't mean to abandon you, but I do need

to go now. I was just about to consult again . . . with the constabulary . . . and I'm sure you wouldn't want me to . . . delay?"

"No," Beauchamp said, nearly spitting. "Oh, the park force has
dawdled quite enough." He breathed hard through his nostrils, and
added: "And I can't *do* much with my squad if we don't have proper
police control of the situation, can I? Go!"

A picture-perfect quintessence of assholedom, she thought with
some satisfaction.

There was, abruptly, a tremendous "knock" and a shattering-
glass sound, very definitely from inside the zoo. Everyone gathered
on the Broad Walk—the autonews producers, the freelance writer,
Beauchamp, Astrid—looked in the same direction.

They heard a man cry out, "DRYSTAN! DRYSTAN!"

"What the bloody munkers was that?" Beauchamp said.

"I don't know. It's not a 'what'—it's a man, surely. Still," she
managed to say, her voice quavering a bit, "we'll need more backup,
just in case, and I better get on the comm-port, right? I need more
support."

Beauchamp sniffed at this. "Yes. Support," he said with a simpering nod. "And we're not going to forget the animals, are we?
Don't forget that. Yes, go. Go, go. Nip along, please!"

ASTRID DASHED BACK to the Paladin, where she found Atwell
and Dawkins in the backseat, talking in friendly tones and warming
themselves a bit, outwardly unmindful of the chaos around them.
She wondered why Omotoso was taking so long to get back.

She tapped on the imagiglass. Putting her lips to its warm, tickling, invisible force field, she explained to Atwell, breathlessly,
that—with jackals on the loose, the automedia out in force, the zoo's
AnimalSafe Squad assembling, and two potentially endangered
people (Dawkins's sister Una and a vagrant) still in the zoo—the

operation was necessarily going to be expanded. They would need to summon more PCs from the constabulary, and escalate with the Met, too, who still hadn't arrived.

"What we need now is air support," Astrid said. "Everything is moving too slow. The Watch have eyes in the sky. The autonews have them. The officers in charge? We have David bloody Beauchamp."

"Has Omotoso got back?"

"Still . . . no," said Astrid. "I'm a little surprised. Perhaps he knows already, and he knows something we don't. I don't know."

Dawkins asked, "When am I getting my Diet Vanilla Coke?"

"Patience," Atwell said, "pa-tience," lengthening the syllables in soft susurrations.

"Oh god," said Astrid, shaking her head at Dawkins. "Like it or lump it, you've got to wait. Will you cut us a break?" Turning to Atwell, she added, "Perhaps the guv'll try to keep this whole operation small and nimble. I wouldn't be shocked if he says manage this yourselves and tell the media to give public affairs a bell in the morning."

Atwell said, "I hope you're right."

"Inspector," Dawkins said sheepishly, shaking his head. "I didn't *mean* anything when I was on about *you* lot and that crazy bloke's cheekbones. It's just doing me head in a bit, Inspector— this night."

"Hasn't it already been done in quite properly?" teased Atwell.

"I know," said Astrid, trying to reassure Dawkins. "It's OK."

But she'd begun to wonder more about this stranger in the zoo. There was the faintest feeling of connection.

"Drystan?" she said to herself. "What a . . . name?" Something about "Drystan" sounded mysteriously familiar as well as beautiful and natural, too, like a dark soil she could push her hands into— dark soil, and speckled with gold. She didn't know why, but Astrid felt a new, peculiar sense of duty, too—something that went far beyond her professional obligations—to look after the man, whatever that might mean. And he was desperate, plainly. She didn't want to embrace the feeling, but she looked at it, with surprise and a respectful distance, as one might upon seeing, in a walk through an English forest, an otter.

the next two seconds

AS ASTRID STOOD BESIDE THE PANDAGLIDER, Chief Inspector Omotoso at long last contacted her via Opticall audio. She wanted privacy, so she quietly stole behind a mottled green-and-white plane tree, hunching down to take the call. (Since WikiNous implantation and corneal electronics had first become a public right, then the law, humans had developed a seemingly instinctual, distinctive way of "ducking" to answer Opticalls, colloquially called the "OptiDip.")

"Inspector? Are you there?" Omotoso said. "Inspector? Astrid?" His voice wasn't groggy at all. It was as if he'd been up for hours. (As a matter of fact, he had been awake for exactly twenty-two minutes, and he had been fielding the most outlandish series of Opticalls of his professional career.)

"Sir, very, very sorry. I'm here. This situation, at the zoo, we're trying to—"

"Yes, yes," Omotoso said, interrupting her—something he rarely did in their usual banter. "I've had several other Opticalls. Speak—fast now. Astrid? Brief me—very briefly." His usual good-natured paternalism was gone. She could hear another Opticall bleeping in the background, on his end.

"Honestly, I hadn't, at first—sorry, sir—I hadn't grasped the gravity of the problem within. I thought, 'It's the zoo, innit?' But yeah. I cocked it. There's an intruder—and another vulnerable person. And there are animals out. I've got Atwell here, but—sir. Sir, the media's here, in force, so to speak. This is more than we can handle, clearly. We need more officers. Beauchamp seems to have called every outlet. In, like, Britain." She cleared her throat. "I think I saw SkyNews just now."

"Fucking hell." Omotoso gasped. "The animals on the prowl—I heard that bit already. I'd hoped the reports were a load of cack. I thought it must be stray dogs."

"I know, sir. It's unheard of. But I doubt it's cack. At least not pure cack."

"Sod it all!" bellowed Omotoso. "How could this happen? You and Atwell are the only constables there, Inspector?"

"Yes. Sir, I wasn't here until a short while ago. I was only on-call tonight. And when I got here, it . . . it was hard to tell what was going on. It all struck me as routine. Initially. The Watch had a frightcopter up—but they—"

"They always put their useless frightcopters up. I know. Never a help to *us*, mind you."

"Yeah, guv. But still . . . it had seemed routine." She felt like the night was a blur at that moment. "See, Atwell had Opticalled me earlier. I was in the Docklands. And we saw the head of a goat and chewed up and—"

"The fecking head of a goat? And you thought that was routine, Inspector, did you? *You?*"

A raw humiliation flushed Astrid's cheeks, and she found herself almost unable to talk. She felt a strong desire to punch herself in the head.

"Sir, I'm sorry, sir. We're trying to secure the perimeter," she said. "Beauchamp's idea. Does that sound wise?"

Omotoso sighed loudly on the phone. "Yes," he said. "The parks minister wants the Met to declare a major incident. We'll have the Met's SO19* units coming—and that's not all. This all looks bad—we—*you* should have declared it, Astrid."

"Yes, sir, I know, sir. I know." She felt grievous self-reproach. Why had she treated Atwell's initial call with anything other than deadly seriousness? It was as if a Flōt relapse were already derailing her life before the drink touched her lips.

Omotoso made a long fricative noise with his teeth, an extended hissing that melted into the white noise of the Opticall line. There was silence. He finally said, "Look, I *am* a bit hacked off, but I've just been awakened in the middle of the night and told that there are chimpanzees in Baker Street and ITN or Sky are there and I'm the officer responsible for it all. Only I am not now."

"Yes, sir."

"We just need to get on with it, right? I just hope no lives are lost." He was quiet for a few seconds. "So, let's see. You and Atwell—hold the position. Try to help Beauchamp get his people together, but keep that bastard in his place. And get the bloody autonewsmedia into their gliders for now. There *are* animals on the loose, aren't there?"

"I believe so, sir," said Astrid.

"Then now is not the time to lose your bottle, right—I mean—in a manner of speaking—sorry, bad choice of words. Sorry, Astrid. I respect your recovery. Deeply!"

"No worries," Astrid said.

"And you're officer in charge of the scene, at least for the next two seconds, right? You're liable to see a huge crush of new person-

---

* Specialist firearms police units

nel, and I've asked for all the parks constables to come in. For a little while, you'll be in charge of the scene. Good luck."

"Right. Sir."

"That's it then. Steady now. Bye-yee!" He signed off.

Indeed, far from "losing her bottle," Astrid felt she was heading for one all too fast. A small part of her was beginning to worry that this whole night was nothing more than a phantasmagoric waking dream, an extended psychotic fugue brought on by insomnia and second withdrawal. Or perhaps she was already spiring, after eleven years clean? Had she already gulped an orb, and this was the ensuing nightmare in which she rode some feral bear into the shadowlands?

"No," she said aloud, trying forcefully to steady herself, as if she were her own FA sponsor. She wanted frantically to feel the confidence that Omotoso still somehow placed in her. "I'm still sober. I can do this."

automatic news no more

WALKING BACK TO THE PALADIN, ASTRID COULD not help but marvel at the sheer number, variety, and sirening intensity of emergency vehicles that had begun to arrive, so precipitously, since her Opticall with Omotoso.

The idea of a crisis seemed to have been communicated to the highest authorities, and probably, Astrid reckoned, without Omotoso's direct knowledge. Those powers had responded with unusual vigor and alacrity, a fact that corroborated, for her, that neither she nor the constabulary were any longer in charge.

Meanwhile, as a sort of case in point, Atwell and Dawkins seemed to have conceded their respective professional roles. Together, they had left the Paladin to have "a gander at the faff," as Dawkins then put it, like common rubberneckers. Astrid thought of saying something, but it seemed futile.

Two new Met solarcopters now thumped very low in the sky above everyone, their huge spotlight beams chopping anxiously across the zoo. The small autonews drone Astrid had seen earlier in the cabcab backed away, immediately, and the Red Watch fright-copter ascended to a high, observational altitude.

Half a dozen yellow-and-green checkered paramedigliders, one after another, shot up the Broad Walk, all slamming their brakes when they neared the growing vehicle logjam. A flabbergasting range of white and fluorange "jam butty" fast-response microglid-ers, ARV vans, estate gliders, and Met police saloons muscled into the area where Atwell had parked the lonely Royal Parks panda.

All the fluorescent stripes and squares on the vehicles left blind-ing scintillations of digital orange, green, and yellow on the night air. Soon, various shiny, cherry-colored appliances from the Lon-don Fire Brigade also appeared, including the renowned, seventy-person staffed Rescueglider NHS Prime hospital. Half a dozen gliderpumps began edging slowly up the Broad Walk, their huge 100-boson engines knocking and shuddering, their fat glider-pads flattening the park grass, all the hulks crawling along with the colossal hospital gilder like blind red elephants trying to squeeze down a garden foot-pavement with their fat mama.

Throughout, an out-and-out swarm of news fotolivers and vid-eographers poured forth from every direction like some massive, imploding galaxy sucking itself into the darkened hole of the zoo. Two of the news crews came in white transit-gliders with their round satellite discs starting to flip upright even as they came to a stop; the words SPOTLIGHT—LIVE AUTONEWS BY SATELLITE was emblazoned on the van from the BBC.

ASTRID DECIDED TO MARCH to the tightest cluster of report-ers, where she expected to find Beauchamp jabbering at its sticky center to anyone who cared. The new command structure meant she would have to withdraw her casual offer to be at Beauchamp's service—the old principle of police primacy would obtain from here on out, no more casual "arrangements" with the old, compliant, incompetent parks police pals.

She suspected that the whole Royal Parks Constabulary that *could* be rousted at this hour, a corps numbering close to 150 officers, would be assigned to the traditional supporting role of creating a filtered cordon around the "incident area," which would be no easy task at this point.

Meanwhile all looked pure chaos. Astrid knew about how the Gold-Silver-Bronze system worked, but only in the abstract. Like nearly all her colleagues on the parks force, she was right out of her depth when it came to the intricacies of the king's new Royal Emergency Services Liaison Panel, or RESLP, plan for major incidents. Gold was strategic, Silver tactical, and Bronze ground operational level. But until a commanding officer appeared and made himself or herself known, there was little to do but, as Omotoso put it, "hold the position" and get people to safety.

"Sorry, sorry," said Astrid, gently trying to nudge reporters aside and feeling mortified in doing so.

When she finally got to Beauchamp, she found him holding court within a scalding panopticon of direct-to-WikiNous camera lights. She felt oddly comforted to see him; Beauchamp at least was acting true to form, if nothing else in the world was tonight.

"Heya," Astrid said, jostling beside him. She inadvertently pushed him off-center. He slipped down to his knees; he rested there for a moment like a churchgoer, blinking in surprise until she helped him up. The accident earned Astrid a prize frown.

"So, so sorry," she whispered. Then, turning to the throng, she said: "Listen, people. Everything's changed. A major incident has been declared."

Not a soul seemed to have heard her. Beauchamp started smirking, and said, "What? A major what?" He was nodding his head. He leaned in close to Astrid and said in her ear. "I see your 'support' is here, although I should think you had nothing to do with that, did you? And now I can't even find my squad. God bloody knows how they'll find me in this mess."

"Just shut it," Astrid said in a stage whisper. Beauchamp's expression didn't change. He seemed content to be spoken to in this way—as if used to it.

"The public's safety is the priority here," she said, "followed closely by the welfare of your animals. Isn't that what you would expect, or is there something else you're after?"

Turning toward the reporters, Astrid cleared her throat. "Listen!" she shouted. "Right!" There was, at least, a modicum of quiet. A great array of lights immediately turned upon Astrid, making her squint. "People, I need you to please get into your gliders and other vehicles. And I would appreciate it if you didn't quote me. The Met's public affairs department will be handling questions from here on out."

There was another pause, then a gruff voice, a journalist's, called out, "On your bike, Mrs. Plods!"

Several reporters guffawed, but one of them responded to the first, saying, "Why? Why insult the officer, you lot of shite-for-brains? You'll ruin it for all of us." But his tone was ambiguous, even sardonic.

"Hang on," said another. "This isn't a restricted area, is it? I'm my own gaffer, and I've got a bloody press card—we all do, I should think. Not even the king can stop us."

"Careful!" someone with a gulping, frog-like voice warned. "Sedition!" he stammered. "You're up . . . you're up . . . you're up to your ears in it."

"Shut it, you fecking royal tool," another responded.

"Harry9 can suck my eyes!"

Astrid felt panicked by the open defiance in the air. She didn't grasp the sense of bitter irony the reporters all seemed to possess.

"I," she started to say. She felt her heart skip and then flutter and jerk into an awkward gallop. For a moment, the edges of her vision grew cottony and white, and she thought she was going to faint.

"God damn it," she seethed, not quite inaudibly. She was furious at her weakness, her wilting under pressure, but unable to summon that anger and bring it out where it might have been useful to her. The rage seemed to knock her heart back into a normal if fast cadence, but she still felt overwhelmed. She could not think of a time when she felt more scrutinized.

"There are bloody animals out!" she spluttered. "Are you half soaked?"

"Yeah, yeah, yeah. Animals shanimals. We 'eard that one already."

"The major incident alarm's on," she said. She tried hard to soften her tone but felt beyond control, too, as if steering an airbike with its handlebars abruptly pulled off. "You—*you* lot need to protect yourselves. There's a mobile control room will be arriving here presently. Do you understand, people? You're standing in the hot zone. We're all in danger. You've got your press freedoms, but you're at your own risk."

Astrid felt, for a moment, a sense of feeble power.

"We heard you, officer," said an older woman reporter with short white hair. "But we've had it with being cowed. We're sick of it. There's something very, very funny going on here. The Watch will be here and start neuralpiking us just as soon as the animals do anything to hurt us. We're supposed to—"

"We can't protect you if you stand out here," she said.

They were looking at her more seriously now. They seemed to respect her assertiveness, inept or not, although it was clear they wouldn't roll over for her. As her eyes adjusted to the light of the cameras, she began to see some of their faces. Many were different from what she would have imagined. The parks police rarely dealt with rank-and-file grunts behind the automedia, and Astrid never had. Their eyes gleamed with an unexpected perspicacity, and their faces wore expressions of genuine concern. It made her think of how the news supposedly used to be, in the days of "investigative reporting" (the term had fallen into disuse) and long-form magazine journalism, a kind of probing rough-literature that had vanished with the Property Revolts.

These autonewsers looked grubbier than the stereotypes. The men seemed to be wearing the same sort of stolid nuplastic-fiber jackets and organum-blend shirts that her male colleagues bought from M&S. The women reminded her of herself on her days off: hastily made up, dressed almost uniformly in off-the-shelf black crylon garments. Some wore their hair back with the same crooked multibarrettes and "living" bio-fiber-hairbands she used. Everyone appeared either just wakened or indeed, half-spiring. She had always figured that the scruffy journos from Canary Wharf who occasionally appeared at her Seamen's Rest FA meetings were exceptions, not the rule.

A few of the reporters started glancing around, scrutinizing nearby hedges and trees. One of them, a white-haired warhorse in an old-fashioned Barbour wax coat with frayed cuffs, hunched slightly, then began lumbering around, spinning a bit, and nearly falling down until he completed a full 360-degree inspection.

"And that, my pretties, is my pirouette—en dedans!" he wisecracked.

Another journalist, a woman grasping in one hand her long autoreporter's zoom-microphone and an opened bag of "masalaflavored" algae crisps, said, "Sorry, but I don't feel threatened." She was shaking her zoom-mike at Astrid as she spoke. "Looks like there are some new authorities around here anyway," she added.

"I'm concerned," Astrid said lamely. "I would think we should all be careful. Do we really know what's in the zoo? What's really there?"

"What's there is a story. And animals. Animals extinct everywhere else on Earth."

Then an autojournalist who seemed to be gazing, involuntarily, at the ground, his lower Hapsburg lip trembling, began to shake his head no. He said, "Yeah, piss off! Just—just—just tell us when the press—press—*press* conference starts! All right?" He sounded both stern and petrified. He kept flexing his fingers and making weak fists—open, closed, open, closed. He looked up and gazed into her wired eyes.

"I'm packing in the 'automatic' news," he said acerbically. "It can f-f-f-*fuck* off. I'm going to find out what the hell's going on, and I'm going to write about it—m-myself."

Astrid found herself admiring his courage.

She wanted some of it.

an omen in the heavens

THERE WERE A FEW MINUTES OF STANDING AROUND
and grumbling while an even greater—and far more dangerous—
chaos seemed to encircle the media group where Astrid stood. A
horde—police officers from the Met, firefighters, plainclothes officials, as well as the scruffy members of the AnimalSafe Squad who
had been trickling in for rare duty—all these people seemed to be
trying to figure out what to do next. There was, as yet, no sense of
a command structure.

Suddenly someone shouted "Look! Bejesus! Look! Look!"

Astrid expected to see some gorilla or wild jackass galloping
toward them all, but there were no animals and indeed no spatial
focus of the crowd's attention. Holding still and closing her eyes
slightly, she tried to discern where the man who was shouting
stood, for there were now dozens of people milling about in apparent confusion.

"Look!" the man said again, and Astrid turned and saw him. It
was the old reporter in the wax coat, grinning and pointing toward
the sky.

Astrid looked up. "Christ," she said.

What the man saw was indeed shocking. Across the park, just above the tops of a line of sick elms, was Urga-Rampos. It was immense. Its tail of luminous space-dust and ionized gases spumed upward and made the comet look as if it were hurtling down, to Earth, like dying Icarus with his long lustrous hair. It shined with an intensity that Astrid found disturbing.

"Amazing!" said another voice.

"It's bloody, bloody lovely, that is. Nice work, God."

"God?" another said, scoffing. "I don't think any 'God's' involved."

All the chaos of the night seemed to pause. The whole congregation grew quiet and all eyes turned to the comet. The new moon made the comet especially conspicuous, almost shameless, as if a great ball of firelight had been plucked by a giant, crushed in its hands, and wickedly smeared upon the black sky.

The old reporter in the wax coat said, quite sententiously, " 'Exhaled meteor!—A prodigy of fear, and a portent of broached mischief to the unborn times'!"

"What?" asked Astrid. "What's that?"

The reporter didn't answer her, didn't even look her way. His smiling eyes were fixed on the comet.

For a few minutes, most of the WikiNous fotolive camera operators trained instinctively on the comet itself. The crowd's reactions gradually muted. There was a flurry of "OptiDips" and messages to editors, with autonews crews running back and forth to their satellite vans. Soon the autojournalists, all clumped on the eastern edge of the zoo, looked unsure of what to "capsule," as fotolive filming was often called. Many chewed on their lips and fidgeted their toes, taking deep, anxious breaths. News that more animals were on the loose and outside the zoo had trickled in. Cornered, the autojournalists reverted to blinkered form, with several grabbing footage of other autojournalists videoing and fotoliving other autojournalists, and so on. Some aimed 3D cameras and lobbed fotolive lens-bots uncertainly toward the zoo, taking in hedges and partially obscured enclosures with animals mostly in the dark. The density of the hedges and detritus along the fence was such that none of the low-budget lens-bots could make it into the zoo. A few floating lens-bots made it in, but something—or someone—kept downing them. Even in the day, there was little one could see of the zoo from without. A great pall of unease spread across the scene, and inevitably, the autoreporters once again stared at the comet.

"It started off pretty," said one of them. "Now it's filling me boots. I don't like it."

"Something bad's going to happen," said another.

"Please, people," Astrid called to them, but no one was listening. She had never felt quite so impotent in her job. "For your own safety, please get into your gliders."

But only the old reporter heeded her, and even he seemed more motivated by fatigue than any desire to comply. He slouched back to his glider, which was, as it happened, surrounded by other gliders and immovable. He got inside, broke open an orb of Flōt, and spired away.

ASTRID THOUGHT she should go back to the pandaglider and check on Atwell and Mr. Dawkins. Because of the major incident tumult, the Paladin was now well out of the center of things, located on the northern tip of the gathering in a comparatively dark, quiet grove where the Broad Walk seemed—it was an illusion of landscape architecture—to narrow to an arbor. As she walked toward the Paladin, she came upon a rather overweight fotolivographer with a smartly dressed TV autoreporter. They stood there, the reporter banging an apparently broken torch on his knee. He was being illuminated by the blazing light attached to the videocamera. There was an illicit air about them, somehow, and Astrid felt wary.

"May I help you?" she asked.

"Oh, how you can!" said the autoreporter. "We're looking, as it were, for the—front? The main entrance? To the zoo? We understand there's a sign there." He stood up more erectly. "We need an establishing shot?"

Reluctantly, Astrid explained how to get there.

"You see, we also need—" the autoreporter said. He waved toward the fotolive camera. "That's not on, not at all."

"You really shouldn't risk it," Astrid said. "We've not at all got the area secured."

"Of course," said the reporter, scratching his chin, but the two then just silently walked off toward the entrance, as if Astrid simply had ceased to exist.

All at once, again, there was a great human scream from the zoo. "DRYS! STAN! DRYS! STAN!"

"Jesus! Listen! Listen!" the reporter said.

A new flurry of noises seemed to reply, and the call became only one of hundreds of feral clamors in the cooling air.

"Fucking hell," said the reporter.

More and more squeals, chitterings, and yowls came. To most of the emergency workers, zoo staff, and journalists gathered, it sounded as if all twelve thousand of the zoo's residents had been freed and now beset one another. In fact, fewer than fifty were out, and most were simply petrified. But that was about forty more than the metropolis could manage with all its powers assembled in the best case.

As the TV news crew walked away from Astrid, dozens of so-called blue-freqs—the main class of message on the all-London emergency tactical channel—began crackling softly in her ears. Their pale, zinc-tinted hue filled her eyes. The night had gone all metal: *Bronze 7, Bronze 7, this is Silver 2, orders from Gold. New orders from Gold, subdue animals by any reasonable means. Orders from Gold to Red Watch. Repeat, orders from Gold: Red Watch should neutralize intruders.* Astrid saw that she seemed to have been passed over, operationally. Events were hurtling forward, and she had become an onlooker.

But she felt, for reasons she couldn't work out for herself, that she could not let it stay that way. The man inside the zoo had brought her here tonight, and now she needed to get stuck in. She didn't feel great clarity about this, but rather an inexplicable urge to bring *something*, if only her *self*, and to "take a place at the table," so to speak. And there was the matter of Dawkins's sister, Una, too. There was a practical problem. Una needed help. But why on earth had a man calling "Drystan" snuck into the zoo? *Who* was he, and *why* this dawning feeling of a need to see him. Why her? Was it because she was, very simply, out of her mind with withdrawal insanity? Or was there something else—something that couldn't so easily be dispatched? There was a pragmatic problem with him, too, she thought. The Red Watch would kill him, and she felt she must find him and, somehow, *try* to protect him before they swooped in. The man's very vulnerability felt vast to her, like a whole new country, a world of very hard-won innocence, and she, if for no other reason than the kindness of strangers, had been called to it.

relieved of duty

AS ASTRID REFLECTED ON THESE THINGS, THE corners of her eyes began flashing purple—a regular, nonsecure audio Opticall. It was Omotoso again.

"Dear Astrid—I have some . . . strange news. But where are you?"

"Probably less than a hundred meters from you, sir."

"Oh, yes—oh, Astrid, I can actually see you. We're south of you, dropped onto the bloody Broad Walk like clumsy squirrels. It's bunged up with autoreporters."

Astrid spotted Omotoso, dressed in his civvies, waving at her. He wore a tight red and black leather jacket, which meant he'd ridden his cycle-glider, and incongruous navy and close-fitting elegant dress trousers. It felt funny to speak to her superior via optical and auditory neutral interface, standing so relatively close in the distance. But there was a certain intimacy about it.

"Astrid," he said. "We are getting . . . intelligence . . . *reports* from some local psychiatrist—I don't know the fellow, a Dr. Bajwa, and that's confidential—that anyway, there's . . . *he* is concerned the person inside the zoo may be a very old, rather helpless patient of his. The doctor's himself apparently quite distraught about it all. The patient's name, it's Cuthbert—*Cuthbert Handley*. He's a serious Flōter, we're told—and certainly not in any stage of recovery, like you. Totally nonviolent. But this Bajwa chap, he says Mr. Handley thinks he hears animals at the zoo, and he says this fellow might believe they're asking *him*—and I mean the animals—to release *them*. The doctor had heard from Mr. Handley tonight, via Opti-call, and it was clear the NHS Twelve Code 'danger to one's self or others' proviso was met, but the doctor, as I said, he's upset. Mr. Handley's very intelligent and evidently well meaning. But very dangerous in this circumstance, I might add. And, surely, he's got that very English—*you* know—sadness. He claims to have 'special powers'—don't we all? But Mr. Handley, we think, is at the bottom of this whole mess. An old Flōt sot. Astrid?"

Omotoso, surrounded by swarms of people, was looking medi-tatively up into the sky as he spoke, as if stars were the only clear phrases he had to choose from.

Astrid thought of the grandfather she'd never met. He was, her mum said, ancient, caring, crazy, and Flōt-addicted. And there was the murky resemblance between her and Mr. Handley that Dawkins had alleged. She knew Cuthbert Handley couldn't be him—that was impossible, right? There were tens of thousands of crazy old Flōters, weren't there? Yet she didn't feel even remotely less spell-bound by this man for knowing it.

"I . . . I don't quite know what to say. That fits with what the night watchman Dawkins said, sir. He said the man, this Mr. . . . Handley? Perhaps, he did indeed look as if he were spiring. Then he has some very serious mental health problems?"

Omotoso rubbed his cheek. "To say the least."

Atwell had walked up to where she stood. Dawkins was there, too. There was also someone new, a very short woman in a most improbable and campy sort of archaeologist's getup, including a khaki jacket with cap-strap epaulets, a rugged twill skirt, and, of all things, a pith helmet. She wore a kind of brace on her arm made of shiny brass gears. She had a round face with creamy skin and large, mildly protruding blue eyes, with two pieces of copper tubing arcing from her helmet down into her jacket. These features, with her short thick neck, gave Astrid the slight impression of a mechanical female bullfrog. To top things off, she held a small white snake curled in her plump hand. She was a kind of steampunk hobbit.

Astrid kept looking at the woman as Omotoso continued.

"Right. OK, here's the thing of it, Astrid. Do you have any advice? With your community work and all, you know, your recovery meetings and such, how . . . how would you deal with a Flōt sot on the rampage?"

"Kindly," she said. "And I wouldn't say 'rampage.' This is a man whose problems are much bigger than Flōt. If he's in second Flōt withdrawal, he'll be angry. If he's a sot, he'll be in first withdrawal, at best, and that means—well—people get fairly off their chump. If he's had BodyMods, and he's old, and he's still somehow alive and taking a drink, he could . . . yes . . . he could be talking to animals or any number of imaginary friends. But 'rampage'—I wouldn't put it like that."

"Right," said Omotoso. "Point taken."

"Thank you."

"And, Astrid, I've had a think, and here's the hard bit: I, er, I *need* you to go home." For a moment, she said nothing more. "Very sorry. You've had a long day. Just jack in the job, just for tonight, and go home and rest a bit, right? You are—*temporarily*—relieved of duty. *Tempor*—"

"Sir, why? What the fuck is that?" She felt blindsided—and utterly betrayed. "I don't understand. Why? What the fuck—"

"Watch it," said Omotoso. "This is still the constabulary."

Omotoso began shuffling one of his feet and avoiding Astrid's gaze. He looked restless.

"There's been . . . there's been a kind of occurrence, Astrid. I'm sorry. I'm not supposed to tell you anything even if I *do* know. But, er. It's a man. Found badly injured about an hour ago at a small group suicide in Poplar. One of the cults, at it again. This man, he was still alive when the Red Watch got to the house, apparently. He claimed to be from your FA meeting, apparently—Marcus is his name. I think he was—this is rather tragic—he thought the Watch might somehow contact you. I think he was . . . scared. But here's the thing. The same thing's happening all over Britain tonight. At least twenty FA members around the country participated in a self-murder attack. And there are more and more reports coming in."

"Fucking hell. Marcus? I saw him earlier tonight. He was sober. He's kind of a prick, but he's all right, he's—"

"Not anymore. The Watch, Astrid. The bastards neuralpiked him. He was already full of drugs, and they killed him. May as well have done it for sport. They are cold bastards. But your name came up, and I've just been . . . asked . . . *told*, really . . . to take you off tonight's situation, as a precautionary measure. The Watch, they're absolutely terrified of Heaven's Gate infiltrating any of the police forces. If there's a perceived connection, an active suicider, they'll want to have a look. It's nothing to worry about, Astrid. You can understand that, I'm sure?"

"But I thought . . . you know . . . that the king and his lot approved of FA and all? That's not FA. It's not immune, after all, from the same kinds of temptations any other organization has in England. I thought Harry liked us?"

"I wouldn't go that far. Indeed, there are things that concern me—new policies—that are going to touch on FA and hundreds of other orgs, I fear. Your name was in the mouth of a dying cult member. It'll need to be cleared up. It's bollocks."

"Marcus . . . he wasn't a cult member. He was just a Dublin fecker. He was all right."

"I hear you, Astrid. And there's something else. This is why I didn't use the blue-freq system, Astrid. I have . . . heard . . . from people I trust. I have heard that the king—and God knows whether it's even coming from the king himself—but I have heard that there's a Privy Council L7 directive coming. Astrid, FA—the king's people are saying there's a link, with the cults."

"That's a disgusting lie. That's a lie. It's not true, guv."

"I know that. You know me. I know this is all naff. But here's another thing: with the Army of Anonymous on the prowl, too, the whole 'anonymous' thing isn't playing well . . . with the nobility, right?"

"That's crazy. We've nothing to do with AA-UK, with English republicanism, with politics of any sort. God damn it!"

She felt gutted about the directive. She had seen dozens of suicidal men and women saved by the fledging self-help organization. The L7 order would deeply damage if not destroy it. It would mean mass EquiPoise examinations. It would mean the inevitable hoodings, forced "serfing," the reclassification of middle-class members.

"FA *helps* the king. This is a nightmare. And all that you said before, where you asked me for my advice? Were you just splurtin' brown sauce on my chip butty?"

"No! Come on, you. I . . . It's not the kind of thing anyone wants to bring up. Is there someone—one of your FA friends, perhaps?— someone, someone like that you can, you know, sort of have a chat with, too?"

"I'm off FA at the moment, sir. I'm not drinking—but I've sort of gone off it."

"Gone off? That doesn't seem wise. You didn't sound like that a second ago."

"Yes, sir. Off."

"Yes, well," said Omotoso. "I'm—you're not just saying that, because you're afraid of the Watch and the directive?"

Omotoso was now looking at her directly, with the same kind of tolerant expression he might have worn were they standing beside one another. "But that's . . . that's your business, naturally. OK. Go. Go home. Go. Is that clear? Inspector?"

Atwell was standing right beside her now, clearly trying to eavesdrop. She wore a somber expression and kept shaking her head whenever Astrid spoke, which Astrid found both consoling and grating.

"Yes."

"I don't like how you sound. Something's off. You know, Constable, Astrid . . . you . . . I *see* this special thing inside you, like a guardian *ori,*[*] as my mum would call it—a 'head within the head.' And all will be well—for you, anyway. But . . . I'm sorry. I really am. You must go home. Do not delay. Take care of your mum. And yourself. Ring your FA mates, right?"

"I don't want to ring them."

"Astrid. Things look bad now, but you once told me that someone told you 'The best is yet to come.' "

"On that score, guv, I think Mr. Handley . . . I believe he knows something we don't, Chief Inspector."

"Good night, Astrid."

She blinked off, her heart pounding again, her thoughts swirling like blown oak leaves. A crowd of people enveloped Omotoso and he was gone. Astrid felt as if she wanted to embrace Jasmine Atwell, out of fear and pain and confusion.

---

*   Yoruba term for an inner spiritual intuition or spark

The round-faced woman with Dawkins and Atwell was staring at her.

Astrid said, to Atwell, "Constable."

"This is, as you can probably surmise, Una," said Atwell. "She just walked out. Dunno how. There must be an opening in the main gate somewhere." Atwell leaned in toward Astrid. "She's dumb—I mean, she's a mute. And she's very worried."

"I know the feeling," said Astrid. She felt speechless.

As Astrid recounted the conversation with Omotoso, and explained that she'd been relieved, Atwell nodded slowly, with an open expression, surprisingly unperturbed. It made Astrid feel both warmer toward her and, in another way, suspicious. They remained several meters away from the giant media, police, and zookeeper scrum assembled on the Broad Walk along the eastern edge of the zoo. The air had grown considerably cooler. Astrid herself was beginning to feel queasy and chilled. She wondered if the enterovirus everyone seemed to be moaning about that week had finally infected her.

"Listen," Atwell was saying. "I'll drive you home." Her voice sounded a bit hoarse, and she was chewing something, a lozenge perhaps, in an irritated, rapid manner. "Ma'am, I'm ready to spit tacks, honestly. I'm not being assigned to any of the Bronze teams either, it turns out. It's a real slap in the face. I know what's happened with you is so unfair, but, honestly, this was also going to be my big chance. I've not once worked a major incident." She sighed, said, "God *damn* it."

"I'm sorry, Constable." Astrid looked down. "You are as fine a PC as I've ever seen. I don't want to embarrass you now."

"Aww, thanks, ma'am," said Atwell. They were quiet for a few seconds. "What should we do? This is just *daft*."

The commotion—solarcopters, spotlights, emergency gliders,

fotolivers, and the cacophony of the poor animals—had reached such a frenzy, Astrid could barely hear herself think. But when the conviction to do what she did next hit her, she didn't hesitate.

"I'm going in, Jasmine. This man, this Cuthbert, I need to see him."

"In? That's insane. No. You are *not* going in, ma'am. It's not worth losing your career over, is it? Astrid? And there are wild animals about, aren't there?"

"I need to see him." She gave a forced little chuckle, but she couldn't sustain a smile. She felt scared. "I think he may be . . . in a way . . . related to me."

Atwell said, "Oh, dear. You're off the deep end, you are. Astrid. Do *not* go in there."

Astrid looked away from her colleague. She said, in a strained, shuddering voice: "My whole *life*. As a . . . child . . . and a teenager . . . and then an adult, you understand? From the time I was a little kid. Until now, see? I've felt bloody *alone* in one thing or another, almost always alone. I've had it. I've had it! I don't care if what I'm looking for isn't there or not. He's come back for me—*some*one has."

"Who?"

"That's what I'm saying. I don't know. It's Mr. Handley, perhaps? Or it's me? But I feel there's someone in me who's got to come see him—and to help him. It doesn't make sense. And the timing's bad, isn't it?"

She turned toward the zoo fence and began scaling it. "Don't stop me," she said.

"No!" shouted Atwell. "Astrid! Don't!"

She was over the barrier in seconds. At that very moment, when her feet touched zoo-soil, Astrid felt herself beginning to awaken to a world half-created. It had been the most frenziedly un-Astrid thing she'd done in her life. For her to enter the zoo this way—it was a step off a cliff. And she hadn't thought it through, at least not like a human being. She thought of her heavy *Encyclopedia of Mammals* tome back home on her bed, and its chapter called "The Wild Mind"—animals *did* think, it claimed, but it wasn't like Winnie-the-Pooh, and it wasn't like the shark in *Jaws,* and it wasn't what the white-haired Brian Cox said on *Wonders of Life.* It was deeper and stranger, and yet it was not amoral.

The prospect of a drink of Flōt now revolted her. As she ran through a few shrubs, toward the big cats zone, her mouth seemed to water, but it wasn't Flōt she desired. Oh, Jesus, thank, Jesus, she said to herself. She wondered if she was a "thinking animal" somehow now. Whatever it was, it drove her forward. Could she read the jackal mind, communicate with chimpanzees, night-ride the elephant soul? She thought, This is crazy, crazy, crazy, crazy, crazy. But it felt like some new plane, one she would have to walk through and to crisscross to find Cuthbert Handley. It was astral and psychokinetic, a place of tangling dimension-strings covered with fur and reptile scales and timespace flowing with blood. Yet she retained a sneaking inkling that a much simpler explanation existed, for everyone and everything she had encountered in this night were uncannily familiar. In one sense, the zoo's interiors were all her own. Nothing truly had surprised her.

seven

close encounter at the lanterne des morts

"MUEZZA? BARMY CAT? GONE THEN?"

Cuthbert felt a visceral sadness now, his thoughts like skinless pink tubes snaking around his tummy. He also needed to relieve himself. Why did the cat have to go? Muezza was, apart from Baj, the closest thing he'd known to a friend in many years. He spotted the Green Line again, patchy and worn, and he trudged on, but then he started banging his knees together like a boy trying not to pee; he wanted to find a quiet little corner. He was no longer quite spiring. The soft, uplifting fogs of Flōt were wearing thin, and he could feel a stinging sensation in his penis. Recently, he had begun to piss in his trousers. It was a relatively new inclination, and common among older Flōters, and it contained more than a seed of childish rebellion, but it horrified him. He said to himself, 'twas time to put the mockers on the habit, wasn't it?

Up until about four years ago, he could still enter an Indigent pub—that (just barely) worked. He used to favor the White Lion of Mortimer, in Stroud Green Road. It was a famous dive, insalubrious and half its seats ripped out to pack 'em in, but he felt comfortable there. Everybody would be spending their dole and eating algae-flavored Discos and cultured-lamb kebabs brought in from the Kurdish joint across the street. Cuthbert even had a few mates at the White Lion, for a time.

But he got too comfortable, as he saw it now. He began to think he was Drystan again, and started, as Drystan, telling "lies" about his brief time at UCL. He grew garrulous. He boasted about how one day he had "dressed down *moi* tutor, Mr. Fusspot Daniels" over the parts of mitochondria, which was almost the exact opposite of what had happened with Cuthbert. He fussed about petty matters, such as whether he received fresh serviettes with every Flōt orb. He fell behind on his tab payments. Finally, one late afternoon, he wet his pants on a pub stool. He'd simply been too unmotivated to get up and go to the gents'. The barmaid, a Polish Indigent with silky red hair, had started punching his arm. "Damn you," she said. He could still hear her low, succulent voice. "You are too fucking weird for the pub." But what he remembered best was how good it had felt to be touched with feeling. It had been years.

He didn't dare go into pubs now, even if they were generally safe from the Red Watch.

THE NIGHT WAS CLEAR AND COOL, and the stars had diminished with the light pollution he was kicking up. Apart from an aching bladder, he was beginning to feel a bit calmer, even with early Flōt withdrawal daggering and dragging down his insides and the growing presences surrounding the zoo. Perhaps he would just ramble for half an hour and go home, and be nothing more than another Indigent tooling about Regent's Park at night. There would be no jackals, no otters, no unctuous cats, no mellifluous monkeys. He would forget the torn-down fence, the goat's head, the Neuters and Luciferians. He would block out his father's beatings. He would twist out from the strangling yokes of the Wonderments—and he would even put otters behind him.

But he would never get away from the loss of Drystan—not in his long lifetime, and not in another ninety years.

Abruptly, all he felt was that it was time for a slash. He unzipped hurriedly, where he was, and geysered into a sprig of wild mint growing along the brink of the Green Line path. The gibbons began again. "What's that song all about now?" he asked them aloud. As the urine streamed, some other animal howled—a guttural, chittering sort of howl. It was not duet-like; it seemed martial and masculine. Cuthbert felt a little shiver, partly anxiety, partly a pee-shiver, and he looked straight ahead, self-consciously, just as if he were before a public gents' urinal.

He gazed into the sky again for that comet, but a thick, fleeting tuft of cloud again had obscured it. Those culters, Cuthbert thought, arr, they must be gathered inside it now, out of their containers and all, looking down upon the Animal Kingdom, that Neuter Applewhite fellow getting his instructions from Luciferian cabin-mates. Cuthbert wondered what would happen when the craft landed on Earth. The pictures on BBC/WikiNous had shown dramatic tails of high-velocity ice-dust behind the comet. Only dream-skies held such objects, he felt, along with pinwheel galaxies and dripping supernovas. Such things didn't land on planets—they inhaled them.

He considered this Applewhite chap. Creepy bloke—no question. But Cuthbert reckoned that the man in some way connected to NASA, which would account for his confident speeches about space travel in his WikiNous videos. Cuthbert had seen in the *Evening Standard*/WikiNous how Applewhite, who called himself "Ta," had met his middle-aged woman partner, "Do," in Houston "We-Have-a-Problem" Texas. Couldn't be coincidence, Cuthbert figured.

Applewhite's attack on the animals grew from his scatty con-
cept that animals "Below Human" existed as earth's most existential
threat to the Luciferian soul. Animal bodies were spiritual voids
into which the alien soul could, with an erroneous trajectory, sink
like an eight ball. While humans had completed much of Heaven's
Gate's goal of the extinction of animals through the destruction of
ecosystems, the London Zoo and its connected research facilities
remained as the world's most concentrated vector of animal di-
versity. For Luciferians, it was like a giant dish of smallpox germs
would be for peoples.

Earth's Animal Kingdom, for its part, knew more about space
than Applewhite gave credit, Cuthbert knew. Laika the *Sputnik
2* space dog, Little Joe, Felix the Cat—all had been forced into
spaceships, as disposable lives, to guide their countrymen into the
stratosphere. He pictured the jackals being led into some canine-
engineered spacecraft of their own dogingenuity, shepherded by a
Wolf Angel up a great ramp. Cuthbert would have asked the jackals
to eat him before they left. He would be like the sacrificial goat, or
the architect Tecton who had been turned into seagulls, to become
a million pieces of himself, floating in space.

"I'd be a sort of *space* saint!" he shouted. He kept pissing. It was
ecstasy, to let it flow openly here. A crushing shame rapidly came
into him. He thought, once again, of how cruel he had been to that
mongrel, as a child. At least the Russians gave Laika's travails a
purpose. He wasn't worthy of Wonderments. But, perhaps, he could
work toward them.

He spotted, for a moment, a long, tapering knot of light, to the
west, which he thought just might, perhaps, be Urga-Rampos; then
it vanished. Was he only going to get one glimpse in his life? He
tried to examine the sky more closely. He did not know the stars,
their names and such, but why, he thought, should that matter?
There was only one celestial object that mattered now, for him and

for all the world. The Heaven's Gaters, he speculated, were somehow going to "switch on" an eternal death mechanism once the cometcraft landed, and all trapped spirits, great and small, human or not, would be sucked in as if into a Hoover.

It was a war. Cuthbert sniffed and turned around, and he pulled up his zipper. That seemed like a good defensive move, for starters. And he needed some sauce, he did. Where in the zoo, he thought, does a man get tipple?

He picked up the pace a bit, walking briskly northwest. Another set of motion detectors snapped on. He heard the same man as earlier, this time as distinctly as if he were standing across the street. "Help me! Bloody help me!" He heard another round of carnal barks and growls. Cuthbert bit down on his index finger. He felt worried. All his decisiveness had disappeared with the cat. He didn't know what to do, what to say, or whether to say anything. But the zoo was looking a bit more familiar. He believed he was heading toward the main entrance gate.

He turned around for a moment, and looked back. It was then that he realized he had wandered off the Green Line.

He caught a glimpse of the old historic BT Tower, sponging up and vomiting a trillion Opticall beams. It looked like the capped top of a great lager bottle. Wasn't far from UCL, really. Was it, he wondered, another mechanism of the death cult?

"No," he shouted at himself. "Stop, bloody stop—stop!"

It wasn't too late to reverse this tragic night, he thought. He might still send an Opticall to Dr. Bajwa's emergency answering service, or even to the Royal Constabulary. He remembered how he had tugged Drystan's hand with his sweaty little fingers, on the horrible day in 1968, before they plunged into the brook. He had begged Dryst to turn back, away from the Boogles, but Dryst had pushed deeper into the Wyre, screaming "Kill the Mekon!"

But it wasn't too late to stop all this nonsense, was it? With at least a speck of sanity, he understood very precisely that he was getting into a real bungle-muster tonight, and that it would alter many lives irrevocably if he did not stop soon.

The shadowy green peaks of the Elephant and Rhino Pavilion jutted into the horizon, among which the BT Tower, far away, looked especially minuscule and mannered to Cuthbert. Beyond it, the enormous city was only a glow in the tops of the trees. The stubby pachyderm spires were meant to look like elephant trunks, but they reminded him of the coned tops of old, ruined oast houses he had seen in Birmingham as a child—primitive, simple, and tall as ogres.

Without warning, a set of quick, separate *woops* hit out beside him. They were so loud and dense, he felt he had been thumped on the side of his head. He bolted. *Woop, woop, woop!* He ran for his life, in short, sloppy nonagenarian dog-trots, holding bolt cutters high, but unwittingly headed straight toward the source.

It was the work of a single, black-eyed siamang. It hung in its huge, spindly pen raised on plinths, about ten meters or so from Cuthbert. The siamang was warning something or someone to back off —and very effectively, it seemed—puffing its larynx sac into an impious black balloon. Cuthbert saw the ape, dimly, in its web of play ropes. It was fiendish.

He said in a half-whisper, "Hell's bells! Hell's bloody bells!"

Cuthbert spun back around, his hands trembling, and ran away. The *woops* came like sound grenades, more resonant and deafening than the loudest alarm Cuthbert had ever heard. It amazed and terrified him. The message was as clear to his garbled mind as it would be to any living thing: *get away, or I give you a ball of forever darkness.*

Then there were men's and women's voices, from deep in Cuthbert's psychosis. They sounded high-pitched, persnickety, and— for reasons unknown to all but the British Midlands soul—deeply

American. They were repeating certain phrases, *mammals will pass from Earth* and *deactivate the animals* and *render biology void*. The voices slipped down above the siamang's noises, dripping down into the zoo like a kind of contempt for nature, sloshed out of a cup in the sky.

"Oh," Cuthbert mumbled, irritated and feeling harried, jogging along as best he could. "The culters! They've come! I've no time for otters." Surely, the great war of the spirits between the Heaven's Gaters and the Animal Kingdom was about to have its first battle. The sounds were a sign as clear as anything. Otherworldly interiors were moving. Pain, anxiety, and failure were its wheel-greasers. He came to a stop. He could not run farther. He bent down, gasping for breath, his heart tumbling. He walked a few feet more, and when he looked up, he could swear that several indistinct figures in white crossed the path, a little ahead of him, near a shadowy pillar of some kind. He thought he saw their white bodysuits, their white Nikes with black swooshes.

"Oh, I see them, those California bastards! Two of them—with a focking camera gun or something," he said aloud. "Stop, yow focking two-bone Neuters."

The Neuters' apparent cowardice was no surprise. They would not confront him directly. For a moment, the figures seemed to linger round the tenebrous stone column up ahead on the path, then ran off, cowardly, as Cuthbert approached.

Cuthbert gasped, "Who the fuck are you lot? Come on now! Who are ya?" But he knew the answer, didn't he?

He spoke, in a voice full of false syrupiness: "If that's how *yooo* want to be then . . ." He could not work out where the man crying for help fit into all this. And what of the Gulls of Imago? Did the bloke asking for help have an answer?

The dulcet duet of the crested gibbons rose again, as if in response, singing to Cuthbert like choirboys from mahogany trees:

WITHsul, WITHsul, WE with souls, WE with souls, SO-ouls-ouls-oul. Cuthbert felt an intense sympathy for the monkeys. He also felt an odd kind of shame for having fled the siamang. It had merely tried to warn him.

With souls!

"Arr," Cuthbert said, knowingly. "I understand now." He looked at his hands. The empty one was shaking uncontrollably. He stuffed it into his pocket. His other hand's tremors were causing the bolt cutters to snap open and shut.

He tilted his head, as though listening for the subterranean effects of the gibbon song under the path-stones. He said, "Come now!"

He could not wait for an answer. A profound exhaustion was catching up with him. He wondered whether his liver, or some other major organ, was shutting down, defeating its cheap Core-Mods. He had never in his life completed anything important that he had started. The thought riled him. Tonight was going to be different. If nothing else, he would at least like to help the primates have an honest ding-dong with some focking Neuters. He found himself thinking back to his days as an Aston Villa supporter with a firm,* knocking West Brom supporters in the teeth down the pub.

But the Neuters weren't here for a bit of footy roughness.

It occurred to him again that he himself might not survive the night. The idea was not as disturbing as it should have been, but he knew he was ready to do anything to help the animals. What had he to lose anyway, besides the memory of Drystan? These thoughts, so fatalistic, had the effect of calming him. He took his hand out of his pocket. It was still thrutching about, but a bit less than before. He felt very dizzy, and ready to pass out. Perhaps, he thought, he could get a little kip, just a little.

---

* Generic name for a football-supporter organization, often associated with hooliganism

The old walkway he had entered, which formed the main route between the eastern and western edges of the zoo, and roughly connected the area where Cuthbert had broken into the heart of the zoo, had long, evenly spaced flower troughs placed in its center, creating a kind of boulevard. It was the zoo's "High Street" and had been in the same location since George IV. Though the stone troughs were empty for some reason, they were newly whitewashed. Each was three meters in length and just broad enough for someone to lie down in. Cuthbert considered this possibility, pausing and setting his knee on one of the rims of a trough, like a diver preparing to jump off a boat. If he was too lucky, he guessed, he would die of hypothermia in the trough, a primate whose time was done. He could be a ghost here, and but for the lack of drink, it didn't seem a bad place at all, not at all. If he didn't die, he might just be awakened tomorrow and a pretty woman who worked for Westminster social services would stand above him, offering a place in a doss house and a hot cuppa—perhaps a prawn curry sandwich? Or a banana? Perhaps Drystan would even find him? Cuthbert was tempted, but he resisted. Who would release the beasts, if not he? There were still the otters to let out—he could not forget his old friends, the otters! There were the poor penguins, and Tecton and the mystery of the gulls. And what if he were, as Muezza said, a kind of holy being, a "harbinger," with a task in the service of *all* animals? Wasn't he supposed to be on the lookout for the Shayk of Night? Surely he would resolve these matters, provided he stayed awake (and alive) a bit longer.

He focused his gaze on the monument and walked toward it. He felt frightened of the humanoid figures he had seen before. He thought they could rip his soul from his being at the snap of their fingers.

Perhaps, he thought, I have underestimated them. Maybe they were not merely Applewhite followers, but also demons sent by

Satan to capture the Otter Christ. As he got closer to the hexago-
nal column, he saw it was a cross-bearing memorial of some sort,
neatly crafted and built from a fine Portland stone. Six small, old-
fashioned incandescent lightbulbs burned under a small, conical
stone roof. It was the Lanterne des Morts, inspired by the medieval
one at La Souterraine, and placed here after the First World War.
The names of a dozen or so men were etched into a bronze plaque,
bearing the men's regiments and their jobs in the zoo (menagerie
staff, gardener, zoo librarian, et al), along with a couplet, which
Cuthbert read respectfully:

> Till the red war gleam like a dim red rose
> Lost in the garden of the Sons of Time.

He thought of his grandfather, long ago plowed anonymously
under the soil of Worcestershire, and whose place in England was
growing over with pink and white campion. He felt an almost practiced bitterness. Where was his grandfather's shrine then? He remembered his father, boasting that his father-in-law was so tough,
he walked away from the gas attack that wiped out his Worcester
Regiment, smoking a Woodbine.

Here I am, Cuthbert said to himself—the lost grandson of a lost
warrior of the Great War, staring down the face of a new war while
belligerents gather apace around me. I have no weapon, he said to
himself. I have no Woodbine. I have no regiment. I have no cloak
against the coming assault.

"But I have the Wonderments," he said aloud. "And all the
voices of animals."

last stand of order primata

IT WAS NOT SURPRISING THAT ANYONE, ESPE-
cially a hallucinating man, might imagine humanlike shadow figures and soulful monkeys in the area Cuthbert had finally reached.
He had unwittingly made his way to the geometric center of the
zoo, to the core of a long-established district of primates.

Cuthbert came to a set of double doors, the main entrance to the
"pavilion," which seemed no more to him than an ugly black cage
that had "caught" a loose brick-pile. Only a few decades old, it was
hard to see how it improved much on the poles and pits and cement-
poetry of yore. Like many other parts of the zoo, heavy steel grid
fencing and red brick predominated. Each species of primate had
a sign with a phrase. There were SPIDER MONKEYS—THE TAIL
HANGERS; GORILLAS—VEGETARIAN GENTLE GIANTS; SQUIR-
REL MONKEYS—SOCIABLE AND CHIRPY; ad nauseam. Debarked
climbing logs and draping ropes crisscrossed each cage, and yellow
straw covered the floors. The zookeepers worked hard to make this
cramped, leafless penitentiary happy for the animals, but no exhibit
at the zoo was so uniquely degrading.

In the central building, zoo guests could glimpse at the apes through glass windows that looked into the apes' night rooms.

Cuthbert examined a brass, embossed evolutionary tree on the way, showing how *Homo sapiens* and apes shared a common Homininae limb. There was a raised silhouette of a naked man and woman. Someone had rudely stuck a piece of chewing gum on the man's head. Cuthbert pulled it off and scratched it clean with his thumbnail. Below the naked people was a photograph of a prehistoric skull, *Australopithecus africanus*. It was yellow and long, with a tiny brain case and a protruding maxilla with big squarish teeth—it had no mandible. Cuthbert felt as though the human animal in this form could be comfortable—a place for thoughts no bigger than a tea mug.

Nearby, to his right, a brightly painted wood sign bore the message: THE GREATEST DANGER TO ANIMAL LIFE. There was a hole in the sign for a human face—unabashed guests could put their heads in the opening and ask a mate to snap a naff "picky" on their retina-cams.

The happiest of the apes Cuthbert could see was the life-size bronze statue of an old dead London Zoo celebrity, Guy "Fawkes" the Gorilla, set near the entrance of the pavilion. Leaning forward on his knuckles, surrounded by leafy vines, and blessed with plenty of room, Guy looked ready to spring downward and away, out of gorilla heaven, to dole out exploding bananas for all takers.

Cuthbert gave the double doors a jiggle. They were locked tight with a key, it seemed. But the noise roused the smaller residents. The monkeys suddenly cried out with a furious astuteness. Cuthbert was instantly animated by the whole, simian keenness of the pavilion; he could feel it, physically. The "monkeys," he hoped, were doing their part to prepare for the Heaven's Gate war. He would do his.

He was beginning to see much larger numbers of flashing yellow and blue lights blooming in the west, and more sirens. What he thought were the death cult's mini-spacecrafts in the sky—ordinary police and autonewsmedia aerodrone, along with a Red Watch frightcopter, investigating an intrusion and rumored animal release at the zoo—beat their wings of liquid titanium like huge dragonflies. He didn't understand why they didn't begin to attack. The motion-sensitive security lights he had tripped earlier inside the zoo, he noticed, were turning back off, and a pitch darkness enveloped everything near him, except for light beams coming down from the "spacecraft." A blue-black spindly bird flew past above him; it was enormous, and Cuthbert stood with his mouth gaping. It was one of the famous herons from the park's heronry on the lake.

"You," he called toward the bird. "You! Get the Gulls of Imago, will you? Can you help, can you?" But the bird was gone.

The greater apes, late to the noise making, started in just then with a fresh vociferousness. First, a cartload of four chimpanzees, already wide awake in their night room, stormed out into the outdoor exhibit area and began hooing at Cuthbert, sticking their golden, soft fingers through the spaces in the grid-fencing. It was as unusual for them to encounter an interested human at night as it was for Cuthbert. Whenever the night watchman, Dawkins, came through—and that was rare—he typically tapped their cage, listened for a moment, and walked on. But like many of the animals, the chimps were no longer confined to night rooms and holding cells after hours. (In the years before all the other zoos on Earth closed down, many had conceded that since nearly all animals are nocturnal, it was inhumane to keep them locked up all night. And no one had seriously worried about the possibility of a zoo invader like Cuthbert.)

The chimps soon roused the nearby, and most rare, mountain gorilla named Kibali, who was living in isolation because of his grouchy temperament. He was the last wild-born mountain gorilla on earth.

He had arrived from the Congo, via Uganda, the year before, all four hundred pounds of him, and he never quite adjusted. His mother and a young sister had been shot to death before his eyes by Interahamwe fighters where he'd lived, up to then, under a canopy of ayous and sapelli trees. He'd been led away from their bodies on three separate leashes.

Kibali was hobbling in circles around his night room, fingering his lips with a twitchy boredom. The room served as an indoor presentation area in the day. Its brick walls were daubed a pale green, a lame attempt to simulate "rain forest" tonality from an era nearly gone on earth, but a colossal, eight-foot-long window of toughened glass—for viewing—made Kibali look like a glum man at a bosonicabus stop.

He picked up a bunch of wood wool and shredded, lurid junk-food wrappers, which were regularly given to him for nest-building. He pulled the soft wad apart in his long black-nailed hands, and tossed the pieces away. A food-wrapper scrap, stuck in Kibali's neck fur, bore the phrase *you can see that Lena has the goods to please all "passengers" on Bonk Air* . . . Many gorillas in captivity like to construct messy nests before bedding down each night, but Kibali had stopped making nests. He was just throwing bits around. He received no comfort from the hoots of the chimps; instead, he felt compelled to strike things and to beat his chest.

Not long after he had arrived at the London Zoo, he had been introduced to a group of biosoftware-cultured females—his potential retinue. But the females had recently been sent, temporarily, to an animal shelter the zoo operated in Bedfordshire. The exile was for their own safety. Kibali had bitten one of their scalps, and nearly broken another's arm. He was supposed to be having a "cool down."

He made a belching sound, then a set of aggressive chuckles. He ran a few meters, ducking under draping two-inch-thick ropes. He batted at an enormous nylon ball across the cramped, mustard-smelling room. It bounced off the ceiling so hard, it hit the floor once and bounced against the ceiling again; considering the low height of the ceiling, however, the feat was not especially surprising. He scrambled atop a large plywood box in his chamber so that he could peer through a window slit and look out toward the disturbances. He slammed his fist against the wall, and screamed. He felt excited; something was happening, he sensed. He was trying, in his gorilla way, to ready himself.

At the zoo, his depression thrived. He had begun slapping food bowls away and pushing keepers away with a force that bordered on the dangerous. He interacted less and less with the public and sometimes threw balls and giant toys at them. They bounced off the fencing, and the humans had a laugh.

Now Kibali's back was turning silver, but he would never be able to start his own troop. His penetrating, shrewd black eyes mismatched his degraded captivity. He was developing angina pectoris of late, a result of his sedentary life and the chocolate bars and éclairs one errant zookeeper would sometimes give him, furtively. Guests would normally see Kibali through the humiliating window and try to get him to look at them with those eyes; their tapping on the window annoyed him to no end, triggering the ache in his chest and left shoulder.

The chimps seemed to be laughing at him. Kibali roared. He did not like chimp-noise. It reminded him of humans. He ran out of his night quarters into the tall but narrow outdoor section of his living space. When he saw the man, he quieted for a moment, stifling a groan. This human did not seem to hold much hope for him, but he would wait and watch. It was astonishing to be visited at this hour. Something unusual was afoot, and much like this man, he, too, felt he had nothing to lose.

"You," he called to Cuthbert. "You are headed toward the chimpanzees. Do not go there." But Cuthbert could hardly hear the noble gorilla, for his head was now a proverbial barrel of monkeys.

tell them the lord of animals comes

IT NEARLY BROKE WHAT WAS LEFT OF CUTHBERT'S own mangled heart to hear the primates cry to him. "Please now please now please now please now," the putty-faced rhesus macaques kept hollering. "Now now now now now help!" Five golden tamarins, their elegantly styled red manes puffed with anxiety, crowded onto a horizontal tree limb and simply repeated a mysterious phrase—*we promise you*—but at wildly different pitches and volumes, and Cuthbert was beginning to feel unable to cope.

"Hang on then," he kept saying. He could not stop listening, but the more he listened, the more sure he became that the "monkeys" ought to be freed *right* away.

He started with the chimpanzees, who were closest to him, still softly hooing. It was a very bad decision.

As soon as he stepped with his bolt cutters off the cement apron near the pavilion entrance, and toward their cage, the chimps whimpered a few times, then exploded. LIKE US, NOISY AND SHOWY, read their sign. If they were "like us," they were a particularly ear-splitting example of Homininae. Their screams were like the sound of several children being stabbed to death. Cuthbert gave a stupid grin, and with his wobbly hands got to work on the fence. He dimly sensed that he was facing something bigger than he could handle. The four chimps started shoving each other against the fence. One of them, a dominant male named Buddy, climbed right up the back of a smaller, younger teenager, and grasped the fence. He glowered down at Cuthbert, slapping his hand against the cage. The teenager, Ollie, peered up and barked at Buddy, whipping his head from side to side. Cuthbert wasn't sure whether the chimps were scared or angry or both.

The indoor viewing window and the building's main doors were armed with loud, guardhouse-notifying alarms, but the outdoor cage itself, which served all the different primate exhibits, was not, and Cuthbert's bolt cutters flew through the fencing with little effort. Within minutes, he had created a rectangular door, loose on three sides, and before he could finish a fourth, the chimps had shoved the door open a few inches.

Ollie sidled toward the gap and pushed his arm through. He managed to grab hold of the sleeve of Cuthbert's jumper and tore it asunder as if pulling a tissue from a Kleenex box. The chimps shrieked and passed the sleeve around. Cuthbert was a little shocked and engrossed for a few seconds, but he kept working. With every new cut, he loosened his "door" to the greater structure, and the chimps drove it open more. Finally, Ollie heaved himself nearly through, but just as the young chimp was about to clear the cage, Buddy vaulted down, and yanked Ollie back, jealously. Ollie scraped his forearm badly on the fence's jagged opening, and screamed banefully.

What happened next came with a grim celerity. The injury somehow turned Cuthbert into an enemy in the chimps' eyes. All four of the chimps piled out of the cage, and set upon him. They knocked Cuthbert down and Buddy bit him viciously on the nose, tearing a nostril away from his face. Cuthbert barely seemed to feel it; he wisely rolled onto his stomach and balled up. The others made *waa-bark* noises, as if egging Buddy on, but Buddy broke off the attack and stepped back. He whimpered again a few times.

There was a comparative silence, and the chimps seemed to be checking each other's fur for something, inspecting. They began hooing again.

Buddy finally spoke. He said to Cuthbert: "You stay away from us, geeza, you stay away." Cuthbert raised his head cautiously. He could barely open his eyes, and blood dripped fast off his face. He pressed the heel of his hand, shaky as ever, against the ripped nostril. It did not hurt, but a squinty feeling filled his eyes.

Cuthbert said: "A'm not your enemy, I'm not. I'm your *ally*."

Buddy shook his head. "Don't talk to me. Don't ever say a word to me, geeza. You are a friend of the otters, and the cats."

One of the other chimpanzees grabbed the bolt cutters and jammed them into the ground between Cuthbert's feet. Cuthbert was astonished, frozen with wonder. The chimps' dexterity and cleverness were beyond anything he expected.

Then Buddy and Ollie each took hold of one of Cuthbert's arms, and he gripped his bolt cutters. They dragged him past the gorilla exhibit, the cutters banging, across a concrete verge, to the macaques, THE ALL-ROUNDERS, according to their sign. They dumped him down in a pile.

Their strength had given him goose pimples, and he wore a weird smile. It seemed he had always only seen old pictures of chimps in powerless or sweet poses: Ham and Enos strapped to their flight couches on the Mercury test flights; nameless *pan troglodytes* being given HIV-filled jabs in some Swiss lab; Jane Goodall cradling an infant chimp in her khaki arms, sticking a milk bottle in its mouth;

Emily the "Chimp Wife" sneaking into the British Museum. But these London chimpanzees seemed powerful and confident and malicious.

The macaques were different. When Cuthbert managed to get to his feet, he gazed at them in their cage, still holding his nose, trying to stanch the blood. The three of them gazed back in silence. Two crouched on the floor of the cage; the other was curled in a motorcycle tire that hung from a chain. They were all a long-tailed species from Vietnam, and they had short, bristly hair the color of tropical honey and bright pink faces. They seemed to be waiting for him or the chimps to make a move.

Buddy told Cuthbert: "Let our friends out, geeza, or we'll kill you, you *cat*-fucker." Cuthbert got to work on the cage with his cutters. When he took his hand away from his face, the blood dribbled again, but less than before. His black jumper camouflaged it a bit. There was a dark, shiny patch across his stomach, and a streak down his leg to his foot. It was as if a hidden rage had burst out of him, messily. Yet he did not mind being told what to do by Buddy—there was a comfort in it, a sense of relief he had heard some of his ex-con acquaintances on the streets of London mention about prison life.

The black-painted caging was the same as the chimps'. Cuthbert snipped methodically, biting his lower lip and squinting.

Meanwhile, Kibali, the last silverback, had come out of his night room and was observing the whole situation from a few meters away. The chimps always made noises when he looked at them during the day. Once, at night, he had seen them with an unlucky rat that had somehow got into their cage. They passed it around, each taking a bite.

As Cuthbert snipped away, the macaques began to stir. One of them with especially large red-gold eyes, just inches away, pranced past him with its little chest puffed out, and scrambled away. The one inside the tire had climbed atop it and started to jerk the chain, causing the tire to sway slightly. They all started to make a kind of clucking-chirpy sound; he could see their pale tongues touching the roofs of their mouths. It was a threat-alert, but to Cuthbert it seemed strictly reproving.

"What are you saying?" asked Cuthbert.

Buddy punched the back of Cuthbert's thigh, and this time he could feel the pain.

"Do not address our friends, geeza," said Buddy. "You are human waste."

Kibali said, "Human. What are you doing? Don't open that cage."

"Piss off," Buddy told the gorilla, leering at him. "Fatty."

The moment that a square of metal fencing fell away, the chimpanzees trooped into the macaques' dwelling. What happened next should not have surprised Cuthbert, but the horror of it was unbearable. The chimps seized the big-eyed leader and beat and finally strangled him. The other macaques shot out of the cage and into the darkness. (One of them ended up being attracted by the helium-inflated aerial lens-bots that had been cast into the zoo by autoreporters, and she made a game of popping every single one between her hands.)

Cuthbert backed away, shaking his head. He began to cry out, again, "DRYS-STAN! DRYS-STAN!" Driven into a terrified passivity, he had regressed pathetically to childhood—lost in the Wyre, unable to find his lost brother.

As Cuthbert retreated, he noticed that Buddy was looking at him strangely.

"What is 'Drys-stan,' this thing you say?"

Buddy's lips were pursed and pushed forward and red with blood. Ollie and the other chimps stepped a few feet away from the dead macaque, making openmouthed "play faces," and hooing again.

"He's the most beautiful thing in the world," said Cuthbert.

"He can't be human," said Buddy.

Almost instinctively, as though seeking his protection, Cuthbert went to where Kibali, flat-faced and quiet now, sat watching the devious chimps. Kibali scratched his forearm. He seemed unperturbed.

"Help me," said Cuthbert. Without Drystan here, he thought, who else was there to ask?

Of course, he was speaking out of his hallucination and toward a hallucinated personality he had grafted onto a real gorilla. But a real gorilla really *was* standing before him, and its name *was* Kibali. Setting aside all Cuthbert's delusions, the fact was, whether imagined or not, he had now managed to release four jackals, three wild sand cats, a large leopard, and half a dozen great apes and monkeys.

The gorilla opened and closed his long, dark hands, as if they were stiff. He nodded, and said to Cuthbert: "This is not as bad as it looks. They have slain a spy, I am sure. They had never trusted the macaque, and neither did I—though I am no friend of the chimpanzees. The macaque was a favorite of the keepers and the other humans. He was, as one might suspect, trying to become human."

Kibali leaned forward and looked into Cuthbert's face. He continued: "The spy did little ignoble tricks for people. He had no shame. He was always being given treats by the keepers— pound cake and treacle and chocolate milk. He would do his lordly trot—*la dee da!* He would steal the keepers' sunglasses, and they would find him, later, wearing them, and they would praise him for this, and give him sweet pasties. We got nothing—slices of green nutra-bread. 'It's good for you, Kibali,' that lot would tell me. The keepers, always, keeping us down, making us more animal than animals."

Cuthbert shook his head. He said, "The chimpanzees did not need to kill him. There's a war about to start, there is, and you need friends."

"Hah!" said Kibali, rousing out of his chronically depressed torpor a bit. "What planet are you on? Have you forgotten that there is *another* war going on?"

Cuthbert considered this. His entire arms were tremoring and his neck ached badly. There was a peculiar barrenness in his head. He felt that at any moment he might flop down onto the ground and convulse, as though he had become unrooted from all concrete things, depersonalized. He watched the police lights, revolving yellow and blue glimmers, and the frantic solarcopter searchlights, hoping they would hook into him somehow, tangle him up in their stabbing points. He turned and glanced around. The macaque cage was empty, he noticed. The chimps had spirited the body away, and vanished. It occurred to him that, indeed, he was losing track of the war.

"Why do you keep saying this 'Drys Stan' thing?" asked Kibali.

"He's here—in the zoo. My brother. My poor brother. He called me here, you know."

"He is magic, human?"

"He's more than that. He's sacred," said Cuthbert. "It's what my gran said—or something like that. 'E's the Christ of Otters—the Green Lord of Animals."

"I want to know him," said the gorilla.

He looked at the gorilla, and said: "You will, Kibali. If it's the last thing I do in my life, I'll find him. Do you know about Heaven's Gate?"

"Yes. Of course," said Kibali. "They are anyone, *anyone,* who hates themselves so much that they try to kill off their own nature. Follow them like a doorway to paradise—that's what they think. But the humans treat us, even in their so-called humanity, with the *same* contempt and fear. That is *your* war on us." The gorilla touched his index finger to the fencing. "It is time that you remove this. The chimps, they will not come back. You are safe, for now."

Cuthbert hesitated for a moment. He was not worried much for his own well-being—after all, his whole life had been about damaging his well-being, and chopping out his own violent inner "gate" to the stars.

"You must promise me something," said Cuthbert. "You're strong, really strong, you know?"

"I know what you're going to say," said Kibali. There was a look of despair on the gorilla's wrinkly dark face, and he groaned. "You want me to wait. Yes, I will wait here."

"No, that's not it. There will be no more waiting, ode bab." Cuthbert began to cut the fence open. "Do not hurt any animals, right? No more of that. I can't take it anymore, right? You are being freed to stop an expected attack from the comet people, so you can protect yourself. You cannot die, Kibali. But you can't kill, either."

The gorilla did not say anything in response at first. After a while, he said, "Hah! Friend! There is blood all over you. I did not cause the deaths. I warned you. And *I* didn't hurt you. You're your own worst enemy."

Cuthbert said, "Ah, that's nothing." He could not see that he was now badly disfigured, missing one entire nostril, and still indeed bleeding profusely. All he could see, really, was that slick patch on his jumper.

"Tell any animal you see. Tell them tonight. Tell them no animal is safe. But tell them the Lord of Animals is coming."

Kibali nodded and rubbed his chin. "I suppose we would not be talking like this, human, if not for some cause. I want to *know* this Lord."

"You will," said Cuthbert.

"I must. Do not years and years of dark gorilla wretchedness add up to something? Is their worth so far below that of human suffering? Shouldn't animals like myself—I am so alone, in every world on earth—shouldn't I be allowed to see this Lord just once?"

"Arr," said Cuthbert. "Sweet gorilla, yes—but beware of the night. And I have a question: have you heard of the Gulls of Imago?"

"Ah," said Kibali. "You've been to see the penguins. They are stubborn things. I know nothing about the gulls, except that, I am told they're white—and not very beautiful, and that they like to eat chips and rubbish."

When there was a hole of sufficient size in the cage, the animal stepped daintily out and made for one of the lime trees beside the zoo's perimeter fence. Cuthbert watched the beautiful animal heave itself up to a thick low limb, pull itself across the fence, and drop out of sight. Kibali did not need to be shown the opening Cuthbert had made earlier. Nor had the chimpanzees, who had already crossed Regent's Park and reached Baker Street. But when Kibali crossed the perimeter fence, the whole night went public. More Met and autonews Skydrones would be dispatched. The Red Watch, undoubtedly, would begin a general crackdown on any nearby Indigent "disorder." There was now a four-hundred-pound gorilla loose in the city. It was the stuff of *King Kong* and "The Murders in the Rue Morgue." Even King Henry would have to be awakened.

canonization of a drunk

CUTHBERT DECIDED, AT LONG LAST, THAT HE needed to find the otters, before it was too late, before the dream of finding Drystan ended. The sounds and sights of battle were growing around him. He managed to find one of the pedestrian tunnels that led to the northern areas of the zoo. The green painted line went right into the tunnel. Three strips of tiny blue bioluminescent lights dimly lit the way. Cuthbert felt strengthened when he saw the pastiche of Paleolithic cave art that covered the tunnel's walls. Rusty orange-colored aurochs—a kind of extinct cattle—trotted along with black hooves high, as though eternally jumping something. The zoo fences—that's what they were jumping, he thought. They were free, these big orange bulls.

If things got very bad, here was a good place to hide, he thought. As he exited, he saw one of the ancient red phone boxes off to the side of the path, and he hesitated.

"OK, Dr. Bajwa," he said aloud. He went into the box. There were only a few such call boxes left in Britain, and the zoo kept it as a kind of nostalgic throwback for tourists. It was audio-only and featured a real working handset. It offered no WikiNous interface—just direct audio Opticalls to people. The overhead light remained on around the clock. The box was strangely pristine inside—none of the things you could find on the kind of phone box Indigents used for cheap WikiNous interfacing—no stickers or cards for prostitutes, no smell of urine, no chewing gum wads pressed all over the glass panels. It also took coinage, something only older people, like himself, tended to use.

He picked up the handset. It felt strangely big and unwieldy. He dug the £1.30 out of his pocket and, unnecessarily, inserted all of it into the Opticall coin slot with a shaking hand. He uncrinkled the piece of paper Dr. Bajwa had given him with his WikiNous cryptograph. He punched it in with shaky hands. The phone rang twice and a woman with a singsongy voice answered, "NHS Élite Doctors' answering service. May I help you?"

"Ar. Tell Dr. Bajwa I'm . . . in the zoo. I've come for the otters and all."

There was a coughing sound, then the woman said, "Excuse me, sir. What's your name, sir?"

"Cuthbert Handley—savior of animals."

"Um, well. Handley, is it? Can you spell that, surname first?" Cuthbert did.

"You're Dr. Bajwa's patient?" she said. "This is an emergency? Dr. Sarbjinder Bajwa?"

"Arr, ma'am." He was slurring again. "Tell him a'm in the zoo right now. Am yow g'ttin' this?"

"It's all going down," said the woman. "I believe the doctor's down in Kent for the weekend—flying his solarcopter or some sort."

All at once, Cuthbert fell backward, pulling the bright yellow handset down with him. Such was his weight that the handset, cord and all, detached like an old banana picked off a bunch. The door of the box flung open and he found himself halfway in and half-out on the ground. He felt dizzy. He threw the phone away and got back to his feet, using his big cutters to help himself stand up, like a crutch.

"There," he said. "It's done."

And then he heard them, reminding him of his task—the otters, surely:

> *Gagoga maga medu, gagoga maga medu,*
> *Remeowbrooow, Cuthber-yeow,*
> *Anglish water ish arg forever groad,*
> *Cuthber-yik-yik-yik-yik, mray for rugrus!*

Gagoga maga medu meant what? He did not know, he thought, and he might never know, but the rest he could work out. It meant, in otterspaeke, *Remember, Cuthbert, English water is our forever road, St. Cuthbert pray for us!* Three separate thoughts, gurgling and un-gilled. It was the end of meaning at the moment just before drowning. For Cuthbert if for no one else, the nonsense meant *exactly* that there was still reason to hope in Britain in 2052.

"Arr, I'm coming," Cuthbert said aloud. "Sweet, sweet boys, a'm coming at last." He started walking again.

A police solarcopter's spotlight found him and trained its shaky beam on his every move, and with the light from the heavens streaming down, Cuthbert reckoned time was running out.

He began to hobble along more quickly, toward the otters, but after a minute of pressing on like this, he found he was lost and out of the spotlight—his normal state, really. The solarcopter's pilot was inexperienced and applied too much pressure to one of his rudder pedals, and the spotter lost Cuthbert and couldn't seem to find him again, for now.

"Shit," Cuthbert said. "Thank god."

He wished he could find one of the zoo's map-signs. He did remember that the otters were located at coordinates "2B," which Cuthbert interpreted as a kind ontological code.

Through shivering lips, he said, "Or not to be—that's the palaver."

The air had turned frosty as a great western fold of stratus clouds finally scudded away for good.

Urga-Rampos had become shockingly visible. When Cuthbert saw it this time, it hit him like a kind of antibeatific vision. Its center showed feathering gradations of light, dozens of overlapping white petals. Its long arms had turned into two pallid, satanic horns. The comet itself seemed to be aiming straight for the ground, tearing the sky open. It looked constitutionally *wrong* for England. It was too big and showy and nocturnal, a multifoliate rose from an evil galaxy far away from the Milky Way. Nothing very English about that.

With one nostril missing, a body racked by Flōtism, insanity, and poverty, and his clothes in dirty, torn strips, Cuthbert faced the comet with what could be regarded as astonishing courage. He held his blood-caked fists up and shook them at the comet. He screamed, with a hoarse voice, "In the name of Saint Cuthbert! You've no right to come here!"

He fell down again, in exhaustion, on all fours, his bolt cutters clanking down, and said, "And we've got otters! Good English otters!" He was beginning to suffer acute liver failure. In fact, his skin was turning a sickly yellow-greenish hue, and Cuthbert's life was ending.

At last, Cuthbert had become the Green Saint, just like the statue in the old churchyard where his grandfather's grave was lost. He held a new power now to bring others, too, into his shimmering faith. He was the al-Khidr, the Mahdi, and now he knew it as much as he could know anything. He grasped, too, that his identity in England had always been written in the water of Dowles Brook, and in the songs of the otters since the Day in 1968 when he left the world and become someone else. Ever since, he had awaited this moment—this canonization.

St. Cuthbert the Wonderworker, the harbinger of a new animal Christ, had arrived.

LIKE MANY OF THE ENCLOSURES, the oriental small-claw otters' exhibit was deceptively hushed at night. The otters' nocturnal habits were only in part disrupted by the zoo's diurnal cycle of daytime visitors and nighttime imprisonment. They remained active denizens of the dark and tended in the wee hours to inhabit parts of their enclosure not seen by zoo guests.

St. Cuthbert's arrival was anticlimactic—at first. Much like at the Penguin Pool, he encountered no movement, no sound. On the sloped walls of textured concrete that made up the fake riverbank were tarry spraints of the animals, smeared and rubbed in by successive paws into marks that looked like a frenzied Sumerian cuneiform. The spraints released a strong, distinctive smell, like jasmine tea. The dung's smell of wildness gave St. Cuthbert confidence and calmness, and he was quick to act on it. Gripping his bolt cutters by their foam handles, he bashed beak-like hardened steel blades against one of two thick glass panels, which allowed guests to view the otters' underwater antics. The effort paid off instantly. A divot of glass popped out and water spouted out onto the walk. St. Cuthbert began jabbing the beak into the hole and easily worked open a gap as wide as a stove. Green water sluiced out in a roar, and St. Cuthbert stood back, staring fixedly and biting his lip. It took about two minutes for the entire enclosure to drain. The California comet aliens were everywhere now, swirling in the sky, screaming through crackling megaphones, roving the zoo to obliterate the souls of all living beings in Animalia. But St. Cuthbert, the water coursing over his feet, stood now in his little islet of English sacred reverie, his psychotic Lindisfarne.

The moment the water stopped rushing, the entire romp of the London Zoo's small species of otter appeared and leaped down through the gap, pouring out in one quivering, shiny, river-bottom-colored whoosh. It was as though they were, together, the last and most precious thing in England to be emptied from it, a half-water and half-earth being made of golden-brown jewels and smelling of stolen foreign flowers. They were seven animals in all, with the huge and now fully pregnant female at the center of the family, swanning forward with a certain lumpy majesty. Two males, "on point," as it were, and yikkering softly, fronted the romp, thrusting their noses out to smell for food and danger and water.

The big female turned to St. Cuthbert. He dropped to his knees. He slapped his hands onto the wet pavement of the walk. He thought he heard her say, "*Gagoga maga medu,*" but he couldn't be sure, could he, really?

"I, I, I, I, b-b-b-b-b-beg you," Cuthbert stammered, falling over and curling up. The cold air, combined with his withdrawals, was making his teeth chatter, his tongue turn to fluttering leaves. "Take away my—my—my sick head. It dunna work royt en-*nay* more."

You have freed us, the otters said. *Look at yourself, St. Cuthbert—and call for the Christ of Otters.*

But my Flōtism? What about that?

Go to the lions. They will take away all your misery. You will save England and all its animals tonight.

St. Cuthbert began to weep. It seemed clear the otters were suggesting his martyrdom.

No, he said. I dunna want to see en-*nay* loyns.

It's the only way to stop the soul-mongers. Through your salvation alone, St. Cuthbert.

No, he said. Tell me, tell me a different way. Can't I find the Gulls of Imago? He said aloud, repeating the song of the penguins, "Seagulls of Imago, yow're song shall make us free . . . from Cornwall to Orkney, we dine on irony . . . along with lovely kippers from the Irish Sea." He belched.

You will free the lions, and the gulls will come, and they will set right the arts of the world, at least for many years. They will put the machines of evil back to their original, good purposes.

Must I die? When? Why? What do I do?

But the otters weren't stopping to chat. Long used to the hundreds of incongruous scents in the zoo, they nonetheless sensed the great disturbances in the night. They were keen listeners, and the sounds of the solarcopters and the screaming chimps particularly terrified them. They moved as one, first west, then south toward the unmistakable smell of the dank water of Regent's Canal. Before St. Cuthbert could lift his head, they were out of sight.

He felt mournful and newly devastated and very tired. He could see, indeed, that his skin's color had darkened to a distinct green. It may have been magic, but it was also multiple organ failure.

As he stumbled south, through the cave-art tunnel, keeping off the paths now, and made his way toward the area of the big cats, he stopped at every enclosure, paddock, and cage he could, releasing as many animals as opportunity afforded. He swung open the great rear gate of the elephant paddock, and Layang, Dilberta, and the fierce Mahmoud came lumbering out. The giraffes and nervous okapis proceeded from their large faux-African diorama gingerly. A threesome of yipping fennec foxes from Algeria came out in a playful sprint, tumbling over each other, ready to cavort with any creature that was game. The shy black-and-white tapir named

Gertie, from Malaysia, had to be pushed along from its leafy pen by St. Cuthbert, then shoved, but it soon returned to the safe-smelling imported plants, cowering. The cow-like anoa from Sulawesi, a pair of Andean pudús, and a quintet of pert peccaries from southern Mexico—all of them trotted out quite happily and expectantly, as if their enclosures had merely been expanded.

As the saint walked on, freeing all manner of mammal, reptile, marsupial, and bird, a question he hadn't counted on began to trouble him: had all these animals really *ever* spoken to him?

Yes, answered the lions. *Don't be a fool, for at the sound of our roars, sorrows will be no more.*

But he wasn't so sure. For a few moments, he began to suspect that his mind, under the influence of decades of abuse, had been playing an extraordinary, elaborate ruse. There was a strange feeling of unreality almost suffocating him, as if every part of the whole crazy night itself had been thrown into outer space, and all he had left was a dark, unbreathable vacuum in every direction for a trillion miles.

BY THE TIME St. Cuthbert had reached the Asiatic lion compound, the London Zoo was being overrun. Because much of the hubbub from the police and autonewsmedia was near the northeastern end of the zoo, the animals naturally fled in the opposite direction, toward its southern tip, where St. Cuthbert had so effectively created his huge hole in the main fence. It was a funnel, and through it the screaming beasts were about to spill into London like unruliness itself, in scalding streams.

At the same time, in St. Cuthbert's mind, there was another, even scarier presence invading the zoo. More and more, he could see flashes of white-bodysuited Luciferian Neuters, gliding unnaturally, as if on wheels, and drawing silver quantum contra-fluxal staves that popped out of their wrists like long daggers. St. Cuth-bert knew they were coming for the animals, and that both he and the Red Watch must do everything to try to stop them.

His nemesis, his abuser, his pursuer—the thuggish Watch—now shared the same enemy as he.

"The Watch and I—on the same squad," he said, snickering. "That's not *on*, not *on*."

father drury and his "dogs"

AFTER LEAVING REGENT'S PARK, THE JACKALS RE-
leased earlier snouted around for a long time in a shadowy rubbish
collection point behind a gastropub on Marylebone Road. They
scrounged among lemon rinds and stale loaves of *pain de campagne,*
and licked sweet dark oil leaking from a broken deep fryer. The canines would dart away whenever any of the workers came outside to
dump bottles and cans or to take cigarette breaks, but always drifted
back, more nervous and irritated. Eventually the jackals managed
to tip a giant blue recycling bin filled with lager cans and the huge
clatter scared them away. But the pack was in a bit of a state now, a
peculiarly canine blend of curiosity, fear, and bloodlust.

They ran south, into Marylebone proper, staying close together
and attracting almost no attention. It was May Day. An emaciated
young hedge fund trader who normally monitored the Asian markets at night was crouched, wide awake, in his new red Bayerische
glider outside the famed London Clinic. He had taken off work to
wait for an appointment at 7:00 A.M. He had been unable to concentrate on his accounts. He was trying to eat a carton of Kung

Pao Prawns and crab puffs picked up in Chinatown. It wasn't going well. Like Dr. Bajwa, he had metastatic lung cancer, although he had never smoked, yet unlike Dr. Bajwa, his had been discovered cruelly late. It seemed to be in the air, like radon gas. His appetite had been absent for weeks. He kept putting prawns to his mouth and taking them out. When he saw the jackals, he rolled down the window and clicked his fingers to attract them.

"Allo," he said. "Come on, busters, let's have a pet."

The jackals at times showed few inhibitions around people if it served their purposes. One trotted up and began licking the traces of sweet, peanuty sauce off the trader's bony fingers. The man was lonely. He had faced his disease, so far, with great valor, but he was far away from his family and friends in Yorkshire. He thought of his small collie, Barney, from his childhood—a loyal little animal, who used to chase hares in the beetroot field across the lane. He wondered if he ought to move home to die.

"You're right good sorts," he said. "Right good tykes."

The other dogs surrounded the hand and the good smell wafting from the Bayerische.

"That's it," he said. The trader looked around the street. He saw no one. He turned the carton upside down and let all the food fall on the pavement. One of the jackals lunged forward, snarling at the others, bullying them back, but they resisted, and every jackal managed to get at least a mouthful. The viciousness of the animals took the trader aback.

"Steady," he said. "Steady, boys."

Then the jackals ran off, south again. Their loyalties were only to the pack.

Humans were one thing, but as the night wore on, the roars of cars and lorries were making them increasingly angry and jittery. The pulsing thrums of internal combustion engines were shocking to them, like a distant background noise they had always heard in their captive lives suddenly turned up to maximum volume. Eventually they fled over to Harley Street, which was relatively quiet at this hour—nearly 4:30 A.M. The unseasonably cool, dry air of the night, passing over the warm, damp streets, had created a thick layer of fog. They stayed on the wide, clean pavements, which had none of the Mars bar wrappers or the scraps of the *Sun* found in most London byways. The place smelled of old, strange human skin to them, skin rinsed of the body odor and sex and food scents they could detect on their zookeepers. They had made fast work of the goat from the petting zoo, but they hadn't been able to eat much. They felt more relaxed and hungry for blood again, and they were yipping faintly, *happyfury, happyfury*.

The iron fence fronting the doctor and dental offices on Harley Street had all been painted recently in the same glossy black enamel. The consistency and predictability of the fence bars gave the jackals confidence. They had latched onto a kind of geometry that fit the canine mind. In their color-blind vision flashed steady ticking of bars, like the demisemiquavers of thirty-second notes. And what was that music? It went like this: *find-kill-find-kill*, trilling in the speeding heart of dog-time.

They ran faster now, a bit furiously, down to New Cavendish Street, where the fence bent perpendicularly to the right. *Tick tick tick tick*, flashed the fence. A black cab clattered into the road and down a very narrow lane toward George Street. They gave chase. They had lost all their caution. Eventually, the dogs came to the High Anglican Church, St. James, an exquisite neo-Gothic structure built on the site of a chapel where Spain had, four centuries before, tried to organize a coup d'etat against Elizabeth I. The doors were wide open, strangely, and alive with human scents.

A very old eccentric priest, one Father James Drury, had risen early, as was his custom, to pray for all airline travelers in the night skies. He knelt with difficulty near the altar. At age eighty-six, he had been under persistent pressure from the bishop to retire, but Father Drury felt pride in saying the occasional liturgy he was permitted to lead, and he had strongly resisted moving from the rectory, to the point of frank irritation among his younger colleagues. He had just unlocked the main doors and flung them open, as he always did. Often, at this hour, one or two rough sleepers would find their way up from the maelstrom of Soho and enter the church for a kip in the pews. Father Drury never asked them to leave. Tonight, he knelt down near a man bold enough to use a sleeping bag. He had started his long prayer, asking for those ten miles up in the sky, who hurtled at the speed of sound while watching edited versions of *Dreams of Antarctica* and *Bone Arrow 2*, to be protected "from all danger of collision, of fire, of explosion, of fall and bruises, and evil, through Jesus Christ, our Lord, Amen." Who knows how many souls Father Drury's intercessions vouchsafed for that morning meeting in Brussels?

When the jackals came into the church, they scampered right up the nave toward the chancel, their tongues hanging out. The nave's pale colonettes of Purbeck marble and the faultless groining of its arches again gave the jackals a feeling of calm.

Another homeless man, one Father Drury hadn't known was present, had seen the animals. He arose from a pew and simply left the church, carrying a small red rucksack and saying nothing.

The sound of the man caused the priest to look up. He doddered carefully up to his feet, gripping one of the marble altar rails, and the jackals immediately surrounded him, sensing weakness and his rich, salty skin.

"Brothers," said Father Drury. "I suppose you have done harm in the world. But you also will be forgiven." He began walking down the main aisle, toward the door. "Now get along."

The jackals followed along. When Father Drury reached the narthex, he felt a great fatigue grip him. He sat down on an oak bench beside a silver dish of holy water set into a carved font, and he sighed.

The jackals crowded around him.

He could see them panting rapidly, and he felt pity. "You're thirsty," said the priest. "You mustn't irritate others now—do I have that promise?"

He worked the silver dish out of the font as he did every Tuesday to gather it up for cleaning, carefully avoiding spills. It looked like a simple mixing bowl. With some difficulty, which made his ribs and back ache, he hunched over and placed the bowl on the stone floor.

The jackals lapped the water greedily.

Father Drury made the sign of the cross five times, once over each animal, blessing it. When the jackals finished drinking, they ran out, excited, and finally traveled in separate directions to join London's thousands of strays. It was the last time wild jackals were seen on earth.

MEANWHILE, JUST NORTH OF THE ZOO, a ginger-haired autoreporter and his corpulent fotolivographer neglected to turn left on the Outer Circle road, and instead came to a bridge over Regent's Canal. Moored below them were some of the long canal boats that plied the old waterway for recreation in the day. The only aspect of the zoo still visible was the boxy concrete zoo administration and research buildings of the quiet northeastern quadrant of the complex.

"Oooo, good," said the fotolivographer. "We ain't getting an establishing shot over here, are we? We can shoot pretty boats, fuck-all. Let's go back. We need that entrance, Jerry."

Just as they turned around, the otters scampered out in front of them. The autonews crew was slightly interposed between the zoo and set of concrete stairs that went down to the cut, and the

otters could not see any way past. They were squeaking and mewl-
ing loudly, running forward and back in narrow, angry loops.

"Holy fuck, shoot them, shoot them," said the reporter named
Jerry.

The fat man with the camera said, "What? Who wants to see
this?" He hoisted the 3D camera onto his shoulder and trained it
on the otters. Jerry dropped a few lens-bots to "capsule" footage
behind the otters.

"Shoot 'em, you ninny," said Jerry. "Shoot the fucking things."

When the fotolivographer switched on the powerful lights of his
camera, a great bloom of light appeared over the whole area.

"Ooooo, now we're doing vérité," said the fotolivographer.
"This is bollocks. Don't we want tigers or hippos or something—
something *not* like rats in Southwark?"

"They're not fucking rats."

But then Jerry saw, down the stairs, the real source of the otters' disquiet. The big female had given birth. He could see at least
six naked little otters in a makeshift den, like pink fingers, and the
mother licking and licking them. He slapped the camera operator's
shoulder and pointed toward the bridge.

"Let's get up there. We need to get out of the way. The other
otters, they're protecting her. It's beautiful. It's horrible," he said.

"It's bollocks. No one wants to see this."

"I don't really bloody care," said the reporter. "Shoot the damn
thing. It's what we've got."

The light shined down like an exploding star. Christmas brought
Christ, but May Day delivered otters—six of them.

raid on the wax museum

LIKE MANY OF THE RELEASED ANIMALS (MOST OF which were moving south, toward central London), Buddy and Ollie, the two chimpanzees who had killed a fellow ape, quickly reached Marylebone Road and crossed it, attracted by the green dome of the London Planetarium. When they reached the venerable building, they almost immediately lost interest since, as they stood close to the structure, the dome vanished from their meter-high view of the world. But there was much else to pique their curious minds.

They began pummeling the doors of the attached Madame Tussauds building, screeching loudly under an enormous *T* banner, which might as well have stood for *Trouble*.

Ollie, smaller and more compact than Buddy, smacked at the glass with his sweaty long hand, hooing lightly. The loudness of his pounding despite the weakness of his effort testified to his muscularity.

The whale-bellied night security guard, sitting inside at his kiosk with his shirt open, startled to attention. He'd been looking at a WikiNous stalk called "Peaches," using a SkinWerks screen sprayed onto his stomach, flicking numbly through thumbnail foto-lives that showed naked women, in a range of ages, all in Venetian masks. Most of the women were expertly inserting sliced pieces of fruit into their own vaginas. The guard's SkinWerks panel was de-livering the sensation of a massage, but his free hand was on his penis; he let go and tapped around the desk for his torch. He grew instantly incandescent, toward himself and at the kids outside.

"Fuck me!" he gasped, struggling to button up.

Buddy kept running up to one array of entrance doors and kick-ing it, which produced a shattering clatter, stirring Ollie to make a series of terrifying *waa*-barks, a noise chimps make to signal a disturbed state of spectating. Buddy was in a state of sheer *Pan trog-lodyte* euphoria. He remembered the coming of the night human, the murder screams of the treasonous macaque, and his and Ollie's vaulting escape. He had found himself, in Marylebone, in a kind of ape heaven, a complex interzone of a million illuminated things to touch and climb and pull to pieces.

What had become of the other two members of his band and the other macaques (whom he still considered cousins), all of them free now? He did not know, and there was too much to do to worry over it.

The guard started to close down the WikiNous, but his hands were shaking so badly (less from fear of the noises than of being found wanking at work) that he left the title page on his stomach. Instead of tapping 999 onto the skin panel, he decided he would give these fucking louts, whoever they were, a scare. He would go out there, say a few choice words, and get the doors resecured before the automatic alarm went off.

Standing as tall as he could, pulling his shirt closed, pushing his shoulders back, he shoved one of the doors open and screamed, "I'm going to kill you, you bloody fucknuts."

The chimpanzees instantly set upon him. Nearly ten stone heavy, Buddy leaped onto his head and began chewing at the man's cheeks. The guard staggered back into Madame Tussauds and fell, and Ollie joined in, immediately going for the man's genitals (still not packed away). It was all surprisingly silent and fast, the guard's death, and far more merciful than many human-on-human homicides. The guard's last sight on earth, projected on his belly in 3D, was a Peaches fotolive of a forty-two-year-old woman from Toronto with a sequined rabbit mask and thighs as effusive as molten caramel. As his stomach rose and fell forever, she seemed, he thought, to be holding him close.

Afterward, Buddy started whooping with an irate joy, spinning around on the man's swivel-chair. He saw the image of a peach still on the WikiNous stalk's front page on the dead man's belly. His muzzle and hands still covered in the guard's blood, he reached down and tried to pluck the fruit off the screen, daubing the man's torso red. Ollie came over and, seeing all this, began making submissive pant-grunts—he wanted a taste of that peach, too.

So Buddy began to strike the screen more forcefully to remove the fruit. It stayed put. An alarm bell started clanging. Buddy and Ollie picked up the corpse and heaved it toward one of the wax figures in the foyer of the museum, in this case, none other than Elizabeth Bowes-Lyon.* The screen-belly whizzed just over the barrel-shaped woman's shoulder but knocked her royal blue hat, white netting and all, straight off, pulling her silver wig along with it. Bald, she looked even sweeter, really, like some benevolent wrinkly alien from the Windsor Galaxy.

But Buddy and Ollie were livid. They scuttled down dimly lit hallways, knocking over figures in a rage. The hated humans did nothing to resist, and this only angered Buddy more. Their most

---

* Queen Elizabeth The Queen Mother

molested victims weren't quite random—tall or portly figures seemed to attract the most ire or curiosity. The wax heads of the inventors of the Opticall neural interface, Jacob Glieb and Varghese Raja, were pitched through the nearest window. Morrissey's clenched hands were torn off and thrown at Muhammad Ali, an act Morrissey's own fists would never dare.

As they ran about, heads, arms, and various props, from dumbbells to stethoscopes to Geiger counters, were hurled willy-nilly and torn and bitten and ape-slapped. Buddy felt a kind of fuming glory. At one point, he grabbed the hoary head of Sir David Attenborough, chucked it down, and stamped it to oblivion.

But new worrying sounds began echoing from the halls—the foe, Buddy knew, and now they were moving. A team of keepers from the AnimalSafe Squad and the firearms experts of the Met's SO19 had been alerted by the alarm and done the math.

The Met specialists, gripping their matte-black neuralzingers loaded with lethal rounds, crept into the museum's foyer carefully. They gasped at the sight of the guard's blood-soaked groin and shredded face. One of the keepers there, an Irish man named Kieran, looked like an Army of Anonymous member. He had long blond dreadlocks dotted with blue bioluminescent pearls and one shaven eyebrow. He only looked down sadly and carried on. He was a bit arrogant and hurried, but this struck those present as a good thing. The officers felt they were in uncharted terrain, and Kieran seemed to know what was what.

"Buddy's here," he said, in a chillingly flat tone, upon seeing the corpse.

"Buddy?" one of the officers said.

"He's . . . troubled. Even animals can be a bit malevolent, in their way. The other ape is not. Ollie worships. That's his flaw."

Kieran knew Buddy's handiwork. Though he hadn't ever hurt a human being, he had become more and more abusive toward his fellow apes, going well beyond displays of dominance. Kieran had been urging the zoo to expel him, but these matters moved slowly. No one wanted an evil chimp.

So, Kieran felt both a responsibility and his own strange urge to deal with Buddy, but he wanted—desperately—to try to save Ollie, who was known as a submissive ape who occasionally, as it were, "aped" naughty behaviors. Ollie mostly liked to eat fresh figs imported from Italy.

Kieran spoke to the officers with unrestrained clout, despite having no rank over them.

"Get your torches on and follow me. Do not shoot, right?"

He held his own Austrian-made neuralzinger in front of him, loaded with stun rounds. He had gone to the range more often than the other keepers, and he knew how to hit the circles on the holographic man's solar plexus.

"You gonks be careful," said Kieran. "This is the last time I'm going to say it."

The chimps, by now, had bolted into the darker, cooler air of the Chamber of Horrors, and there they had settled down a bit. They were exhausted and confused.

Buddy had begun to whimper and cry. He was thinking of his mother in the forest, how she would pick ants from his scalp and put them in her mouth, and nuzzle him gently and cuddle him. He thought then of the day his father was murdered by a strange chimp from another band, how terrified he had felt, how the new chimp had beaten and strong-armed him and his siblings into terror until his mother, the new chimp's new bride-widow, had literally beaten the invading male into a state of deference, down on the leafy, dangerous, hot floor of the jungle. Now, he thought, his entire troop— all but he—were perished, and the jungle was no more.

The French Revolution display, one of the oldest in the museum, intrigued Buddy and Ollie. The gory guillotined heads arranged on pikes—with Marie Antoinette's dishwater hair in a frizz and Robespierre holding one crooked eye open—caused Buddy to begin hooing respectfully, as though coming upon a musanga or fig tree in a Congolese forest. Blood and gore dripped in the same way from the leaders' mouths and necks, whether aristocrats or radicals.

Buddy reached up to touch the queen's head. She looked to him so peaceful, sleepy, and empathetic. These were things he did not associate with humans, whom Buddy saw as, above all, intruders in the chimp heart.

Ollie was beginning to bark nervously.

"Buddy," said Kieran, aiming the gun at his face, approaching. "We can help you, Buddy. Buddy, Buddy—"

But Ollie, fatally, started hopping violently and screeching, and in doing so, he knocked forward a recently debuted wax monster named The Crick from the new Andrew Lake series. Misty red fear-bubbles actually sizzled into the air above and around The Crick, causing marked anxiety to all nearby. It was the kind of cheap thrill Tussauds depended on these days. Buddy went bonkers, and one of the younger officers reacted, too. A long, thunderous burst of rounds was choked from his neuralzinger, and then the other specialists let loose. Buddy crouched into a pathetic ball as the rounds tore into him. Ollie, terrorized, tried to reach for Kieran but went down with a round to the mouth. The muzzle-flashes lit the Chamber of Horrors like lightning.

"Nice one," said Kieran. "You stupid, stupid fucks. You stupid fucks."

He began to weep, and he covered his eyes with his hand.

deep in the paved forests

IN THE DAY THE SIX HECTIC LANES OF MARYLE-
bone Road—part of the central London Ring Road—presented a
hazardous, ugly barrier for any rough beast seeking to cross between Regent's Park and the rest of the Borough of Westminster. It
was the shell of a dying ovum of humane governance, and within
lay Buckingham Palace, the Houses of Parliament, Westminster
Abbey, etc.—none of which much interested any animal apart from
Homo sapiens.

Cuthbert himself always made for the zebra crossings, such was
the fearful alacrity of the taxigliders, commuters, and coaches on
the thoroughfare, many on their way to Euston Station or to trendy
Islington. At night, however, the road was sparsely trafficked and
superbly desolate. The Green Line within the zoo seemed far, far
away. It was just the sort of place a depressed gorilla such as Kibali,
the silverback, might take a stand simply to breathe in the air beyond what he regarded as the small "forest" of Regent's Park.

And he had done just that, testing his new state of autonomy, and
only a few shocked drivers passed.

Freedom. He grimaced. He scratched his massive mandible with a long, shiny finger. He felt suspicious of what he saw.

Freedom—and where are the trees?

He was one of thousands of hurting creatures in the metropolis, but no one would ever know his story. He wished he could hide somewhere, under the green trunks of ayous trees. Were the Interahamwe militia nearby? He remembered everything from his last days in the wild. Obscured by foliage, he had seen the fighters cut open brown-eyed little ones, human and gorilla, like they were nothing more than papayas, and toss them aside. He did not expect better treatment here, for even his keepers had not respected him, he felt. They had often spoken to him impatiently. "Get *bloo*dy up and around, Kibali. *Please*, cocker."

And there was something else—a kind of shadow, an umbrageous sleekness, following him. He turned around, several times, to look—nothing.

He finally crossed Marylebone Road to the west of where the chimps and jackals had. He had indeed been followed, too, and by beings not shadowy at all. Behind him, two of the three elephants released—Layang and Mahmoud—were thundering right along, treating him as a sort of guide.

Now he was knucklewalking down the middle of Baker Street, throwing forward his furry black arms, as big and strong as mastiffs, in perfect alternation with his legs. There were no trees on Baker Street, no green lines. He felt disorientated. He looked behind him—the elephants wagged their heads, angry or excited—he did not know, he did not care. He felt angry and unable to catch his breath. There was something more dangerous than these animals. There was a true hunter near—he could smell its hot, sweet urine. Where were the other apes of the zoo he sometimes called to in the night? Where was his old friend, Thin Lips? Where was his cousin, bred in captivity, Small Girl? Were they all dead?

That the jackals could still be mistaken for dogs was understandable, but the sight of a four-hundred-pound ape trailed by two Asian elephants was fairly distinctive outside the Sherlock Holmes Steak House. The light flow of late-night traffic on Baker Street rushed onto the pavements like waters parting. Doors were hurriedly locked, 999 calls breathlessly made, and escape routes worked out. The one exception, the N74 night bosonicabus operator, who truly had seen it all, after trying to Opticall in (the local networks were jammed), managed to navigate carefully around the animals, then speed on, extraordinarily unfazed—she had a schedule, didn't she, and she 'adn't time for these scofflaw Hollywood film people you get at night, or whoever it was goofing on her route with animals—without a proper permit, obviously. "Flaming Nora," she hissed. "What's all this, now?"

But not a soul dared approach the beasts, who indeed did find themselves without permits.

At Portman Square, Kibali's pounding heart rose. There were trees, at last. He could hardly catch his breath now, but he wanted to go home, to the northeastern Congo, and at that moment the enormous lime and plane trees seemed the closest thing. Just as he approached, the unpredictable elephant Mahmoud stood back on his haunches and trumpeted the kind of powerscream he had not heard for years.

Kibali whipped around to look, in terror and in glee. Now the fighters would come for him, wherever he went, he thought. Perhaps the shadow-creature he had sensed earlier would make itself known, too—perhaps as an ally, if not a friend. In any case, he felt driven away from Portman Square, and funneled southward, toward the unknown.

As he lurched onward in Baker Street, his chest aching, the confidence of the aristocratic and moneyed world confronted him. There were restaurants called Texture and Blueprint North; a toy shop known as Petit Chou; a beauty shop named Elemis Spa. It all struck him as refined but oddly lifeless. There were no good urine stenches. There was no hair on the necks of the mannequins he saw. Soon, running as fast as he could, he crossed Oxford Street, which was mostly deserted, over to Orchard Street. He could see, farther ahead, a beautiful green-blackness—no gliders, no machines, no buildings, just dark sanctuary. It was Grosvenor Square, of course, the home of the American Embassy. (A replacement chancery had been built in south London in 2017, but it had been twice flattened by terrorists.) Grosvenor was the only other big patch of forest in the vicinity, and beyond it the treetops of two great royal parks, St. James and Hyde, yoked together into a giant green-brown sky-arcade. *Follow the Green Line*, he found himself thinking, in gorilla, as if the spirer Cuthbert's thinking was now spreading to other creatures. Mahmoud had stayed at Portman Square, to fight perceived aliens and to trample cars and to bellow for justice (until he was shot by snipers), but Layang had followed Kibali, sensing the growing threat behind their little herd.

the lions warn st. cuthbert

CHANDANI AND THE THREE OTHER LIONESSES
stalked the central court of their dirty enclosure, cutting back and
forth like tongues of blown fire. They looked enlivened by the return of Cuthbert, but angry, too, to be stuck. The haggard male,
Arfur, sat in their midst with his paws extended, as smugly inert
as they were uneasy. As for St. Cuthbert, he was tired. He felt the
stumpy-legged daze of fading Flōt. There was, again, that peculiar,
disassociated sense that the entire night was unreal. He leaned up
against the main wall of the enclosure.

Behind the enclosure, the gathering lights of dozens of emergency gliders set the lime trees and hazel shrubs and ivy banks
aglow like green lamp shades of all sizes and sorts. The entire
horizon burned with yellow and blue radiance, and the two colors, striated through the shrubbery, combined into a distinctive
emerald green.

Since Cuthbert left them earlier, the lions had also caught
glimpses of the Neuters, and instinctively, they recognized them as
a somewhat detestable prey for the hunt—but prey indeed.

"I said I would return," St. Cuthbert was telling the great felines.

"The hour's late," said Arfur, shaking his great, tawny head. "Let
us out, holy man. The Gate—the Heaven's Gate—is soon to open."
Arfur jumped to his feet, and he continued: "One side is here, beside
us, somewhere in the zoo, and the other is somewhere south—near
Grosvenor Square, we are told. Once the Gate opens, it will destroy
us all. We must stop it!"

"Calm down," Chandani instructed Arfur, approaching the old
male with a limber, menacing gait. "It's *almost* late."

"Late? Or early?" said St. Cuthbert. "It must be three in the
morning. And I still . . . I'm not sure. I know what will happen. Or I
know what's *supposed* to happen. And if you're free, I will surely be
the first to die. I am still waiting for him—for the Christ. Of Otters."

"Ha!" scoffed Arfur. "I would've thought that a saint cannot
perish."

Chandani snarled at Arfur. "Show respect," she said. "This
blessed man can help us."

But Arfur held his colossal paws up toward the huntress, bar-
ing pinkish-yellow claws. He threw his head back. "While Rome
burns, you and this old man are talking about otters?" The other
three lionesses sneered at Arfur. St. Cuthbert feared a fight was
about to erupt.

"You say," St. Cuthbert asked Arfur, trying to understand, "that
the second part of the Gate, that it will appear . . . at Grosvenor
Square? Why? Near the American Embassy? And we're beside the
first part—here, in the zoo? That bit makes sense, of course. But ah
wouldn't have said Grosvenor—never that. Are you sure?"

"Grosvenor, it is," Chandani said in her low, sweetleather voice.
"Already, we *feel* the invasion under way, holy one. Not American soldiers, of course—but Americans nonetheless. Californian

comet-worshippers. So many have laughed at them, but they will do real harm, and it won't amuse anyone, and it—"

Arfur broke in: "No. No. No. No. No. Not since those dipsomaniacal French felons landed at Fishguard has British soil been under the feet of invaders—but *now* look. We English lions, you surely know—our blood would boil if even an Argentinian center forward stepped into Wembley. So—"

Chandani interjected: "What my husband wants to say is . . . we *are* under . . . quite some duress . . . now."

Arfur nodded, looking satisfied. He said, "And I ask this: If you are a holy man, why will you not sacrifice something—or someone—for us, to stop the invaders? What are you waiting for? Where is this . . . *Christ* . . . of Otters? Mark my words: any great battle will end here, near us, the absolute omega of all earthly animal strife—where the lions live. Is anyone calling me the 'Christ of Lions'?"

"Arfur!" Chandani scolded.

"Yes?"

"I must say," said Chandani, "that the simpleminded Arfur is right about one thing. The equivalent of the Légion Noire[*] will come to us, and they *will* come here." She added, with a noble note of recognition for a dreadful enemy, "We must face them, bravely, first with devotion, then with our paws. *Here*. But someone still must go down to Grosvenor Square, I am convinced. Perhaps— that is where your Otter Messiah will be needed most. And His prophet—*you*."

"I . . . I . . . I don't know," said St. Cuthbert, filling with a new wave of self-pity. "This is all too much for me." The lions' paws suddenly looked to him like huge golden pastries. "A'm a Flōt sot,

---

[*] The Revolutionary French raiders who landed in Wales in 1797

when it comes right down to it, and I doubt a'm going to be much of anyone's miracle-maker or giant-slayer. Oi can't even get me donnies on a seagull—and we're only an hour from Southend."

"Let us free," said Arfur, "and you will have all the winged beings you will ever need. Indeed, a great eagle will carry your savior to you."

Chandani rolled her eyes.

"I don't want to see *them*," said St. Cuthbert. "But I did hope to see my brother before I 'shuffled off this mortal coil.' And I can't find Drystan anywhere. That's all I really cares about. More than the animals—no disrespect meant. More than England. I need to see him, see? There's summat I've got to tell him, right? My brain's deceived me. Or the Flōt."

And then, as if on cue, something astounding occurred, at least from the perspective of one grubby saint, and the lions, too. Out of the narrow forest at the zoo's fence, out of the twinkling green lights and sparrow nests and bowls of darkness, out of his gran's porcelain thimble and deadly Dowles Brook, out of his drunkenness and sorrow and shame and a loneliness no one but a Flōt sot could know, out of an endless night of kitten games and enclosures drained—there came a being from St. Cuthbert the Wonderworker's deepest anguish—the Christ of Otters. The Lord of Animals came because, in the end, St. Cuthbert needed a Lord.

St. Cuthbert stared in wonder. His long lost brother's hair was longer, and his eyes more fearful and feminine, but here he was, risen from the dead, walking purposefully, and looking every bit like Drystan . . . if . . .

If.

If, thought St. Cuthbert. If, if, if, if, if.

If he were a *woman,* in her late twenties or early thirties.

"Drystan?" asked St. Cuthbert. "I knew it. I knew it. I knew it. I knew it."

Arfur roared with a bellicose grandeur that could have been added to the *Oxford English Dictionary* as the very definition of *leonine*.

It was, of course, a Royal Parks Constabulary inspector, a woman, and her physical resemblance to the Handley brothers was indeed, as Dawkins had put it, "the spit." The black-brown eyes, the high cheeks, even the freckles taken from the dappled downs of Clee—she was as close to a doppelgänger as one got. It was the face that had that night launched a thousand scripts in St. Cuthbert's head.

But she was different, too, from the Drystan whom St. Cuthbert had been imagining all night. She was calmer, and more professional, and less delicate. And she had very long, wispy, obsidian hair.

"Drystan? Are yow the Christ of Otters?"

"I'm Inspector Sullivan," the woman said. "And you're Mr. Handley, aren't you? Cuthbert?"

"Yow'm my brother," he declared flatly to the woman, shaking his head, gasping to catch his breath. "*Gagoga maga medu,*" he said. His eyes were wet with tears. He nearly comprehended, in his rough way, that this constable, the utter stranger, wasn't the *boy* who had died so many, many years ago, but it was hard for him to accept that it wasn't somehow a kind of Drystan—changed, yes, hidden in the shape of a beautiful woman—but Drystan.

"Are yow 'im? Dryst?"

"No, I'm afraid I'm not," she said. She felt tears slipping down her face. "But if you want to call me that, you should. I work for the Royal Parks. The constabulary. I'm a special sort of officer."

"If I say something to yow," he asked her, "does he hear me?

Does the Christ of Otters? Are yow 'possessed' by 'im, loik, as it were?"

"I don't know—Cuthbert. I don't know if it works like that," said the woman. "But I'm very interested to hear about all this. Are you hurt?"

"T'snothing," he said. "But you must leave me now and get down to Grosvenor Square, if you're the Christ of Otters."

With that, St. Cuthbert pulled the remake Undley Bracteate from his pocket, the talisman he had tried years ago to give to his cousin Rebekka. He placed it into Astrid's hand and closed her fingers on it.

"Treasure it," he said to her. "The animals tell me I've become a kind of saint. St. Cuthbert. I don't know 'bout that. But this talisman, it *will* keep you safe, Drystan—or whoever you are."

She looked at the medallion, long broken from its key chain. It showed the two brothers, Romulus and Remus, drinking from the teats of a wolflike creature. There was the inscription, in ancient Frisian runes, *gægogæ mægæ medu*, and Astrid rubbed her thumb over the ancient incantation, and smiled gently at the man.

She reached then into her own pocket, and pulled out her old pearl rosary. It was her own most precious possession, and she hung it around St. Cuthbert's neck.

"There," she said. "Now you're a proper apostle, aren't you?"

She wanted now, dreadfully, to believe this homeless man might somehow be connected to her in a more direct way. And if she couldn't be "Drystan" or an Otter Messiah, couldn't she, perhaps, be the lonely granddaughter of the poetical drunkard who had spent a night with her grandmother, and vanished from her and her mother's lives, so long ago? Could that not be what drew her toward him tonight? Might this peculiar ancient sot not be her grandfather? Was it so impossible? In his state of inebriation and need, she observed, *he* seemed content to let such questions live in golden unanswerability. But she reckoned she would need more of an answer.

"Why did yow come here?" he asked her.

"To help you, I suppose," said Astrid. "And maybe for another reason. I don't know. You have caused an awful load of worry for many people, you know, Mr. Handley. " She put her arm over his shoulder to steady him, and unusually for him, he didn't fight it. "Do you understand that . . . Cuthbert?"

Just as the old man seemed poised to answer, an orange-freq unexpectedly flashed across Astrid's corneas, its flames whipping up in the purple-yellows of a gas fire.

Eep, eep, eep, eep! Zunga-gunga-gunga!

"Fuck!" she said, squeezing her eyes shut.

Astrid read the text. *Special notice: Detention and suspension order. RPC Inspector Astrid Sullivan, white female, aged 32, 5'10". Please detain. Considered armed and possibly dangerous. Caution. Possible tie to terrorists.*

It felt like a punch in the stomach. Her career, now, was ruined. The orange-freq would have been seen by every law enforcement officer in Greater London.

"Am I . . . in trouble?" asked Cuthbert. "For trespass? And . . . quite a few other . . . things?"

Astrid touched her eyebrows and switched off all freqs.

"Let's not worry about any of that for now, Cuthbert."

"But I'm not finished here. Nor are you. Really, *you* must get down to Grosvenor. Are you nicking me then?"

"Well, no," she said. "I don't think that's quite appropriate."

At that, the lion Arfur growled with approval.

"We need to get you to a safe place," she said.

"A'am safe," said St. Cuthbert. "*Yow've* come. But the animals of the world are not. Please—go to Grosvenor Square. I don't need yow—*thay* do."

There was some movement in the same spot in the hedges where Astrid had come through, and a new figure came strolling from the shrubbery. He wore a dark orange *dashar** on his head. He ducked through the branches, lifting them very high, and looking back a few times as he walked toward them, as if trying to verify that he had indeed just crossed the zoo's fence. He grimaced at St. Cuthbert and Astrid. It was none other than Dr. Sarbjinder Bajwa.

"Cuthbert!" he called. "You . . . it's you!"

It had been only a few weeks since St. Cuthbert had seen Dr. Bajwa, but the doctor looked noticeably thinner and less muscular. It was obvious that his cancer had worsened. There were no magic cures. His eyes were sunken, and there was a pastiness about his clove-colored skin. He wore a curved little *kirpan,* or ceremonial dagger, on his belt in a scabbard gleaming with purple and green garnets. In fact, he'd just come from his brother's wedding celebration, where the guests had reveled late into the night.

At least a dozen more constables and Met firearms specialists, tigered in green and black TotalCamou™ suits, filtered out from the shrubs near the fence. They were hard to make out, presenting a visual facsimile of everything directly behind them (in this case, murky foliage). They carried glossy-white tactical autozingers as well as scoped neuralzinger rifles, both of which obviated TotalCamou's effects. (Indeed, the strange sight of guns apparently floating through the air by invisible beings tended to draw attention.)

"Let's stop this, Cuddy," Dr. Bajwa said to his old patient. "Please. I have some—some rather extraordinary news, but it . . . it will take your cooperation, Cuddy." He bowed very subtly toward Astrid. It was clear they didn't know one another, but the doctor must have heard about Astrid's gambit.

"Officer," he said.

---

* Sikh turban

"Doctor . . . Bajwa, I presume? You're the flying GP?"

"Right. I suppose I am. It's just a hobby. I'm . . . I'm here . . . to help? If I can?"

"See, Cuthbert," said Astrid. "We're all here to get you help."

"Cuddy, oh," said Dr. Bajwa. "I was so worried." He leaned toward St. Cuthbert, who moved closer to the ledge above the lion pit.

"Lad, please. Can we move away from the edge a bit? Are you all right? You've been hurt. There's blood. On your face, Cuddy. Looks like you've been in the wars."

St. Cuthbert nodded, but he didn't betray any real appreciation of the words. He said, "Baj—here he is—Drystan. I tell you, this constable woman. She's Drystan."

"Yes," said the doctor, humoring him. "You must listen to me, Cuddy. *Listen*: that NHS psychiatrist who tested you . . . Dr. Reece? His recommendations have all been rescinded. He was bloody overruled somehow." He squinted at St. Cuthbert, as if waiting for a reaction. "I don't know why. It's unusual. But it means . . . it means, it *means* you can go back to your flat."

The doctor looked around, as though fearful of a tiger springing down from a tree. "After this, er, incident has been cleared up. You can live at home. And come see me. You don't need to run, Cuddy. You don't need to be afraid."

"But I'm not afraid," said St. Cuthbert. "Not one little bit. Not for meself, anyway." It wasn't quite the truth. He feared death, and he feared Flōt withdrawal, but he feared more the annihilation of all he held dear.

St. Cuthbert turned and said to the inspector: "We and those who know must stop the Neuters. They're already mixed in with us. I've seen a few in the zoo. The lions and the otters say I must make a sacrifice. For the souls of all animals. Or the Neuters will have them."

"The who?" she asked. She shrugged toward Dr. Bajwa, and he shook his head.

"What's this 'Neuters,' Cuddy?" The doctor smiled cordially. "What do you mean by that? When did that start?"

"The invaders—from outer space. The Luciferians. The animals 'av warned me all about them. They are opening a giant Gate to death. The lions understand. And there's a little sand cat around here. He understands, too." He pointed his thumb toward Astrid. "And Drystan does."

There was a long silence. Astrid motioned with her hand for the camouflaged men with hovering neuralzingers to stay back.

Dr. Bajwa finally said, "Cuddy. Come with me. I will take you to hospital. You need to be seen to, my friend. At the very least, we need to get away from here. The animals, they're everywhere, they said. You could be hurt. Please, my friend. I care about you, my friend."

"It's good advice," said Astrid.

"I don't understand," said St. Cuthbert, pursing his lips. "You talk as if you don't know a single *thing* about the Luciferian plan— *thay* aim to do in all the animals on earth. You're the one we've all been waiting for."

The officer and the physician shook their heads, wearing a similar pitying expression.

"It's the Flōt, Cuthbert," said Dr. Bajwa. "You've got hallucinosis, my friend. We can get help—at the hospital. We don't hear lions speaking with words. We don't hear otters. We don't hear little cats. We're not *awaiting* anyone. All we hear is a man desperately in need of looking after. A man almost destroyed by Flōt."

"Flōt."

"Yes, Flōt. It makes you see things."

Astrid said, "But, Cuthbert. I know this will sound unbeliev-

able. But I care about you. I don't even . . . well, I think I may
know why." She smiled, but sourly, shaking her head in tight little
wiggles. "Or not. A *bit* why. Maybe? But you've . . . you've drawn
me here tonight. And I . . . I *want* to believe you. And I want to
help you."

Cuthbert felt his heart begin to gallop unevenly, and a vise-like
pain shot up his chest. He looked up in the sky. There was the comet.

"The co-co-comet," he said, in a daze. "Thar's a spaceship in
there. Hidden."

Again, the officer and Dr. Bajwa looked at one another. From
above, one of the Red Watch's frightcopters trained its spot beams
on St. Cuthbert and Astrid.

There was a voice from above: *You are commanded by the Yeoman
of His Majesty the King to remain where you are.*

Astrid waved her hand, as if trying to swat midges away from
her face.

"Cuthbert," said Astrid. "Our time's running out. You know,
I came here tonight, and now I've lost everything, but I wouldn't
change it. You see, I don't know who you are, but I knew I had to
find you. I *look* like you. Anyone would see that. And I wonder if
I think like you? And feel like you? I'm a Flōt sot, too, and I'm in
second withdrawal, and you know there aren't many of us, and the
statistics for me are bleak, but I am here. I think, Mr. Handley, I
think you *could* be my granddaddy. Maybe."

St. Cuthbert gasped. "Yow? How can that be?" He stood totter-
ing on the edge of the enclosure, knotting his fingers. "It's impossible. *Sullivan?* Irish? You're bold and brave, Inspector. Irish blood
and English heart?"

"Oh, far better than that," she said. "Are you from the Black
Country? And your family's from the Marches?"

St. Cuthbert nodded.

"Did you know a barmaid from Bermondsey? And you spent a night? A long, long time ago?"

The bits about the Marches and the Black Country made sense, but the rest was entirely foreign to St. Cuthbert. He never knew any barmaid from Bermondsey, at least not one he could remember.

"Do you see someone in me?" Drystan asked. "Someone else, too?"

But St. Cuthbert needed no further proof of a connection than to stare into the dark eyes of this woman, at something far deeper than genes. Her questions felt like a sweet vine pulling through him, even if, in his mind if not his heart, it kept hitting snags. She was, surely, looking through the same strong eyes he hadn't seen since his gran Winefride Handley lived so long ago. And that meant there was another human being in Britain who would, one day, be able to speak animal. She would possess the Wonderments. She was a he was a she. She *was* Drystan. She *was* the Christ of Otters. St. Cuddy no longer would have to carry the burden himself. He was beautifully, perfectly, finally sacrificable.

A hot streak of Red Watchmen was now spidering down from their dark, hovering scarlet frightcopter on black nylonite ropes. When they touched down, they gathered themselves for a few moments, folding and unfolding their arms in arthropodal jerks.

Astrid, Baj, and the other officers watched anxiously as the ropes retracted like hissing black asps. The frightcopter remained rigidly in place, about forty feet up, its solar-electric engines thrumming in near-silence. Looking over his shoulder, St. Cuthbert leaned over the edge of the lion enclosure, peering down into the moat.

"Move back from there, Cuthbert," said the doctor. "Please, Cuddy."

The Watchmen—there were three of them—extended their extra-long golden neuralpikes. One of them cracked open a black nerve-bar instant prison at their landing site. The other two Watchmen began to stomp toward Astrid and Baj, their pair of pikes jutting ahead of them, the tips charging with red glows. The pair together were a single massive satanic head, swaying forward and back with ox-like unstoppability. They seemed to know exactly what—or who—they wanted—and only Astrid and a GP with lung cancer stood between them and their quarry.

"Cuthbert, run," said Astrid. "Get out of here."

"I won't," he said, smiling sadly. "I can't."

These were no ordinary Watchmen, Astrid fearfully realized. Suicide cultists and street-rousing republicans were generally left to the regular Watch. These Watchmen belonged to a special new unit, the Scots Coldstream Aristocratic Regiment, or SCARE. They were deployed for high-level political or strategic-level hits when Harry9 wanted to make a special, showy example. They wore the red and gold House of Windsor mantles of the regular Watch as well as the glossy scarlet body armor associated with the king's own Yeoman Protection Command. SCARE's distinctive, bulbous mantis-eyed helms hid their faces.

"Cuthbert Handley and Astrid Sullivan," said one of the approaching Watchmen, warning through a fuzzy speaker. "You are both hereby placed under the custody of His Majesty and you—"

"Just croak that cunt," said the other.

St. Cuthbert swung one of his legs over the relatively low enclosure wall. The moat below, between the wall and the exhibit area, was the chief barrier between visitors and the lions. The saint sat upon the wall like a novice skier, leaning forward a bit for balance, trying to hold the wall between the palms of his hands. He kept glancing between the Watchmen and the lions down in the enclosure.

"Cuthbert! No!" cried Bajwa.

The Met officers and firearms specialists, still in TotalCamou, backed away ominously, a set of receding floating guns, and Astrid knew she was in gravest danger. The other Royal Parks constables, some of whom Astrid knew well—fat Jenkins and young Hopper and the jokester Sergeant Raheem—seemed either confused or paralyzed with fear. They remained rooted along the bushes.

The doctor, instinctively, had dropped to all fours. He was a picture of appalling befuddlement, crawling toward his wayward patient, then stopping, looking back like an impatient pony, and cantering back toward Astrid.

No one, not even registered law enforcement, took stands against the Watch, and its SCARE units possessed an especially fearsome reputation for outrages against civil decency. Their favorite quarry were British republicans and followers of Anonymous UK, and their pop-up prisons ended up securing the bodies of "terrorists" as often as live prisoners. Indeed, anyone they killed was, ipso facto, a terrorist.

"Behind me," Astrid said to the doctor, struggling to get herself in front of both the doctor and Cuthbert. She plunged her hand into her trouser pocket. She clutched her neuralzinger. Still loaded with nonlethal gangliatoxic rounds, she remembered.

Before Astrid expected, one of the Watchmen hurled himself forward. He stabbed out at her with his pike's searing red tip, stretching his arm so far he became unbalanced. The pike hit the pavement beside her foot with a chittering *zhe-zheeng!* A fist-size divot of pavement concrete spurted up. The missile hit one of the sheepish Met officers in the knee, and he fell hard, moaning.

"It begins," said St. Cuthbert. "It begins."

Astrid stepped back. She knew now that the Watchmen were trying to kill her—to kill them all, probably. She drew her neuralzinger, gripping it tentatively with just her one hand.

"Please. Move back," she said to the Watchmen. "Please. *Please.* Let's all kotch a bit."

But then her pistol went off. It kicked back and up, almost flying from her hand. She'd pulled the trigger all right, but it hardly felt willed. The living gangliatoxin's visible gray net grew as wide as a shark's mouth before hitting its target. It stuck to the one Watchman's armor, a dull shroud now silvering with white sparkles. There was a second's pause, and everyone assembled stood dumbly, petrified; then the victim staggered over in mortal agony. He screeched through his helmet's speaker as his brain opened millions of pain receptors.

"Jesus fuck," cried Bajwa. "Inspector, you didn't have to—"

"You fooking bitch!" shouted the other Watchman with a neuralpike. "Now you're dead, you slag."

The frightcopter, humming above, descended abruptly. It thudded upon the pavement, its feathery rotor blades folding up and inward. When this happened, the other Watchman with a pike, and the one still fussing with his pop-up prison, retreated a few steps toward the compacted frightcopter, which sat like an enormous black scarab, ticking with heat, its two giant neural cannons slowly gliding toward Astrid. It presented an implacable, story-ending foe, and Astrid knew it.

"Listen! I'm sorry!" she hollered. She crouched down, pulling the doctor to the pavement. "Get down," she whispered to Bajwa. "Down! Crawl toward the copter!" She did feel sorry; hurting anyone felt repugnant to her, but she also needed to stall them. "I didn't mean . . . I didn't . . ."

Astrid motioned to St. Cuthbert and the other constables and Met officers. "Get down!" She glared at the frightcopter with steely anger.

But now the other SCARE pikeman, bolstered by Astrid's proximity, was barreling heedlessly toward her and the doctor, his weapon's tip fully charged. This time, a hunkered Astrid held her neuralzinger with both hands, like the trainer she was, and took down the pikeman.

The Met officers, who had switched off their TotalCamou for safety, began scampering toward Astrid and Bajwa, too. The parks constables started to make more tentative, parallel moves on St. Cuthbert.

"She's bloody off her chump!" one of the Met officers screamed. "I tell you, she'll kill us all!"

There was a shrill *zhinging!* sound as the grounded frightcopter fired its neural cannons. First, for a fraction of a second, white tracer laser-lines landed on St. Cuthbert and just above Astrid's head.

"No!" screamed the doctor.

Then, two darkening fat columns of air, wide as smokestacks, puffed out all along the laser-line guides and turned into the equivalent of million-tubed synaptic extruders. The deadly columns of swirling gray-black plasmas swiped back and forth like windscreen wipers and at once shrank off.

As Astrid had calculated, the shots ranged safely above their heads, but instantly and silently, they had liquefied the brains of all the Met officers and parks constables around the lion enclosure. She and Bajwa watched in horror as the men's eyes turned into orange sockets even as they timbered to the ground.

The last Watchman scrambled into the eight-by-eight-foot pop-up prison, which he was now treating as a spur-of-the-moment fortress, or at least a kind of safe room.

The winged red doors of the frightcopter flew open.

Astrid felt she had no choice about her next maneuver. She must subdue the frightcopter's pilot before he killed them all. She sprinted toward it. She ducked under one of the copter's hot red and gold-crested nacelles. She pushed her back against the main engine cowl, inching toward the door, weapon drawn. As she crouched and rolled into the open, aiming for the pilot, she saw the reason that she and the doctor were still alive: it was empty. The Watchman inside the prison was controlling it remotely.

"You will be hunted down," the Watchman said to them. He took off his helm, and he clearly considered himself safely ensconced. He was a sallow, weak-chinned, balding man with tiny blue eyes and an incongruously noble roman nose. "But I'm going to kill you first."

Dr. Bajwa stood up behind Astrid. "Distract him," he whispered. "I've got nothing to lose, have I?"

"What?"

"Distract the idiot in the box."

So Astrid said to the Watchman, "You can't, er, see it . . . from your angle, but above you, chap, I see . . . *I* see the king's own frightcopter. It's all pretty-ditty Windsor golds and scarlets, and I don't think His Majesty's going to be pleased with your performance. You've murdered your colleagues. He's landing down, my friend."

"Oh, piss off," the Watchman said, smiling greasily. "You're lying. King Harry! And now you better hope your affairs are all in order." He began tapping the aerosol touchscreen on back of his armored hand, and frowned. "What the bloody hell?"

Dr. Bajwa popped his head out of the frightcopter's cockpit. "I've disabled the remote," he said. "I've got an NSeven solarcopter certification. Almost. It's ours now."

"It's a bloody frightcopter," the Watchman hissed, his face grown incandescent red. "It ain't some weekend whirlybird."

"Well, we'll see, friend. I've been to Philip K's Solarcopter Flight School. In Kent, mate, in case you're wondering." He nodded and grinned. "And if you don't mind my saying, you look like you've gone for a burton, old chapper."

"You'll all die," the Watchman spat back.

"I won't argue that," said Bajwa.

Astrid and the doctor looked toward the lions. "Cuthbert!" they shouted, nearly in unison.

They ran over to the enclosure and looked over its edge. There he was—St. Cuthbert, slid halfway down the inside wall, up to his thighs in moat water. He was using his bolt cutters like a climber's pick, keeping himself above the moat. A full inch of bright emerald algae covered the water, so much it hardly rippled. Only four or so feet deep, it posed little danger to adults, but it was cold, and Cuthbert was old, sick, and he'd had a few knocks. The lions gazed at the spectacle of him with interest, but not any sort of bloodlust.

"Cuddy," said Bajwa. "We'll get you out of here. Can you stay there?"

"Oi'm St. Cuthbert, my old friend. Oi'm going nowhere. Yow must—yow *must* get down to Grosvenor Square—with Drystan. Ar, it's *past* time. I shall begin my . . . my last prayers."

"But we can't leave you," said Astrid. "You'll die."

"Yes, yes," said the doctor, nodding.

"Drystan," said St. Cuthbert. "I will call you 'Astrid.' It's only two letters off 'Drystan,' and one of them is '*T*'—and I'm here, ain't I? Ha-ha. But the animals. If I can hear them, so must you because of who you are. *Listen* for them. They will not hurt me any more than people have already. Go. Go to Grosvenor—now, please. And then come back."

"But you won't be safe," said Astrid.

"If you don't go, there's no future."

"No." Astrid turned to Baj. "We can't do this. We shan't leave him."

St. Cuthbert, his words smearing together, said, "Please*please*-gonow. Oi'm just a voice in tha wilderness of the streets. Yow're the glory. So go. Gogaga-gogo. Go."

Smiling down at his patient, battling back tears, Dr. Bajwa said, "Well, Cuddy, I guess this is, officially, going for a burton."

"Yes," said the saint.

It was with heavy steps, and crushed hearts, that Astrid and Dr. Bajwa climbed into the frightcopter.

"I can't believe we're doing this," said Astrid. "It's utter madness."

"Yes," said Dr. Bajwa, pulling up the hovering touch-controls. "Isn't it wonderful?"

And they whirred into the busy London night sky.

eight

always england

MASON GAGE WAS A LONG WAY FROM HIS HOME IN Mingo Grove, West Virginia.

The chief security officer at the American Embassy, still a little grumpy at getting awakened at 4:00 A.M., couldn't believe his eyes. He was standing in what was officially called the Central Confidence Module, or CCM, but most everyone called it the Roost. Apart from the sound of air whooshing through a ventilation register, the dim room was cool and silent, despite the twenty or so people packed in.

He took his spectacles off. He wiped them on a paper serviette he kept folded in his wallet. He could never get the last smears of facial oil off his lenses these days. Something about London. He put his specs back on. In his hands, he clutched three reports about the night, printed on sticky-feeling, dissolving TemPaper, like all classified communiqués of the Company. The latest report read:

NORTHERN EUROPE-WIDE CLASSIFIED UPDATE 20520501.1
UK / CROWN SOURCES CLAIM SEVERAL NON-DOMESTIC

RARE LIVE ANIMALS ON STREETS ACROSS CENTRAL LON-
DON. POSSIBLE LINKS TO ENGLISH TERRORISTS OR US-
BASED DEATH CULT ACTIONS OR (EARL OF) WORCESTER
INSURGENCY. ADDITIONAL REPORTS: GORILLA NEAR
GROSVENOR COMPLEX. ADVANCED ROYAL WATCH ASSETS
DEPLOYED. THREAT BLUE. STRICT LEVEL H PROTOCOLS IN
RISK ASSESSMENT / CONTAINMENT. REPORT ENDS, 202061-33.

No report could have prepared him for the surrealism of the
facts at hand. Animals in London—everywhere. And there was a
dang gorilla on the loose!

He didn't like the tie-in with the nutjob cults. He didn't like re-
lying on Crown intelligence sources. And he really didn't like the
gorilla.

Mason wasn't classic Foreign Service, even within the comparably asperous milieu of the diplomatic police. He was a God-fearing,
foulmouthed, bona fide Allegheny grit, a coal-dusted rut-buck
hunting hillbilly from Pendleton County, West Virginia, who considered anything smaller than a .30-06 Springfield a squirrel gun.
He kept a fourteen-point set of whitetail antlers on his dresser beside an old picture of his mama in a pink housedress, standing in a
kitchen in slanted sunlight, holding Mason up proudly as a toddler,
kissing his black flyaway hair.

Beyond a seated row of Diplomatic Security Service agents,
a bank of screens showed various feeds from low-light and deep-
infrared videocameras around Grosvenor Square. On several,
a Royal Watch frightcopter was hovering erratically above the
square's lime and plane trees.

"That's cockeyed," Mason said to himself.

The pilot seemed unable to keep the aircraft evenly pitched. It
looked like a big red, black, and gold Easter egg, rocking and tip-
ping and threatening to take a great fall.

"Watch that chopper," Mason said aloud. "Something's . . . something's just *off* there."

"Yessir!" said several voices.

"And please, will someone please 'ring the Circus'* and find out what the *fuck* is going on?"

Much of Grosvenor Square, particularly the road and square itself, was surveilled from within the Roost. Faces, cars, trucks, and DVLA number plates could be put on-screen, magnified, and analyzed with a suite of recognition and consciousness-probing technologies that could penetrate facial BodyMods and even, it was rumored, insert understated, subtle ideas in targets, although in Britain a Crown Court order was—strictly speaking—necessary for cognitive interventions, and only to British subjects.

The shaky frightcopter lowered itself in one of the corners of the enormous square. An attractive, dark-eyed young woman with long black hair alighted from the copter, and the frightcopter immediately shot back up to the safety of the air.

"What the fuck is this?" asked Mason. The woman's uniform resembled a minor British police agency's. She certainly wasn't Watch.

"I want to know who that woman is," barked Mason. "I want to know why she's here. I want to know what brand of organic strawberries she slices into her muesli for breakfast. Jesus fucking shit. Is this the animal catcher?"

Mason was not an arrogant man, but he felt better than this animal silliness. The entire spectacle struck him as too sloppy and absurd to be professional or terror related. The ambassador and her family were on holiday in Greenland—one less headache. But the frightcopter and this woman and the animal reports worried him, if only because of their absolute total fuckedupedness.

"Seriously, get me some data, people!"

---

* MI6, Britain's Secret Intelligence Service

Astrid's face popped onto half a dozen screens. She seemed to be looking for signs of something, but tentatively.

A squinty-eyed, frail-looking cognitive specialist, a so-called Cog on loan to the embassy, sat nearby in one of the "meat chairs"— it used a lab-cultured flesh whose bioware flaps, skin-to-skin, partially garmented the Cogs. He said to Mason, "Sir. I'm getting into her now, a little. I think she's . . . a British citizen. Astrid . . . Sullivan."

A new group of people, about a dozen, began shuffling in through the steel doors of the Roost. The Cog flinched a little when he saw them.

"Excuse me. Who are you?" Mason asked.

One of the newcomers, a tall man with short cropped hair, rehearsed the pass-phrase: "If you want to make an apple pie from scratch," he said, sounding oddly amused with himself, "you must first invent a universe." It was from the old twentieth-century astrophysicist Carl Sagan; Mason had seen it on yesterday's last brief.

"Well," said Mason. "OK. But we're busy here, folks. Are you . . . ?"

"Yes," the tall man said, grinning at Mason. "Tertiary operations. We're everywhere." The man snickered.

Mason said, "Just, please, try to stay out of the way."

The Cog was waving at Mason. Cogs were highly trained if far more conventional cousins of the controversial, shriveled-legged mutant PreCogs he had heard about. Although trained in NYPD's PreCrime Agency alongside PreCogs, the Cogs were only faintly empathic—a little empathy went a long way, as Mason saw it— yet far less vulnerable to directed brain attacks than PreCogs. Still, Mason didn't like them much. All the cognition stuff rubbed him the wrong way. The Cogs could see inside anyone, after all—and mess with things. He'd had enough messes.

"OK, lessee," said the Cog, petting his meat chair's pink armrests in a way that unnerved Mason. "An inspector with the Royal Parks Constabulary. She's upset. Under stress, sir. The Watch . . . they're looking for her. I don't know why. Possibly mixed up with the cults. And there's something else: I'm feeling . . . um, lessee . . . an incursion of some sort? Really vague. Possibly one of the cults, sir. She's not . . . uh."

"What?" asked Mason. "Come on, man. Fuck the 'vague' shit." The Cog looked at Mason, wincing bitterly, and started jiggling his knee.

"She's not carrying *guilt*—at least, not normal guilt."

"What's that mean? Who cares about that?"

"What I'm trying to say is . . . she's . . . she's—I don't know. That's it. I'm out now."

"Stay on it," said Mason. "If she's cult, I want her kept at a distance. I want her to be thinking of nests of baby bluebirds and nothing else."

The woman's flowing black hair swayed as she drifted along the edge of the square, gazing off into the mottled sycamore stands, up toward the sky, then all around the building facades. She appeared both otherworldly and sprung from earthy soil and water, and Mason found himself entranced. A faint nimbus of green—raw, vernal, and fecund—reflected off the budding limbs of the sycamore and lime trees, enveloping her. She hadn't looked at the chancery with any more interest than the rest of the square, and Mason now felt convinced that this Astrid Sullivan, whoever she was, posed no threat to the embassy.

Astrid now seemed to be looking straight into some of the hidden cameras, in a way that didn't feel quite human to Mason, and he got a hard, close look. She wasn't young or lithe, but tall and powerfully built, with the liquid muscles of a swimmer that swelled against her white and dark navy uniform.

In this woman's face, Mason saw something larger than another

entitled aristocrat's or angry republican's call to arms. It was deeper
and stronger and older and more *British* than just about anything in
England Mason saw. It was more than some ridiculous *through blood
and law* catchphrase.

Some of the diplomatic cops in the Roost were astir.

"Shit! Look, shitheads," one of them was saying. "It's that god-
damned monkey."

"Not a monkey, dumbass," said another. "Ape."

Mason had also seen flashes of the gorilla's face, and the humped,
retreating backside of an elephant, and the giant legs of elephants,
and now the gorilla again, with a strange, pained expression, looking right into one lens. There was another animal, too, but it was
harder to make out—a tiger? No one had said anything about
tigers.

The gorilla's face came up again on several screens, but Astrid
seemed to vanish.

"Britain's under attack—by its own zoo? But now I don't see the
woman—this Inspector Sullivan," said Mason. "We've got lots of
gorilla." The animal looked sad and frighteningly sentient.

"Nope. Not a face we're going to find on the databases," he said,
turning to a square-faced black rookie agent from Baltimore who
was manning the master CCTV console. Mason really liked this
rookie, Navas, an agent who also had strong empathic skills (it
was getting to be a trend in FBI and CIA recruitment). But Navas
wasn't exactly trained in using them, and for Mason, that made him
far more trustworthy.

Navas smiled and shook his head, then asked in a serious tone,
"What about the woman?"

"I think we're sort of stuck," said Mason. "I don't actually see
how her presence rises beyond a UK internal security matter. But
I'm still thinking we've not seen the end of this. I hope she's OK. I
see no threat with *her*. I just don't—but, for now, I think we've got

to leave her to the fucking Watch. Damn shame." He hesitated for a moment, then turned back toward the squinty-eye Cog.

"Is she or is she not a threat to America?" Mason asked the Cog.

"I don't . . . think so?"

"OK," said Mason. "But the Crown doesn't like her."

"Good 'ole King Harry," Navas muttered. "If he's after her, she must be competent."

"Damn right," Mason said, leaning down toward him.

"Heh-heh," said Navas, smiling awkwardly. Several of the CCTV monitors were swinging wildly in a way that made it impossible to see what they were recording. "My concentration's shit," said Navas. "I'm losing focus. I'm feeling like there's something in the chancery building. Sir?"

Mason took a deep breath. He said, "What do you mean?" He glanced over at the Cog, frowning.

"What do you say, Cog?"

"I don't know. I notice . . . something, too? Something's in my thoughts. Something's in here."

"What the fuck do you mean, 'in here'?"

"I don't know. I think . . . my thinking's . . . it's like it's sort of rippled, sir."

Mason looked over toward the group of newcomers who had come in with the pass-phrase.

It could be nothing, Mason knew, but a Cog's distraction usually meant trouble. For all his dislike of Cogs, he recognized that they possessed a talent. They would clamp onto others' minds like sharks and never let go.

"OK," said Mason. "Let's sweep the building." He nodded to one of the few actual armed U.S. Marines who stood guard in the Roost. "See if there's anyone in the building who's not on crew—or authorized."

"The woman," said Navas. "We should help her. We have to."

"Maybe," said Mason. "It's complicated. Is there a valid, concrete threat? Where are these . . . animals?"

Navas spun around, back to his console, and worked his cameras. A blur of images from the square—sycamore leaves, black bollards, mullioned windows—flashed across the screens. Finally, two big shots, at separate angles, of an exhausted pachyderm appeared on the main CCM screen, its trunk held rigidly out like a visible bolt of anger.

"OK, sir. Got one. It's *outside,*" he said, with a sigh of relief.

"Fuckinay," said Mason. "This is—goddangit—it's England, isn't it? That's what this is all about. Y'all think? Why does this kind of shit *always* happen here?" He leaned in to look at the screens more closely. "Anybody read *War of the Worlds*? Typical Englishness."

A different, boyish agent turned around, about to speak.

Mason interrupted him, "That was rhetorical."

It seemed to him now that the newcomers—austere-looking goobers with ultrashort haircuts as tidy as helmets—were crowding around the screens. Where did all these folks come from? Mason wondered. Few wore the dark bland wool suits and ties of his agents. Mason didn't want to overthink their presence; one of the hassles you learned to tolerate in security around the Company was being monitored and visited by shadowy, parallel organizations within the service. (And the pass-phrases were redundantly protected and knowledge of them sacrosanct.) But Mason felt nervous. He noticed that many of the kooks also wore the same white Nike trainers. They were in one of the most secure rooms in London, six floors below the surface (not the commonly believed three), encased in a full ten-foot-thick socket of lead and steel-buttressed well-being. They could survive a direct hit from most hydrogen bombs—for a few hours, at least. Apart from the mysterious newcomers, they all adored Mason. He was cantankerous and popular, and he inspired loyalty. But something was slipping past him.

"Seriously," he suddenly announced to all, "the pressure's sort of off on you all." Not everyone turned around to listen.

The Met and the horrible king's special paramilitary units were working this weirdness, he explained to the crowd in the room. American security personnel—diplomatic police, a small, specialized marine detachment, the CIA agents and liaisons, and a few British security "contractors" whom everyone accepted as MI5— would spectate. No one seriously believed that an embassy attacker was going to fill an elephant with ammonium nitrate and attach an Opticall detonator.

"Gorillas are buckchuck cool," said the boyish agent. Everyone looked at him. He zoomed in with one of the deep-infrared cameras, making a red-orange bloom fill the screen. "That's its brain. Lot of energy there."

A soldier standing by the door laughed.

And that was about the time when Mason's own brain, still recovering from a deep sleep, truly awakened.

"Holy shit—the applicants, the fucking visa applicants!"

A collective gasp arose. *No* one had remembered. Even as early as 4:00 A.M., there was always a queue for the visa services section of the embassy. Men, women, often children—usually Indigents— huddled in blankets, walked in place to keep their feet warm, whispered reverently in a hundred languages. The problem was, they normally gathered so close to the front of the chancery, they were not visible, on-screen, until the embassy officially opened for business at 8:30 A.M., when they would filter into the building's indoor battery of metal detectors and snaking queues and undergo a terrific, multitiered, marginally legal scrutinizing.

Mason said, "Goddamnit, we need to get the *fuck* out there." He could see the *Mirror/*WikiNous's headline already: HEARTLESS YANKS LEAVE REFUGEES TO BEASTS.

He looked at the marines in the Roost. "Jesus. Wait a second.

You can't go out there." What to do, precisely, turned out to be not so simple. The applicants stood on British soil, for now.

U.S. soldiers could not go out onto the pavement with weapons to protect foreign nationals on English territory. Even assigning diplomatic police to the pavement could cause an international row. The "special relationship" between America and the United Kingdom had long gone. If nothing else, Henry IX was majestically, deviously fickle. You just never knew what was coming next. Last year, Henry had actually lobbied to reopen the Treaty of Ghent; there were some twenty million acres of mineral-rich Maine and Upper Michigan that he felt Canada, now a Crown colony (apart from Quebec) again, had a historical claim to, at least in part, and tensions between the two countries were rising. Weeks later, he was calling the struggling America of the twenty-first century "a continuing inspiration for all."

"You could invite them in," said the British contractor. "The people, obviously—not the elephants."

"No, no elephants," Mason nodded, smirking. "That's good." He turned to one of the diplomatic police officers. "*Do* it."

The officer started patting his neuralzinger belt.

"Goddamnit," said Mason. "Do it fast or I'll cut your cock off with a dull deer antler."

A few of the men laughed. The Cog was shaking his head in apparent disgust.

"Yes, sir! Sorry, sir!"

The officer ran out of the room.

"Open the main doors!" A voice was shouting up a stairwell. "Let the applicants in."

Mason turned to Navas.

"What a mess. Get Five and the Circus up to speed. Tell them that we're getting our *logistics* in place, that we've got a few minor jurisdictional queries out to Legal—wait, no, wait, don't, don't do that. God, we'll never hear the end of it. The 'rights of Englishmen' this, EU treaties that. Wait till Harry gets a hold of that! Just request assistance."

"Sure," said Navas. "What about the woman—the inspector from the Royal Parks? The one the Watch is hot for?"

"I don't know. I'd like to talk with her. I think I need to get out there."

"Are you fucking nuts?" asked Navas.

"Well," said Mason. He punched in the code on a rectangle of numbers by the door of the lift. The lift, which had just two stops— ground level or six floors below to the Roost—opened with a sibilant *woosh*.

"I'm good with animals," said Mason.

The applicants needed help. Mason remembered Ephesians— how it was important to "be ye kind to one another, tenderhearted." He himself had come up hard from the impoverished hamlet of Mingo Grove, a foggy holler in the shadow of Spruce Knob Mountain. After high school, he joined the air force and excelled. He later worked his way through the state university, managing a Body-Friendly's ice cream restaurant at night to pay the bills. Despite the stereotypes of insular Appalachia, Mason's attraction to "furn service," as his family called it, was admired around his pine-forested, precipitous home. Getting out was the right thing to do, as everyone said once you'd done it. The applicants had it much worse, he knew. There was no comparison.

As for animals, he had grown up around aggressives, both sentient and otherwise, and he loved them. His older sister had bred and sold at half-market price Perro de Presa Canario puppies and kept, of all things, a pet bobcat, called Snaggle, caught as a kitten in the hills. Snaggle had grown up to be dangerous; it had once attacked Mason's mother and killed a visiting Presa stud as well as another pet in the Gage home—a big raccoon. Still, no one, especially not Mason, thought for a moment that Snaggle didn't have a place in their household.

As the lift opened to an anteroom of the chancery and Mason loped out into the square to survey the applicants, he felt a keen sense of destiny—and confidence to a fault.

Tenderhearted, he had to repeat to himself. *Tender. Hearted.*

the brave man from zanzibar

OUTSIDE THE CHANCERY, A QUEUE OF AROUND two dozen people, mostly men from sub-Saharan Africa, South Asia, and central China, seemed to be standing with remarkable poise. Few of them came from places wealthy enough to implement the Seoul International Open-Comm Accords, which made Wiki-Nous flesh-implantation a human right. Consequently, almost none of them understood what was going on in the rest of London. When the gorilla and elephant—and something else—entered the square, they froze.

But it wasn't composure. It was terror.

"*Dà xîngxîng*!" a Chinese woman finally began screaming, and a clamor of cries and shouts followed. "*Dà xiàng!*"

Suleiman Ghailani had been sitting upon his "Ghana Must Go" bag,* as some of his queue mates kept calling the huge plaid nylon tote, which contained all his possessions on earth. These mostly comprised secondhand clothes from charities in Zanzibar whose supply of ugly, ancient polyester clothes from Kentucky and

---

* A large hold-all sack

Bavaria was apparently inexhaustible. (The world had plenty of T-shirts and garish jumpers for Africa, Suleiman had discovered, long ago. To Zanzibari eyes, the old prebiodegradable fibers seemed to last decades longer than the inscrutable fashions they chased. There were things more injurious than poverty. Who in the world needed tight purple leggings with twelve zippered pockets?) There were also a pair of very weathered Reverend Awdry's Railway Series books to help him learn English (the haughty blue engine, Gordon, made him laugh), and two packages of his cherished ballpoint pens, which he had purchased prematurely (and expensively) upon arrival at Heathrow. He planned to post the pens back to his father and young sisters in Tanzania as soon as he finally made it to America. (No one attached to the WikiNous/Opticall web used pens or pencils, but the poorest parts of the world treated them with reverence.) He would put a crisp, new $500 note in the letter, too, as he had seen done in the kung fu movies everyone in Tanzania watched on the old electric *dalla-dalla* buses. Once safe in the USA, he was going to make his family feel big.

When he saw the first animals, he leaped up to his feet and backed against one of the Portland stone columns that helped support the chancery's facade. He was shocked. There were no gorillas on Zanzibar—the only primates left were a few colobus monkeys tourists paid to see in special reserves he himself had never cared to visit. As a young child, he had seen some of the last of the wild elephants, and like most East Africans, he respected the *tembo* more than any other creature, even *simba*, the lion—also now extinct in the wild.

After a moment, Suleiman stepped forward, toward the *tembo*. If he could attract the animals' attention, it might save lives.

"*Fee amaan Allah,*" he whispered. "*Inshallah.*"

Suleiman was very bright, but in coming to London he had catastrophically depended on someone who turned out to be unreliable, and now he was down to his last £400, staying in a B&B, and filled with anguish. He was supposed to have stayed with a very religious acquaintance from the neighboring island of Pemba, a man named Abbas who lived in Finsbury Park and attended the Aga Khanian mosque there. But Abbas, strangely, had disappeared, and when Suleiman had knocked on his flat door, a bearded young Pakistani man in a long linen prayer shirt answered and smugly told him that Abbas had disappeared into hell. He never explained what that meant.

"Brother," Suleiman had said. "I am lost."

The man smiled and nodded knowingly. "Come back tomorrow and I will give a new way of life. You need to hear our imam. He's friends with the Caliph Aga Khan, you know? He's like no one you've ever heard. He will help you, *rafiki*."

A fanatic, Suleiman thought.

So Suleiman had changed course; all the Africans he had met in London—nearly all from West Africa—urged him to "visit" New York City and simply overstay the "leave to remain" passport stamp. You could hide in Queens or Newark forever. The rest of America could be safely ignored.

"Go to the Big Apple, my nigga," a fat path-manager from Lagos had said, laughing his head off. "I'm going back next week just to buy some new shoes. This London—it's five thousand percent rip-fucking-rippa-dip-dip-*rip*-off!"

The elephant very pointedly stopped and faced the visa applicants. Suleiman turned and saw several of them try to squeeze behind the column. But it was hopeless. Too many people, too little protection.

"*Toka, mama tembo*," Suleiman said to the elephant. "*Toka, mama lady.*"

Meanwhile, the gorilla regarded the entire scene, shaking his head mournfully. He looked up at the facade's massive grill-like

Eero Saarinen design of reinforced concrete cells. (Its precise, offset rectangles, along with the thirty-five-foot-wide gold eagle above the building, inspired and intimidated visitors—it made America seem like a country of the distant future, a splendid but remote post-human society, oddly complementing the tidy math of the Georgian buildings around it.) But something about the rectangles riled the gorilla; there was a cold blandness and lack of fire about them, a total ensnaring of aggression, from grid point to grid point, the opposite of animalism.

Hoping for a closer look, Kibali jumped onto one of the dozens of new, larger stone bollards, ancient tank traps installed decades before in front of the embassy complex. They were ugly, disordered trapeziums, like the reactive-armor bricks on Russian T-120 tanks, and they completely perverted Saarinen's light touch. Amid this angular clutter sat the ape, perched on one of these stone fists of national fright, hunched in anxiety as the doors of the embassy flew open. Nearby, he saw the giant plane trees, so thickly and horizontally limbed that Kibali felt he had perhaps found a safe, comfortable, murky home in this strange world.

A spectral being then drifted up and out of the green shadows that Kibali was contemplating. It resembled Astrid, but it was larger, untamed, like a wild, long-limbed yew tree spotted with tiny red berries. Astrid's long black hair seemed to have turned a golden green, and floated in the air between the embassy and the animals, sparking little fires from which baby kestrels and whipping adders and speeding tiny stoats burst forth.

"*Gagoga,*" said the creature. "*Gagoga maga medu.*"

And those close to the vernal being, who heard the words, bowed their heads.

But not Mason Gage. He came out of the chancery building with his arms behind him, his head lowered for other reasons. Such was his focus on the notion of saving the vulnerable visa applicants from the elephant and gorilla, he did not, for quite a while, even notice the being. He'd merely struck a sort of improvised submissive pose, something he remembered in dealing with his sister's feisty Perro de Presa Canarios; it could not have contrasted more with the imperial golden eagle statute six floors above him, and the gesture looked particularly odd on Mason.

The angry elephant turned its head toward the being, calming for a moment, but it trotted straight through the green fog, and bucked a bit, then squared off against Mason, so close the young man could smell the high, sweet reek of its shit.

A phalanx of nearly identical-looking men in coveralls the color of yoghurt stood behind Mason, too, emerging from the interior of the chancery, and looking pressed for time. By contrast, Mason had thrown on a simple navy blazer and old black DreamUp jeans, which supposedly could be slightly adjusted through telekinesis (but this never worked, buyers soon learned). He kept a neural-zinger pistol with nonlethal rounds holstered under the blazer.

Several of the men had their hair cut in the same cropped, androgynous style. Their appearance threw him off a bit, but they'd come from the chancery's offices, and he implicitly—and imprudently— trusted them as legitimate. There were, after all, a very few tertiary aspects of embassy operations in any major world capital— everything from toilet repairs to heating duct maintenance—that even the chief of security didn't fully grasp. Mason's mistake was that he saw these people as one of them.

"Who are you? What unit?"

None answered.

Mason decided that they must be some kind of foreign outside building contractors. He would address the issue of the white-suited caretakers or whatever the fuck they were at the next security team meeting, and they looked funny, didn't they, and shouldn't they know some basic English?

Moving out into the square, toward the elephant, Mason walked right past the black man who had stepped forward.

"Go inside," Mason told the man, pushing his eyeglasses higher on the bridge of his nose. He held his hand out toward the anxious, angry pachyderm, behind which the green fog was gathering again. Mason glanced back for a moment at the rest of the visa applicants, and a feeling of protectiveness arose in him—but the elephant's stolid, fearful gaze preoccupied him more. If pushed to choose between human and animal, Mason was a person who could not be depended on to stand up for his own species.

"It's OK, sugar," he was saying to the elephant. "It's OK, darling." Some of the men in the white coveralls leered at the scene, as if they thought Mason must be joking.

"Thar, thar, sugar," he said to the elephant, smiling genially. "What're you all put out for?"

The men in coveralls began waving the visa applicants inside. Some of them were reading off SkinWerks notes glowing on their hands, in reflexive voices: "Inside! Inside! Welcome! *Huanying guanglin! Bienvenue!* Welcome! *Huanying guanglin! Bienvenue!* Inside!" A 3D holographic sign with the same words, in puffy lettering, was, in a flash, projecting from above the doors.

Suleiman, who had dawdled, and who didn't like the looks of the men in white coveralls, knew immediately that the navy-jacketed man from the embassy was making a profound mistake by getting so close to the *tembo*. When Suleiman was a child, his elder cousin, Amani, had been lucky enough to live and work seasonally at one of the game preserves south of the capital. When Suleiman had visited, he saw Amani carefully drive wild elephants away from the touring Land Rovers by smacking their feet—but it was perilous work, and one risked death. But this American man, he acted as if he had never seen a *tembo* in his life.

When the elephant began to charge, Suleiman watched stunned

as the man ran *toward* it. He did not know why, but he too began running toward the animal. There was perhaps a vague sense that he must start acting larger than himself—is *this* American, this running *toward* a monster? But mostly, Suleiman simply heeded an innate decency and courage he himself did not know he possessed.

"No!" he shouted. "*Toka!*"

Layang let out a sneezy, squeaky cry—the splurty sounds of a knotted cornet—then knocked Mason off his feet with the base of her trunk. His eyeglasses went flying. Everything happened so fast, Mason was still smiling, still believing, when the animal's front feet slammed down only inches from his knees. He had made no sound. He felt nothing. He still held his hand out toward the animal and was almost laughing, with a strange sense that his cropped hair had suddenly grown miles long and caught fire.

"Oh," he finally said. "Hey."

Then there was Suleiman over him, trying to wrestle with one of the elephant's feet. "*Toka! Mama tembo, toka!*"

Suleiman had never been so close to a *tembo,* never touched one. The softness and warmth of the animal's huge ankles surprised him—he had expected a kind of hard rubberiness. He realized he didn't know what he was doing, but Layang seemed to respond to him, and backed away, but only for a moment. Suleiman turned toward the man and tried to lift him up. Layang had risen to her hind legs, preparing to pounce down on Mason with a 1,500-pound coup de grâce.

Suleiman spun around and staggered back, positioning himself between the angry elephant and Mason. The beast moved its head side to side in a brutal fashion, as if trying to shake its own brains out, and glared down at the humans. Suleiman was able to pull the man up to his feet, looping his arm around his chest, and yank him back. For reasons he could not grasp, the man was resisting him, pulling at his forearms fiercely.

"I'm OK," Mason seethed. "Let me go!" But Suleiman had no intention of letting him die. He kept trying to heave him away from the elephant.

Mason, trying to regain his balance, thumping the heels of his own trainers down on a short set of three cement stairs, could see the blaming, sweeping rage in the elephant, its ears engorged with blood, its reddish-brown eyes furious. The unfamiliar tenderness of the man, the unplanned human-to-human connection, was humiliating to him. He didn't want to be rescued. It was a goddamn elephant, not a suicide bomber.

Still, as they stood back now, watching, Layang all at once thrust her feet down so hard on the pavement the nearby trees rustled. Then the elephant seemed to back off.

"Thanks," said Mason stiffly, gaining a footing, gazing at the small, lean man, who was grinning. The dark blue insulated coat he had been wearing was missing an arm, and all he wore under the coat was an old faded-red T-shirt that read OPERATION GET DOWN—DETROIT, MI.

"Go inside now," Mason said. "It's OK. Just go in." He wiped some of the dust off his saggy khakis. He knelt down, retrieved his broken spectacles, and reset them on his nose. One of the lenses was shattered; he popped it out and let it fall on the ground.

The gorilla had moved off the bollard and into the little central garden in Grosvenor Square. He was watching all the people in front of the embassy with a look of unyielding confusion and distress. He kept placing his long hand over his solar plexus—in pain, it seemed. The elephant remained in the street, just beyond the tank traps. She was taking deep breaths, making her curved flanks flare out visibly in the half-darkness under the canopying boughs of enormous mottled plane trees.

Once again, the trees seemed slowly to exhale a verdant fog that was itself unspooling and forming a larger, and utterly bizarre, tree. It was the great, weird Yew of Wyre, beside which many a local witch had tried, secretly, to raise spirits. It had germinated in deepest Worcestershire, thousands of years ago, and now it thundered up and out into the square as summoned. The vapory limbs began spiraling, too, into various half-human forms of the forest and stream—dryads, wodwos, and sylvan sprites, all made of sand-colored basalts and pink feldspars and river pebbles polished to a shine by centuries of inland flow toward the mighty Severn. When any of the Neuters came near the tree's green vapor, they would quiver in place until they melted into puddles of white jelly. Amid it all, Astrid's form emerged, her skin shaggy with lichen, her clothing falling off in tatters, with a set of eyes blacker than a riverbed, and her hair growing into the golden-emerald limbs of a great, tortuous-rooted, ever-spreading tree.

"*Gagoga maga medu,*" she began saying, in a voice more plangent and piercing than her own but hers nonetheless. "*Gagoga maga medu.*"

Then the yew began receding rapidly again, and Astrid felt herself phasing into reality. She fell onto her knees. A new physical sensitivity, neither hot nor cold, began coursing up and down her limbs. It didn't hurt, but it forced her to hold her arms out. It was like unripened electricity, budding from the soil and the leaves, and bleeding green from her palms.

"Please," she said, moaning. "Please."

Astrid was naked, too. She climbed back to her feet shakily, forcing herself to take slow, halting breaths. Her pale, teacup-size breasts rose and fell visibly as she steadied herself. There were green patches of sticky sap dappling her skin, and it trickled down from her head and shoulders, past her glistening navel, down the smooth curves of the middle of her back, then all along the ogees formed by her narrow waist as they broadened out to ample, potent hips. An accidental coronet of holly and ivy ringed her sopping head, and she held a craggy yew stick like a staff. All those in the square who glimpsed her saw an athletic, tall, beautiful woman, emerging like a kind of green Diana birthed from the trees.

Mason Gage, standing slightly back, was spellbound. "Easy," he said to her, gingerly edging closer. "It's OK."

She herself felt crushing vulnerability and bitter coldness.

"Oh my God," she cried, stepping toward the embassy, hands in front of her as if she were blind, balancing the yew stave on her shoulder. "Oh mother Mary. Help me, someone. I'm in Flōt second-withdrawal. Someone." She could not seem to speak above a whisper. She began waving her hands at the man in the navy blazer.

"Jesus," said Mason.

She wasn't quite, but she was close.

the luciferian offensive

SULEIMAN HAD NEVER SEEN ANYTHING LIKE THE green woman, but he felt her power and her unruliness keenly, and these things frightened him, and the nudity, well, that created a kind of panic in his brain.

"*Allahu, allahu, allahu*!"* he kept repeating.

Suleiman turned toward the glass doors. He saw the gleaming whites and golds of the chancery's reception area, all pale marble and honey colored. It reminded him of the small, filigreed gilt and ivory jewelry boxes from Oman that one could find in Stone Town on Zanzibar. They were ingenious contraptions made to swallow pieces of sparkling beauty, and they often outshined their contents.

Also in the anteroom, most peculiarly, was a kind of ad hoc bar set upon a table, with fine orbs of Flōt and an arrangement of top-shelf liquors and red-sashed magnums of champagnes, a spread of crackers and brie and Stilton, silver bowls of grapes and figs. He felt ashamed of his disheveled appearance.

---

* A Sufi chant: "God is truth"

Mason stood rapt, watching the naked woman, quite unable to move, rubbing his hands together, partly to dust them off, partly to cope with a rising anxiety. It soon dawned on him that the tree-woman was just Inspector Sullivan, and her twisted face betrayed her own terror, and whatever he thought he saw, must simply not have been real. It couldn't have been, could it?

He finally trotted toward Astrid, sniffing, trying to regain his prepossession.

"Inspector? Sullivan?"

"Not an inspector anymore."

Mason put his arm around her paternally, tenderly, but she began to shrug it off.

"My skin—it's extra-crazy sensitive. That's not going to help," she whispered. She looked up into the man's eyes. He seemed kind and strong, and she began to weep with relief. "I'm a recovering Flōter. It's second withdrawal. The Death. Do you know what that means? You can't save me."

"I don't know what it means, but I guess it means you are in danger," he said. "I can help get you warm. I can . . ."

"You know," said Astrid. "If you only did what other primates do for each other, that would be great," she said. She kissed his cheek. "But thank you, kind sir."

Suleiman had managed to pull an old Detroit Tigers hoodie from his Ghana Must Go bag, and he and Mason swaddled Astrid in the hoodie, and she accepted this.

"What happened to you?" Mason asked her. "What's going on?"

She said, "I'm afraid I don't know. But I . . . I felt like I—I *feel* like I am here for a reasons that goes way beyond myself. I'll say this, too—I've had king's bulletin Opticalls and black-freqs going off in my eyes like nuts in the last ten minutes. We're . . . in trouble. In Britain. Something's going on . . . a kind of attack."

Mason motioned toward one of the nearby rank-and-file diplomatic police officers, while nodding toward Suleiman. He said to the officer, "Make sure this gentleman gets his visa—whatever he wants. He saved my life. He's one of the good guys. *Make sure.*"

Mason glanced inside; the sight of the table of Flōt and champagne and hors d'oeuvres startled and disturbed him. "What the shit?" It snapped him out of the reverie he felt toward Astrid, which was making her uncomfortable.

"Who's having a fucking party in the middle of the night?"

Something newly bewildering was unfolding. The officer Mason had ordered, a tall man with red hair, was being led away by one of the people in white coveralls—a Neuter. The red-haired officer was distraught, and so was Mason. Astrid was holding on to Mason's arm, more from a desire for warmth than fear.

"Hey," Mason said to the Neuter. "What the hell's this?"

One of the Neuters, smiling broadly, bashed Mason's collarbone with a neural-coshstick, flattening him, taking his breath away.

"Are you ready to go to the comet ship?" the Neuter asked Mason, in an absurdly courteous voice, still grinning numbly.

"Wait!" said the officer, trying to pull away. Mason tried to rise back to his feet, and the Neuter hit him again in the middle of his back, knocking him back down.

"Ah!" he screamed. "You sumbitch."

Another white-suited Neuter appeared and took the red-haired officer's free arm.

"What did Chief Gage say?" said the officer. "Asshole, stop! Get your fucking hands off me. Who the fuck are you people?"

Before anyone could say another word, the Neuter's jaw was hit so hard, it seemed to move sideways off its hinges. In a single swing of her stave, Astrid dispatched two others and gave the Americans a brief haven.

As Mason got back to his feet, he realized how desperately he had failed in his own sacred duty to protect the embassy. The Neuters had somehow infiltrated the chancery, emerging from within. Some of them, it seemed clear, had to have been in the diplomatic security detail.

Now the Neuters, who had come to England to obliterate all animals and to force mass human suicide, who seemed to be replicating themselves by the second, were acting with cruel force, using shoulder-dislocating jerks to haul everyone in the embassy out into the square. They had fanned out across the square and started to invade the rest of central London, surrounding every animal they encountered. There were also new Red Watch frightcopters and a few autonews drones in the sky, too, but the Neuters were shooting them down with a kind of sticky-roped plasmatic harpoon.

Indeed, by this time, all across central London, men, women, and children—aristocrats first—were being dragged out of bed by the Neuters and compelled to return to Grosvenor Square. A nightmaric invasion had begun in earnest, just as the sand cat and the lions had warned St. Cuthbert. With its hundreds of living and frozen gene banks, the last zoo on earth—more Noah's ark than Noah's—would be the supreme, but far from the only, target.

Suleiman was in a daze, but he was incongruously free of fear. He did not understand what was happening. He actually believed the appearance of the Neuters was all part of some eccentric embassy procedure. The naked woman—well, he didn't know *what* to think there. But he felt in her a sign or symbol of good luck or power that he didn't need to grasp. He had always stood little chance of getting the visa, but now that was secure, as this Chief Gage man had said. And Suleiman could not stop grinning. He had barely noticed the attackers; he was still half-focused on the *tembo*. It was still there. Someone needed to trap it now, he thought, smiling. It looked settled and compliant, but exhausted, its trunk hanging limp making tweedling squeaks and low, muculent rumbles. Perhaps someone could give it some of those crackers he had seen on that intoxicating American table of plenty?

Mason grabbed Suleiman's hand, and Mason's rock-hard grip frightened him, and for the first time, he saw what everyone else did; hundreds of the white-uniformed humanoids were spilling out of the embassy now.

"What is this?" Suleiman said, in a halting English. "Is the embassy . . . is it angry?"

"I don't know," Astrid said to him. "But it's not good."

Thousands of London's citizens were pouring into Grosvenor Square, all pushed and prodded by the beings in white.

The cellular artistry of Eero Saarinen's chancery was revealing itself as something, indeed, not of this Earth—it was serving, literally, as hell's, not heaven's "Gate" for the animals.

A great plasmatic quarkbeam suddenly exploded from the roof of the embassy. It curved high above central London. It flowed parallel to the ground for a mile or two, and bent down again, somewhere north, toward the zoo, a plunging finger of doom. It formed a colossal arc of nervous subatomic particles, a sort of white suitcase handle with which Atlas might have picked up the borough of Westminster and hurled it into the stratosphere.

All the rectangular panels of Saarinen's soulless facade immediately were illuminated and began to glow a lurid red. In each of the cells, Astrid could see mammalian silhouettes slowly appear and dissolve. Kudus, tree shrews, frogs, corgi dogs, porpoises—they flickered and were gone. The mammoth, satanic soul-eating machine had started to suck in all the souls of living animals of earth. It was just as the sand cat had warned St. Cuthbert. Here was the device "from outside the desert," a product of some distant intergalactic malfeasance, switched on like the demon Baphomet's vacuum cleaner.

Some of the white-suited Neuters, meanwhile, had opened long silver staves that smoothly glided up from their soft pale wrists to deliver powerful quantum contra-fluxal shocks. Then the cultists began to work the staves, like stock prods, blue sparks flying out, jabbing the applicants and CIA agents and analysts and police officers, even some of the autoreporters who had shown up, herding them toward the table with the alcohol. There the shepherded were made to imbibe from blackberry-colored orbs of Flōt. It was dosed, Astrid suspected, with barbiturate. This was how the Heaven's Gate cult killed you. Did they, she wondered, as they murdered you, slip their famous enigmatic $5 bill into your pocket right then, the currency meant perhaps to pay the toll of some intergalactic Charon, thus ensuring a steady stream of souls to their comet world?

The red-haired man was still resisting until he was thrust down and held in place with at least three of the alien stock prods. One of the cult members began to beat and shock him aggressively until he stopped moving, stopped making noise, and when that happened, Astrid felt sure that she was next.

Amid the chaos, the leader of the cult, Marshall Applewhite III, appeared in the door of the lift that the security team had used. He wore the same silvery tunic Astrid had seen him wearing when she watched the telly with Sykes at the Seamen's Rest. It was a ridiculously campy garment one might see on some Venusian high priest from an old science fiction B movie. His tall frame and shaved head would have made him seem menacing, but his large blue fawn eyes, his good posture, his expression of barely repressed merriment, offered a sugared charisma. Astrid could almost see why so many followed him to their deaths. Almost.

"You're freakstyle," she said. "I must be close to the end now. You are the Flōt withdrawal talking. You're a figment, you are."

"I'm sorry," Applewhite said, moving somehow closer to Astrid. "I'm as real as the comet," he added, pointing toward the sky. "I'm sorry—do not be afraid. You'll see. Everything is *fan*-ta-stic!"

Astrid wanted to shove the creep away from her, but he pre-empted this by moving himself along.

MOST OF THE PEOPLE being driven like cattle were only zapped a few times before taking their potion willingly. Applewhite himself was touring the operation like a kind of foreman inspecting the factory floor. He nodded and smiled and patted people on the back in a starchy, awkward way, and even tried to comfort prospective victims, giving quick hugs and laughing. "Exiting isn't death," he said. "In Level Above Human, you'll all get new, eternal bodies built—and they're so beautiful!—for space travel." But if those herded and prodded ones did not become pliable, the Neuter soldiers squirted poisoned Flōt or champagne down their throats, sometimes stuffing in a handful of crackers and pills and a fig for good measure. At these ugly scenes Applewhite merely gave an exaggerated pout of sympathy and walked on.

"Let's all be nice," he said at one point.

Some of the regular embassy personnel queuing at the table didn't appear rankled at all and required no abuse—indeed, they politely waited their turns.

Astrid herself felt the allure of the Flōt and the champagne. She was convinced that little of what she saw before her was really happening. Could a drink or two hurt? It would end the anxieties of the Death in an instant, and as she saw it, end this entire phantasmagoria of a night. Couldn't she just get a sip, a little taste, of some Glenfiddich, and stir in a splash of Flōt, and a bite of cheese, without the downers? She pulled her hair into two thick tails and twisted it into a splayed chignon. The humidity of the chancery had given it waves, and it was as flyaway shiny and distracting as ever.

Marshall Applewhite III glided right in front of Astrid.

"Yes, it's sooooooo OK," he said, in a sibilant, not unfriendly voice. "We're inside you, after all. We know you. We know about your unhappiness and your loneliness. And all those years of having no one but your mother, and now she's dying of Bruta7, poor dear one, and it's become so hard to believe in anything in . . . in this . . . this dirty *world* of petty kings and animals running amok and people acting like animals. Go ahead—drink away. It's liberating, Astrid."

Applewhite frowned a little. He showed Astrid a purple orb of Flōt and two shot glasses. She put her hand to her mouth, as if guarding it.

Out in the square, she heard a loudspeaker babbling about King Henry's sins, and the death-groans of neuralpike victims, and the screams of an elephant. She was still without panties or trousers, her muscular legs still dripping with green sticky sap. She felt appallingly exposed but almost beyond embarrassment.

"This corrupt manimal," said the loudspeaker in a nasally, bloodless tone, "this selfish manimal—this earth-bound manimal—this corrupt manimal—he has—corrupt manimal—he has appealed to Britain's worst nature. Corrupt manimal. Let Harry9 die. Let him be gone with the rest of earth's animals. *Let* him—" and on and on the voice droned. In the distance, Astrid could also just make out a new and alarming sound, both musical and corrosive, like the gold-throated shrieks of hundreds of dragons. Applewhite, too, seemed to hear it, and squinted suspiciously.

"Oh," she said. "Oh, god."

After a long pause, she said, "But there's St. Cuthbert." She began shaking her head, taking a few steps back from Applewhite. "He thinks I'm his brother. Or some kind of forest messiah. He says I'm the Christ of Otters." She turned away from Applewhite. "Cuthbert's crazy, but he means something . . . to me, at least."

"What's he to you? He's a stranger. He's nothing. He's a part of your second withdrawal from Flōt. Your unnecessary withdrawal. Your unnecessary 'struggle' with your human container."

"But he's not. Leave me alone. You don't care about me. Cuthbert—he's no stranger. I've even an idea that he might be my granddaddy. He shouldn't be a stranger. Not to anyone in England."

"But you don't realize," said Applewhite, beaming smugly, holding one of the glasses toward Astrid, "that this saint is merely *second withdrawal?* Don't you see? There is no *Saint* Cuthbert. He's just another city drunk."

Astrid pulled her hair down again and shook it out.

"I don't care," she said. "For all I know, we're all just the ghosts of one another's deepest needs. But there is this helpless old Indigent who says he has come to save Britain's animals, and he may be crazy, but tonight, this first of May, in the reign of King Henry the Ninth, in 2052, in London, England, he is Saint Cuthbert."

"But you . . . what about you? What are you to him?"

"I am . . . I am the Christ of Otters."

Applewhite grimaced sadly. "Oh, child," he said, chuckling. "You've been, well, between withdrawals for so long—and that's such a scary thing, I know!—that you're easily taken in. And that's OK. We'll help you. I really, really, really, really think you're at the Evolutionary Level Above Human. You're as *unanimal* as they get. And you're *so special*. That's why you're not being forced . . . like the others . . . see? We know you well, Astrid. I'm sorry, but I have to say this: you're completely ready to shed your container. You *are* ready to ascend to our home in the comet. Drink, friend, drink."

Lifting a filled shot glass in his wrinkled pink hand, Applewhite drank one of them, wincing slightly.

Astrid said, "I will not, cunt."

"Then you've wrecked your*self*, Astrid," he said, gasping a bit. "You can stay in your world of giant vaginas and shit. You *will* die tonight. If the Death doesn't get you, my Neuters will."

There was a kind of popping sound, and a flash of red lights, and Applewhite, mysteriously, was gone.

rage of the leopard

ASTRID ALL AT ONCE FELT VERY DIZZY AND clumsy, and she fell again to her knees, right beside the banquet table of Flōt and champagnes and Stilton and foie gras, still naked from the waist down. And her heart seemed to be struggling to beat, as the gorilla's was. Had the cultists somehow slipped her the fatal ingredients, too? she wondered. She did not have time to speculate—she soon found that the redoubtable Mason was by her side again.

"Can I help you up?" he asked, his lip quivering a bit.

"No," she said. "Yes."

And when with his arm he pulled her to her feet, for a moment her legs straddled his thigh, and a shudder of pleasure hit her, and she nearly pushed Mason back to the floor so that she could take him inside her.

He seemed to scramble for a few moments, as if twisting and weaseling away from her.

"Fuck," she said. "For some reason . . . I'm really hot for you. I'm sorry. It's . . ."

He pulled her to her feet, and she spun around. She looked all around herself.

"It's OK," he said. "I just—I'm kind of slow, you know? And you're so . . . you're beautiful. But there's something going on with you."

"He's . . . left?" asked Astrid.

"Who?"

"The creepy cult man, holding the shot glasses."

"Um, sure," Mason said, in a way Astrid read as *sure, whatever you say.*

Astrid leaned hard against Mason, trying to calm herself, to still her body—but a big part of her remained like an unsocketed eye, looking everywhere helplessly, unable to move, stuck upon Mason. She wondered if this helpless nakedness, this abject dependency on the animal warmth of another, was somehow a sign that she had indeed cleared the last hurdle of the second withdrawal, and that a new life could unfold from here. She hated the feeling of need. She longed to be the otter queen again, with legs as big and hard as the trunks of oak trees and a mind as big as the sky.

"You saw him?" asked Astrid.

Mason just smiled at her and said, "We need to get you some trousers." In his own buttoned-down and overly competent way, he felt oddly liberated, too. The *loop d'loopers* in matching white had taken the night into realms beyond the diplomatic service. Questions swarmed his mind: Was America also under attack? Had he been drugged? Was he somehow mentally ill? Was he alive? He didn't see a way that the events of the night would *not* leave his outlook forever altered. But delusions or not, drugs or not, live or dead—he, for one, wasn't going to let an obviously suffering woman walk around half-naked in the chancery without getting her some clothes.

He opened Suleiman's giant bag and dug out a pair of ancient, tattered *Phineas and Ferb* pajama bottoms. They must have been half a century old. Astrid jumped into them gladly.

"Now," said Mason. "I want to see about the animals."

"Come with me," Astrid said to Suleiman and Mason. "Let's try to move them into the center of the square. We need to move away from here."

At that moment, not far beyond the trees west of Grosvenor, and growing closer and closer, there arose again the chilling noise Astrid had heard earlier, like a phalanx of holy dragons, puffing purgatorial fires and spitting sizzling golden bolts.

"Jesus," said Mason. "Let's go. That doesn't sound like it wants to be our friend."

"But my visa," Suleiman said.

"You'll get the visa," said Mason. "We can't stay here."

The three of them began to move down the chancery steps and into the crowded square. The elephant Layang was raging again, bucking up and screaming. *Help me*, the elephant said to Astrid. *Take me to a warm country.* As Astrid moved toward her, the elephant almost instantly settled down.

Astrid looked back toward Mason and Suleiman. "Oh my god," she said. "I just *heard*—I *heard* the elephant, speaking to me."

Mason said, "Oh boy."

Astrid didn't get to enjoy her new interspecies linguistic skill. When she saw some of the Neuters' faces now, a new horror hit her: *all* of them seemed to have become Marshall Applewhite. All wore the same blue-eyed, thick-browed look of happy, gelded contempt for her.

"He's going to kill me," she said. "He'll try to kill all of us. We need to go!"

An old-tech gunshot cracked out from the crowd and Layang

the elephant dropped into a gray heap beside Astrid, with a thud so powerful the trees of the square rustled and windows rattled. Mason and Suleiman felt it in their knees. The shot seemed to have come from a tumult of rowdy Indigents, but it was hard to tell. The animal's death was instant and monumentally total. No limbs quivered, no ears twitched.

"No!" cried Mason, running toward Astrid and the elephant. "Goddamnit, no!"

Who? he asked himself. Fucking who? Marines, the police, these Neuter people, or an ordinary Londoner? And why? *Why?* "Don't shoot," he shouted. "Stop, you fucking fuckers, stop!"

There was an odd, new noise, in the trees, like a wooden saw made from living flesh.

Hur-haw! Hur-haw! Hur-haw!

It was at that moment when Monty, the melanistic leopard, the Shayk of Night, as the sand cat called him, dropped from one of the plane tree boughs. He hung down for a few seconds, draping like a scarf of luminous black silk. Then he fell onto the backs of two of the Neuters. Monty had been following the gorilla and elephant—stalking them—but other prey would do.

Astrid looked up, and a sense of unaccountable relief filled her. The balance of power seemed to move toward the animals.

"*Chui!*" Suleiman gasped. "Leopard!"

The leopard began to slash into the Neuters, and any humans within reach. He was a power beyond any of their machines, any of their programmed incantations. A violet-blue liquid spumed out of the Neuters' necks as if from broken lawn hoses. It was not blood. It was ice cold, and it tasted bitter to the cat. It made the animal more determined to bring the infidels to heel.

The gorilla, Kibali, watched from a distance, shifting his weight fretfully from one foot to another, back and forth, back and forth.

"Stop this," the gorilla called to Monty. "Please, let us take the paths of peace, my friend. Friend!"

"The Mahdi comes!" Monty screamed, beyond reason, swiping and gnashing and tearing into any spot of creamy white flesh its claws could hook. "For everyone, for all, for now, for you!"

Astrid could hear every word of the creature, although she wasn't sure she understood them.

"Brr-row-brr-row-brr-rowowow!" snarled the animal. "Bow down and pray before the Mahdi!"

"The Mahdi?" Astrid asked the great cat.

"He waits for you, at the zoo," said Monty, pausing from battle, yet somehow speaking to her intimately and alone, even as many melees spread around them. "You, the princess of all things untamed, and the force 'through the green fuse'—you, the Otter Christ."

"That can't be," said Astrid. "I am just a lonely drug addict in London, and you're nothing but a symptom of the Death."

"You will see," said Monty. The black panther vaulted into the air and slammed onto a Neuter.

"Inside! Inside!" the Neuter repeated, trying to chop at the black cat's hot muzzle even as its cold heart ceased its slow, steady, quantum-powered ticking.

"Down! Bow!"

It was Abrahamic religion versus www.heavensgate.com.

Some of the citizens in the square decided to surround Kibali, and they began to hurl objects at him—plastic bottles, belt buckles, shoes. "Fuck," said Mason, huddling close to Astrid and Suleiman. "Fucking idiots."

"Why they want to hurt the *sokwe*?" asked Suleiman. "He hurt no one."

"Let me die," Astrid could hear Kibali pleading. "Let me go."

These weren't the Neuters, who had indeed planned, later, to put the gorilla down. This was the human mob.

Astrid and Mason now saw poor Kibali fall to the ground in the square, just across the street from the embassy; the ape lay on his side on the grass, clutching his chest in pain, and Mason ran toward him. Astrid and Suleiman followed.

The noble silverback was having a myocardial infarction. The appearance of the white-suited aggressors, the stress of the escape, the spurting violet-blue liquid, the years of sedentary anguish, those éclairs from the well-meaning keeper, and finally, this insult of ordinary people—it had been too much.

Kibali felt crushed by what he had found outside the zoo. Humans were not only his foes, but they also were not even as minimally decent as animals. He would be hunted eternally. The entire city was merely an outgrowth of the zoo, and he would never be allowed to escape.

All around Kibali were the voices, too, that Cuthbert had heard in the zoo—the high-pitched, fussy, and deeply cloying treacle-tones of Heaven's Gate. They were repeating certain phrases, *The mammals will pass from the earth*, and *Deactivate the animals*. Surely, thought Kibali, the Interahamwe soldiers could not be far behind, and in an odd way, he knew he would prefer them. In being cut to pieces with a machete, one died at the receiving end of real emotion, of something both animal and human. Here, by contrast, was detached, digitalized, mob slaughter. Here was the truth of the comet Urga-Rampos, bringing the possibility of holocausts beyond the nightmares any of previous millennia. If he had only made it to St. James or Hyde Park, or to the Wyre Forest—perhaps from there he might have ducked under the cover of these beautiful English trees, and he might have proceeded slowly ahead, from green patch to green patch, until he arrived in the Congo. Oh, if he could only die under the ayous and sapelli trees, in peace, with ants tickling his knuckles and his family around him, how content he would be to leave this world.

He could not breathe. He tried to pull the air in, but nothing came from the effort. He felt dizzy.

Mason held Kibali in his arms now, cuddling the big, sad beast against him while Suleiman, in turn, placed his hand on Mason's shoulder. Mason had held dying bucks he'd shot like this before in Pendleton County. He would tell them the same words: "It's OK, fella, it's OK."

At that moment, Astrid felt sure that she saw the golden eagle atop the embassy awaken, too, tearing the bolts from its talons like annoying thorns. The steel bird of prey flew down to the four animals huddled in the square, and hovered above them. It was an America-within-an-America, an animal core and inner spark like Omotoso's Yoruba *ori*, a guardian disguised as art, that would never fit into any death cult's plans.

Under the shadow of the eagle, Kibali spoke to Mason, too, for he also had listened very hard to animals his whole life, and at last he could hear their words now, at least for this night.

Kibali said, "I say to you both, '*Gagoga maga medu*.' That is the life-phrase by which the survivors of today will know one another. I give it to you from the animal world. It's the voice against the rushing-in of death. It means, 'I want to live.' "

Then the gorilla, his eyesight dimming, his heart trilling to a stop, looked up at Astrid, who, in his eyes, seemed to be floating above him, and he said to her, in the stalwart gorilla tongue, "*Gagoga maga medu*, Astrid. Live! *Live*, sweet messiah! You are almost past the Death. And you are the last holder of the Wonderments on Earth. You are the princess of the wild, the Otter Christ of England. You will save our country, and you will save our world. But the cost of avoiding pain and grief is annihilation, I assure you. Just as you cannot trap an animal and expect it to survive, you must not go back to Flōt. You must keep imagining the green world, and you must walk toward it—and we will be by your side, on the road of happy destiny. Help the stranger, in the zoo. That poor crazy man who thinks you're his brother. He may or may *not* be your grandfather, Astrid. Why does it matter? The fact is, he *can* be."

"I hear you," said Astrid. A fresh set of king's bulletins and orange-freqs *eeped* in her eyes, but she dismissed them all without reading.

"If I could only gouge out my eyes," she seethed. "Bugger!"

The golden wings of the eagle covered them all like a feathery shield, kicking up a cloud of dust around the square, hiding the creatures under its wings—three *Homo sapiens* and the *Gorilla gorilla*—and keeping them safe. They were pulling together, Astrid saw, as though circling the proverbial wagons, but soon the Heaven's Gaters would find them and drug them and force them into the soul-swallowing machine. They must leave or perish, she suspected.

Suleiman, unsurprised but heartbroken, felt sure now that he would not make it to any new country. These American immigration demons, as he decided to think of them, had them surrounded. The only dim hope he felt was the Shayk of Night.

Apparently immune to the Neuters' silver stunners and to bullets and mob-hurled projectiles, the black leopard had grown frantic and exceedingly lethal, screaming in leopard language, ripping the pale demons to pieces like so many rotten white peaches.

Under the beating eagle's feathers, Astrid felt herself kissing Kibali's forehead as he lay there, struggling for breath.

"You wake up," she said, her licorice-colored hair falling onto and tickling his face. "Wake up." Such was the fantastical tenor of her swirling brain in second withdrawal, she had to wonder: was she really talking to a gorilla, or to herself. "Please!"

Kibali's own last thought was of his dead mother, named Long Stander, the matriarch of his father's troop in the verdant hills of eastern Congo. He saw leaves in her hair, felt her pulling him closer to her, there under the ayous trees. As he expired, he heard her singing her burly ape lullabies with a might beyond the human heart.

releasing the spirits of animals past

AND NOW THE EMBASSY'S "EAGLE" WAS PULLING
Astrid deeper under its wings, and dragging Mason and Suleiman
upward, too, as the Shayk of Night battled on in the square. Astrid
felt herself rising into the sky, and she wondered if this journey, this
spiriting away by an eagle, would finally—*finally*—be the end of
second withdrawal.

Saved by an eagle. That's how good fantasies always end, she
mused darkly. Perfect.

But it wasn't an eagle. The creature had doors, and the doors
had sprung open, and human arms had emerged to yank her inside.

The "eagle," it turned out, was merely another, larger frightcopter—a troop transport—with a very ill, grinning Dr. Bajwa pilot-
ing it. The good GP had come to rescue them from the square. He
sat working the holo-controls with an expert's ease and comfort,
and a weekend pilot's lavish joy.

In the cargo area of the frightcopter, the three unhelmeted, regular Red Watchmen who had lifted Astrid, Mason, and Suleiman
into the copter were trying to help them into their seats.

"Get your fucking hands off me," said Mason, drawing his neuralzinger from under his blazer, and rolling himself in front of Astrid and Suleiman like a giant, awkward jelly roll. He waved his pistol at the Watchmen, holding his arm out stiffly, but he was still lying prone.

"Hey, jeez, jeez, jeez," one of the Watchman said. "Keep your hair on, mate. We're awright."

"It's OK," Bajwa assured everyone. "People, sit down. You are safe. Inspector, the Crown has . . . for now . . . seen the error of its ways. These gents—Jake, Nigel, and Lawson—they're on our side. The Watch is fighting the cultists."

"You can count on old 'Arry," said the one named Nigel. " 'E'll get these suiciders. I hear that 'e's even brung Æthelstan's Bliss out for this do, yeah? That's the noisy sort of mortar what toys with time? With those pink arms?"

"I've heard the . . . tales," said Mason, slowly holstering his sidearm. "I thought you might be more of . . . those people."

"The cultists?" asked the doctor. "It's unprecedented. They've finally gone too far. Even the English republicans—and the Earl of Worcester!—have allied themselves, for now, with King Henry."

"I can't believe it," Astrid said to the doctor. "But the Neuters want to destroy us all. It's the animals they want most."

"Erm, yes," Dr. Bajwa said vaguely, as if not quite grasping what she meant but wanting to show politeness.

"The suicide cult," said Mason. "They're not human."

"What?"

"He's right," said Suleiman. "I saw them. They all look exactly alike."

The most senior-looking of the Watchmen, Lawson, abruptly turned to Astrid and said, in a stone-mouthed, sea-blasted West Country accent: "I've just had a new freq, miss. Incredible." He blinked his eyes a few times, clearly reading his corneas carefully.

"His Majesty 'Arry9, I've been asked to relate, says he's sorry for any misunderstandings, m'om. And you needn't *warry* about any re-class-ifi-cation. And we're getting *hope* for yar mum with her Bruta7, ar-right? You'll not need to *warry* about the P-Levs, either. Right? Oh, and EquiPoise 'as been told their off yar case. And, erm . . ." He paused for a moment, glancing above himself, and tapped his eyebrows a few times. He was reading off his corneas. He scratched his chin. "I think that's it. M'om."

"Well," said Astrid. "Thank bloody God." Out the window, she could see the great white quarkbeam sizzling across the sky. Despite the light pollution, the comet Urga-Rampos wasn't actually any harder to see. Indeed, it was now luridly luminous, as if it had lowered itself toward Earth.

"Thank His Highness," said Nigel, who sounded more local—perhaps from south London.

"Whatever," said Mason.

"We need to hurry," said Astrid. "The longer the beam runs, the more species we lose—forever. To the zoo!"

"I'm one step ahead of you," said the doctor. "Just two minutes, and we'll be above the lions."

"But the beam, it's a kind of energy weapon," said the local Watchman. "What do you mean, 'species'?"

"Animals," said Astrid.

At this, Dr. Bajwa turned around from his holo-controls and looked at Astrid quizzically.

"I don't understand," said the doctor. "You're sounding, Inspector, like—my patient. Cuthbert."

"St. Cuthbert."

Dr. Bajwa peered closely at Astrid's face. He asked, "Did you do whatever it was you needed to do . . . to humor . . . to help, you know, our friend, Cuthbert?"

"I didn't need to humor him. Something happened to me, something that made me understand Cuthbert better, but it's something I may never understand myself. I was 'the Christ of Otters,' as Cuthbert might say. And I can hear animals speak now."

Dr. Bajwa felt so startled, his manipulation of the holo-controls slipped, and the frightcopter dipped down hard.

"Oh no," he said. "Cuthbert's delusional. It's got to be Flōt withdrawal. This is classic Flōt. You're in second withdrawal?"

She said. "Yes. It may be the Flōt, but others saw it, too."

"Others *saw* it?"

"We saw it, too," said Mason. "The inspector—she turned into . . . some . . . being. And, I think—I think—it was almost like I heard the gorilla. *Speaking.*"

"Huh," said Suleiman, his lips trembling. "I saw the woman, too. She was like a kind of forest, come to life. She held the *sokwe* in her arms as he died, and he looked into her face as if looking at his own mama-*sokwe*. But I did not *hear* him."

The frightcopter stopped above the zoo now, with a slight shudder, and it began hovering quietly on top of the lion enclosure, where the earlier deadly confrontation had taken place.

"We're here," said the doctor. "As for your story, I can only suspend my disbelief. But this is all very, very strange!"

"Shite!" Nigel yelled. "Look out the window, where we just was—that fucking *thing*!"

And that's when all the passengers glimpsed the source of the earlier draconine noises—it was King Henry's rumored Æthelstan's Bliss. It was as big as a small cathedral, and just as tall. Its main platform crawled on massive titanium caterpillars, crushing everything in its path. Only its glowing pink tentacles, waving and screeching and erasing clusters of Neuters and anyone else it came close to—and playing a very risky game with time—were visible to the copter passengers.

Trained on enemies within its grasp, the Bliss was at once folding and scrubbing timespace of members of the suicide cult. It not only killed, it nullified a human being's moment in the universe while, simultaneously, mopping up the dimensional residue of her or his existence.

For every cultist the Bliss "unexisted," there was the potential for any animals "exited" by a cult member to be restored. The problem was the staggering "collateral damage." Each time a whipping rose-colored tentacle even brushed the back or forearm of an innocent bystander, that person's entire identity—in the flesh and online—dissolved. Worse, all the lives connected to that person would be smacked by ripples of alternate timelines. Whole families could be wiped out. If a boy who would one day pull a fire alarm at his school was accidently touched by a tentacle, droves of burn victims might appear.

"If that's what I think it is, anything can happen tonight," said Mason. One of the tentacles—they were actually "fired" from the base of the apparatus—nearly hit the frightcopter, which it veered to the right violently.

"Fuck!"

"We need to land," said Baj. "It will destroy us!" Astrid noticed that the pilot-physician sounded a little different, his voice more sonorous and low. Strangely, too, he looked considerably heavier than he had earlier, as if he had gained two stone.

The frightcopter plunged again, sprang up, and shimmied side to side for a moment, but then Baj got it back.

"We're OK," he said. "Perfectly OK."

"Your king is a fool," Mason said to the Watchmen. "You don't fuck with time."

"Piss off," said Nigel. "You can fuck right off, Yank. You fucking Americans, you—" And with that, Nigel disappeared.

"No!" cried Lawson. "Holy fuck!"

Mason shook his head. He said, "Not good. I guess the Bliss just erased someone in some way tied to the life of your poor friend, and when he was cleaned from time, he went, too." He sighed. "But there's a chance he's not dead, too. He could have just been moved. I guess we'll find out."

Astrid said, "Any one of us could be next?"

"Yes," said Mason.

"Not Cuthbert, I hope. Not poor Cuthbert."

"The gorilla—the thing he said: '*Gagoga.*' We'll say it. Say it. What can it hurt?"

Nothing. So they did, again and again, and the two Watchmen left in the frightcopter looked at them as if observing two mental patients.

When the group disembarked and approached the lions' enclosure, they came to a huge crowd of others standing around it, looking on helplessly.

Astrid pushed her way to the wall around the enclosure, just above the moat, and there was Cuthbert, out of the water now, a giant ursine mess of a man, stumbling quickly toward the halted lions, bolt cutters in hand.

"Cuthbert," she called. "Come back. Come back!"

As the lions themselves had predicted earlier in the evening, this was where the night of the animals would end, in their strict orbit.

Locomotion still felt gluey and slow to Astrid. When she turned around, for a moment, she thought she saw Atwell and Omotoso in the dimness, far behind her, sprinting, but the tenebrous figures didn't seem to move nearer, oddly. She felt a panicked sense of clarity: it was *all* Flōt withdrawal. Everything and everyone—figments!

But she could not stop herself now. She beelined for a red alarm box that stood just outside the lions' enclosure. It had not once, in the zoo's history, been used. And despite the fact that one of the largest and fastest assemblies of police and public safety forces in British history now ringed the zoo, with sirens blasting, solarcopters thumping, whirling yellow and blue lights in inferno mode, Astrid nonetheless felt compelled to punch out the glass and pull down the emergency lever, which no one, oddly, had deigned to consider.

Astrid noticed the peculiar sign above the box:

ALARM BELL

IN EMERGENCY BREAK GLASS

When she did so, a great, uncanny horn sounded out. It was like the sound of all animal voices synthesized into one snarling caterwaul, or the way thunder would sound if clouds were not water but living creatures.

In a bright, aureate haze, the Zoological Gardens of London gave up its ghosts.

One by one, but rapidly, hundreds upon hundreds of tiny, sparkling green-gold animal figures unfolded from some subtle *mundus imaginalis* beyond our quotidian world. As Astrid approached the lion terraces, and dozens of other police officers, reporters, and zoo personnel converged, the little animal souls began to whirl around them all, quickly filling in the general vicinity between the lions and the Penguin Pool. It was as if a wild ark had cracked open, and now out they came, a vast revenant herd of nearly two hundred years of caged beings.

Philosophers and theologians in the West had generally not granted animals souls. Exceptions to this rule among the brainy or blessed were few—a mystic cabalist here, a Christian hermit-saint there. These rarest of visionaries, such as Rabbi Chaim Vital and St. Francis, knew that animals never died. Even the Luciferian death cult, the Heaven's Gaters, feared animals because they believed them to possess, at the very least, weak demi-souls, which threatened their own self-loathing operations. But much of humanity allowed nothing. Toddlers in Florida were told about Peter Rabbit; the one-tusked elephant, Ganesh, was worshipped in Mumbai; the terrier was an object of fetish in Hollywood—but who really, among the humans, apart from the mad and a few brilliant scientists and ridiculed activists, genuinely saw themselves as profoundly *equal* to their sentient cohabitants of Earth?

Now the souls of the animals living and dead in London were coming to try to save humanity—for they were animals, too.

Some of the spirits were notable. There was the famous Guy, the sterile gorilla, clapping his huge hands with excitement—he was ready to slap the cultists back to San Diego; the black bear from Canada, Winnie, walked forth on its hind legs, growling; Jumbo, the colossal African elephant eventually sold out to Phineas Barnum's circus, blasted into the night with a joy it rarely had in life. The sweet Sudanese hippopotamus who set Victorian London ablaze with curiosity, Obaysch, lumbered toward the Penguin Pool. Atop him was the Mexican bird-eating spider Belinda, carefully stuck upon Obaysch's pinkish-golden back. There were lesser-known luminaries, too—Eros, the snowy owl and survivor par excellence, whose unrelenting flight at sea kept spirits up in England's rationed, dour 1950s. There Eros soared, circling above, catching eyes now like a white undertuft of the night's ripped-out fabric. Then came multitudes of the extinct beasts, materializing like passé but beloved angels: a Tasmanian tiger, flexing jaws large enough to swallow a wallaby; a zebra horse, the quagga, whinnying and kicking at the cold air; the giant red-speckled Welsh hare, the largest lagomorph the world had ever known—all of them the last of their kind, all perished at the London Zoo.

The glittering procession of animal souls doubled over and twisted into itself like some living, breathing Möbius strip, like a million wet honeycombs balled into intersecting globules, like an explanation for the seventh dimension, like a religion. It was as if all the powers borrowed from them by kings, nations, by parents, by children, by creeds across human history and right to the Pleistocene, had been ceded back to the animal kingdom. *Here's what we lent you,* they seemed to suggest, *look at it.*

lions' play

THE CATERWAUL CONTINUED BEHIND ASTRID'S thoughts, a steady background hum of shrieks and yowls and barks, but she could also hear her granddaddy—or whoever Cuthbert was—his labored and lagery breath, his hepatic farts, his hopeful misery—as though she were right beside him.

She leaped over the wall and slid straight down into the freezing water.

"Cuthbert!" she said, scampering on hands and knees, up the other side of the moat, slipping badly. "Wait!"

This mucky St. Cuthbert looked so big to her—twenty stone, at least, tall as a standing bear, but ragged and filthy—and huge! And he was covered with the algae from the moat, and green head to toe like the copper-covered statue of St. Cuthbert the Wonderworker in the Worcestershire churchyard where the pauper's grave of Cuthbert's granddaddy, Alfred Wistan Wenlock, had been lost forever.

"It's Astrid! It's Tritty! Saint! Cuthbert! Listen!"

Now Atwell was calling down from above, too, from the enclosure wall. "Come back, Inspector! The specialists are coming. They'll put a stop to this."

"I can't," said Astrid. She made another leap up from the moat but slid right back down. She couldn't seem to extract herself.

Meanwhile St. Cuthbert was on his feet, holding forth in the dirty, algae-covered center-court, surrounded by the five grubby Asian lions. Hundreds of pieces of the crisps and popcorn he had earlier thrown to the lions, with the best intentions, still littered the ground. The algae dangled off his bolt cutters and hung from his clothes. It even slopped from his mouth, giving him a mantle of watery jade that seemed to grow out of his mouth.

"A'am this green 'un, arr?" said St. Cuthbert. "And *yow . . . yow're* the last ones to visit. I said I'd see about coming back. And I've got blessing for all, blessings, I say, blessings for all."

"Cuthbert!" cried Astrid. But he didn't seem to hear her.

"And not a moment too soon," said the matriarch, Chandani, to St. Cuthbert. "The enemy is near. They must not be allowed to gain the upper hand. We will make our stand here, and we will vanquish them. But you need to let us out."

Chandani spoke in her usual velvety tone, but now St. Cuthbert noticed a haughty but exquisitely measured new timbre in it. She was excited, her tail rising slightly, her brow arched. "You have released great beauty tonight—but now comes the discharge of justice and nobility. Only British lions can offer those things. Let us free."

"Oh, come on then, and enough canting," said St. Cuthbert. "Oi've 'ad my share of speeches tonight." He was swaying a bit on his feet, holding his chin out, as if doing that alone might keep him from falling on his face.

Suddenly, both Astrid and St. Cuthbert saw the spectral quark-beam shoot a second time out of the American Embassy. The lashing ray then whipped down again like an angry snake and drove its head into Lubetkin's Penguin Pool. The ramps, somehow restored to their dual-helix "DNA" shape after heavy Cuthbert's damage to them earlier, began to twist around. It was as if the architecture had been switched on; the white, sloped inclines of the Altar of Lost Chances started to whirl around like the wing-blades of death itself. As it turned, Neuters poured out of the Altar, pulling out their stunners and spreading like leukemia.

Astrid felt terrified. But in her and St. Cuthbert's midst, they were beginning to see a counterweight to the cult's artful technologies. The souls of the animals were quickly collecting into an emerald nimbus, half alive, half supernatural, which kept expanding and expanding. Within the cloud St. Cuthbert and Astrid could see all the animals, led by the black leopard, Monty, beginning to attack the white Neuters. It was a gory, glittery battle, and the animals seemed to be gaining an advantage.

"Oh, it's bostin beautiful," St. Cuthbert said, breathless. He turned to the lions. "Where's your door now? Daynt see it here. Quick, quick!"

"Please, Cuthbert. Get out of there!"

The old male with a scraggly mane, Arfur, walked in slow, arthritic steps toward the back of the terraces. There was a small green door built into one of the sort of cement predellas upon which content lions were supposed to display themselves to the public. For safety purposes, it could not be locked on the outside, only latched up, in the event that a keeper needed to escape. St. Cuthbert quickly opened the green door. On the other side of the recessed double-gate staging area was a heavy chain. Getting down on his hands and knees arduously, Cuthbert crawled in, cut the chain, and opened another outer door which, at last, gave the great felids free and clear passage to their beloved country.

When St. Cuthbert came back, Arfur was jogging around a little, as if preparing himself; he kept circling the shiny-leafed Chinese tree of heaven, which had been planted in the lions' living area.

"Go, then," St. Cuthbert said. "Fight!" But the lions did not leave. They seemed to be flexing their limbs, bumping one another, working themselves into a kind of kill-state.

"Holy man," said Chandani. "We are here to save the animal world. You are part of that kingdom—only part. This does not mean we have no needs of our own, nor selfishness, nor desires. We want you. Surely, you could have seen that, long ago."

Then St. Cuthbert turned and finally saw Astrid in the water—like Drystan, so many, many years ago, struggling to stay up. There was something wrong with her limbs now. Whether it was the Death, or fatigue, or a simple lack of coordination, the great swimmer, the queen of Highbury pool, suddenly couldn't seem to swim or even hold herself up above the five feet of water. She slipped below, gasping. The "Christ of Otters" in Astrid was gone.

"Drystan! Bostin! You came! You came! I knew you would!"

Astrid splashed down into the moat water again, coughing, and trying to scramble, again, up the other side, and flailing and slipping and sliding, trying to rise to her feet, but falling again and again. And that was when Chandani leaped onto Cuthbert.

"God, no," shouted Astrid.

"It's OK," said Cuthbert, who was smiling. "Let them have me." The lions piled onto him with such force they rolled en masse down into the moat, but Astrid bravely threw herself at the tangle of man and beast.

They were in the water again, and Astrid grabbed for this ancient lunatic who she thought might be her long-lost grandfather. She could not tell what was lion and what was human—it was all warm and ragged and desperate. The lions were speaking, but

Astrid no longer could understand them, yet, underwater, it did sound like the phrase she'd heard herself saying before, the underwater words, *gagoga maga medu*. And the words emerged in bubbles as the swimming lions reached for Cuthbert and now Astrid with their huge jaws. Astrid felt that the lions harbored no ill will, but there was real rage in their movements. Unlike the Neuters, the lions killed with passion and with meaning, using the same blessing phrase Astrid had heard from Kibali and Cuthbert had heard from the otters years ago in Dowles Brook. Like so much aggression by cats of all sizes, the line between affection and murderousness was both blurry and long. Just as any household Siamese will "play" with a fortuitously caught mouse, the lions' assault on Cuthbert was not without an element of real fondness.

"Don't kill him," Astrid commanded the lions, her voice full of its own animal-to-animal heat. She had never heard herself speak with such conviction. "Do *not*. I will not lose him! Not again!"

And with that, the lions broke off their attack. It was as simple as that. They respected firmness.

"We were agitated," said Chandani, and once again, Astrid could understand their words. "That is all. We have been . . . pent up."

The lions helped drag Cuthbert and Astrid out of the moat, biting down on their shoulders gently, drawing them to safety like two of their cubs, and departing.

"And now you are baptized," Cuthbert said to Astrid. "And I am, too."

Chandani, the strongest one, the huntress, did not join the battle against the Neuters. She craved the purest form of freedom, and she slinked away into Regent's Park. There, on one of the tidy bowling lawns, the lioness chased and harried a Red Watchman until Kieran from the AnimalSafe Squad, freshly returned from the sad chimpanzee business at Madame Tussauds, brought her down with a tranquilizer dart, much to his own relief. It was one of the few happy outcomes for the animals that night.

The other lions, including Arfur, began to head to the Tower of London. The lions had been sent away from the old Lion Tower in 1835. They wanted to go back. It was their right, they had always been told. They made it to towers, but of the brutalist variety in the Barbican, where they were cornered in Lakeside Terrace. A contingent of city police officers easily subdued the distracted animals while they played with the jetting fountains in the round red-brick pools. They could not stop themselves from batting the water jets with their paws, obsessively.

All lived, but only Arfur was granted, by chance, a fate that nearly matched his leonine dreams. All he had wanted was to sit in the Tower and protect the Realm. He was more stupid, lazy, and old than the other lions, but with his long, golden, wonderfully messy mane, footage of him on the autonews apparently caught the king's attention.

"That one," Henry had told one of his consorts as they lay naked in his bedchamber, watching the ceiling autonews feeds. He was up on Flōt, fully His "Highness" indeed. "I'll get *that* one—for next year. He's a rascal, he is—you can see. I shall have an official picture with a fucking lion. '*Dieu et mon droit*' and all that. What do you think of that, then?"

your song shall make us free

AFTER THE LIONS LEFT, CUTHBERT AND ASTRID had lain for a while on the lip of the moat, a green heap of Flōtism and moat slime and blood ties woven in threads of dreams and pain and need. They were a perfect public spectacle, and the autonews-media ate it up.

A roaring crowd of autonews "gatherers" and zoo staff and police surrounded the lion enclosure.

When Astrid began to sit up, that tall, indefatigable autoreporter named Jerry and his chunky fotolivographer encouraged them, rather cynically, to hold still.

"No, you're perfect!" called Jerry. "You better stay put, yeah? Until the paramedics arrive? Perhaps something's . . . erm, broken?"

"There's plenty broken," croaked Cuthbert.

THE SKY WAS BEGINNING TO BRIGHTEN. The Neuters from outer space were quickly vanishing in Astrid's and Cuthbert's minds, and a golden green cloud was spreading over London.

Astrid kissed her granddaddy's clammy forehead, pulling him as close to her as she could. She said, "You mustn't ever leave me again. Never, Cuddy, never," and for Cuthbert, every one of her words seemed to be uttered by Drystan, and he had found what he felt he'd needed for eighty years, since his poor older brother drowned in Dowles Brook.

Meanwhile, Atwell and Omotoso appeared again at the edge of the enclosure, looking down on Astrid and Cuthbert.

"Idiots," said Atwell. "You're a perfect fool, Inspector."

"I second that," said Omotoso.

Soon, Astrid could see the oddly fatter Dr. Bajwa again, shaking his head, but smirking, too.

"You have been delivered, it seems," hollered Dr. Bajwa. "I told you. I told you, didn't I? It's as plain as a pikestaff."

Elbowing into the crowd came Mason, waving bystanders aside with authority, repeating the phrase, "Sorry, security, sorry."

Then Suleiman glided in. For reasons known only to him, the Zanzabari man was wearing on his feet the speedfins one normally saw on kids playing dangerous games of hurtball around the IBs. He was smiling openly, with his American visa now inserted. It was a silver holographic eagle that popped up from the palm, beating its wings in its flight to nowhere.

Mason and Suleiman leaned far over the edge of the enclosure, and Mason called down to Astrid, winking, "Help's on the way. Just hang tough, y'all."

Eventually, Astrid also spotted Tom, her friend from FA.

She felt embarrassed to see him.

"I did not drink," she said, looking down.

Tom seemed unfazed. "Of course you didn't. But it's a miracle. I was starting to think I'd be the only one who did the Death. And now I'm not."

Astrid then took her Cuthbert's hand and kissed it.

Soon, a detail of the king's personal Beefeaters, the Yeomen of the Guard, took up positions near key "battle" sites—the Penguin Pool, the American Embassy—and showily stood sentry duty, all part of Harry9's plan to "own" the night as an exemplar of Windsorian might. One Beefeater came to the edge of the lion enclosure and planted her neuralwave pike with a thud. Few loyal subjects could ever have been as pleased as St. Cuddy to see such an old-fashioned regal spectacle, apparently on his behalf.

The raw video feeds, broadcast from the autonews and spread on WikiNous, were already fashioning a kind of rough narrative— the hands of King Henry's council were behind this—which presented Cuthbert and Astrid as fending off a terrorist suicide cult. Cuthbert's release of the rare zoo animals was framed as a sort of stopgap "tactic." As long as the cultists were dead and their gobs shut, Harry9 was happy.

"Tritty," said Cuthbert as they lay beside the moat. "That's your name? But I'll always see Drystan in you, you know? I'm all done. My body's shot. A'm done for. But you found me. You remembered me. It's all I could have ever wanted. Never forget now, all right?"

Suddenly, a mass of white birds appeared above everyone's heads, singing madly. Seagulls! It was as if a beneficent, reintegrated version of the Neuters had materialized. They had wings. They were not here to harm, but to inspire. They swooped down and began to gobble up the popcorn and crisps that Cuthbert had tossed into the lion enclosure during the night. They screamed for joy.

"Blastid," said St. Cuthbert. "It's the Gulls of Imago. They've come." And finally St. Cuthbert himself sang in his croaking voice the penguin song, all to the tune of "A Hundred Years Ago":

> *Seagulls of Imago, your song shall make us free,*
> *From Cornwall to the Orkney, we dine on irony,*
> *Along with lovely kippers from the Irish Sea.*

Along with lovely kippers from the Irish Sea,
We'll take our daily fill of anguished poetry,
'Til the world becomes zoologically arty.

Seagulls of Imago, your song shall make us free,
Seagulls of Imago, your song shall make us free,
Make it new! Things not ideas! Ambiguity!
And endless lovely kippers from the Irish Sea.

"What does it mean?" asked Astrid.

"Haven't the faintest," Cuthbert said. "Perhaps we need to eat kippers first. That's all I need—and a full English.* And a stomach. I need one of them."

"Yes," said Astrid. "Egg and fried toast soldiers and a tomato. Fried. It's the day."

"It is," said Cuthbert. "Let's wakie wakie then. I've got loads to tell you, Astrid. Loads. It's been so long."

The seagulls dove down, flapping and crying around their heads, and scurrying away with bits of popcorn. Nearby, in Lubetkin's Penguin Pool, which was restored, not a trace of the attack discernible, the penguins were marching up their helical ramps, ready to go anywhere on earth. They had heard the gulls and they were ready to follow them to homes off the tip of southern Africa, at the Cape of Good Hope.

All across the city, everyone began to noticed hundreds of new cloud-doodles in the sky. The children of London had got wind about the night, and their response was to draw pictograms. There were rhinos and zebras with stick legs. There was a giraffe with a

---

* A full English breakfast, typically eggs, sausages, beans, bacon, black pudding, tomato, etc.

neck the length of a football pitch. There was a jaguar with spots that blew away almost as fast as they were drawn by a five-year-old girl in Hampstead named Lucy.

AND WHAT of the other animals?

The Shayk of Night, predictably, disappeared. He would hide in the trees for as long as he was needed, be it days or decades, ready to bring infidels to the true faith. Eventually, he would join the ranks of Britain's cryptozoological legends, a big black felid, sometimes spotted late at night on westerly moors by some excitable retired schoolmaster.

The zookeepers, try as they may, couldn't find Muezza, Monty's little admirer, and it was assumed that he would take up with the feral cats of north London, happily hunting Norway rats for all his days ahead. The other sand cats were eventually rounded up.

The otters, like most of their species, went in different directions. One headed to the Thames estuary. It would swim toward Lindisfarne on the North Sea, where the spirit of St. Cuthbert awaited all pilgrims. Another otter would make its way west, toward the quieter corners of Somerset, and perhaps, one day, even toward Worcestershire, the Severn basin, and the Wyre Forest. The otter pups were in pain—they had been forced to abandon the new mother because such were the forced detachments of the mustelid universe. It was a place where you just swam on. The spirit of St. Cuthbert would protect them until, one day, they re-populated Britain's rivers and streams. Meanwhile, their video likenesses were to be broadcast all over the world, thanks to the ginger-haired reporter, Jerry. For several days, the most popular image projected of the zoo disturbance would be the video of the six newborn otters in their glossy blankets of caul, their dutiful mother licking them clean, with interspersed interview shots of the tiresome David Beauchamp, finally a minor celebrity, explaining how the London Zoo was already planning a "once in a lifetime" exhibit called "Six of One, Half a Dozen of the Otter." "That's my title, actually," he would be heard saying.

AS MYSTERIOUSLY AND BIZARRELY as the Luciferian attack had begun, it had ended up receding, rapidly, in terms of both concrete facts and in what people believed about the night. The white demonic arch that rose from Grosvenor and landed in the zoo's Penguin Pool had flickered off, and the comet Urga-Rampos disappeared from the Eastern Hemisphere. Nearly as soon as the horrors had gone, some people claimed they never existed. The timeline vandalism of Harry9's Æthelstan's Bliss further served to confuse the public.

But some things could not be disputed.

All across Britain, and especially in London near the American Embassy, the bodies of hundreds of suicided "Neuters" were discovered that May Day and in the days afterward. They all wore white coveralls, cropped haircuts, and white Nike trainers. But they were not, as Astrid had imagined, all clones of Marshall Applewhite III. They were ordinary citizens, from all over the Americas, northern Europe, and Japan and Singapore, especially, who had dedicated themselves to the HeavensGate.com cult and decided to end their lives in England in order to "shed their containers" and meet Applewhite in his comet starship. It would be the apex of the suicide cults' powers on earth. In every case, the suicides had imbibed lethal doses of sedatives along with Flōt and killed at least one poor animal, usually someone's stolen domestic pet. All had an American $5 bill in their pockets for the afterlife, which they apparently considered a cut-rate operation. In central

London, as planned, a large squad of Neuter aggressors had managed to murder dozens of other noncult members, in some cases force-feeding victims sedatives and Flōt, and some of the loose animals, did indeed attack them.

But as the autonews reports went out, in the weeks and months that followed, and WikiNous started sizzling with wild rumors about what had happened that night—with tales of mass murder and leopard attacks, outraged reports about the catastrophe of Æthelstan's Bliss, rumors of a subsequent UK-USA diplomatic row over terrorism—officialdom began, slowly at first and then quite aggressively, to suppress the truth. Harry9, for his part, even feared that his indiscipline with the Æthelstan's Bliss had endangered his own throne. He was, for now, a king humbled—but not entirely.

Harry9 still ran a massive disinformation operation. Soon, the facts of the night of the animals became as elusive as the otters of the Severn. Timelines seemed to get artificially resewn. The AnimalSafe Squad's ambitious David Beauchamp led the effort among the zoo officials to downplay and to understate, and in some cases to erase, the evidence. The Met played its part, too, and with the cowed, impoverished automedia at historically weakened levels of investigative nous, the story soon began to evaporate. Still, the Crown instructed EquiPoise's Psyalleviators to steer clear of both Astrid and Cuthbert. The authorities saw Astrid, privately, as a kind of selfless minor hero, and Cuthbert as a chaotic messenger. They were marked as a kind of special case, a Flōt-related aberration, and the night, officially, as a sort of subterranean watershed dividing what could be tolerated from the cults and terrorists, and what threatened the English at their core.

It wasn't, as Cuthbert wanted, all about *all* the animals.

There hadn't been many animals on the loose—not really, it was said. No one but a few soft-headed cultists actually died. SCARE hadn't actually lost any soldiers. Only a few suspect people saw anything like a "green being" near the American Embassy. And apart from a small number of animals hurt or temporarily escaped, nearly all the animals were captured and returned to their enclosures to resume their happy jailed lives.

BY THE NEXT SPRING, in 2053, a year blessedly free of comets, the night of the animals was largely forgotten, and the big news on everyone's corneas was, of course, King Henry, for 2053 marked his silver jubilee. In the monarch's official portrait for the year, Arfur appeared, in the background, prone on a settee of purple velvet brocades and ermine, his muffin-paws in front of him, and wearing an expression of impossible contentment.

nine

incantation in a new tongue

DURING THAT LONG, SCORCHING SUMMER OF THE jubilee, Cuthbert Handley one day realized that he didn't hear voices as often as he used to. In fact, they had all shrunk down to one.

By 2053, there were far fewer animals and species of them on earth. Not since the end of the Pleistocene, when the woolly rhinos and dire wolves died out, had evolution reached such a choke point. Epically closer to home, a hot April and May had hatched swarms of midges, bringing an epidemic of a virulent bluetongue to Albion's sheep and cattle on the king's large collectives.

In London, there were even fewer moggies in the alleys, fewer dog walkers around the silenced swan ponds, and a host of unexpected, strange breeding problems at the zoo. Indigents were no longer permitted pet licenses. While the zoo was still the most precious archival repository of genomes on the planet, research and bioengineering and preservation work tended to hold primacy now. Security increased tenfold, with admission by invitation only. The exhibitions, one by one, were being shuttered, too. In all but a few cases, genomic clones replaced the wild originals, and the London Zoological Gardens—humankind's last ark of the Animal Kingdom—had become, for the most part, a closed shop.

For reasons Cuthbert could not grasp, the animals stopped talking to him. The unexpected great quieting depressed him, and left him with agonizing guilt.

"I *can't* bring 'em in," he would exclaim to Astrid. "I don't know what's gone wrong. Why? Why'd I have to tinker? Why? What's become of the Wonderments? Do you hear them?"

But that was a question Astrid never dared to answer again, not even to dear Cuthbert.

He'd thought, gullibly, that people would have learned after the night the animals saved them. He trusted that the bond between creatures and people would grow inviolate. That hadn't happened at all.

He decided, that summer day, that it was time perhaps that he come in off the streets of England for good.

"I've had enough, haven't I?" he thought, not without real shame. "And I've done my bit for the beasts—and for King Harry. What's the use?"

But this notion of sleeping indoors for good occurred to him as the sweet smell of baking kidneys and puff pastry wafted into his eager face. He was in Astrid's kitchen, in her flat in Haggerston, where he found himself spending more and more time. With shaky hands, he moved a piping-hot pie, still in its tin, directly to an Italian dinnerware plate painted with large red pears and golden quinces. There was a square nuplastic container of burdock greens that Astrid had sautéed with watercress and put away, and she'd made Cuthbert promise her to eat a bit of the greens if he insisted on "those unwholesome pies."

"But the pies, they're good," he maintained. Astrid was vegetarian, of course, just like his gran had been, and he respected that, but he could not bring himself to denigrate a good kidney pie, could he?

Astrid was away at work that afternoon, where she'd long been reinstated and promoted to chief inspector, with Omotoso moving up to the Met, and Atwell taking her old inspectorship. She was only the second person she knew in Britain to make it past second withdrawal from Flōt, and in her FA meetings, she'd become something of an inspiration. Her own "Wonderments," it turned out, had worked in unexpected ways. She wasn't sure she liked or trusted God, or if she even knew how to believe, but her old revulsion was gone.

Cuthbert sat down at Astrid's dark, walnut-grained kitchenette, and he dumped some of the unheated greens, straight from the container, onto the pie. A ray of piercing June sunlight shot across the tabletop, glaring a bit, and he squinted.

Cuthbert covered the whole plate with HP sauce, and he ate greedily. One hunk after another, without pause, he took enormous portions of pastry and the bright jade burdock upon his fork without bothering to spear anything with the tines. He washed it all down with a big honeyed bowl of peppermint and nettle tea, and when it was finished, with a barely concealed exuberance, he burped.

"That's a piece,"* he said.

Oh, she wants me to stay here, he thought to himself. To keep out of the cold—and the heat. Why don't I then?

But could he find a way to leave the Flōt alone forever?

AGAINST THE ADVICE of many acquaintances—for her friends knew better than to say a thing—Astrid had invited Cuthbert after the night of the animals to stay with her without apparent reservations or regrets. It was an odd arrangement, and a big gamble, she

---

* Meal

knew, but she could not get over a feeling of wanting to protect the man, as best she could, or at least see to his creature comforts for a few years.

"He's my grandfather," she would tell skeptics, although she hadn't known that, really. She was, for the moment, content to leave it at that. "I love him."

In the year since, both she and he had, after all, suffered great losses. Even in an era of replaceable major organs, the endlessly patient Dr. Bajwa's cancer could not be stopped. The loss felt cruel for Cuthbert. It turned out that the extra weight and more robust voice Baj had gained on the hijacked frightcopter, right before Astrid's eyes, was an effect of Æthelstan's Bliss. A damaged timeline had somehow shrunk his tumors, added to his fat stores, and given him more months of life, which he gave to the poor of Holloway Road, treating Indigents almost to the end. Eventually, the tumors came back, and Baj died in the winter, sending Cuthbert into a panic. The same month, Astrid's mother, her mind too ravaged by the Bruta7 virus even to recognize her daughter, finally succumbed to complications brought on by it, despite receiving specially ordered NHS Legacy-level care.

AFTER HIS LUNCH, Cuthbert decided to take a little nap. He lay atop the duvet on his plush bed, and he pulled his legs up.

He called, just as his grandmother had, "Kitty-kyloe! Kitty-kyloe!"

Instantly, the little golden cat came running from its hiding place and jumped onto the bed, snuggling into a ball at Cuthbert's feet. He reached down and scratched the feline behind its ears, and it allowed this, for a moment, then bucked away. It would never relax in human hands, but like many sand cats, it was semi-tamable.

"Yow smelled the pie, did yow?" Muezza leaped off the bed onto the floor, as if signaling for a feeding. (He had to be fed frozen mice.)

After the incident in the lion enclosure, and being seen to by paramedics, Cuthbert had spotted Muezza in the hedges, very near its shattered, aquarium-like exhibit. Unknown to Astrid or anyone, the old man had managed to smuggle the sand cat out in his bundled coat, stowing him like a small melon in a grocery sack.

It was unethical. It was illegal. It was unwise. But Astrid had reluctantly let Muezza stay in the flat. For all its standoffishness, the creature clearly adored both Cuthbert and her. It rubbed against their ankles, cuddled with them on the sofa, and did what it could to destroy Astrid's £200 faux-Iranian rug. She knew, someday, the cat would need to go back to the zoo. But not today.

Muezza meowed at Cuthbert, almost provocatively.

"What is it? Use words, my brother. All the animals have stopped talking to me. Are you next? Am I not al-Khidr?"

The cat did not answer, at least not in words.

"Oh," said Cuthbert. "Oh my brother, Muezza. Yow must talk. Or I've lost the Wonderments."

Then they both fell asleep.

ASTRID HAD FIXED UP the room where her mother had stayed, and she gave Cuthbert a key to the flat. There was one rule: he wasn't allowed to drink either alcohol or Flōt in the flat, under any circumstances.

But he was not, strictly speaking, quite sane, even though he didn't hear many animals.

At age ninety-one, with his CoreModded organs updated by the special dispensation from the Crown, Cuthbert might have had another decade or two of life to look forward to if he could stay away from the Flōt. He was *trying*—very hard. He'd make it weeks sometimes, and only rarely need to go, to rest a few days, to the

Whittington detox. He would vanish from Astrid's flat for a week or two, then come back, always remorseful. But he always came back. In so many ways, he still believed that Astrid was his long-dead brother, Drystan, and Astrid didn't have the heart to disabuse him of the notion.

In her own unobtrusive way, Astrid had learned much more about him in the last year—the abuse he and his sibling suffered at their father's hands, his mother's emotional neglect, the inexorable love the two boys received from their witchy gran. Above all, she discovered the deep break in Cuthbert's being that occurred when his older brother drowned.

Earlier that summer, one morning, Cuthbert had asked "for that coin," just to see it again.

"The souvenir bracteate? The one you gave me?"

"Yes."

She snatched the Undley Bracteate from her pocket. She'd learned that boffins at the University of Leicester had decoded the ancient Anglo-Frisian inscription on the coin. It turned out that *gagoga maga medu* meant something along the lines of "Abracadabra—to you, kinsman, a drink of mead." The researchers said it was actually the oldest sentence in English.

Cuthbert glanced at the bracteate for a moment, as if looking for something. There were the two brothers, Romulus and Remus, drinking from the teats of a she-wolf beneath the image of Constantine.

"I've not been as good to yow, Astrid, as yow've been to me. I canna stop missing my brother, Dryst, and I'm sorry for that."

"No," she said to him. "Never think that way. You've helped me—you brought me through the Death, you know?"

"I've done nothing," he said. "It's yow, Astrid. Yow're the angel."

In the year he was with her, all this knowledge helped her come to her own livable terms with what happened to her in second withdrawal, when she herself experienced a mystical encounter, and with what had happened since. She'd come to believe that being the Christ of Otters wasn't a supernatural event; it was subnatural. It was a deeper part of being human.

AFTER HIS NAP, with Muezza at his toes, Cuthbert did something he'd pledged to himself that he'd never do. He snooped around the flat a bit and went where he knew he oughtn't. He tiptoed into Astrid's bedroom, looking behind himself continually, terrified she'd walk into the flat. It wasn't the London Zoo, and there was no malice or prurience, but he hated himself for doing it. He felt compelled only out of a loving, cracked desire to know more about Astrid, whom he still associated with Drystan in a way that was helplessly immovable.

So a few minutes later, the erstwhile saint stood at his Messiah's dresser, and he gazed at the small collection of things Astrid had put there. They struck him as sacred, even in their mundanity. There were the three fotolives, including the one with Astrid as a girl in a red teepee, and extra hairpins. There was a loose gangliatoxic round packed into its cylindrical bronze cartridge. There was a set of blue nuplastic swimming goggles with a precious white band. And there was a carefully folded DNA wipe with tiny number 5's all over it.

Cuthbert unfolded and flattened the wipe out. It was dated from the day before yesterday.

He'd heard of these wipes, but he'd never seen or used one. He felt curious. It felt dry and papery, yet slightly sticky somehow, too. He suddenly recalled that, the day before yesterday, Astrid had gently wiped a bit of cake from the corner of his mouth at tea, using what he thought was a serviette. He hadn't thought twice

about it until now. She *had* looked oddly uncomfortable, he realized, not herself. The wipes were used to establish or prove familial
genetic relationships, and this one indicated that the chance of a
direct genetic connection between whoever had been swiped was
roughly 5 percent. Cuthbert began to refold it, but he couldn't keep
the folds straight, and this—and the sudden dread that she would
reject him—caused such anxiety, his hands shook and the refold-
ing process failed again and again.

Such was the weakness of Cuthbert's hearing, and his distracted state, that when a scrabbling at the flat's front door began,
and Astrid came in, he hadn't a clue she was behind him.

"No," she said. "Don't look at that. Please, Cuddy."

Cuthbert reeled back, utterly humiliated, his mouth gurning
with shame.

"Oh blessed," he gasped. "Oi'm a sorry yam-yam, I am. A'm
sorry, a'm sorry. I'm so desperately sorry." He held the DNA wipe
up. It was balled and slightly torn. "I've just cocked up this important document of yours or whatnot, dear, the one with the fives all
over. I just—I wanted—I was just curious . . ."

"It's all right," she said, speaking with a shaky voice. "It doesn't
matter. But come out of there, you silly old rascal. Let's have a nice
tea now, shall we? Cuthbert? Cuthbert?"

But Cuthbert Handley had fallen down. His big, stupid, cardio-
myopathic heart had trilled into a lethal ventricular arrhythmia.

"No!" Astrid cried. Without a moment's pause, she blinked 999
over her corneas, and sent out emergency double-orange-freqs.

Cuthbert lay on the floor, looking up at the white ceiling, struggling to breathe, but not feeling any real pain. His mind began to
travel.

He and Drystan had been so perfectly happy, so rarely happy,
ambling on a different scalding day in the Wyre Forest. 1968. He
remembered again a little detail from that afternoon, how Drystan

quite inadvertently stepped on a young snake—an adder—and killed it—oh, they should have turned back then, Drystan had said. It was a complete accident, blameless—the snake had been totally hidden—but Cuthbert instantly saw Drystan's recognition that he had tread upon a living forest creature. Drystan had jumped in horror, drawn himself back.

"Oh no," Drystan had said. "I hurt something, Cuddy. Oh, no."

The venomous adder hadn't bitten him, but the thought of what he had done seemed to annihilate him.

"It's only a snake," Cuthbert had said. "Wasn't you, Drystan. It's like a cricket or something, that's all. A snake is a snake. It's not even a *good* animal."

But no consolation seemed to touch Drystan.

Cuthbert remembered how he had run his finger down the cool scales of the snake, whose upper body had been given a grotesque crook. The string of black diamonds on its back were so perfect and ordered, like some optical art. But Drystan would not touch it. He looked devastated, clutching his cheeks and pulling his own ears.

The two boys had buried it quickly, dug a little hole and covered it in pink mallows and purple betony, but Drystan would not stop weeping. Cuthbert had almost forgotten that, and now he could see Dryst's face above him, weeping again. He was a brilliant child, and could go from hard lad to sensitive so quickly, Cuthbert remembered—he could be so terribly sincere. He was a good boy, a very good little lad.

"A'm worse than evil," Dryst had said as they brushed soil over the snake, so genuinely remorseful. "I'll pay for this—yow'll see. Them Boogles will get me. Maybe both of us."

After the burial, they went on exploring the forest. Drystan did seem to lighten up a bit—just a bit, at first. Cuthbert found pieces of old charcoal around some of the old woodland hearths, and he beaned Drystan with them a few times rather beautifully, and eventually Drystan fought back, and they were having fun again. Then they were laughing again, running down that hill in the forest like young puppies, not minding their bearings, speeding through the waist-high maidenhair and bracken, and they ran and laughed and ran and laughed and it was as if they were carving a path through a flood of green and fields of glee that would go on and on and on. Drystan turned around and looked at Cuthbert, and it was the last time he saw his brother's face alive. He was smiling, but he looked sad, too, as if he knew.

He went back in his memories to the terrible walk back to the cottage, after Drystan vanished. He saw, on its hind legs, the same giant river otter he'd seen and heard under the water with Drystan, trying to save him, or to take him to the animal world. There, near a bend in the brook he could see and hear, again, more softly now, more sweetly, how Drystan had called out underwater to him, and how the words sounded like *gagoga maga medu*, at least as Cuthbert came to remember them.

There had been an inquest by the county authorities. The death was ruled a "misadventure." Cuthbert, only six years old, could not be persuaded that "Boogles" hadn't murdered Drystan. His granny said it wasn't so, again and again, until the day she died, soothing Cuthbert as best she could.

"Inna wasn't them Boogles, Cuddy. It wasn't nothing with the forest." But he never wholly believed it, and he didn't think his granny did either.

He thought of his gran for a moment as he gazed at the whiteness above. He wondered if he might see her in the next world. Winefride Wenlock had leaned even more heavily upon "owd" Wyrish folkways after Drystan's drowning. She used to tell Cuthbert that she had been careful to make sure neither his brother nor he had gazed at a looking glass before age one, but somehow she must have failed with Drystan, she must have. She claimed that white birds were a sign of death, and if Cuddy were playing alone in the garden and a seagull or white owl appeared, he was to "scrobble indoors" right away. One time, when Cuthbert was down with bronchitis, his gran came into his room late at night with scissors. Her Alfie had died of pneumonia, and lung ailments in general obsessed her. He felt her bend down and carefully clip hair from the nape of his neck. He asked her, the next day, why she had taken the hair, and she related that she counted out twenty pieces of the sweet brown strands, folded them into a slice of buttered bread, and fed it all to a stray dog. The dog would take the disease "back to the Boogles," she said.

"Astrid," Cuthbert gasped, raising his hand up toward this stranger, this kind soul who had come to love him, for no apparent reason, at the end of his life. The cat, Muezza, sat on the bed, paws in front, looking puzzled and detached.

"Yow, love," said Cuthbert. "Yow. My answer to *gagoga maga medu*. My answer is . . ."

But he was gone.

"*Gagoga maga medu*," she said. "I hear you."

It was the life-phrase, the blessing, the secret otterspaeke of visions. It came from the same eternal underwater world of the forest, where Drystan and his gran and his lost grandfather's body lived, where the Wonderments lived, and where Cuthbert could now return.

It said, take this dream, take this prayer of otterspaeke, take this phrase of a new tongue and new tales, and beneath the many-colored bows in the clouds of the whole world, let not the voices perish.

acknowledgments

WRITTEN ACROSS FOURTEEN YEARS, THIS NOVEL left a deep elephant trail of indebtedness to many people around the world. I suspect that some of those who helped me may have, understandably, long forgotten this project—but I haven't them, I hope.

I wish especially to acknowledge Sheikh Ahmed; Rachael Ashton of Chester Zoo (UK); my brother Patrick Bracken; the late American art historian Bruce Chambers; Hans Coster; James Gardner; Professor Andrew Goldstone of Rutgers University; zoo planner and consultant David Hancocks; my H.P.; linguist and folklorist Alf Jenkins; Mike Jordan of Chester Zoo; Traugott Lawler, professor emeritus of English at Yale University; Dr. Edward Lundeen; Dr. Bryan Serkin; the Royal Parks; founder of the London Emergency Services Liaison Panel, Anthony Speed, CBE; Catherine Slater; and the participants of the VillaTalk.com online forum, who offered generous insights into West Midlands speech and usage.

I thank Brad and Lynn Thompson of Galveston, Texas, for providing a place to write for two summers; and Robert "T" Farris Thompson of Yale University, who adopted me as a resident fellow at Timothy Dwight College, allowing me time and lodging to write.

In Britain, special thanks to Alan Hollinghurst, my thesis committee director and a great general encourager. Certain editors in London offered me interesting and flexible employment while I lived in Finsbury Park, wrote, and hung around the zoo: Paul Finch, of the *Architects' Journal*; Tim Lusher, of the *Guardian* newspaper; and Lindsay Duguid, formerly of the *TLS*.

Three of my colleagues at East Stroudsburg University—Peter Hawkes, Nancy Van Arsdale, and Andi McClanahan—gave the drafting of this novel a legitimate place in my work-life.

I shall remain forever appreciative to my dear friend Marian Thurm, who so reassuringly read early drafts of the novel.

In England, my cousin Kimberly Shaw gave me critical insights into Midlands history, culture, and language. Her father and my friend, Richard T. Elsmore, helped me understand the depth of my own connections to an England of long ago and of tomorrow. My cousin Mary Finnegan assisted unforgettably in helping me travel to London.

The many stories of my father, William A. Broun, mostly set in the Worcestershire and Birmingham of the last century, form the basis of some of this novel's inner mythology.

Lavish credit, served on the best china, must be given to my longtime friend Pamela Diamond for daring me to take on such a vast story and for reading early drafts.

At Ecco, I am deeply thankful (and such phrasing sounds far too trifling) to Megan Lynch, whose ingenious editing and unswerving encouragement have answered many a prayer; to her talented, diligent assistant editor, Eleanor Kriseman; and to the rest of the editorial and art teams.

Almost inestimable gratitude is owed to my mentor, Mary Gaitskill, who has remained an indefatigable friend, and who read and critiqued several drafts of this novel.

Mary also introduced me to my brilliant and life-changing agent, Jin Auh, of the Wylie Agency. I also thank Jin's wonderful assistant, Jessica Friedman, and indeed all the Wylie staff.

I thank my sweet son, Tobias, who taught me much about the two boys at the center of this story, and who put up with a distracted dad far too often. (And I assure you, Toby, that the promised novel about English setters who battle in intergalactic space is coming—someday.)

Above all, I thank my wife, the poet and translator Annmarie Drury. She lifted me up from despair again and again, gave up so much, and inspired me to follow these animals and ghosts out from their cages and into the starry night.

about the author

BILL BROUN was born in Los Angeles to an English father and an American mother. He was educated at University College London and Miami University (Ohio). He also holds an MFA in creative writing from the University of Houston. He is associate professor of English at East Stroudsburg University.

While writing fiction in his spare time, Broun spent many years as a news reporter, music journalist, and news editor, including long stints as editor in chief at several weekly newspapers in Texas. In London, he was employed as a copyeditor at a host of British newspapers and magazines, with staff positions at the *Guardian* and *Architects' Journal*. His own writing has appeared in the *Washington Post*, the *New York Times*, the *Times* (London), the *Times Literary Supplement*, and more, as well as specialty publications such as the *Architects' Journal* and *Publishers Weekly*. He was appointed a resident fellow at Yale University in 2002, where he lectured in fiction writing, advanced composition, and journalism for four years. His short fiction, which often explores the lives of the urban underclass and "working poor," has appeared in journals such as the *Indiana Review*, the *Kenyon Review*, and *Open City*.

Broun lives in Hellertown, Pennsylvania, and *Night of the Animals* is his first novel.